SPIN

by

Bob Steele

Third Edition 2021

Copyright © by Bob Steele 2021

Bob Steele asserts the moral right to be
identified as the author of this work

Chapter 1

Billions of dollars spin through the world's financial markets every day, in a ceaseless dance that casually makes and breaks fortunes in passing. The controls that surround these economic juggernauts are rigorous and the systems supporting the traders are mind-bogglingly complex. In London, giant computers suck in gigabytes of data twenty-four hours a day, digesting and interpreting the portents. But as the ancient Greeks discovered at Delphi, most oracles have a potentially fatal flaw. Glimpsing the future is one thing. Making sense of what you see is something else entirely.

The shirt-sleeved man sitting in front of the bank of computer terminals was young for the responsibility he bore, though stress was already greying his hair and etching worry lines in his sallow face. He was jumpy this morning, not from the adrenaline-fuelled twitchiness of everyday share trading but in response to a deeper unease. The display on one of the screens changed again and the furrows deepened on his forehead. The red of falling stock prices flashed briefly across the biotechnology sector like spots of blood spurting from a knife wound. He glanced at the analysts' reports and press clippings cluttering his desk and tried to ignore the sweat that trickled down his back despite the air-conditioning in the cavernous dealing room. There was nothing specific he could put his finger on, but alarm bells were hammering in his head and he didn't have the luxury of time to dig deeper, not when a potentially catastrophic run might be starting. It might only be seconds, perhaps minutes at most, before others reacted to the trend and left his investments in the sector hopelessly exposed. Doubt turned to certainty and he lifted the phone, speaking urgently to the traders at their desks on the far side of the room.

Moments later, the splatter of red on the monitor turned to a flood as the bottom fell out of the market. The young man stuck his thumbs under his braces and twanged them with a sigh of satisfaction. He'd just beaten the odds again, the way one of the City's leading movers and shakers should and he could harden his heart to those without a chair when the music stopped. Movement up on the mezzanine floor attracted his attention and he saw the Chairman looking down at him from behind the glass wall of the Executive suite. Stanfield didn't often grace the office with his presence these days, but it was uncanny how the old buzzard always seemed to materialise when something major was happening in the market. Still, it was no bad thing for the top brass to see a virtuoso performance every now and again. He allowed himself an enigmatic grin and got up to head for the coffee machine. There was no substitute for the killer instinct and the balls to get the timing right on the tough decisions he thought smugly, unconsciously rationalising the strange fit of the jitters that had gripped him earlier. He would have dismissed as madness any suggestion that his actions had been pre-programmed with the unglamorous precision of a silicon chip.

***

Madness of a different kind was on Peter Conway's mind. The line between obsession and insanity is narrow and his father had been lurching unsteadily along it ever since he could remember. Now, it seemed, the battle that had made his childhood a living nightmare was finally lost. Peter's hand strayed to his jacket pocket and touched the letter that had arrived, unheralded, in the morning post. He'd thought the shackles of family obligation had long since been thrown off, but his father's message had cut through that complacent assumption like a scalpel. The practicalities of coping with a broken mind were daunting and he felt the rage against the unfairness of that burden well up again, as it had on and off all morning. But it couldn't disguise a deeper, more corrosive fear that he could barely bring himself to admit. There was no doubt where he'd inherited his broad forehead that fell to a narrow chin, his grey eyes set slightly too close together and his wiry physique. They ran in the family. What he couldn't handle was the thought that the seeds of madness might run in his blood too.

Like father, like son.

That was the most terrifying prospect of all.

Peter shuddered and forced his mind back to the job in hand. The image in the viewfinder of the Hasselblad 501CM medium format camera was pin-sharp, but it offended his professional eye. The eighty-millimetre f/2.8 Carl Zeiss lens was performing perfectly, as it always did, but the bloody lighting was still wrong, he decided with a grunt of displeasure. He lifted his head and glared at his assistant.

"You'll have to move the umbrella spots again," he said. "I'm still getting too much shadow."

Jack Howson cast a jaundiced eye at the first edition of Dante's 'Inferno' perched in splendid isolation against a battleship grey screen and ventured a protest.

"It looks fine to me," he said. "It's only an old book, for Christ's sake, not the Mona Lisa. How many more times do you expect me to clamber round the junk in this attic and lug the sodding lights about?"

"As many as it takes to get it right," Peter snapped. "We're trying to convince somebody the damned thing's worth buying, not doing holiday snaps for your family album. And don't give me that 'old book' crap. It's a rare work of art, worth a fortune to a collector."

"I know the party line." Jack waved the draft sales catalogue they were using as a shooting list as though it was a piece of dirty laundry. "I can read. And there's no need to scowl at me like that. I'll be buggered if I can figure out why anyone would pay thirteen grand for a pile of moth-eaten paper, that's all."

Peter sighed and struggled to hold on to his volatile temper. Normally, Jack's banter was a welcome diversion, easing the strain of long hours of concentration under hot lights. But not today. Then his eye strayed to the dog-eared object in front of the camera lens and amusement briefly softened the sharp angles of his face. As usual, Jack had put his finger on the heart of the problem. At first glance it really was a sorry looking specimen, but an eye for detail was the essence of a good photographer and getting past those first impressions to find an image worth serious money was what he was being paid for. Fortunately, the faint lines on the leather binding weren't the scuff marks they seemed to be. They were hand tooling by a first-rate craftsman and if he could get the lighting just right the shadows would lift it into relief to make a picture that would hit a potential buyer right in his bank balance. It wasn't a con trick. It was simply a matter of focusing attention on what you wanted people to notice and distracting them from the rest. Ironically, in those terms his job wasn't that different from what his father had done as a reporter with a National newspaper all those years ago, before he had blown it. Again, like father, like son, Peter thought sourly. The past had a nasty way of catching up with you, however hard you tried to escape.

And he had tried bloody hard. He felt a blush rise to his cheeks as it always did at the embarrassing memory of the gauche and pimply novice who had fled to London from the sticks with a camera bag on one shoulder and a large chip on the other. Against the odds and with the help of a few strangers who became good friends he had somehow blossomed into the master of an up-and-coming West End studio. He had talent and was in demand. He had even, most of the time, mastered the emollient skills of keeping clients happy. And now his alcoholic failure of a father threatened to drag him back into that old car-wreck of a life that had killed his mother and destroyed his childhood.

"Where do you want the damn lights, then?"

Jack Howson's question cut across his thoughts and Peter dragged his attention back to the job in hand. He shook his head irritably.

"I don't bloody well know," he scowled. "How am I supposed to think with you pestering me? Anyway, you're the one who's supposed to be the lighting wizard round here. Wave your fucking magic wand."

"Well, up yours," Jack muttered under his breath.

"What's that you said?" Peter demanded.

"I said, we'll have to tidy up the floor."

"That's not what it sounded like."

"Look for yourself." Jack waved at the heaps of books lying higgledy-piggledy where they'd been dumped and, judging by the layers of dust, long forgotten. "If you want to keep playing around with the lighting, we're going to need room to move. This place is like the black hole of Calcutta."

An icy silence fell and Peter saw Jack brace himself in expectation of a withering response. Then he heard the door behind him creak open.

"Tea, anyone? I, er..."

Claire, the youngest of the shop assistants, stood in the doorway clutching a mug in each hand and looking like a rabbit caught in a car's headlights.

"Oh dear," she said nervously. "Sorry. Am I interrupting something important?"

Peter's grey eyes swivelled towards her and he bit back a cutting reply. It wasn't her fault he was in a foul mood and taking it out on such a helpless target would only make matters worse. His conscience pricked and he felt his anger drain away. Jack was made of tougher stuff, but the same principle applied to him, too.

"No, it's OK," he said, forcing a smile. "Just a bit of creative tension, that's all. Tea sounds great."

"Are you sure?" Claire said doubtfully.

"Really, it's nothing a cuppa won't sort out. We were just getting a bit frustrated because we're so tight for space in here. Isn't that right, Jack?"

"Yeah," Jack grunted, accepting the olive branch. "We need to move the lights about, see, and all this junk keeps getting in the way."

Claire giggled.

"You don't want to let Anna hear you talking about her precious books that way or she'll really give you what for," she said, with a mischievous glint in her eye. Then she paused and wrinkled her nose prettily. "I suppose it is rather a tip in here, though, now you come to mention it. Look, I'll give you a hand to tidy up a bit, how about that?"

"You sure? It'll be a mucky old job."

"Why do you think we wear these dust coats?" She puffed out her chest and gave a provocative twirl. "I mean, it's not exactly the Paris fashion show round here, is it?"

"What about us?"

"Don't worry. Mr Conway's nice and slim, he can borrow a spare one of mine. You, though..." She let her eyes run appreciatively up and down Jack's chunky frame and giggled again. "None of the girls are quite your size, but I expect I can find something. Drink your tea and I'll be back in a tick."

Dust in a camera or on the lens is instant death to good quality pictures and Peter busied himself packing the equipment away into its protective travel bags. By the time he had finished, Jack and Claire were getting enthusiastically stuck into shifting the books and stirring up an acrid cloud in their wake. He left them to it, retreating to a corner where the air was relatively clean, though the acid smell of decaying paper still stung his nose and throat. He could not get his father's letter off his mind and before he could help himself it was in his hand. The silky touch of expensive vellum notepaper and the blue-black colour of fountain-pen ink brought old memories flooding back, even though the writing itself had deteriorated to an unfamiliar scrawl in the years since he had last seen it.

The perpetual ranting about shadowy figures spinning a web of lies to ruin his father's life and the story-of-a-lifetime that they had prevented him from publishing was the all-too-familiar wallpaper of his childhood. Fuelled by whisky and bitterness it had left no room for love. Anybody brought up amid the bleakness and disasters of a childhood like that could surely be forgiven for hating their father. Nobody could blame them for severing the ties and walking away to make their own life.

If only things were that simple. The vellum crackled as he crumpled the letter in his fist. At one level, a casual reader might think the words on the paper were rational enough. They spoke of proof of a conspiracy, of hard evidence finally discovered that events of twenty years ago had been manipulated to suppress the truth and ruin a prominent journalist. They were the words of a man whose most cherished beliefs had been vindicated.

To Peter, though, the letter conveyed a very different message. The truth was, there had never been any conspiracy, just a sad fantasy dreamed up by a failure, desperate to explain away screwing up his career and wrecking his family. Now the fantasy had completely and irrevocably taken over from reality. That left just two options. He could turn his back and walk away again, which would be no more than the old bastard deserved. Or he could shoulder the responsibility and kiss goodbye to having a life of his own. The choice should be easy, but somehow it was quite the opposite.

***

Across the other side of the City, the Head of Security at Media Associates was also facing a crisis and contemplating his options. An outsider would have found it odd that a seemingly ultra-respectable public relations firm should employ a security team at all, let alone possess the kind of sophisticated operation that Sam Garvey presided over. But then, outsiders never penetrated far enough to become aware of it. The firm's up-market address, slick front-office set-up and carefully nurtured professional image satisfied any idle curiosity. The select group of clients, knowing a little of how results were achieved, saw nothing strange about the need for tight security. And to the true insiders, whose creature the firm was, the necessity of protecting their secrets was so obvious that it was taken for granted, as was the correspondingly generous budget.

But the money in Garvey's domain was not lavished on fripperies. The open-plan room was starkly functional. The computer equipment was state of the art, but the ranks of grey metal desks separated by cheap chest-high partitions were a far cry from the leather and chrome designer furniture of the client reception areas. At the far end of the room a uniformed guard sat in a sealed-off control centre, monitoring a bank of screens that provided high quality digital surveillance of the entire building and with the ability only a fingertip away to trip the electronic locks on any doorway. The only other enclosed space was a large glass-walled office in one corner, with an uninterrupted view over the whole operation. The man sitting at the desk like a spider in his web was in his early fifties and elegantly suited in black. On the surface he looked every inch the urbane senior executive, though on closer inspection cold eyes and hard muscles told a different story.

Sam Garvey flicked through the file on his desk and again found nothing to reassure him. It was old and dog-eared, but history had a way of turning round and biting you in the arse. He hated loose ends. They spelled trouble with a capital 'T', something his employers would not tolerate and which they paid him handsomely to prevent. Judging from the dossier this particular loose end should have been tied off permanently long ago. However crazy this guy's allegations may have been, they had the potential to inflict serious damage. Back then they'd destroyed the man's credibility cleverly enough if you liked playing that sort of game. But they hadn't finished the job and security depended on certainties, not fancy footwork and wishful thinking. Whichever way you looked at it, this mess had been a ticking time bomb for far too long. Now the explosion was imminent and there was only one way to prevent it. That much was blindingly obvious, but there wasn't a damn thing he could do about it.

Sam snapped the folder shut and scowled at the stark red stamp on its cover. The imprint was smudged here and there and the colour had faded with age. But the words were still plain enough to read and they stood like an iron bar across his way. 'Research Directorate: Restricted', it said and he knew better than to ignore the warning, despite the urgency of the crisis. The old harridan who called herself 'Chief Scientist' was the real power behind Media Associates, whatever the Director and his cronies might pretend. She would tolerate no interference with one of her projects and her fingerprints were all over this.

His fleshy lips curled in distaste. The weasel words in the firm's marketing literature about professional standards and ethics hid realities that were hard to swallow even by his pragmatic standards. It gave him the creeps the way they screwed with people's heads and he felt a flash of something close to sympathy for his current target. The spin-doctors had been pulling the poor bastard's strings like a puppet for a long time and there was no telling what they'd been trying to achieve or why. Whatever their plan was, though, the wheels were about to come off unless they got their fingers out and sanctioned some action. Sam Garvey looked at his watch and drummed his fingers. Time was running out. If he didn't get the word soon, it would be too late.

Mike Arnold's eye caught the movement and he glanced furtively at his boss. It was the tenth time check in the past half-hour and for Sam Garvey that was tantamount to apoplexy. It wouldn't be long, he reckoned, before the lid blew off. It didn't happen often, but then there were few people brave or foolish enough to leave Sam stewing like this. He was a tough son of a bitch at the best of times and when he erupted there'd be blood on the walls.

Mike's immediate objective was to make sure the blood wasn't his, so he kept his head down, re-reading the latest surveillance report. A good inch of typescript and photographs, it was a fine piece of work and he made a mental note to compliment the team. Way out there in the boonies they'd have had to use all of their SAS training to get this kind of close coverage without being spotted. And their conclusions were unambiguous, with none of the usual cover-your-arse caveats. The target had finally pieced enough together a credible enough story to try and cut a deal with the kiss and tell tabloids, who wouldn't care how far-fetched the story was but only about how much muck their lawyers would allow them rake. He'd been dumb to give his game away like that, though. He should have figured out that the firm had key players in all the major news outlets on the payroll.

Mike Arnold flipped through a few more pages, but it was a pointless exercise going over the material yet again. It was obvious what had to be done, whatever the headshrinkers said, so what the hell was Sam pissing about for? The decision should be easy, but somehow it seemed to be quite the opposite. He forgot himself sufficiently to stand up and walk over to the open door of Sam's office to make the point, but the bleak expression on his boss's face froze the words in his throat.

"What?" Sam snapped at him.

"I... er..." Mike struggled. Then the phone on Sam Garvey's desk rang and the tricky moment passed. He watched the frown on Sam's face deepen as the one-sided call went on and braced himself for a backlash.

"Arrogant prick," Sam Garvey muttered under his breath as he slammed the phone down. He wasn't used to being told in detail how to do his job and didn't like it. But whatever his opinion about the rest of the agenda, he had no quarrel with the first item on the list. "Mike," he said sharply. "Is the field team ready to go?"

"Yeah, they're on standby. Everything's in place."

"Well what the fuck are you standing there for then? Boot them off their fat arses and tell them to get the job done."

While Mike Arnold made his phone call, Sam leaned back in his chair and stared at the ceiling. The Research Directorate, hidden away in its own building on the other side of London, was a law unto itself and he was not amongst the privileged few who had been admitted into its innermost secrets. But the voice on the phone had let slip that all this was part of some sort of complicated test of new techniques. What was that fanatical bitch of a Chief Scientist really up to this time, he wondered. That was a much more intriguing problem than killing off one crazy old troublemaker.

Chapter 2

The hard-bitten ex-Sergeant in combat fatigues acknowledged his new instructions and killed the satellite downlink. About bloody time, too, he thought. His team had been hanging about here far too long already because the armchair warriors at head office couldn't make their fucking minds up. He slid the binoculars up to his eyes and with minimal movement scanned the target area one more time. There had been no activity other than the random wandering of grazing sheep for a couple of hours now and he was as certain as he could be that there was no threat of detection. He squeezed a switch and spoke softly into the microphone of his lightweight headset.

"All units. Phase four. Go now. Repeat, phase four, go now."

The acknowledging signals came quickly. His men were alert and probably just as keen as he was to get to a pub for a few pints, with this job done and dusted. His teeth bared briefly in a vicious grin. He'd have their balls if any of them were over-enthusiastic and cocked up now. The first three phases of the plan - infiltration, installing the surveillance equipment and monitoring the subject - had gone like clockwork and that could breed complacency. But termination and extraction were always the trickiest parts and any lapse of concentration could have dire consequences. Not from enemy action; this wasn't the military any more and no bullets would be flying. The risks were real enough all the same. As he'd said to the men in his pre-op briefing, jail for life was as grim a threat as incoming fire and they'd damn well better remember it. The Sergeant gave his equipment a final check, then slithered out of the hide that had been home for the past couple of days, eradicating the remaining signs of his presence as he went. The sheep continued their grazing undisturbed and if the tall grass on the hillside moved, it was only in response to the gentle breeze coming down the mountain towards the cottage in the valley below.

On the opposite side of the valley, a battered old Series III short wheelbase Land Rover swerved off a narrow country lane into the space afforded by the entrance to an overgrown track. The driver, looking even scruffier than his vehicle in muddy overalls and Wellingtons, clambered out and bent over to inspect the front offside wheel, cursing loudly and fluently. The obscenities covered the sound of the air being let out of the tyre, just as effectively as the immobilised vehicle now eliminated any possibility of unexpected visitors reaching the cottage a mile away down the track. The driver straightened and looked around as though to be sure that other traffic would have room to pass by in the lane. Then, satisfied there were no immediate threats, he fetched the makings from his pocket and casually rolled a cigarette. He flicked away the match, took a deep drag and started to rummage in the back for a jack and wheel brace. He was in no hurry. The flat tyre was a watertight excuse to be where he was and nobody was around to complain if fitting the spare took some considerable time. Meanwhile, the action team's flank was secure.

Entering the cottage was easy. The garden was a riot

of untended shrubbery, pressing up hard against the walls and the three men slid through it soundlessly and invisibly. They materialised abruptly only feet from the open front door and moved through it without the slightest hesitation, led by the Sergeant. Behind him, one soldier angled right to secure the kitchen and study, while the other strode left towards the stairs. Their rubber-soled boots made no sound and no word was spoken or necessary. They had taken objectives like this a thousand times in many countries and the only difference today was the lack of weapons in hand. Armed resistance was not an issue here and they were supremely confident in their ability to handle anything else with their bare hands. Moments later they returned to the living room, each crisply announcing 'Target clear'. It was the first sound to break the silence, apart from an anguished grunt from the grey-haired old man who until a few seconds earlier had been dozing peacefully in his chair.

The grunt was caused by the Sergeant pulling tight the Velcro fastenings of a 'Humane Wrap', an eight-inch wide band of tough, two-ply cotton webbing encircling the victim's torso and clamping his arms immovably to his side. An American invention, designed to allow policemen and prison officers to immobilise violent criminals quickly and easily, the politically correct bullshit of the trade name on the label caused the usual brief flicker of amusement in the Sergeant's eyes. The lightweight, compact devices were a vital part of his team's restraint kit, but 'humane' had never figured amongst the many practical reasons for immobilising his victims. A quick tip backwards of the chair helped deployment of a second Wrap, this time locking the legs together around the knees, to complete the job. There would be no possibility of a struggle, no thrashing about to cause bruising or other injuries that might interest a nosey policeman or pathologist. Afterwards they would peel away cleanly, leaving no forensic traces and no evidence that the subject had been under constraint.

A few curt words directed one of his men to retrieving all the bugs they'd installed and making good so that no traces remained. The other set about a rapid search of the house. The surveillance tapes had revealed most of what to look for and where and the black plastic sack quickly filled. Years of rigid Army discipline made the sanitisation process thorough and ensured that he left each room tidily squared away in his wake.

The Sergeant ignored the old man's feeble cries for help. There was nobody within earshot, so the noise was immaterial. He reached out with his gloved hand, delicately picked up a tumbler from the table by the old man's armchair and raised it to his nose. The whisky dregs smelt fresh and he smiled. Half his job was already done, by the look of things. He reached into his pack and lifted out a bottle.

"Be quiet, now," he said firmly. "You and I are going to have a little drink, that's all, while my mates do their business."

He was a convincing liar when he put his mind to it and his disarming smile was tentatively returned. He broke the seal on the bottle and poured a hefty slug into the glass. Taking care not to smudge the fingerprints, he raised it to the old man's lips.

"There you go. Your favourite brand of Scotch. Nothing to worry about."

The old man took a first gulp and the Sergeant smiled again, encouragingly. So far as he could figure out from the surveillance intercepts the guy was nothing more than a deluded old crackpot, but that wasn't for him to judge. Some important people were obviously highly pissed off and there was no room for pity; business was business and this was easy money compared to some assignments. It would not be long before his victim was past noticing what he was swallowing. Then it would just be a simple matter of pressing his fingerprints onto the medicine bottles and feeding him the pills.

***

Jack Howson dusted himself down and strolled across the room towards his boss. He read the body language and decided this was not, after all, the moment to take the piss about certain people being too posh to get their hands dirty.

"Are you okay?" he said.

"What?"

Peter looked up and seemed surprised that the attic walls had all but disappeared behind neat ramparts of musty books, leaving a large clear area in the centre. Jack looked at him quizzically and gestured at the crumpled letter in Peter's hand.

"Problems?"

Peter folded the letter and put it away.

"Not really. Just family stuff."

A load of bollocks that was, Jack thought. Something

seriously heavy duty must be going down to take his boss's mind off the job like this, he was usually focused to the point of obsession on his work during a shoot. But whenever the subject of family came up it was like hitting a brick wall. Except, he mused, on a couple of rare nights out when Peter had forgotten his usual aversion to getting pissed and accidentally let slip a little of his family past. Poor sod, losing his mother like that because his dad had taken to the bottle. That was no kind of childhood. His own family had never had two pennies to rub together, but though life had been tough they had always been close and looked out for each other, the way things should be. The way he'd like it to be with Peter if only the stubborn bastard would open up a bit.

"Well, fair enough then," he said. "If you're sure. You've only got to ask, if I can help with anything."

"Yeah, thanks, I know. Grab those lights while I set up the Hasselblad again, will you? We've got a job to finish."

"Sure," Jack replied laconically. "You'd better get your mind back on photographs, though, if we're going to get it done by the end of the week, let alone today."

***

The camera shutter mechanism clunked heavily and the room vanished in incandescence as the synchronised Courtenay Colourflash units fired beneath their silvered umbrellas. Like the aftermath of a lightning strike, silence fell and a pungent smell of scorched dust permeated the air. Peter Conway repeated the sequence twice more, bracketing the exposure one stop either side of the flash meter reading for insurance against the gremlins that lurked in any mixture of film emulsion with light. Then he let out his breath in a sigh.

"Right, that's it," he said, inserting the blanking plate into its slot and unclipping the film back from the camera. "Jack, will you pop downstairs and tell Anna we're all done up here?"

Peter eased his back and watched the spiky hair and broad shoulders of his assistant vanish through the door. Life was bloody strange sometimes, he thought. On the face of it, nature had intended Jack Howson for a building site or a boxing ring and not as a candidate to be one of the pillars of Spectrum Studios. When he had turned up at the door about a year back looking for work, displaying all the awkwardness of the youthful unemployed, it had seemed like a charity case. But a couple of hours a week for odd jobs, offered with misgivings in a moment of weakness, revealed a surprising talent with studio lighting that had quickly become indispensable. More astonishing yet, he felt they'd become friends. Peter was still struggling to work out how that had happened. It wasn't something he had much experience with.

"Mrs Stein says she'll be along in a minute," Jack said, reappearing like a genie through the low doorway. "Assuming she can squeeze her way up those bleeding stairs, that is. They're steep as hell and narrow with it."

"I expect she'll manage," Peter chuckled. "She should be used to it; she's been here long enough. And call her Anna, everyone does."

"Sure," Jack said absent-mindedly, looking around at the screens, lights, tripods and other paraphernalia of the day's filming. "That's not going to make it any easier to get all this stuff back down to the van, though. I'm still knackered from carting it up here."

"Think of it as a work-out. It's a damn sight more productive than pumping iron in that gym you go to. Anyway, you didn't even break sweat fetching it in this morning."

"That's not the point. I can't figure out why we've gone to all this trouble instead of using the studio. You don't need to run errands these days."

"Habit, I suppose," Peter said slowly. "This was the first commission I ever got, you see and I've done the catalogue every year since. Believe it or not, coming here was the only thing that kept me afloat when I was starting out."

"Maybe so, but ..."

"I know, things have moved on. I guess you're right, I probably shouldn't be doing this kind of work any more. But there's more to it than that."

"What happened to the ruthless young tycoon? You were rabbiting on only the other day about how you had to move up-market, go for the movers and shakers with their fancy fees. Something about covering your overheads, as I recall."

"This is different."

Jack sniffed disdainfully.

"Bang goes my bleeding pay rise then, I suppose. You're too soft."

"Loyalty cuts both ways. I've come close to packing

the whole thing in a few times over the years when things were rough and Anna helped me through. She's been like a guardian angel and introduced me to some of my best clients into the bargain. Nobody's going to accuse me of walking away from debts like that."

Besides, he thought, Anna was a poppet and the closest thing to family he'd had after he'd escaped from his father's clutches to strike out on his own. Then the poppet in question marched through the door, all bosom and beads, interrupting Peter's train of thought.

"All done, then, young feller-me-lad? About time, too. I kicked the last punter out of the shop an hour ago. Bloody PPP merchant. Place has been crawling with them today and it's past time I went home."

Peter smiled. She'd not changed from the first time he'd met her, except that her flowing auburn hair had a few more streaks of grey in it. Matronly and sixty-something, with a dress sense that seemed to have got stuck in the age of hippies and flower power, she had all the bashfulness of a Regimental Sergeant-Major and a voice to match. The kind heart behind the bluster was another story, but the unfortunate customer was unlikely to have seen that far under the surface, he thought, suppressing the giggle that threatened to erupt.

"A what merchant?" Jack said, looking puzzled.

"PPP," Anna said with a grunt of amusement. "Stands for 'Pick up, Put down and Piss off'. They're the bane of my life, bloody browsers cluttering the shop showing no inclination to reach for their wallets. I have to keep swatting them off like flies."

"Isn't that what a second-hand bookshop's all about? Getting people in to browse, I mean."

"Wash your mouth out, young man." Anna stuck her hands on her hips and glared at Jack. "Second-hand books, indeed. I'll have you know this is an antiquarian bookshop. I sell literary treasures, not recycled garbage. You're not one of those limp-wristed Mills and Boon types, are you?"

"Most of Anna's customers are serious collectors," Peter explained hastily, before Jack rose to the bait. "Believe me, she charms the pants off them, real red carpet treatment. Isn't that right, Anna?"

"Of course it is. You don't think they're going to pay such outrageous prices just on the strength of a few measly photographs, do you? Some of us have to work to earn a living."

"My heart bleeds for you," he said with a grin. "I suppose you're in a rush for the prints as usual, all the same?"

"Of course I am, dear boy. Can't afford to have these damn books sitting around gathering dust, you know."

That was a laugh, Peter thought, considering how the musty smell was still lingering in his nose and he could taste the acid in his throat, despite the cups of tea that had been flowing all day.

"I'll have the proofs back to you for checking in three or four days, then, if that's OK."

"Don't be silly," she said with a frown. "I'm already a week late getting the bloody catalogue to the printers. Tomorrow would do nicely, though."

Peter sighed.

"I can't perform miracles," he said. "Not even for you.

I'm tied up tomorrow afternoon with Viscount Stanfield, sorting out pictures of some new property development he's involved with down at St. Katherine's Dock and the rest of the week's pretty hectic, too."

"Billy Stanfield? Are you still working for that old rogue?"

"Actually, we've grown quite friendly since you first introduced us. And yes, he's a regular client now, too, so don't even think about asking me to cancel the appointment."

"That still leaves tomorrow morning," Anna said with a stubborn look on her face. "I'm sure you could shuffle your other commitments as well, if you really wanted to. Or are you so high and mighty now that your old customers don't matter any more?"

"Come off it, Anna, you know me better than that. Look, I suppose I can get your stuff to the lab first thing and hope they can fit me in," Peter said, thinking quickly. "Even then, the best I can offer for getting the proofs to you is the day after tomorrow and I wouldn't do that for anyone else."

"That whingeing little man at the printers will just have to wait a bit longer, then, won't he?" she said with a careless shrug of her shoulders that set her necklaces jangling. "But you tell Billy Stanfield when you see him that he's messed me about and he owes me one. I'll expect him round here with his chequebook to buy something nice and expensive for his collection by way of compensation."

"I'll tell him you're pining away from neglect," Peter agreed, suppressing a twinge of sympathy for the unknown owner of the print shop, whose scheduling problems had just multiplied. "Now, if you've finished twisting my arm, perhaps I can get on?"

He turned to start dismantling the equipment, keeping his thoughts buried under a professional smile. He'd have to juggle his appointments book again and dishing out the soft soap to keep everyone happy was part of the business he detested. Life would be a whole lot sweeter if customers, Anna included, were capable of planning ahead and being flexible about deadlines. But they never were and that was that.

Wintry darkness had already fallen as he helped Jack load the equipment into the back of the van. The alley off the Charing Cross road that housed Anna's bookshop was deserted and the last of the commuters were scurrying across the junction with the main road a hundred yards away, heading for the station and the comforts of home. He knew how they felt. The thought of the hour or so it would take to go back to his West-End studio, pack everything away and lock up was suddenly too much. He reached into his pocket, pulled out the bunch of keys and chucked them across to Jack Howson.

"Here, Jack, will you take the gear back for me, lock up the studio and everything? I've had it for today."

Jack looked at him and raised an eyebrow.

"Quick pint first? Thirsty work under those lights. I know a good pub just round the corner."

Peter smiled. Jack appeared to know a good pub round every corner in London and it was never just one pint. Every once in a while they'd had a memorable evening together, but having a drunk for a father tended to put you off booze.

"Not tonight, Jack, thanks. I've got an early start tomorrow to get these pictures to the lab and I don't trust them to get the colour balance right unless I watch them like a hawk. I'll see you at the studio about lunchtime, okay?"

***

The forty-five minute journey to Tonbridge was the customary amalgam of lurching bodies, sharp elbows and stale sweat, but Peter had long since acquired the seasoned commuter's ability to ignore such intrusions on his personal space. Instead, his mind picked away relentlessly at the scar tissue of his past and his fears for the future, just as, presumably, his fellow travellers were doing behind their averted eyes and expressionless faces. It was a relief when the front door of his two-up, two-down Victorian terraced house in Woodside Road slammed shut behind him, leaving the rest of the world comfortably outside. He kicked off his shoes, threw his jacket and tie untidily over the spare armchair and peered unenthusiastically at the hamburger and fries he'd grabbed at the McDonald's outside the station. The chips were already cold and limp and his appetite vanished. Instead, he poured himself a large Southern Comfort before settling into his Scandinavian leather recliner. The first sip of liquor burned the dust from his throat and the tensions of the day started to drain away.

At half past eight, the telephone rang and put an end to all that. Peter put down his drink with a curse and pressed the mute button on the TV remote control, cutting off Inspector Frost in mid-sentence. He snatched the phone from its cradle.

"Conway."

"Is that Peter James Conway?" The voice sounded flat and official.

"Yes, speaking."

"Son of Francis Albert Conway, of Pike's Cottage, Michaelstone?"

Peter froze. The intrusion was like something straight out of his nightmares.

"Hello? Are you still there?" the caller insisted.

Peter took a deep breath and gathered his wits.

"Yes. Who is this? What do you want?"

"This is Detective Sergeant Williams from the Hereford police. I'm calling in connection with your father…"

"If the old man's in trouble again you can leave me out of it," Peter interrupted. "Whatever mess he's got himself into this time, it's his own funeral. Nothing to do with me."

There was silence for a few seconds and the sound of DS Williams clearing his throat came down the line with crystal clarity.

"Er, just a moment, sir, if you don't mind. It's not that he's in trouble. Er, well, not with us, that is, exactly…" The official voice had clearly been put off its stroke and was tinged with embarrassment.

"What is it, then?"

"Well, sir, we've been given to understand that you're his next of kin." Peter felt something twist in his gut at the words and his knuckles whitened on the phone as the policeman continued. "I'm sorry to have to tell you that your father was found dead at six o'clock this evening."

"What do you mean, dead? That can't be right. I had a letter from him this morning, for God's sake. Do you mean he's had an accident?"

"I'm sorry, sir. I know it must be a shock, but I assure you, we don't make mistakes on matters like this. We were called to his home by a neighbour late this afternoon and we were able to get positive identification."

"But how... I mean... what happened?"

"I'm afraid you'll have to wait for the Coroner to establish the exact circumstances," the voice continued inexorably in his ear. "In cases like this the law requires a post-mortem and an inquest to be held. I am permitted to tell you, though, that there's no suspicion of foul play. Our preliminary findings suggest your father took his own life."

"Jesus. I, er... I don't know anything about this sort of thing. I mean, do I have to come down there, or what?"

"The Coroner's office will be in touch, sir. They'll explain everything."

"I see. Er... thank you."

"All part of the job, sir. In the meantime, please accept my condolences. If there's anything further I can do to help, give me a call at Hereford police station. Just ask for Detective Sergeant Williams."

Peter put the phone down and let the implications sink in. He was free of the old bastard at last and relief fizzed through his veins like champagne. Then the selfishness of that thought took his breath away, but he searched his conscience in vain for kindlier sentiments. There were too many things he could not bring himself to forgive or forget.

Chapter 3

Two weeks later, Peter drove the hundred and seventy miles to Hereford and found a car park not far from the city centre. The 'Pay and Display' machine swallowed his coins, wheezed and disgorged a ticket. He frowned again at the sign proclaiming the maximum length of stay was two hours, wondering how strictly it was enforced. He'd no idea how long the inquest would take and today's ordeal would be bad enough without the aggravation of having the Porsche clamped. Then he shrugged, stuck the ticket on the inside of the windscreen and walked off. The one-way system was a nightmare and he didn't fancy another white-knuckle ride through the city traffic to look for different car park, so he'd have to hope for the best.

At the exit, he turned right without thinking then stopped, perplexed at the incongruity of his action. In the car he'd felt like a stranger, but on foot it was different. He knew where he was and where he was going. The memories were still there even after nearly ten years. The family outings were fewer after Mum died and fewer still after Dad took seriously to the drink, but there was the cathedral ahead of him and round the corner to the left, out of sight, would be the Green Dragon hotel where they'd always had their cream teas. The crooked buildings lining King Street seemed smaller and shabbier and some of the shop fronts were unfamiliar. Otherwise little had changed, perhaps not since this end of the cathedral collapsed one Easter Monday in seventeen hundred and something.

He chuckled, remembering how he'd always given the structure a wide berth after Dad told him about that. Then his smile died in confusion. He couldn't recall the last time he'd thought of his father with anything but loathing and a few happy memories didn't count for much against that reality. Somewhere nearby a clock chimed the quarter hour, startling him out of his daydream and reminding him he needed to get moving. After coming all this way he didn't want to be late, at least he was still certain about that.

When he found the coroner's court it was far from the imposing edifice he'd imagined. Outside, the brass plaque was in danger of being squeezed off the wall by a flashier offering from an adjacent solicitor, while inside a narrow corridor led to an area more akin to a Victorian schoolroom than a court of law. None of it had been troubled by redecoration within recent memory and he wrinkled his nose at the smell in the air. Perhaps it was the drains, he thought, settling himself on one of the benches at the back of the room, or maybe the loss and guilt attendant on unnatural death had their own stench that had soaked into the fabric over the years. The thought made him uneasy. Smell or not, he recognised those emotions stirring in himself and shook his head at the vagaries of human nature. They were not feelings he had expected to associate ever again with his father. But he had little time to dwell on it before people started to file in and the proceedings got under way.

The evidence of the police was brief and unemotional. They were summoned to Pike's Cottage at approximately five thirty on the twenty-seventh of

September. The door was open and there was no evidence of forced entry. They found a body, later identified as the occupier, Francis Albert Conway, in an armchair in the sitting room. The police surgeon was summoned and confirmed life extinct at about six p.m. There was no evidence of foul play. A whisky bottle and several empty pill bottles were found and submitted for forensic examination. The coroner's officer was notified and the body removed for a post mortem. Next of kin were informed. Routine enquiries revealed that the deceased had a history of drunkenness and irrational behaviour. No note was found, but the police were satisfied that Francis Albert Conway had taken his own life.

The pathologist was even more economical with his words. The cause of death was asphyxia from the inhalation of vomit, caused by a fatal dose of aspirin and paracetamol ingested with whisky. The physical evidence was consistent with the drugs being self-administered. Death occurred some four hours before the arrival of the police. And that was it. Open and shut. Suicide while the balance of his mind was disturbed. Fifteen minutes, Peter Conway noted, was all that it had taken to recount the life and death of his father.

Apart from the officials, the two witnesses and himself there was only one other occupant of the room. At first sight he looked like an elderly tramp, his shirt grey-edged around the collar and the tie askew beneath a roughly patched tweed jacket, though a few desultory scribbles he'd made in a notebook suggested otherwise. There was little by way of comfort here to attract a drifter off the streets so maybe he was a local reporter at the fag-end of his career. If so his demeanour suggested that the proceedings would fail to merit so much as a mention in the 'wed and dead' column and Peter felt a surge of irrational anger. The man obviously neither knew nor cared that the by-line of Frank Conway had once been feared and respected on the front pages of the National press. Now this hack, scraping a living at the bottom of the journalistic barrel, was dismissing his passing as not worth a line of print. Surely a man's existence should leave more of mark than that.

The urge to lash out at such indifference and put the record straight overtook him and Peter was on his feet looking for trouble when reason prevailed. This was not the place to make a scene. Besides, it would achieve nothing except a minor scandal for the press to gloat over and he wouldn't give them that satisfaction. He bit his tongue and brushed past the reporter, ignoring the man's half-hearted attempt to catch his arm and say something. At the door, one of the court officials intercepted Peter, guiding him into an office to complete some final formalities and by the time he emerged the place was deserted and the moment had passed.

It wasn't that simple though to throw off the bad taste the incident left in his mouth. He brooded all the way back to the car and was still full of conflicting emotions as he drove across the Wye bridge and headed south-west towards the hamlet of Michaelstone. Pike's Cottage was another bloody problem he could have done without. He'd never understood why Mum had left it to him in the first place on condition that Dad could occupy it rent-free for life, but the fact was he had to decide what to do with it now and it would be daft not to give it the once-over while he was here. He gritted his teeth, not wanting to be reminded of happier days when it was the family's retreat from the rigours of a reporter's life in London and Dad had been a man to be reckoned with. Much of his work had been penned there, scribbled longhand in the stone-flagged study, cutting to the heart of the issues of the day and conceding nothing to the softer rhythms of rural life. If only things could have stayed that way...

***

Peter cursed and stamped on the brakes as he almost overshot the entrance to the track that led to the cottage. The potholes were deeper than ever and he slowed to a crawl, fearful for the exhaust and wincing at the sound of the untrimmed hedges scraping the paintwork. The Porsche was his pride and joy and he'd be damned if he was going to wreck it for the sake of saving a couple of minutes, but despite his care there was a harsh scraping of metal on stone as he negotiated the hump of the bridge spanning the river Honddu. He swore again and slowed even further for the hard left turn through the gateway. Peter switched off the engine and stared at the cottage in dismay.

It looked cold and dilapidated, hunched beneath the mountain ridge, with an air of abandonment highlighted by the wilderness that had once been a garden but now pressed up against the walls in a riot of tangled growth. Paint was peeling off the window frames and the porch, showing the grey of weather-beaten wood underneath. Faded curtains at the windows, obscured by streaks of dirt on the glass, reinforced the mood of neglect and the feeling of wrongness that had been nagging at him all day strengthened. There was something unexplained here, not just about the squalor in which Dad had lived out his last days and the manner of his death. Something deeper. As a child, he had never looked for explanations behind the bitterness and drunken rages that had destroyed their family life. The hurt left no room for reason. But now as an adult he found himself compelled for the first time to think about the forces that had smashed a respected and successful man and brought him to this. And he realised that he had no answers.

Peter reached across to the passenger seat, tore open the manila envelope containing his father's personal effects that he had picked up from the coroner's officer and pulled out a bunch of keys. He jumped out of the car and strode over to the front door. The lock turned easily and he ducked under the lintel, stepping through into the gloom of the sitting room.

It had always been a dark room, he remembered, with its small windows shaded for much of the day by the loom of the mountains nearby. Without the crackling flames in the inglenook fireplace it was dank and cheerless and he shivered. Oddly, although the furnishings were battered and threadbare, it was tidy. If there was anything left that might speak of what had happened he wouldn't find it here. His eye strayed to the right of the fireplace to the rickety door that led to the study and he hesitated. That was his father's domain and the inhibition against entering without permission was still strong even though his head told him the rule was irrelevant now. Then, tentatively, he walked across and lifted the latch still half expecting a whiplash reprimand from the figure that should be sitting inside.

Fifteen minutes later Peter Conway was back in the study, sitting in the Grandfather chair behind the desk and feeling perplexed. His memories were of an arrogant man who dismissed tidiness as a preoccupation of petty minds and had lived accordingly. But not any more. Everything in the house was in its place. Even the desk in front of him, always a mass of scribbled notes, half-finished manuscripts and files, was clean. Like a stage set, he thought; how a stranger might expect to see it rather than how Dad had really lived and worked. Then his eye caught the Parker Duofold fountain pen that was lying in the desk-tidy and he leaned forward to pick it up. The barrel was dulled with years of heavy use and his lips twitched with amusement as he recalled the way Dad had always referred to it as his sword. It was blunted instrument now, but in its time it had cut down to size many of those who saw themselves as the great and the good. He slipped it into his pocket and twined his hands behind his neck. There was an enigma here and nothing seemed to add up. Someone driven to take their own life would hardly spend their last hours doing the housework they despised. Broken mind or not, the old man couldn't have changed that much.

He settled back in the chair, letting his thoughts

wander and his gaze drift round the room. It was full of familiar friends from the early days when he had been permitted to sit in the corner, over there on the milking stool and watch his father's flying hand create the words that would be tomorrow's headlines. Here, on the bottom shelf of the bookcase, was the leather-bound edition of Roget's thesaurus, next to the ranks of the Oxford English Dictionary. On the next shelf, the presentation volumes of "Who's Who" and the Encyclopaedia Britannica awarded in recognition of some long-forgotten journalistic triumph. Above that, the brassbound box containing the homeopathic medicines that Dad swore by to cure all ills.

At the sight of it Peter's lips curled in revulsion. Those herbal potions had always been dispensed liberally and most tasted so disgusting that even the memory made him feel queasy. But like it or lump it there was no alternative, except the occasional pill handed out by the nurse at school and never admitted to. Conventional medicines were banned. Chemical poisons, Dad called them with a vehemence verging on fanaticism. It was bloody odd to put it mildly that he would choose to take such drugs to kill himself. Aspirin and Paracetamol were so commonplace that nobody had questioned their presence, yet in this house it was as startling as finding the Koran in a synagogue and there were plenty of natural poisons he could have used that would have been much more in character.

Then his thoughts came to an abrupt halt. In character? That was ridiculous. Bitter and twisted the old man might have been. Drunk and lonely, too, living with past failure and loss. But live with it he had and remained true to his convictions however wrong-headed. It was not in his nature to be suicidal but to attack adversity like a terrier shaking a rat. And if that was the case, just where had those pills come from and why had his father denied the beliefs of a lifetime to take them?

A creak from the ancient roof timbers startled him and the hairs prickled on the back of his neck as the room darkened. He fought back the urge to leap out of the chair and get the hell out of this dismal place. It was nothing, he persuaded himself, just the shadow of the mountains creeping over the house as the sun slid down behind them. Where the hell were Dad's papers, though? There must be something that would provide a clue to what had been going on in the old man's mind. He ransacked the desk drawers but they were empty apart from a few stray paper clips and he slammed the last of them shut in frustration. Presumably the police had taken everything, though it was peculiar that they hadn't mentioned it.

His gaze strayed back to the medicine chest. A distant memory nagged at him and he struggled for a moment before it surfaced. Dad had kept a few of his most important documents safe from prying eyes in there, that was it. A secret compartment, which had caught his imagination when he was a kid. Peter pulled the box off the shelf, fumbling around the base to find the barely detectable notch that marked the hidden mechanism. Press it just so, he remembered Dad patiently explaining and then twist like this... With a quiet click the base came away in his hand and a bundle of papers covered in Frank Conway's characteristic scrawl fell into his lap.

For an instant he felt his father's presence, as though the old man had stepped into the room and was looking over his shoulder. He shivered superstitiously and scrabbled the documents together. His imagination was running riot, but the chill was real enough and this time the urge to get back out into the fresh air was irresistible. Hurriedly, he stacked the thesaurus and the dictionary on top of the medicine chest. The rest could stay, but those he would take as keepsakes. He lifted the pile with both hands, clamping his chin on the books to steady the load. The smell of damp paper and leather filled his nostrils and he stifled a sneeze that threatened to spill everything to the floor. At the front door he had to bend his knees to get under the lintel and he edged awkwardly through, arms aching from the strain of keeping his grip. Then he saw the door of the Porsche hanging open and frowned. He didn't remember leaving it like that.

Two black-clad figures materialised with shocking speed, one on each side of him. From the left a fist crashed into his kidney, doubling him up in agony and scattering the possessions he'd salvaged all over the pathway. The second assailant, equally muscular but lighter on his feet and perhaps more particular about his workmanship, took careful aim and bashed Peter's temple with what seemed from the corner of his eye like a baseball bat. The sickening crunch of wood on bone was the last thing he remembered before the earth seemed to open and sucked him down into a bottomless black pit.

Chapter 4

Peter Conway stared into the open grave and shivered as the wind sliced through his overcoat. It was not the cold, though, that was getting to him. It was the certainty that nothing he had been told about his father's death made sense. What if the old bugger hadn't been mad after all? Perversely, the possibility was no less troubling than the alternative and he shifted uneasily. Another gust ruffled the wreath of lilies on Frank Conway's coffin and filled his nostrils with the musty smell of fresh-turned soil. He hunched his shoulders, clasping his arms tighter across his chest. Winter was coming and they were bleak here in Michaelstone, where the rocky escarpment of the Black Mountains defied the storms and sent them roaring down the valley. The fabric of the church and the graveyard were crumbling under the assault, just as the family had disintegrated in this lonely place. But it was where his father had chosen to be buried and the harshness of it was no more than the old bastard deserved. Peter had no doubt on that score though so much else seemed wrong. He shuffled his feet, trying to get the blood circulating and contained his impatience. Soon, he'd walk away from these memories and return to tending his studio and taking his photographs and smiling at his clients. The thought was comforting and he tried to cling to it. But the seeds planted deep in his subconscious had taken root and allowed him no peace.

"Ashes to ashes, dust to dust."

The words shook Peter Conway out of his reverie with a start. The vicar's tempo had picked up dramatically as the service drew to a close, stimulated by the thought of the warmth of the vicarage, or perhaps simply by the lack of a receptive audience. You couldn't blame him Peter thought, casting a jaundiced eye at the small group huddled around the burial plot. The only other mourners marking the occasion were the undertakers whose black tailcoats and sombre expressions were strictly professional, bought and paid for as part of the funeral package. For them, too, the sooner the formalities were concluded the better.

As if reading Peter's thoughts, the funeral director coughed into his gloved hand and jerked his head meaningfully towards the grave. His cheeks were pinched and bloodless and the message that his fee did not cover much more standing around in the cold was unmistakable. Peter stepped forward and looked down at the coffin, gritting his teeth against the pain of his sore head and bitter thoughts. Absolution was asking too much, though compassion, maybe, was possible if he could bring himself to understand how things had ended this way. Dad had always fought for the truth and it was not the truth that was being buried here. The lump on his temple and the stabbing pains in his side every time he moved were an eloquent testament to that. He reached into his pocket for the worn fountain pen and let it slip from his hand into the open grave. At least the bastards who'd attacked him hadn't stolen that and a warrior should be buried with his sword whether the fight had been won or lost.

As the pen disappeared into the earth Peter felt his resolve harden. The Hereford police hadn't given a shit about the assault; nothing of value stolen, not even the Porsche; a sore head but no permanent damage; probably some young hooligans having a laugh, sir, so sorry and here's a crime number but don't hold your breath for an arrest was all they had fobbed him off with despite his best efforts to stir them into action. And no they hadn't taken any papers from the cottage, why would they? As for questions about aspirin and paracetamol, they'd looked at him as though he was mad. So much for 'anything I can do to help'; Detective Sergeant Williams of the unctuous official voice had proved a broken reed after all. But the mugging was too slick to be the work of amateurs, which meant that coincidence was out of the question. It had to be connected with Dad's death. That made it personal. So was the shattering humiliation of it all, coming round with his face in the dirt unable to remember where he was or what he was doing there, then realising that he'd not even landed a single blow in his own defence. The books, the medicine box, the manuscripts, even the manila envelope from the car had gone, too. All of it. Someone was looking for something and whatever it was they wanted it very badly. Badly enough to risk leaving him for dead in the middle of nowhere with a broken head. He'd be damned if he'd let them get away with that. The police were useless so it was down to him. Nursing his anger Peter Conway turned on his heel and left the graveside without a backward glance.

"So you're Frank Conway's son?"

The gravelly voice came from the shadows at the side of the lych-gate and made Peter jump. The gate slipped from his grasp and groaned as it leaned over tiredly, the bottom hinge hanging free where it had torn away from the post. He grabbed it quickly and heaved it upright. The last thing he needed right now was a confrontation with the vicar about the destruction of church property.

"Christ, you startled me. This bloody place is falling to pieces." Peter scowled at the crumbling woodwork that was all that remained of what had once been an imposing entrance to the churchyard. "Yes, I'm Peter Conway. Who are you?"

"Simon Milward. Look, don't worry about the gate. It's been rotting away for years like everything else round these parts. Including me, I'm afraid to say. But that's beside the point. I need to talk to you about your father."

Peter stared suspiciously at the figure emerging from the shadows, then recognised the man with the notebook from the coroner's court. The tweed jacket looked even more tattered and disreputable in the daylight and the tracery of broken veins in the sweating face suggested a long-standing dedication to drink.

"What the hell are you doing here?" he said brusquely. "I'm not interested in talking to the press. The local rag will have to make do with whatever you came up with at the inquest. Not that you seemed to be taking much notice of the proceedings when I saw you there." Peter turned to go and then hesitated as the man grasped his elbow.

"Wait a minute, please." The note of desperation in the voice caught Peter's attention in a way that nothing else could have done. "You don't understand. I'm not a reporter. Not any more, anyway. I was a friend of Frank's, going way back. I have to speak to you about his manuscripts, the work we were doing together."

"My father was working with you?" Peter snorted and shook his head in disbelief. "Pull the other one. He hadn't done a serious day's work for years apart from unscrewing the cap of the next bottle. If you knew him at all you'd know that. Now let go of my arm. I told you, I'm not interested."

"No, I won't let you just walk away." Peter recoiled as the sweaty face thrust close to his and a gust of sour breath tainted with whisky assaulted his nostrils. "I know you and Frank didn't see eye to eye but he was a good man, one of the best. None of what happened to him was his fault."

It was too much, coming on top of the funeral, his splitting head and his already turbulent feelings. Peter's temper boiled to the surface.

"A good man you say? What the bloody hell do you think you know about it?" He grabbed the lapels of the tweed jacket in both fists and pulled viciously until he was eyeball to eyeball with his adversary.

"That good man killed my mother with his drunkenness and self-pity as surely as if he'd stuck a knife in her," he yelled. "I'll never be able to forgive him for that. And he damn near wrecked my life too. Would have done if I hadn't managed to find the courage from God knows where to get the hell out of his clutches and make my own way."

Peter's knuckles whitened with the ferocity of his grip as the suppressed rage continued to boil out.

"Just who the hell do think you are to be lecturing me about a man who was so obsessed with his own screw-ups that he could do that to his family?"

The face in front of him had turned a sickly grey and Peter realised that he was shaking the old man hard enough to rattle his teeth. Suddenly disgusted with himself, he released his grip and pushed Simon away.

"Now why don't you just bugger off," he said. "You don't know what the hell you're talking about. My father's none of your business so just leave it alone."

Simon Milward staggered backwards wheezing and coughing, looking as if he was about to collapse with a heart attack. Peter felt a surge of alarm, his anger suddenly evaporating as he realised he'd half throttled a defenceless man who was old enough to be his father. He winced at the crassness of the cliché that had automatically sprung to mind and held his hand out, half in apology and half in support. Simon cringed and backed away behind raised arms as if he feared another attack.

"No, please, I didn't mean any harm." The voice was tremulous and it cut through Peter like a knife. There was no excuse for losing control and taking out his anger on such a pathetic victim.

"I'm sorry," he said curtly. "You picked a bad time. Are you all right?"

"Jesus," Simon spluttered. "You scared the shit out of me." Colour was slowly coming back into his face and he tugged ineffectually at the crumpled lapels of his jacket, still eyeing Peter warily as if expecting another explosion. "Frank always said you'd inherited his temper. He certainly got that right."

"Don't start on that again," Peter warned. "I've told you, my father is none of your business. Anyway, how would he know about whether I've got a temper? He never gave a damn about me or how I behaved."

"You'd be surprised. He followed everything you did. Talked about you all the time. He was real proud of you."

Despite himself Peter felt the colour start to rise again in his face. Simon took a step backwards and held his hand up as if to ward off a blow.

"Okay, okay, I'm sorry I spoke. Keep your hair on. I'm not trying to poke my nose into your affairs. But Frank made me promise that if anything happened to him I'd get in touch with you and tell you about the work we've been doing together. He helped me out of a few holes over the years and I owe him that much. But it's up to you what you do about it. All he wanted was that you should be told the truth."

"The truth?" Peter said contemptuously. "Now that really would be a first. I've heard all his crazy stories till I'm sick of them. I don't think he knew what truth meant any more and I'm damn sure you don't." Peter turned away and started walking down the gravel path to the lane. "Forget it," he said over his shoulder. "Let the old bastard rot in peace."

There was nothing here, Peter thought, which would help him answer the questions that were nagging away at him like mosquitoes on a summer evening. Certainly not gossip from a local drunkard. The answers, if there were any, were back in London, long ago and far away. Simon Milward was still bleating in the background but he was wasting his time. He had nothing to say that was worth listening to.

Then Peter Conway stopped suddenly. It was like running into a brick wall. He looked back up the path in shock.

"What did you just say?" he said, not believing his ears.

"I said, don't you want to know who murdered your father and why? Buy me a drink and I'll tell you."

***

The public bar in the King's Head, just a short stroll down the lane from the graveyard, was dingy and deserted. Peter watched as Simon, his Adam's apple bobbing furiously, dispatched his pint of bitter without a pause.

"Ah, that's better." Simon belched and put his glass back on the table. "Another one of those would really hit the spot. And perhaps with a large Scotch as a chaser?" He glanced expectantly at Peter.

With a shrug of resignation, Peter put down his own glass, barely touched and got to his feet, ducking to avoid the oak beams. The place could have been attractive, he thought, with a modicum of care and attention. The makings were there with the exposed stonework and massive fireplace. But the firedogs were littered with yesterday's cold ashes, the carpet beer stained and the ceiling had acquired a patina that only uncounted years of cigarette smoke could produce. It was dirty and unloved and the licensee's slovenly habits clearly also extended to serving his customers. As he shambled over to fill the order Peter could not tear his eyes away from the roll-up cigarette that was glued to the man's bottom lip. A half-inch of cold ash, wobbling gently with the exertion of pulling the pint, threatened to drop into the beer. If it did, Peter wondered briefly, what would he do? The unshaven face, heavy build and uncompromising expression suggested that complaints from strangers would not be well received. But to Peter's relief the laws of gravity were defied just long enough and the landlord brushed the ash off his stained shirtfront after he thumped the glasses down on the bar.

The whisky vanished in a gulp and Simon was reaching for the beer when Peter reached out and grabbed his wrist.

"Not so fast." he snapped. "We came here to talk, remember? Now give. What did you mean back there at the church?"

Simon sighed and leaned back in his chair.

"Well surely you didn't believe all that drivel in the coroner's court? You know, about Frank being mentally unbalanced and killing himself?"

"It didn't seem to me to entirely stack up, no. But that's a long way from saying he was murdered. Over recent years we weren't exactly on speaking terms but I do know that 'mentally unbalanced' is putting it mildly."

"That's bollocks," Simon said crudely. "He was never crazy. Angry and bitter, sure. He'd every right to be. Drunk, too, more often than not and who could blame him for drowning his sorrows."

"Me for one." Peter struggled to contain his rising anger. "He had a family and responsibilities. He screwed up, then took it out on us and ran away into the whisky bottle. Whatever happened he'd no right to do that to Mum and me."

"Maybe not, but he had his reasons. Frank was one of the best reporters of his generation until he got shafted. How would you feel if you were kicked out in disgrace from the work you loved best through no fault of your own?"

Peter gestured in disgust.

"Look, I can do without all this crap. I know what my father was like. I suffered it long enough and I don't need you apologising for him, making out he was something he wasn't. Now if you've got something sensible to say about his death just spit it out."

Simon Milward looked at Peter in disbelief.

"Jesus," he said, slowly shaking his head. "You really don't know, do you? I mean, what actually happened to Frank all those years ago and why."

"For God's sake, will you stop going on about ancient history and get to the point?"

"But that is the point. It's all part of the same thing, don't you see?"

Peter glanced at his watch. This was a waste of time, just a drunk playing around to get a few free drinks. It was time to get the hell out of here; the backlog at the studio wasn't going to sort itself out.

"No, of course you don't see," Simon continued, oblivious. "I'm being stupid. Sorry." He picked up his beer and took a hefty swig. "Look, it's a long story, right? What I'm saying is that the same people who did for Frank before have done it again. But this time they shut him up for good. He was getting too close to exposing them and he wouldn't let go."

Despite himself Peter found his interest beginning to awaken. It was just possible the old fool did know something useful. But he wished Simon would stop rambling and tell a coherent story.

"You're not making any sense. Getting too close to what?"

"I'd better start at the beginning, I suppose." Simon put his hands behind his head and stared at the ceiling. "It must be nearly twenty years. You'd have been five, or maybe six at the time. God, how time flies. Frank and I were both journalists then on the 'Globe' and we worked together a fair bit. We were good mates, too, although he was something special, a real rising star and I was just one of the pack. The paper was buzzing in those days. One of the heavyweight national dailies, not the sleazy tabloid it's degenerated into now. You wouldn't remember but I tell you we had a hell of a reputation for digging out the top stories. And Frank was the guy behind most of them. Like a terrier, he was, never let go once he got his teeth into something and the paper's young firebrand of a proprietor Rodney Hardcastle was out of the same mould, backing him all the way. We all thought we were invincible…"

Peter snorted.

"Well that didn't work out too well, did it? Look, I told you already I've had Saint Frank up to here. It's what you said back at the church that I'm interested in, that he was murdered. For Christ's sake just tell me who you reckon did it and why."

Simon shrugged.

"The who is easy. It was an outfit in London called

Media Associates that Frank said were out to get him. On the face of it they are a big Public Relations firm, you know, bullshit for Britain, sinners into saints, all that kind of spin doctor stuff, though underneath the glossy exterior they are something altogether nastier. The why is more complicated, though. To understand that you have to go back to the beginning, like I said."

"Well go on then, if you must. But keep it short, will you? I've got to get back to London tonight."

"Okay, look, Frank had this bee in his bonnet back in the day about a guy called Robert Maxwell who built a publishing empire after the last war and made a fortune by cornering the rights to German scientific and other publications. There were all sorts of rumours about dodgy deals and some people even reckoned Maxwell had an inside track with some of the top Nazi scientists about their secret projects at the end of the war. Anyway, Frank got his hands on a diary supposedly written by one of the Nazis' top scientists, a real bigwig called Oberberg, which he reckoned would nail Maxwell to the wall."

"So that was the big story he was always banging on about? The one he reckoned they prevented him from publishing?"

"Yes." Simon smiled wryly and spread his arms as if in apology. "I never knew the details, Frank always played things very close to his chest when he was onto a scoop. All he ever said to me was that he'd got Maxwell on toast. But that was Frank all over. His nose for a headline was infallible, never more so than when smelling the opportunity to expose the sins of the rich and powerful. No target was too big, no name too awesome to attack when the truth was at issue. It was his greatest strength and perhaps his greatest weakness, too, that he never stopped to calculate the consequences or the risks. But in Robert Maxwell he found an adversary more cunning and ruthless than he bargained for."

Simon shivered at the memory, broke off his narrative and leaned forward earnestly.

"It was that combination that finished him, you see. He had no idea at the time how deep it went and how powerful the vested interests were. Or how far Maxwell and his cronies would go to cover things up. Knowing Frank, it would have made no difference even if he'd known, but at least he might have been better prepared. As it was, he was like a lamb to the slaughter when they came after him."

The passion that had crept into Simon's voice gave Peter a glimpse of the ambitious and confident young journalist that time had buried beneath the raddled old drunk he'd thought he was dealing with and it shook him up.

"What the hell do you mean, 'how deep it went'?" he said uncertainly.

"Frank went directly to Rodney Hardcastle with the outline of the story. The following day his place was burgled and the diary was stolen. And before you ask, the police got absolutely nowhere tracing the manuscript or the burglars."

"And you think it was some sort of conspiracy?" Peter scoffed. "That's pretty thin."

"Nobody else knew what Frank had at that stage. Like I said at the beginning, it's up to you what you believe.

I'm just telling you the way it was. What happened to Frank afterwards was no accident, though."

"What was that?"

"When the Maxwell thing fell apart Hardcastle had him assigned to follow up a tip-off about a fraud in one of the City banks. The evidence dropped into his lap, sweet as you like and he spread it all over the front page. The problem was it turned out not to be true. They threatened to sue the paper for millions and Frank carried the can. They said he'd been negligent, got his facts wrong."

"Jesus wept." Peter whistled and shook his head. "So that's why his career went down the pan. I never knew. But what do you mean that it wasn't an accident? If he screwed up that badly he only had himself to blame."

"That's where you're wrong. He was set up."

"Come off it. A reporter's most basic responsibility is to check out the information and make sure he's got things straight, even I know that much. He must have got careless."

"Not Frank. He never did a sloppy job in his life. I'm telling you, he was suckered. But it was worse than that. A load of stuff came out about him trading in the bank's shares, trying to make a killing on the stock market."

"What the hell are you talking about? That has to be bullshit. He knew nothing about stocks and shares. The way I remember it, he could barely understand his bank statement."

"Exactly. There was no way he could have dreamed up a scam like that even if he'd wanted to," Simon said emphatically. "But they produced contracts showing he'd bought share options ahead of his story being printed. I don't understand the technicalities but the idea was that if the share price fell he'd make a fortune. And it was obvious that as soon as the news about a fraud hit the street those shares were likely to fall hard."

"Contracts?" Peter frowned. "I thought you said..."

"They were forgeries. I mean, the contracts were real enough. But Frank never had anything to do with them." Simon waved his hand dismissively. "Oh, they had witnesses, handwriting experts to verify his signature, the works. But it was all lies. They stuffed him like a Christmas turkey."

"But there was never any prosecution. Not that I remember. That sort of thing's criminal isn't it?"

"It never came to that. Frank didn't know at the time but he found out later that Media Associates was behind it. What they had in mind was much worse. They didn't want a court case and a potential martyr. They wanted him quietly ruined, written off so nobody would take him seriously if he ever tried to point the finger at Maxwell."

Peter frowned.

"What the hell did a PR firm have to do with it?"

"Sorry, didn't I say? Maxwell was one of their founding partners. Frank reckoned it was the perfect cover for his dirty work."

"Wait a minute." Peter's throat worked convulsively as he struggled to come to terms with what he was hearing and find the words to protest. "Look, I've always believed... I mean, I was told that he'd made mistakes, that what happened was all his own fault."

Simon took a deep breath, like a man about to step reluctantly into uncharted territory

"I know it must be hard to accept," he said gently. "That was what your mother chose to think and nothing Frank said could change her mind. But I've got no reason to lie to you and Frank insisted that if he should die unexpectedly you should be told the truth. Believe me, I'd just as soon forget the past. I told Frank it was too bloody dangerous to rake up all the old ashes again but he wouldn't have it. I'll happily shut up though if that's what you want."

It wasn't the reaction Peter had expected and it forced him to stop and think. Then he shrugged.

"You've got this far," he said. "If you're going to turn everything I thought I knew about my own family upside down you might as well spit out the rest of it."

"OK, then, if you're sure. It wasn't pretty, though, the way those bastards got their teeth into him. The talk was all of breaches of the journalistic code and prosecution for insider trading, which was bad enough to make him unemployable. But oddly it turned out it isn't an offence to lose money on inside information, only to profit from it. But Frank's relief they couldn't prosecute him was short-lived. The share options purchased in his name turned out to be a very sharp two-edged sword. If the share price fell you made a fortune, but if they rose you lost the same fortune and more. And seemingly by coincidence, not only was the fraud story killed too quickly for the market to drop but a sudden stream of good news in the media pushed the shares up to record levels. Suddenly Frank was faced with impossible demands to settle huge debts.

When the dust settled it wasn't just his reputation he'd lost. Your father was an undischarged bankrupt without a penny to his name to the day he died. There was no escape. He had no money for a legal battle and no way to prove he'd never signed those contracts. The writs and the bailiffs took care of the rest. All except the cottage, which was in your mother's name. That's why she left it to you, you see, so your Dad's creditors couldn't get their hands on it."

The detail about the cottage was the final straw. Peter put his head in his hands. It felt as though it was about to explode as he tried desperately to absorb the shock. It was true, he knew in his bones. Too many other small things from the past were suddenly tumbling into place and the foundations of his life were rocking as old preconceptions shattered.

"Why?" he muttered through his hands. "Why didn't he tell me? All those years I thought..." Peter's voice tailed off as he recalled all the spiteful things he had said and done in his ignorance.

Simon leaned forward and put a sympathetic hand on Peter's shoulder.

"He was a proud man, your father. Too proud to admit to you of all people how he had been made a fool of; he was desperately ashamed of that. He wanted to protect you. Yes and perhaps protect himself as well. His worst nightmare was that you would find out and think that he'd really done those things."

"But I wouldn't..."

"Wouldn't you?" Simon said grimly. "You were sceptical enough a few minutes ago about what lay behind it all and without that where's the motive for anyone to go to those lengths to frame him? Nobody else ever believed his claims that he was set up. Why would he expect you to be any different?

"I'm his son. I had a right to know."

"Maybe so. But remember, Frank watched the stress and humiliation kill your mother and he couldn't forgive himself for that. I can understand why he wouldn't put the same burden on your shoulders, can't you?"

"He should have found a way."

"Oh, he did. His way was to search out the truth of what had happened and why and he never gave up on that. To expose the facts about Media Associates, the way that made him one of the best investigative reporters of his generation. Then he'd be able to prove to you that he wasn't the pathetic failure you thought him to be."

"My God," Peter said incredulously, "Is that what you meant when you said you were working with him and he was murdered because he found out too much?"

"Yes." Simon said tersely. "Oh, don't get me wrong. There was little enough he'd let me do, just some legwork now and again. It was his work through and through. He found out the sons of bitches were still at it, you see."

"Still at what?"

"Manipulating the financial markets and screwing people, of course. He tracked down and interviewed a number of other poor sods whose lives were ruined by Media Associates, just like his. He had videos, affidavits, all sorts of stuff."

"You reckon he really did have proof, then? It wasn't

just some sort of delusion?"

"Delusion? No way, Frank Conway had his scoop all right. He called me the day he died and told me. He'd finally nailed the bastards, he said. It was all written down and ready to publish. Enough to blow Media Associates wide open."

Simon's words exploded into Peter's mind like tracer bullets and burned away the last of his doubts. He'd had that manuscript right there in his hand, Peter realised with a shiver and he hadn't even bothered to read it. Proof positive, dropping out of that secret compartment in the old medicine chest. Then like a damn fool he'd delivered it straight into the arms of his father's killers.

"Did he tell you who those people he interviewed were?" Peter said urgently.

"Nothing very specific. Like I said, he always kept his stories under wraps."

"Did he mention any names? Think, man, he must have let something slip."

Simon scratched his head in thought and Peter held his breath.

"There was one man he kept going on about," Simon said slowly. "Damned if I can remember his name though. But he was some sort of scientist who'd been conned out of his business. Something to do with biotechnology if I remember right. "

"Nothing else?"

"No, I don't reckon so. Like I said, I was just doing bits and pieces of the legwork for him. Sorry."

It wasn't much of a basis for nailing down a bunch of murderers, Peter thought. But at least it was a start.

And he owed it to his old man to finish the job.

Chapter 5

Simon Milward stared at the inch of warm, brown liquid that was all that remained of his pint. He'd reached that familiar but unwelcome predicament of having drunk enough to become maudlin, but not yet enough to forget his troubles. Now that Peter Conway had buggered off back to London in his fancy car and taken his wallet with him, the equally familiar problem of finding the money for the next drink was adding to his woes. He rummaged through his pockets, came up with the same depressing result as the last time and once again cursed his lack of foresight in not cadging a few quid while he'd had the chance. The story of his life, he reflected self-pityingly, as he drained the last drops and put the mug down with exaggerated care. A missed opportunity and an empty glass.

Selfish bastard, he thought, fingering the marks left by Peter Conway on his still crumpled lapels and allowing the alcohol to fuel his indignation. Youngsters these days had no respect for their elders, no gratitude for services rendered. He'd gone to a lot of trouble to put Frank's boy in the picture and it was surely worth more than a few measly pints. Things would have been different, he reckoned, if he'd been able to produce that damned manuscript Frank had boasted about. That would have been worth a tidy sum of anybody's money and his back stiffened at the thought of exchanging it for a packet of crisp notes. Then the vision faded and his shoulders slumped.

There was no chance, he thought dully. Whoever had taken care of Frank would have made sure of that.

The barman of the King's Head watched his only remaining customer get up and walk a trifle unsteadily towards the door. His eyes glinted slyly behind the creases of surplus flesh that surrounded them and he shifted his bulk from behind the beer-stained counter to peer out of the window. He took careful note of the direction taken by the battered Ford Fiesta as it left the car park and grunted in satisfaction. There was only one route it could follow from there, along the back road across the mountain where all the locals knew that the chances of being breathalysed were as good as zero. He touched the wad of money in his trouser pocket, enjoying the crisp texture and the pleasant crackling sound of the new notes as he caressed them greedily. More money than sense, these city folk, he thought, thinking of the strangers who'd come into his bar looking for information earlier that day. But perhaps there was more where that came from. He peeled the soggy remnant of his cigarette from his lower lip, tossed it into a dirty ashtray and headed for the telephone.

The Fiesta was struggling as it weaved its way up the last pitch to the top of the ridge, but despite the low speed Simon had his work cut out to keep it out of the ditches that bordered the single-track road. The damn thing was clapped out, Simon thought derisively, keeping his foot hard down and leaning forward again to scrub ineffectually at the mist that kept creeping over the inside of the windscreen. He cursed as the car lurched towards the hedge, prompted by his unintentional movement of the steering wheel and his knuckles whitened as he wrestled for control. Then the road started to fall away in front of him and the car accelerated on the downhill stretch towards home. To his left, the lights of isolated farmsteads twinkled deep down in the valley, where the tree-clad ridge fell away sharply, but otherwise it was as black as the ace of spades. The beam of his single working headlamp was barely up to the task of picking out the tarmac strip snaking its way elusively down the steep gradient and Simon hunched forward over the wheel trying to concentrate. But by the time he reached the hairpin turn halfway down, his mind had drifted and he was thinking longingly of the hoarded half-bottle of Scotch that was waiting for him at the end of the journey.

Without warning, the flare of headlights on full beam hit him straight in the eyes. Blinded, he flung up one hand in front of his face and yanked the wheel instinctively to the left to avoid the oncoming vehicle. The last thing Simon Milward remembered was the immediate, hopeless realisation that here, in this precise spot, that was completely the wrong thing to do.

The two men in the stationary black Jaguar watched the Fiesta tumbling down the escarpment, gouging out young trees and disintegrating as it went. Its passage terminated abruptly with a grinding crunch of metal on stone, followed by the thump of petrol vapour igniting. Far below them, a new light started flickering in the blackness and the crackling of resinous pine catching fire carried to their ears in the sudden quiet. Then a black-gloved hand reached forward, flicked the switch to dip the headlights and turned the ignition key. The heavily built figure in the passenger seat turned his head fractionally.

"London?" Mike Arnold enquired economically, over the purr of the motor.

"London," Sam Garvey confirmed with a satisfied nod, sliding the car into gear. "We're all done here, nice and tidy. We can finish the rest of the job back up in the Smoke."

"We're going after Peter Conway, then."

It was a statement, not a question, but Sam hesitated uncharacteristically before replying. He'd still not figured out what was so important about Peter Conway that he'd been instructed to leave him alone. But only a fool made the same mistake twice and the young brat had found that manuscript those damned idiots in the action team had missed at the cottage. That made him just as much a danger as his father had been. All the same, defying the Research Directorate wasn't a thing to be done lightly, especially when you didn't have all the facts. He'd be putting Mike's head on the block, too. Then he chuckled. Life wasn't worth living without taking risks and he wasn't about to let a bunch of bloody bureaucrats stand in his way.

"Damn right we are," he said calmly. "The chances are he read Frank Conway's manuscript before we nicked it. And he spent long enough with this Milward guy to get chapter and verse. You know my motto."

"No loose ends," Mike said. "Yeah. I reckon you dragged our asses down here instead of leaving it to the troops because you expected something like this. I just hope you know what you're letting us in for with the spin doctors, that's all. It's not part of the job description to screw around with them."

"You're not going soft on me, Mike, are you? I need your support on this."

"It'll cost you two favours," Mike said, leaning back in his seat and closing his eyes. "Stop asking me stupid questions. And wake me up when we get there."

***

The paperwork was a pain in the backside, literally as well as metaphorically. Peter Conway shifted awkwardly, trying to ease the discomfort of sitting cross-legged on the floor sorting through the piles of bumf. But VAT inspections were an unavoidable evil and he knew from bitter experience that the desk wasn't big enough to accommodate twelve months' worth of bureaucracy. Every year, he swore he'd keep the files in order and up to date and somehow it never happened. Then he'd vow to get organised well ahead of the deadline, with no last minute panic. But there was always something to screw that up, too. This time, it was Dad's death and all the distractions that went with it, but if it hadn't been that it would have been something else. And so every year, when it came to the crunch, the only recourse was to tip the jumbled mess onto the floor and start again. It was the only space in the studio big enough.

He looked sourly at the classy 'Spectrum Studios' logos on the headed paper and forms. Anyone would think they signified a smoothly oiled enterprise, buzzing with accountants and suchlike to take care of administrative chores. Peter snorted derisively. That was exactly the impression they were intended to convey, but smoothly oiled or not, he was it. Chief cook, bottle washer, paper-pusher and Grand Panjandrum of everything else. It wasn't what he'd visualised when he'd agonised over selecting an up-market name and a fancy letterhead to impress prospective clients. But perhaps it was poetic justice. In a photographic business, image really was everything. And he could hardly complain when it worked, even if the penalty of success was yet more paperwork and red tape. All the same, it was a good job his clients couldn't see what went on behind the scenes.

Footsteps approached the door and Peter started guiltily at the sudden coincidence with his thoughts. Then he relaxed at the sight of Jack Howson.

"Fiddle the books time, is it then?" Jack said, taking in the scene with the smugness of someone who knew the chaos wasn't his problem. He tossed the morning mail in Peter's direction. "Here's some more of the rain forest they've hacked down for you. Picked it up from the postie on the way in."

"Thanks a bunch." Peter groaned and clambered stiffly to his feet. "How about doing something useful, like making a cup of tea?"

"Sure," Jack said, heading for the curtained-off alcove where the electric kettle perched cheek-by-jowl with a microwave. "Check out the posh envelope, though," he added laconically over his shoulder. "Smells like money to me."

When Jack came back a few minutes later with a mug of tea in each hand Peter Conway was standing by the window, the embossed envelope discarded at his feet, staring at a sheet of hammered vellum notepaper as though it was a poisonous snake.

"Here," Jack said, thrusting one of the mugs at his employer. "Get yourself outside this." He twitched an eyebrow and inclined his head towards the letter. "Bad news?"

"What?" Peter looked up. "Oh, thanks." He took a sip of tea and shook his head, frowning. "No... Not exactly. It's a reply from that mail shot about producing advertising literature we sent out a few weeks back. You remember, we sent out hundreds of the bloody things to everyone we could think of in the City. One of them wants to take me up on the offer and do some pictures for an in-house marketing brochure."

"So how come you look like someone just pissed on the doorstep? Is it the Iraqi tourist board or something?"

"Nothing like that. It's one of the top London agencies."

"So what's the problem?"

"See for yourself." Peter thrust the piece of paper at Jack, who pursed his lips and let out a low whistle as his eye caught the elaborate letterhead.

"Say, aren't these the guys who...?"

"Media Associates," Peter confirmed. "The same people Simon Milward told me screwed over my Dad and probably killed him. It could be just a coincidence, but..."

"You said in the pub the other night that you were going to finish what your Dad had started and no mucking about," Jack interrupted. "You telling me you've changed your mind?"

Peter's thoughts drifted back to the drive home up the M4 after he'd left Simon. The Porsche had been steady as a rock cruising at ninety, barely more than ticking over. His feelings were another matter, seesawing between rage and shame as the miles flashed past. Rage at what had been done to his father and shame that he could have been so wrong in his judgements for his entire life. He'd condemned a lousy father and instead it turned out he'd been a lousy son. He should have tried harder to believe, to understand and forgive. To help, even, with the fight that his Dad had never given up on. To embrace the father he'd always wanted and hoped for, but thought he'd never had. A caring figure, an innocent victim of circumstances, striving to protect a family he loved from those seeking to do them harm. Hatred of the people who destroyed that man and made his son's childhood a misery swelled as if to choke him and he could almost taste the desire for justice and revenge. But another part of him insisted on remembering the unforgiving reality of what his father had become and how easily his enemies had driven him to despair and drink. There could be no doubting the danger of picking up the fight. The closer he'd got to London, the scarier it all seemed. There was something about the down-to-earth cut and thrust of negotiating the Bracknell by-pass and the M25 to Tonbridge that made a mockery of any pretentions to be a conquering hero. By the time he'd reached home, he had at least been sure of one thing. He could choose to put his own future and his business on the line, but he'd have to come clean about it with

Jack and give him a fair chance to bail out first.

Peter dragged his thoughts back to the present and shook his head.

"Not me." He took the letter back from Jack's hand and waved it for emphasis. "But these are serious people and as I was about to say, this may not be a coincidence. If they are after me already things could get nasty damned fast. I've got no right to drag you into any of this."

Jack sniffed. "Bollocks to that. Like I said in the pub, you gave me a chance and took me on here when thousands wouldn't. They bring you down, they bring me down too so now it's payback time for me as well as you, innit. Besides, if anyone mucked about with my old man, I'd kick his fucking head in," he said bluntly. "No messing."

Peter looked up in surprise. It was uncharacteristic of Jack to volunteer an opinion, especially in such vehement terms.

""Well, if you're sure, I'm not going to argue. I can use all the help I can get. So what do you reckon our next move should be?"

"That's bleeding obvious. You know this Media Associates outfit is crooked, but you've got naff all by way of evidence. That letter means you've got a perfect chance to go and find some. From the inside, like. Bugger all you can do otherwise, I reckon. Either that or forget it and walk away."

Peter Conway's jaw dropped.

"Terrific. You want me to go in feet first on the off chance that they've conveniently left evidence lying about and then steal confidential client information to beat them about the head with. That's one hell of a smart plan. Have you any idea how uptight people in the photographic business get about confidentiality? Nobody would ever touch my work again if I pulled a stunt like that on a client."

"From what you've told me, I'd have thought if they catch you poking around where you shouldn't your reputation as a photographer would be the least of your worries. Look, I never suggested you go and make a fool of yourself," Jack said. "I'm not a muppet. All I'm saying is take their money, do the job and keep your eyes open. Who knows what will turn up? I don't see how you've got anything to lose so long as you're careful."

As Peter struggled to find a reply, the phone rang, making them both jump. Jack was nearest and reached out to grab it. He listened for a moment and then held the receiver out.

"Anna Stein for you," he said with a grin. "Wants to know, have you got your finger out and become computer literate yet?"

Peter held the phone a judicious half-inch from his ear. Anna still worked on the assumption that to be heard across London on the phone meant you had to shout.

"Hi, Anna. What can I do for you?"

"Peter, dear, I've had this ghastly Japanese man on the phone. They want to print my book catalogue over there, in Japanese, would you believe it."

"Sounds like good news. What's the problem?"

"Well, of course I said 'yes', but he was wittering on about wanting an electronic tiff for his computer. Something to do with your photographs. Silly man, I didn't understand a word, never had time for all this new-fangled nonsense. But you're young. You must know something about computers."

Peter smiled. He'd just finished building himself a new system, assembling it from the ground up with the latest AMD Athlon processor and enough random access memory to handle high-definition digital imagery from a professional grade Nikon scanner. It was all sitting in the attic room at home, waiting until he could find the time to start experimenting with the new release of the Adobe Photoshop software.

"I know a bit," he said modestly. "I do some work restoring old photographs and suchlike with the computer. I even play around with a digital camera occasionally, though I reckon it'll be a while before they're good enough to replace the Hasselblad."

"There, I knew I was right," Anna bellowed in satisfaction. "You'll know all about it, then. What he needs, I mean."

"I expect he meant he wants digital versions of my photographs in a TIFF file format. That's what printers usually prefer for computer based colour separations to go on the presses."

"If you say so, dear boy," Anna said doubtfully. "It's all Greek to me I'm afraid. But he was very insistent that pegs weren't good enough. At least, I think that's what he said."

"That's okay. That would be 'jpg' or 'j-peg' files. It's a compressed format, easier to handle on less powerful machines but the quality isn't usually acceptable for professional work. I can take care of all that, though. Do you have a list of the photos and details of where you want them sent?"

"I've got a fax here somewhere." Peter heard scrabbling and muttered imprecations and he imagined the papers flying on the cluttered desk and the dry smell of dust rising. "Damn, look," Anna said finally, "I can't put my hand on it right now. Why don't we meet for lunch and I'll give you all the details then? How about that fish restaurant at Hay's Wharf, you know the one I mean. Say one o'clock?"

As he put the receiver down, Peter glanced at his watch and then at the pile of papers on the floor. If there were no more interruptions, he thought, he might just get the VAT paperwork sorted before he had to leave to meet Anna and Jack could keep himself busy with a long-overdue film stock check.

After a couple of hours hard labour Peter slapped the final file on top of the stack on his desk and sighed with relief. That was a boring job well done. He headed for the door feeling good. Lunch with Anna was always a laugh and he reckoned he'd earned it today.

"I'm off now. Expect me when you see me," he shouted over his shoulder towards the walk-in store cupboard where Jack was still doggedly trying to get the numbers to tally and received a grunt in reply.

Peter paused for a moment in the hallway, enjoying the elegance of his surroundings. The antique panelling and the elaborate plaster cornices were a legacy from the days when this must have been the home of an aristocrat, which had somehow survived the conversion to more mundane business uses. But it made for an impressive impact on clients, despite the fact that Spectrum Studios occupied just one, albeit the largest, of the downstairs rooms. The front door made a satisfyingly solid thud as it closed behind him. He stood at the top of the marble steps, ignoring the noisy bustle of Buckingham Palace Road and glanced smugly up at the front of the building. It was expensive, but it oozed prestige, he thought, from the Georgian sash windows and brick facade to the chiselled stone balustrade around the edge of the roof, four stories above. He'd come a long way and this was just the beginning.

Peter frowned slightly and some of his good humour evaporated as his eye caught the brass plate beside the door. As usual, it was covered with dirty fingerprints beside the bell push, despite his long-running battle with the janitor to make sure it was cleaned regularly. It was a battle he was losing, he thought with irritation. Perhaps it was because he was a photographer and used to spotting details that passed most people by, or maybe he was just pernickety, but the marks offended his sensibilities. A dirty sign gave an impression of sloppiness that was bad for business in a profession where attention to detail was paramount. It had become a habit to give it the once-over every time he went in and out, but he still resented the chore. Peter reached into his pocket and pulled out his handkerchief, making a mental note that it was time for another go at getting the bloody caretaker to do his job properly.

As he scrubbed at the gleaming brass, Peter's gaze strayed across the street. The traffic was more congested than usual, snarled up by a black Jaguar double-parked while the driver talked into his mobile phone. Behind it, opposite where he was standing, the sheer glass front of an office block rose like a mirror and his photographer's eye was caught by the reflection of his own building captured on its canvas. It would make a dramatic picture, he thought, with the stark contrast of the old superimposed on the new and his brain started automatically assessing angles and exposures.

Then there was a blur of movement and the composition of the picture he was looking at inexplicably began to change. While his brain was still registering the reflection of a chunk of the rooftop balustrade sagging outwards and yielding to the pull of gravity, Peter Conway's world dissolved in a thunder of noise and rubble.

Chapter 6

"I was damned lucky not to be killed," Peter said, feeling the trembling threatening to start again at the recollection of just how close it had been.

Anna Stein leaned forward and took his hand, her green eyes wide with sympathy. They had odd silver flecks in them, he noticed inconsequentially and the touch of her fingers felt strange, as though it was part of a dream. Perhaps it was, he thought. The lunchtime bustle in the Balls Brothers restaurant had the same unreal quality.

"God, how awful for you," he heard Anna say. "Shouldn't you be in hospital or something?"

His mind was still reliving events back at the studio and the words didn't register. He couldn't remember any conscious thought, just the instinct that had made his body vault over the railing onto the steps next door. If his eye hadn't sent its message directly to his nervous system, he'd be history. He shuddered again at the mental image of a huge chunk of masonry crashing down exactly where he'd been standing only a fraction of a second before and fragments exploding outwards from the crater caused by its impact.

"Peter, are you all right?"

This time, the worry in Anna's voice caught his attention and he looked up.

"Yes, I'm fine," he lied, fingering the tear in the collar of his jacket. If destiny had moved the razor-sharp lump of stone a few inches to one side it could just as easily have taken his head off. The knowledge that he owed his life to a quirk of fate was devastating, but he'd be damned if he'd admit as much, even to Anna.

"You look terrible. Didn't the medics give you anything for the shock?"

"I didn't want any fuss, so I just sneaked away."

"But that's crazy. I mean, just to come here for lunch as though nothing has happened, what on earth were you thinking of?"

"I told you, I didn't want to get mixed up in a lot of silly commotion over an accident. It would have been a nightmare."

"Well, I think it's appalling," Anna said indignantly. "At the very least you should sue the landlords for negligence. Get yourself a good lawyer and you could take them to the cleaners."

"Maybe so, but it's not my style. I'm okay. There's no harm done and I really don't want to get involved. I've already got more than enough my plate since Dad died."

To Peter's surprise a wistful expression fleeted across Anna's face and he saw tears appear in the corners of her eyes. She turned her head away from him in embarrassment and rummaged in her handbag for a tissue.

"I was so sorry to hear about that," she said, dabbing self-consciously at her face. "For all his faults, he was a lovely man. Life was so cruel to him and he deserved better."

The emotion in her voice caught him unawares and Peter was momentarily stunned. He'd trodden on a nerve and suddenly here was another mystery about his father. Every time he turned around at the moment it seemed like another chunk of his past got torn apart.

"You knew Dad, then? You've never said anything."

"No, I didn't think... I didn't want to risk...   I mean, it was all such a long time ago and I knew that you and he didn't get on. It seemed best to leave things alone."

A feeling of detachment overwhelmed Peter again as he tried to absorb the implications. The buzz of conversation at the tables, the bustle of waiters and the glint of candle-lit crystal receded, as though he was watching a make-believe world. With an effort he forced his attention back to Anna, but she was waiting, ill at ease, for his reaction and refused to meet his eye. She was still a handsome woman, he observed dispassionately, with the kind of delicate bone structure and well-proportioned features that defied the advancing years. Subtract a couple of decades, replace the shapeless purple pullover, casual trousers and old-fashioned jewellery with a designer outfit and she would have been a beauty in her day.

In a sudden leap of intuition, Peter understood that there was much more between Anna and his Dad than the simple admission that she knew him signified. Had they been lovers, he wondered? If they had, how did he feel about it? And was her support for him and his business over the years nothing more than a kind of catharsis of some past guilt? He didn't know the answers. But in any case, it didn't matter. Perhaps it was just too many shocks in the same day, but life was too short to spend it looking at the past and jumping to conclusions. Especially when nothing in that past seemed to be the way he'd believed it to be.

"I'm beginning to realize I didn't know Dad at all," he said quietly. "But I'd like to. No, damn it, more than that. I need to understand more about his life and how he died. The way things really were, not the half-truths and lies I've been living with. I'd like you to tell me what you know about him, if you will. "

Anna looked at him uncertainly, but said nothing, turning in relief to the waiter who arrived at the psychological moment to take their order. As the man departed, Peter took a bread roll from the basket in front of him and started picking it to pieces with unconscious intensity.

"I'm serious," he said bluntly. "I want to know about my father."

"Why now?" Anna said, dabbing her reddened eyes again with the tissue. "You've never been interested before. Quite the opposite, you've always got angry if the subject even came up."

"Yes, I know. It's never occurred to me that you knew him. But I learned a few things when I went down for his funeral. Things that made me think I've been wrong about him all these years."

"What things?"

"That the crazy stories he used to tell that he was the victim of some sort of conspiracy weren't so crazy after all. A fellow called Simon Milward, who reckoned he used to work with Dad, collared me at the church and I've not been able to get what he told me out of my head."

"Simon?" She whispered the name and the blood drained from her face. "You met Simon?"

"Yes," Peter said, puzzled by Anna's reaction.

"What's the matter? Don't tell me you know him, too?" Her hand was shaking, he noticed, as she lifted the glass of wine to her lips and took a long swallow.

"The three of us, Frank, Simon and me, we were a team in the old days." She straightened in her chair, remembering. "Back on the Globe, before... before everything went wrong."

"Bloody hell, you mean you worked with Dad back then? I didn't know you were a reporter. How come you never said?"

"It was a long time ago," Anna said sadly. "It's something I prefer to forget, really. I've always loved words and print and I was young then. I thought we could reach out to people, make a difference. It was exciting, fulfilling. You can't possibly imagine unless you'd been there. But when Frank went, it all fell apart. We couldn't go on without him. And now Simon..."

There was an arid silence as her voice tailed away and Peter could almost touch the desert of unfulfilled dreams and shattered hopes that lay beneath her words. It was a glimpse into her unguarded soul, as shocking as if she had suddenly stripped off her clothes. Peter found himself squirming in embarrassment, unsure how to respond. The sudden clatter of their food arriving and the pantomime of Dover Sole being peeled off the bone on a salver at the side of the table gave him time to compose himself. But as the fillets of white meat were laid deftly on the plate in front of him and the appetising aroma assailed his nostrils, he found he could not summon up any enthusiasm for eating. Much as he hated causing her pain, he had to find out what she knew, even if it meant dredging to the surface a host of memories that she would clearly prefer to leave buried. Peter nodded his thanks to the waiter and pushed the fish idly round his plate with his fork.

"What about Simon?" he insisted, suppressing his misgivings. "Is there something I should know?"

Anna raised her eyes from her plate and looked at him. They were once again brimming with tears.

"He's dead, too" she said brokenly. "I'm the only one of the team left now."

Peter dropped his fork with a clatter, ignoring the glances that Anna's tears and his own reactions were generating from the adjacent tables.

"What do you mean, dead?" he objected. "That's impossible. Christ, I was only talking to him just after Dad's funeral. He was fine then."

"Please, Peter," Anna raised her finger to her lips, "keep your voice down. It's true. I've got a friend who keeps a bookshop down near there, in Hay-on-Wye. He sent me a copy of the report from the Hereford Times. They said Simon was over the limit and drove his car off the road on his way home from the pub. It was an accident."

"When?" Peter said urgently. "When did it happen?"

"Just over a week ago. Saturday night, they said."

"But that's..."

"Yes, I know. That's the day you buried your Dad. It's just a horrible coincidence."

Peter shook his head. "I was with Simon that evening in the pub. It can't be right, no way was he that drunk. I should know, it was me buying his booze for God's sake, to keep him talking."

"Simon was always a hard drinker. Perhaps he carried on after you'd gone?"

Peter stirred in his seat, spurred by the suspicions that were bubbling up in his brain. There were too many coincidences, too much happening, all linked to his father's death. And perhaps, he thought with trepidation, also linked to Simon's tale of what lay behind it all.

"No, he couldn't have. He told me he'd got no money. I thought at one stage he was going to twist my arm to give him some, but he must have thought better of it. He'd had a few beers, sure, but he was perfectly OK to drive."

Anna raised an eyebrow. "Are you sure?" she said. "I mean, the legal limit is pretty low. You must have fed him more than that."

"Are you suggesting..."

Anna held up her hand and interrupted the outburst. "I'm not suggesting you're to blame or anything. Of course not. But don't forget I knew Simon. He was an artist at cadging drinks from anyone who'd listen to his stories."

"Well, maybe so. But I can damn well see if someone's pissed. I'm telling you, he wasn't anywhere near being incapable." Peter spoke vehemently, hoping it was true. Anna had a habit of putting her finger on uncomfortable issues and he'd not be human if the thought that he might have been to blame hadn't crossed his mind. It had. And he was finding it hard to dismiss it.

"What are you saying happened, then?"

"I don't know," Peter said miserably. "I truly don't.

It's all too bloody much to take in. I mean, first Dad is supposed to have killed himself in a way that doesn't stack up, then I get mugged and some of Dad's things get stolen, then Simon tells me Dad was murdered to cover up some bloody conspiracy or other. Now he's dead too and that doesn't seem to add up either."

"Mugged? Murder? Conspiracy?" Anna whispered, glancing furtively at the nearby tables. "What on earth are you talking about?"

"You tell me," Peter shot back. "You knew the two of them and what happened when Frank lost his job at the Globe. According to Simon, it all went back to that." He leaned forward over the table, where their forgotten lunches were growing cold. "Listen, I'll tell you what Simon reckoned it was all about..."

As he related the story, Peter found part of his mind wandering. Until a few weeks ago, his life had been straightforward, focused like millions of others on getting ahead, making some money and having fun where he could. Now he seemed to be surrounded by violence, death and mystery. There had to be some simple explanation. Stuff like that just didn't happen outside Hollywood, he thought. Not to ordinary folk like him. But it was like a nightmare. The more he tried to escape, the deeper he seemed to sink into the mire. Like the accident this morning. It could happen to anyone, he supposed. It was an old building, constantly under attack by the weather and the corrosive effects of pollution. Crumbling stonework was almost inevitable and something had to give sometime. But why now, on top of everything else? And what were the odds against it happening precisely when he was standing in the line of fire?

What if it wasn't an accident? The thought came from nowhere and shocked him. He lost the drift of his narration and stuttered for a moment before he regained the thread of what he was saying to Anna. But the insidious idea wouldn't go away. Like most photographers, whose job depends on noticing every detail with the same clarity as the camera lens, he had an unusually strong visual memory and the images of those few seconds were suddenly crowding back into his mind's eye, jostling for attention. The reflection in the glass across the street wasn't perfect, he remembered. The distortions were a vital part of the picture composition, but there was something not quite right about the roof, something that spoiled the dramatic contrast he was looking for between the old and the new. He concentrated harder and the image sharpened. Then he spotted it. There was a blur of movement behind the elegant stonework, enough to show on film and mar the effect. That would have been the moment, he thought, when the weakened mortar gave way and the stone started to tumble. Registering that split-second picture was what had saved his life.

Or was it? The images in his head stubbornly refused to conform to his rationalisation and he struggled to pin down the inconsistency. Then it clicked into place and Peter sucked in his breath sharply.

"What's the matter?"

Anna's voice cut across his introspection and he realised that he'd stopped talking and was staring blankly at her. But his heart was pounding and he was trapped in his memory, unable to respond. He'd seen two movements. Sure enough, the one that had saved him, had prompted him to jump, was the stonework beginning to topple. But before that, there was another motion, behind the balustrade. Somebody had been up there, directly above where he had been standing. Someone who might have deliberately levered the masonry over the edge. Someone who wanted him dead.

"Peter." Anna was tugging insistently at his sleeve across the table. "Peter, what is it? Are you all right?"

"Uh...Yes," he mumbled.

Cold sweat was trickling down his spine beneath his shirt and he was gripped by suspicion of everything and everybody. Even Anna. By her own admission, she was part of the original team that worked on the story with Dad and Simon Milward. He no longer doubted that was at the root of things as Simon had claimed and now she was the only one left apart from him who knew what had happened. There was no way to know if that made her a potential victim, or one of the conspirators. One thing was certain, though. While he'd been plotting to avenge his father, the killers hadn't been sitting idly by. Someone had been waiting for him up there on that roof and you didn't have to be a genius to work out how long it took to get from Buckingham Palace Road to Hays Galleria for a one o'clock lunch appointment. Anna would have known, almost to the minute, what time he'd be leaving the studio.

He pulled himself up short. That didn't prove anything and she was a friend, damn it, a good friend. Paranoia wasn't going to help. All the same, the smart thing would be to keep his recollections to himself and try to find out how much she knew.

"I'm sorry," he said. "The truth is, I guess that accident shook me up more than I realised, that's all."

"You poor dear," Anna said, her voice full of concern. "You should go home and take things easy."

"No, I'm fine now. I want to finish up what we were talking about. Where had I got to?"

"You were saying that Frank had got proof of his claims and had written a story about some outfit called Media Associates."

"Yes, that's right. That's what Simon reckoned. He said Dad had phoned him about it just before he died." Peter hesitated, then decided it would be safer to keep quiet about the papers he'd found. It was academic anyway; he'd not had the chance to read them. "There was nothing in the cottage when I looked around, though," he continued. "That's about all there was to it, really. Simon just started repeating himself after that and I had to get back to London, so I left him there, in the pub. But what about you? You must have known what was going on back then."

Anna leaned back in her seat and pushed her plate away from her with a gesture of distaste. The lunchtime crowd was thinning out and the hubbub at the other tables had begun to die away. Dredging up her affair with Frank and its aftermath was painful. He was the only man she'd ever fallen for and there'd been no half-measures about it. She'd been hopelessly in love and the memories still burned, despite all the years of trying to forget, of trying to reconcile herself to what had happened to them both. The choices she'd had to make were hard. And it was harder still to explain it all to his son. How did you tell someone that you'd seduced his father, deceived his mother and then hidden the truth while pretending to be a loyal friend? No, she thought stubbornly. Not pretending. Peter was a friend and she cared about him deeply. She owed him the truth, or at least those parts of it she could allow herself to talk about, now that his father was gone and he needed to know. She took a deep breath and hoped that she wasn't about to destroy their relationship and with it her last link to Frank Conway.

"I wasn't as close to the story about the fraud that brought Frank down as Simon," she began hesitantly. "But from what I do know he seems to have painted a pretty accurate picture of what went on. Certainly, the way his career fell apart, the bankruptcy and so forth, that was true enough. Frank was a broken man at the end, but he always swore he'd done nothing wrong."

"But what about the people behind it?" Peter pressed. "What do you know about them?"

"I can't add much to what you already know. Frank was convinced Rodney Hardcastle put the knife in where it counted. Rodney was certainly a megalomaniac of the first water. I worked for him, you know. Research, he called it, but it was more like spying, making sure he knew everything that was going on so he could shaft anybody who stepped out of line. He had lots of us doing it, officially and unofficially, like some sort of secret police."

"Sounds grim. Why did you go along with it?"

"You had no choice if you wanted any sort of career.

Besides, nowhere else was much different. People who own newspapers don't buy them for fun, you know, or even to make money. They've all got their egos to feed and their nasty little axes to grind."

"You're very cynical about it."

"So would you be if you saw what actually happens in the newsrooms of the national dailies. Rodney Hardcastle was a pretty extreme example, though. What turned him on was power and using it to destroy people as viciously as possible when they got in his way. Or even just when the fancy took him. I don't suppose he's any different now he's got the knighthood he was chasing."

"Why did he turn on Dad? That's like killing off the golden goose, if he was as good a reporter as they say."

"I don't know. Oh, make no mistake, Frank was good, perhaps the best. He was Rodney's blue-eyed boy until it all went tits-up. But Rodney knew Frank and I were... well... close." Anna's eyes misted over and she hurried on to find safer ground. "Whatever his reasons, Rodney wasn't about to let me in on them. He knew it would get back to Frank."

Peter saw the telltale signs confirming his suspicions about Anna's relationship with his father. He should be outraged, he thought, but the reality was different. Even as a child, he'd known things weren't right between his parents and after all these years his memories of his mother were vague. It would be ridiculous to take offence now, to pass judgement on emotions and motives he knew nothing about.

"Did you come across anything about this outfit Media

Associates that Simon mentioned?" he said matter-of-factly.

Anna read the play of emotions on Peter's face and silently blessed him for accepting what she and Frank had experienced together. The danger that it would come between them and destroy their friendship had been very real and the knowledge that a critical obstacle had been successfully negotiated was like a tonic.

"All I know is that Frank reckoned Media Associates was the key to his story," she said. "He discovered Maxwell had set the organisation up and that Rodney Hardcastle was also involved in it in some way. That's why he believed they were both behind the frame-up, I suppose, but if he had any hard evidence he never told me."

"Nothing else? He must have said something about what he thought they were up to."

Anna shrugged and shook her head. "I'm sorry. He didn't talk about that. Not to me, anyway." She paused and chewed reflectively at a fingernail. "There was something else, though, now you mention it."

"Go on."

"Well, the big story Frank was after at the start of it all was about Maxwell, as Simon told you. Maxwell was in the Army during the war and seconded to Berlin as an Intelligence Officer in 1945. His job was interrogating people, sorting out the Nazis from the civilians and digging out any secrets that would be useful to the British government. Just twenty-two months later, he comes back home and makes himself a fortune, except nobody could figure out exactly how.

That's what got Frank sniffing around in the first place. Then this woman turns up, with a diary she claimed was from a top Nazi scientist. Well, back then stories about mad Nazi scientists were two-a-penny, but Frank reckoned this one was different. It turned out she was the daughter of a scientist called Oberberg."

Peter nodded at the name.

"Yes, Simon mentioned him. The diary got stolen didn't it?"

"Yes, but it's what happened just before that sticks in my mind. Frank was spending a lot of time with this woman - Magda was her name - and I got a bit ratty about it. But he said he had to get her to trust him before she'd hand over the diary. He was desperate to get his hands on it, because Magda claimed it gave chapter and verse on a deal with her father that if he handed over a top secret archive of his scientific research Maxwell would make sure she and her father would be given new identities and looked after. But as soon as he got the papers Maxwell welshed on the deal. Her father had been arrested and died in a prison camp and she'd been left destitute. It would have ruined Maxwell's reputation if it had come out."

Peter whistled softly. "That's pretty conclusive as a motive to shut Frank up."

"It was the smoking gun that Frank had been searching for. But the odd thing was, when he did finally get his hands on the diary he more or less lost interest in Maxwell himself. He reckoned he'd found a bigger story, to do with the research Oberberg had handed over to Maxwell. He called it the Kaiserhof Archive. It was the key to one of the most dangerous and closely guarded secrets of his generation, he said. He was convinced that Maxwell had never handed it over to the British government, but had used it to set up Media Associates under his own control."

"To do what?"

"Anna shrugged.

"He never said."

"And you just let it go? What sort of bloody journalist were you?"

"Of course I didn't just walk away. We had the mother and father of all rows about it, but Frank was a stubborn bastard when he wanted to be. He clammed up, said it was too dangerous to get me involved any deeper. He reckoned he was doing me a favour and the way things turned out, perhaps he was right. Magda was killed in a car crash shortly afterward so I couldn't follow up with her. The police said at the time it was an accident, though I have my doubts. But one thing I am absolutely certain of. Whatever Frank thought they were doing with this Kaiserhof stuff, it scared him shitless. And your Dad wasn't a man who scared easily."

***

Later, Peter watched Anna head off through the archway towards London Bridge station and her train up to Charing Cross. He stood irresolutely by the mobile sculpture in the middle of the Hays Galleria plaza. It depicted a galley, oars splashing with mechanical futility in the middle of its artificial lake, while fountains played. His own situation was much the same, he reflected. All at sea and wound up, but going nowhere.

A flight of marble steps to his left led up to the riverside walkway and he drifted up them, deep in thought. At the top, he paused to take in the panorama of the City across the Pool of London. The bulk of HMS Belfast, framed by Tower Bridge, loomed to his right, a relic from the war with her blanked off guns pointing menacingly fore and aft but no longer offering a threat to anyone. Was there really another legacy from that same past corrupting the very heart of the City spread out in front of him? It seemed incredible. But what he'd learned over lunch had all but confirmed that it was true, even if the evidence was still circumstantial. And like his father before him, he was tangled up in it whether he liked it or not. Someone had tried to kill him. It was outrageous and it was terrifying, but maybe it was just a warning. If he walked away now and minded his own business, perhaps the threat would disappear.

He leaned on the railings and stared down at the river. His future seemed about as clear as the mud-banks left by the ebbing tide. He shivered, remembering the finality of the sound of masonry smashing to the ground. There could be no illusions about what he was getting into; he no longer had any doubt they were trying to kill him. Yet the compulsion to put himself further into harm's way burnt in him like a forest fire from which, once lit, there was no escape. This wasn't how things were supposed to be. Up to now, the biggest risk he'd taken in his life was leaving home and that had been to run away from trouble, not to go looking for it. He wasn't cut out to be a crusader and only a few weeks ago he wouldn't have given a toss about what had happened to his father. Perhaps he really was going crazy. He'd be damned if he could think of any other explanation. But all the same, the foundations of his world had shifted irrevocably and his new-found passion would not be denied. Whatever the cost, he could not betray his father a second time. He had to go on. Come what may.

Chapter 7

Being stalked was a mind-wrecking experience. The worst part of it, Peter Conway decided, was the unremitting tension that pervaded every facet of his life, even the most mundane activities. The fear of what might lie in wait around each street corner or behind every closed door was obsessive, but ultimately manageable. The part he couldn't handle was never knowing who was watching or when they might strike.

He heard the rumble of a tube train and felt the blast of air through the archway connecting the two platforms, which signified that it was approaching on the other side. Peter tightened his grip on the folio case containing his presentation materials and pressed his back more firmly against the curved wall of the westbound tunnel, well away from the edge of the platform. His heart started to pound and he strained to avoid furtive movements of his head while his eyes anxiously scanned his fellow travellers. The rush hour was over and the tube station wasn't crowded. Nobody seemed to be paying any particular attention to him, but that meant nothing. Professionals wouldn't give themselves away so easily. The hard-looking man in overalls and heavy boots might seem engrossed in his copy of the 'Sun', but he was a prime suspect. He'd been no more than a few paces behind all the way from the ticket machines at the top of the escalator.

There was a screech of brakes on the eastbound platform and the doors of the train rumbled open with a swoosh of compressed air. Timing was critical now. With so few people around, it wouldn't be there long. Peter counted to ten. Then he sprang into the connecting tunnel, sprinted across to the other platform and jumped onto the waiting train, his ears straining to detect any following footsteps. There were none and a glance along the platform as the doors thumped shut at his heels confirmed that nobody had tried to match his move. The knot of tension in his stomach eased as the train lurched into motion. He was safe for now. Probably.

His eyes were gritty with lack of sleep and the black coffee he'd breakfasted on was swilling around his gut like battery acid. He reached into his pocket for the Rennies, popping another couple into his mouth with a grimace of distaste. He'd been eating them like sweets, but they weren't dealing with the heartburn as advertised and his chest still felt like it was packed with barbed wire. The emotional roller coaster he was trapped on turned every stranger into a potential threat and had him continually looking over his shoulder fearing the worst. It was out of control and the stress was killing him without any outside help. It had to stop, he told himself for the hundredth time. The only way to do that was to find the evidence to settle things one way or the other and reducing himself to a gibbering idiot wasn't the way to go about it. All the same, a small, shrill voice deep inside refused to be silenced as he hung onto the handrail against the lurching of the train staring at his fellow passengers suspiciously. He'd nearly been killed the other day. There was no getting away from that.

Peter Conway's journey ended uneventfully at Bevis Marks, the narrow City street just a few hundred yards from Aldgate tube station that housed the headquarters of Media Associates. Prestigious high-rise office blocks obscured the sky and the pavements were crowded with men in suits, hurrying about their business with mobile phones clamped to their ears. But for the first time since leaving Tonbridge that morning, Peter didn't feel as though he was the centre of attention. That honour fell to a white van parked in front of the gleaming stainless steel and glass revolving doors of number 46. It had attracted a crowd, as the driver ignored the attempts of a uniformed commissionaire and several minions to move him on. With a sinking heart, Peter recognised the rebellious figure of Jack Howson and the Spectrum Studios logo on the van. He picked up his pace and pushed through the crowd towards the eye of the storm.

"What's the problem?" Peter demanded.

Jack turned to face him, looking sullen. "You finally made it, then. This bloke's being a right pain in the arse. Won't let me take our gear inside."

The commissionaire's head swivelled like a gun turret and he fastened his eyes on Peter. "Is this your van, sir?" he said, as though it was a piece of particularly obnoxious litter that had been dumped on the doorstep. "I must insist that that you ask your driver to remove it at once."

Peter bridled at the tone and suppressed the urge to snap back. There were plenty of reasons to keep a low profile and a shouting match on the front doorstep wouldn't be a good start.

"I'm sorry, I think there's a misunderstanding," he said patiently. "We've got a contract with your marketing director Philip Williams to do a photographic session here today. You can call him if you like. We just need a few minutes to unload our equipment."

"I told him that already," Jack grumbled loudly. "He's not listening."

"Cool it, Jack," Peter hissed out of the corner of his mouth. "I'll handle it." His eyes were still fixed on the uniformed flunky and his instincts were twitching. The man's forehead was covered in beads of sweat and the expression on his face didn't look like the usual arrogance of petty officialdom. In fact, it looked strangely like fear, tinged with desperation. A five-hundredth of a second at wide aperture, say f.2.8, taken medium close-up to catch the facial details against a background blurred by the narrow depth of field, would produce a classic shot of someone looking at an impending disaster, his photographic brain automatically told him. But there didn't seem to be anything here to warrant such a reaction.

"What's the problem?" he repeated, trying to sound conciliatory. "We don't want to cause any hassle."

A flicker of relief crossed the commissionaire's face. "I've got to keep this space clear," he said, unbending fractionally and accepting the olive branch. "There's a board meeting this morning. The chairman will be arriving any minute, see and there'll be hell to pay if his driver can't pull in. I can't accept any deliveries till after."

"That sounds fair enough." Peter forced a sympathetic

smile onto his face. "But look, I've got problems, too. I'm due upstairs in the next few minutes and I need my equipment. Tell you what, is there somewhere else my assistant can park up and unload? The stuff's too heavy to carry far, though."

After a hurried but amicable negotiation, they struck a deal. Peter Conway watched the van move off, trailing a cloud of silent protest from Jack Howson, but bearing a security guard whose electronic pass would open the doors to the private underground car park and the internal service elevator. He turned to say a diplomatic 'thanks', but the doorman's attention was rigidly fixed on a light blue Rolls Royce that had just come into view. That peculiar, strained expression was back on his face. And not just his, Peter noticed. The sight of the car had sent a noticeable wave of tension through the yuppies milling about on the pavement. Not just bystanders, then, he thought. A reception committee of some sort, which meant that whoever was in the Rolls carried a lot of clout. But it was the facial expressions and the atmosphere that fascinated him.

There was real drama unfolding in front of his eyes and Peter automatically drifted back to a good vantage point, reaching for the digital camera he always kept in his pocket ready to capture such unexpected visual gems. The light was reasonable, he noted subconsciously. Good. That meant no need for flash, all the better for candid shots and for staying unnoticed in the background. Photographers weren't always welcome, as he knew to his cost, especially when peering uninvited into people's souls, recording unflattering realities they spent a lifetime trying to hide. But getting beneath the mask and capturing the uncensored truth was what good pictures were all about. There was a swirl of activity as the car pulled in and Peter clamped the viewfinder to his eye, his finger hovering over the shutter release.

The grey-uniformed chauffeur leapt out to open the rear door. A short, overweight man, with an air of barely suppressed fury at the world in general, exploded onto the pavement, barking instructions over his shoulder at an aide emerging behind. The way magically cleared in front of the beetling eyebrows and outthrust jaw, the crowd of acolytes parting like the Red Sea and then closing in behind as the imperious figure strode towards the entrance, still firing off orders as he went. Peter looked in vain for any sign of acknowledgement or appreciation of the staff's efforts to smooth his path. This was clearly a man who paid no heed to such trifles. It wasn't that he hadn't noticed. Quite the reverse, Peter thought with distaste, as he mentally reviewed the images his clicking finger had captured. Those darting eyes had missed nothing, feeding on the fear of his subordinates like vultures gorging on their prey.

The retinue disappeared into the building, leaving behind a curious silence like the aftermath of an earthquake. Peter tucked his camera away and sidled back up to the commissionaire.

"Who on earth was that?" he asked.

"That's the Chairman of the Board. Sir Rodney Hardcastle."

"Is he always that... er... energetic?" Peter said,

smothering his dismay at the revelation that this was the man he'd decided to attack. He didn't know what he'd expected, but it wasn't such an elemental force.

"He's a busy man, sir. Always on the go. Anyway, sir, if you take the lift to the eleventh floor, I'll call ahead and have Mr. Williams' secretary meet you."

Despite the neutral phrasing, it was confirmation enough that Sir Rodney's behaviour was not exceptional. And it was salutary, Peter mused as the lift carried him upwards, that the fear underlying the scene he'd just witnessed wasn't the kind you'd expect from people worried about mere job security, even under the harshest of bosses. There was nothing you could produce as evidence in a court of law, but it was more akin to the terror of someone confronting a rabid animal. The battle to control his inner forebodings suddenly became a good deal harder.

***

An hour later Peter looked across the table at the smiling face of Philip Williams.

"So you're happy with my ideas for widening the scope of our initial contract?" he said, gesturing at the litter of papers from his portfolio scattered in front of them. "I know they go well beyond your original brief, but the results will be spectacular, I assure you."

"I think they bring my marketing concept to life," Philip responded with a burst of unexpected enthusiasm. "I've always told the board we need something more adventurous, more... er... compelling." He paused for a moment. "If you think you can do it, that is," he added with doubt returning to his voice. "It's tough to capture what really goes on in a firm like ours. We'd have to find a way to get across to potential clients the expertise we bring to our projects. Make the messages about quality and commitment jump off the page at them."

"As I said, I'm sure I can do that if you let me work in depth with one of your project teams. I'd have to be there, a fly on the wall so to speak, as they're working through the issues from start to finish. Once they get used to me, I'm sure I'll be able to capture the images to bring out the essential messages very powerfully."

Peter watched Philip scratch his chin thoughtfully. The hunted look was back on the client's face, his high forehead creased into the nervous frown that seemed to be his trademark.

"That could be difficult. For us, I mean. Most of what we do is pretty confidential, you know. Clients can be very funny about that sort of thing."

Peter suppressed a sigh. They'd been round this loop before and he wondered if Philip Williams was actually capable of making any sort of decision.

"Maybe so. But a firm like yours needs a marketing brochure that's innovative. Nobody buys your sort of services on the basis of glossy pictures of offices and computer terminals, whatever fancy words you wrap around them. You've got to get under the skin, show them what makes you different."

"Well, yes, but there are risks..."

"Look," Peter interrupted, seeing the project extension beginning to slip away from him again, "I'm happy to sign confidentiality agreements or whatever if that's what's worrying you. Surely your clients would agree to that?"

Philip brightened. "Would you? That would make it easier. But there's the cost, too. What you're suggesting is a lot more expensive than a straightforward shoot. I might have trouble getting the board to agree to a bigger budget."

Peter thought quickly. He couldn't let this kind of opportunity to worm his way much deeper into the organisation slip by and he was so close. Fees weren't an issue, though he could hardly say that. How could he close the deal without giving the game away? A bit of flattery and humble pie might help.

"Perhaps I can meet you half way," he said tentatively. "It means a lot to me to work with a top agency like yours and I'm willing to take a chance. How about if I do it at my own risk?"

"What do you mean?"

"I'll take the formal pictures you've already agreed. The cost of that will be within your budget and that's all you'll be committed to pay. But I'll also do the other shots, working with your people, on the basis that you'll only pay the additional cost if you're happy with the results."

"You'd be taking quite a risk."

"It's worth it to me to get your business," Peter said, trying to look sincere. "Anyway, I'm confident you and your colleagues will see the added value, in which case I'm not out of pocket. But there's no downside for you. How about it? I can't say fairer than that."

Afterwards, Peter strolled down the corridor towards the spare office where Jack was waiting, unconsciously rubbing his hand on his trousers to rid it of the residue of the clammy handshake that had sealed the deal. But to be fair, there was nothing limp or indecisive about the ensuing action. A compact digital box of tricks materialised and took only seconds to produce a plastic security pass embossed with his likeness. It was a novel experience to find his picture being taken, for a change. The integral magnetic strip, he learned, was programmed with the codes to give him access through the electronic locks which protected all the main doorways and the pass had to be worn visibly at all times while in the building. A whirlwind tour of the premises and some furious scribbling gave him a working draft of the key scenes, angles and lighting requirements for the stock shots and usefully embraced the toilets and the cafeteria en route. Then it was down to business with tripods, lights and flash meter, plus the usual banter to keep the human elements of the photographs cooperative and looking natural.

Peter was struggling with a tricky but spectacular shot of the atrium through a fish-eye lens when he felt a tap on his shoulder. He grunted irritably and straightened up from the viewfinder to confront a smartly dressed young man of about his own age.

"Sorry to interrupt. You must be Peter Conway?"

"That's right."

"I'm David Tyler."

The handshake this time was firm and dry, which was a distinct improvement, but the smile bristled with unspoken reservations.

"Hi, David." Peter gestured towards Jack. "This is my assistant, Jack Howson. What can we do for you?"

"It's more what I can do for you, I think. I manage several of our key accounts. Philip Williams tells me you're looking for some sort of in-depth session on one of our projects, is that right?"

Peter was suddenly all attention and he looked David up and down discreetly. He didn't look like part of a sinister conspiracy. More like an advert for motherhood and apple pie. He was tall and thin, his clean-shaven, tanned face and twinkling brown eyes conveying an impression of artless honesty. The carefully groomed hair, pinstripe Versace suit and black Churches lace-up brogues were a subtle statement of competence and professional integrity if you believed in Shakespeare's old adage that the apparel proclaims the man, although the colourful silk tie hinted at just a touch of rebelliousness. David Tyler had all the attributes you'd expect to find in a top PR executive. Or in a snake-oil salesman, Peter thought cynically. No one knew better than a photographer that images were only skin-deep and could rarely be trusted. He'd have to watch his step with this one.

"Bit young for all that responsibility, aren't you?" he said with an edge in his voice. "I was expecting someone older."

David smiled easily, as if it was a remark he fielded regularly. Which it probably was, Peter realised.

"That makes two of us, then," David replied without visible offence. "Your work has a depth and maturity that usually only comes with long experience. Just goes to show that age isn't everything, doesn't it?"

There was no answer to that and Peter found himself reluctantly warming to this young man.

"Touché. Sorry, I didn't mean to be rude. You've seen some of my photographs?"

"Yes, I went to an exhibition at my local photographic society. I'm quite a keen amateur photographer. Nowhere near your class, though, I'm afraid."

"You'll understand what I've got in mind for this brochure of yours, then. I suppose Philip explained the background?"

"Not really. He was just touting for volunteers and I thought some of your expertise might rub off if we worked together." His gaze wandered around the equipment and back to Peter's face. "You won't mind if I pick your brains? The chance to work alongside a professional photographer doesn't come up very often."

Peter paused, thinking fast. Flattery was all very well, but too much attention would cramp his style when it came to poking around. On the other hand, an enthusiastic volunteer would be more forthcoming than a reluctant conscript.

"OK, David," he said. "Why don't you start by telling me which of your current projects you think might fit the bill?"

"I don't know. Philip was pretty vague about exactly what you're trying to achieve. Something about a new perspective on how we work with clients was all he told me."

"Dammit, I didn't think he grasped what I was driving at," Peter frowned, forgetting his hidden agenda for a moment. "I'd have thought a marketing director would be smarter at thinking outside the conventional box."

"He's a words and politics man. No visual imagination.

I expect he gave you the limp-wristed treatment? That's what usually happens when he's out of his depth."

"Well, I wouldn't exactly say that."

David laughed at the confirmation in Peter's voice.

"No, I suppose it wouldn't be diplomatic, would it? Don't worry, though. He's decisive enough when he wants to be and he knows what he likes when he sees the finished product. In the meantime, why don't you try your ideas out on me?"

"Fair enough. When would suit you?"

David glanced at the jumble of equipment and then at his watch. "It's getting on now and it looks as though you've still got a bit to do here. I've got a few things to sort out as well before I pack up this evening. How about tomorrow around ten? You'll find me and my team on the third floor."

Peter stared at the departing figure, wondering what was really going on underneath that smoothly packaged exterior. Perhaps he'd just fallen lucky and what you saw was what you got. For sure, if there was a conspiracy to manipulate the financial markets and wreck peoples' lives it would be a jealously guarded secret, held by a few key men at the top. It was improbable that someone at David Tyler's level would be in on it. But not impossible. Spin was an everyday tool of David's job and at some point the reality of how it worked must become inescapable. The bottom line was that he had to assume the worst and trust nobody.

His stomach churned again at the prospect and the urge to pack up and get the hell out while he still could was almost overwhelming. It was self-disgust at his weakness that came to his rescue. The game had barely started and he was already on the verge of giving up. It was pathetic. He was inside Media Associates, ideally placed to worm his way into their confidence. He'd be an idiot to throw that away for nothing more than a bout of nerves. Peter pulled himself together, trying to ignore the dry taste of cowardice in his mouth and turned back to the image in the viewfinder of the Hasselblad. It was total crap, he thought, feeling the frustration boiling up. A blind man could see that the lighting set up and the angles were all wrong. Jack Howson should damn well know better than that by now and if he didn't pull his bloody finger out and use some sense, they'd never get the job done.

***

By the time Peter got back home, after another episode of hide and seek across London, he was shattered. Even the stoical Jack Howson had been moved to anger at his irrational behaviour, marching off in a huff that had brought the day's shooting to an abrupt and unhappy end. It wasn't the first time the stress of a new job had led to a falling out, but this was more acrimonious than usual and Peter cursed his capricious temper. It was worse then useless to take his troubles out on Jack, even though he was a convenient lightning rod and would have shrugged it off by tomorrow.

The microwave pinged to announce that his dinner was ready and he plodded through into the open-plan kitchen. Traditional beef stew and dumplings, straight from the freezer, was on the menu tonight. 'Meal for two' it said on the discarded packet lying on the work surface, but they'd have to be two pretty meagre appetites for that to be a practical proposition. Or perhaps it just meant two recognisable pieces of meat, which seemed to be about the average contents. Either way, it was no banquet, washed down with a glass or two of plonk from the box of supermarket special that was always lying handy. But it was hot and filling. And no washing up, he reflected with satisfaction, as he slid the container onto the breakfast bar and pulled up a stool. The wine glass and the fork didn't really count. He ate mechanically, anxious to be done so he could check out what he'd captured on the digital camera this morning.

The attic room was akin to an operating theatre, immaculate and silent apart from the hum of the cooling fans inside the computer case. In some ways it was an apt parallel, Peter decided, considering the surgery he performed here on digital images. The idea that the camera never lied was a hopeless relic of the past. With modern software, you could cut and paste images seamlessly at the touch of a button and create any effect you wanted even if the original picture was flawed. The technology bug had bitten him deeply and it was rapidly becoming an indispensable weapon in his armoury, although many of his fellow professionals still scorned it. More fool them, he thought. The alternative of laboriously airbrushing flawed or scratched negatives with photographic dyes was a mug's game when you got better results digitally in a fraction of the time. And it was magical to be able to call up and manipulate images without messing about with chemicals and darkrooms.

He plugged the camera into the USB hub on his desk and watched with satisfaction as the images downloaded and sprang to life on the colour monitor. The new Athlon processor was lightning fast, just as he'd hoped. His worries receded as he lost himself in the pleasures of playing with composition, contrast and colour saturation, seeking out the exact effects he wanted like an artist with his paints. Some of the shots were stunning, conveying the tension and drama of the moment even more powerfully than he remembered.

One in particular stood out, of Sir Rodney Hardcastle, outside the Rolls and eying his waiting minions, just about to start his march into the building. Peter tapped the keyboard to zoom in and the screen filled with the power and arrogance of the man. Caught as he tensed to move, the pose was like that of a leopard about to pounce on his prey, accentuated by the curl of the narrow lips and the gleam of white teeth. The grey eyes were chips of ice and the snarl on the face might have been carved in granite. Peter shuddered. This was one for his private portfolio, a portrait of raw brutality. The real man, whose veneer of civilisation had slipped for an instant.

He zoomed out to a full screen view and studied it, trying to decide the best crop lines for the composition of a final print. As he did so, his eye strayed to the left hand edge, behind the Rolls. There was another car, one he'd not noticed at the time. A black Jaguar. There was something about it that demanded his attention and he dragged a window over it to bring up the detail. At that magnification, the picture was grainy but still clear enough. A muscular-looking man in a black suit was caught in an awkward pose, back to the camera, halfway out of the passenger door. But it was the driver's head, framed by the open window and partly obscured by a mobile phone, which rang a bell. He'd seen that image before, recently.

He racked his brains, but the memory refused to surface. Peter scanned through the other photos for the two men, but they appeared only once more and it didn't help. All that showed was their backs, disappearing through the revolving doors in the wake of Sir Rodney's entourage. That must mean, though, that they were part of his team. Bodyguards, perhaps? They certainly looked tough enough to take care of any dirty work, he thought idly.

Then it clicked and the shock fizzed through him like a lightning bolt. It was outside his studio that he'd seen the picture before. The black Jaguar, blocking the traffic while the driver talked into his phone. Just before he'd nearly been killed. The face wasn't clear, but the profile matched his memory of a square jaw-line and prominent beaked nose, topped with groomed black hair streaked with the kind of silver that added gravitas. And the other man could easily have been the figure on the roof, taking telephoned instructions about the location of his target. Suddenly Peter was certain. He was looking at a photograph of his would-be killers, the ones he'd been checking over his shoulder for every minute since that horrifying day. There was no room for doubt that like him they were working for Sir

Rodney Hardcastle and his life wouldn't be worth a bent penny if they made the connection with Spectrum Studios. Assuming, he thought with horror, that they hadn't already done so.

Chapter 8

The grey light of morning creeping through the gaps in the curtains brought little comfort, except that Peter could give up the pretence of trying to sleep. Exhaustion had driven him from the computer keyboard in the early hours, but his nightmares had denied him any rest. He threw aside the sheets and padded through to the bathroom. The spearmint toothpaste took care of the vile taste in his mouth and a shower dissipated the worst of the cotton wool that his head seemed to be stuffed with. Only a gallon or so of coffee was going to do anything for the dull ache behind his eyes, though. He pulled on the most anonymous of his business suits - today wasn't a day when he wanted to stand out from the crowd - and headed for the kitchen.

Half an hour later, he summoned up his courage and left for the station. The red pillar-box at the end of Woodside Road swallowed the product of his night's labours without excitement and so far as he could tell without any of the early commuters scurrying towards the trains paying any attention. He'd expected the small act of defiance would make him feel better, but it didn't. There was cold comfort at best in documenting his suspicions - you could hardly call it evidence, even with the photographs - and sending the result to Anna Stein for safe keeping in case anything happened to him. Last night it had seemed a sensible option to take out some kind of insurance, however feeble. But the chill of the morning brought home the hollowness of a gesture that would only have meaning if he was killed. Perhaps not even then, he thought, feeling scared and slightly sick. Writing it all down hadn't done Dad much good, had it? His lips twitched in a thin smile as he walked down the steps to the platform. It was ironic that he'd been driven to follow in his father's footsteps after a lifetime dedicated to avoiding that very thing. Words were no more than scribbles on a piece of paper, not the sword and shield Frank Conway had imagined them to be.

The familiar screech of tortured steel as the Hastings to Charing Cross service hit the curve on the approach to the station reached his ears and he glanced up. The headlight of the approaching train cut through the gloom and a blue lightning flash from the live rail underlined his thoughts. This was where Dad's path and his diverged, as they always had. All the words in the world wouldn't solve his problems. Only actions could do that. He stepped into the carriage and slammed the door behind him with a note of finality. It wasn't that he felt heroic, far from it. He'd been left with no choice.

At 46, Bevis Marks, the atmosphere was calm and businesslike and Peter felt the demons of the night retreating into the shadows. The papers from his portfolio were once again spread over a polished mahogany table, albeit a rather smaller one than graced Philip Williams' office, but this time they were receiving a more enthusiastic accolade. The concept of trying to capture in photographs the inspiration of a PR team in full cry appealed, it seemed and David

Tyler's reservations about introducing an outsider to the mysteries of his work appeared to be evaporating fast.

They had successfully galloped past the 'what' towards the 'how' of the project and Peter was explaining that the Hasselblad, with all its attendant studio lights and paraphernalia would have to be discarded. It would be far too intrusive. Indeed, Peter reflected, he'd already made his peace with Jack Howson after yesterday's altercation and dispatched him and the vanload of gear back to Buckingham Palace Road. He fetched the Nikon F1 out of the bag by his feet to demonstrate. It was a much better tool for spur-of-the-moment work, with its interchangeable lenses and the motor drive for catching the fleeting images that would tell the story. A fast Tungsten film, perhaps 1600 ASA, would eliminate the need for flash and overcome the problematic orange 'glow' that artificial lighting generated on conventional colour film stock. The downside would be some graininess in the negatives, but that was acceptable since it was unlikely that large blow-ups would be called for. In any case, he wanted the flexibility to use the 35-70mm zoom lens and couldn't afford to drop below 1/125th of a second shutter speed because of the risk of camera shake with hand-held shots. That combination left him no other choice of film. The key to it all was that David's team had to forget that a photographer was there. You had to blend into the background to catch those moments when the masks dropped, when the true emotions and motivations emerged.

"I could use you at my board meetings if you can do

that, lad."

The deep voice with traces of a Yorkshire accent came from the open door behind them and made Peter jump. He turned and froze. There was no mistaking the identity of the figure standing there.

"Good morning, Sir Rodney," David Tyler said smoothly, apparently unperturbed by the interruption, "Let me introduce you to..."

Peter's brain raced as he recognised the potentially disastrous consequences of what David was in the process of saying. The grey eyes that were staring at him from the doorway were twinkling with amusement and the voracious predator of yesterday's photograph was wrapped in a cloak of bonhomie. So they hadn't put two and two together yet. But that probably wouldn't survive an instant if he heard the name Conway. He stepped forward smartly with his hand held out and cut across David's words.

"It's a real privilege to meet you, Sir Rodney," he said enthusiastically, taking the other man's hand in a firm grip and pumping it up and down. "I'm from Spectrum Studios. We're just putting together the outline for your new marketing brochure and I must say I'm deeply impressed with the operation you and your team have got here. It's such a pleasure to be working with the best in the business."

One of the bushy eyebrows twitched quizzically and Peter hoped he wasn't overdoing the flattery.

"So you're the up and coming photographer Philip Williams was telling me about?" The twinkle momentarily vanished from Sir Rodney Hardcastle's eyes and they went flat and hard as he brought his full attention to bear. It was like a cold shower and Peter felt goose bumps down his spine at the intensity of the scrutiny. "I gather you're going to expose our innermost secrets, is that right?"

Peter forced a laugh, though his heart was hammering and it didn't come out quite as casually as he intended.

"That's exactly what I'm hoping to do, sir," he said. "Show your clients what it means to work with top-line professionals, bring to life the kind of dedication they can expect if they put themselves in your hands."

"Aye, well," Sir Rodney grunted sceptically. Peter felt the stare switch off like an inner door slamming shut, as though he'd been catalogued and pigeonholed as not worthy of further consideration. "You'll have your work cut out, then." He gestured at the table. "I've got a couple of minutes. Show me what you've got in mind."

After a brief explanation, Peter watched in silence as the specimen photographs in his portfolio were examined one by one. The chairman's face was inscrutable and he began to fear the worst. It would be a disaster if the project fell apart now, before things had even got off the ground. He glanced appealingly towards David, willing him to say something positive. The message got through, but was met with a smile and a slight but unmistakeable shake of the head. Peter's heart sank. No help would be forthcoming from that quarter. It was not surprising. David's interests were bound to be in his career and it would be a foolish move for him to risk second-guessing his boss, especially such an obviously unforgiving one as Sir Rodney.

The silence stretched on and he opened his mouth to make a last-ditch attempt to salvage the situation. From the corner of his eye, he caught a warning glance from David and another firm shake of the head. He hesitated and then it was too late. Sir Rodney tossed the prints back onto the table and looked up.

"You seem to know your business, lad, I'll give you that. I thought the proposal was rubbish when it came up at the board," he said bluntly. "But you can have your chance to prove me wrong."

Peter was nonplussed. "I... er... thank you. I'm glad you like my work," he managed, weakly.

"Don't count any chickens. A chance, I said, that's all." He turned and marched toward the door, then hesitated and looked back shrewdly at Peter. "I'm throwing a party on Saturday. My daughter's twenty-first birthday. Come and bring your camera. My secretary will give you the details."

The room felt strangely empty after he left, which was a measure of the way Sir Rodney's personality had dominated it, Peter supposed. He looked across at David Tyler in confusion.

"What the hell was that all about?"

David laughed. "We call it being 'RH'd'. That's either Royally Hassled or Rodney Hardcastled, according to your taste. Anything new, he gets to hear and gives it the once over personally if he thinks it's significant. You'll get used to it if you stay around for long."

"He didn't have much to say."

"That means he really liked your stuff. You don't know your luck, I've seen him chew people up and spit out the bones when the mood's on him. That's why I was trying to tell you to keep your mouth shut. He makes his own decisions and any bullshit just sets him off big-time."

"Strange way to run a business this size. Getting involved personally at this sort of level, I mean."

"Maybe. But he's the Boss with a capital 'B' around here and he never lets anyone forget it. And that includes firing people if the fancy takes him. What the hell, though," David shrugged, "it works. You can't argue with success."

"So what was that stuff about photographing his daughter's twenty-first? Was he serious?"

"Oh, yes, he was serious all right. Thank your stars you're not a builder, or he'd have had you putting a new roof on the house or something. He does it all the time with contractors, like a pay-off for giving them his business."

"It's a freebie, then?"

"Sure. He may be rich as Croesus, but he's still a Yorkshireman at heart. It's a pretty small price to pay to get on the right side of him, though and you can bet it'll be one hell of a party. You don't have a problem with that, surely?"

***

The Hardcastle residence was deep in the Oxfordshire countryside and Peter drove up the M40 that Saturday evening not knowing what to expect. When he got there, the extravagance of the place wasn't a surprise, knowing a bit about the owner, though he figured there must be a hell of a big hole somewhere nearby to have provided that much Cotswold stone. What he had not expected was the laser lighting flickering across the Georgian facade, or the boom of heavy-duty pop music, which even at the gates was loud enough to make his teeth itch. Either there were no neighbours within earshot, or nobody gave a toss about their feelings. Lines of lights wound their way up the slope towards the mansion, flanking a drive that seemed long enough to merit a service station and by the time he pulled up in front of the Palladian columns of the portico, he was feeling thoroughly intimidated. At least the Porsche lent him a veneer of respectability, he thought, as a uniformed valet opened the door for him and held out a white-gloved hand. He hesitated, suppressing the instinct to shake it. That didn't seem right. Then his eye caught the traffic-jam of exotic vehicles being marshalled in the stable yards at the side of the house and he flushed, realising all the man wanted was his keys. Thank God he hadn't brought the van, though. It would have stuck out like a sore thumb and he'd probably have been shunted off to the tradesman's entrance into the bargain. He tugged unhappily at the sleeves of his dinner jacket, which seemed to have shrunk a size since he'd tried it on at Moss Bros. This wasn't his scene and he felt wildly out of place. But there was no going back. He took a deep breath, slung the Nikon over his shoulder and marched up the steps towards the throng of merrymakers.

Inside, sipping the champagne that had been thrust upon him, Peter paused to take stock. It was clearly open house and, absent any introductions, the first order of business was to work out who was who and what was where, so he could start photographing the right people. The entrance hall was big enough to play tennis in, although the built-in audience of marble statues didn't look the types to applaud any such activity. In front of him, an oak staircase rose to a galleried landing and to either side double doors opened into the main reception rooms. Most of the noise was coming from his left in what must be, he calculated quickly, the West wing and there was a definite absence of grey hairs and decorum in the gyrating bodies he could see through the open doorway. That would be the birthday girl and her friends, then. The East wing, in contrast, exuded the fragrance of Havana tobacco rather than the garden-bonfire smell of less legitimate materials and the hum of conversation seemed altogether more in keeping with the crystal chandeliers and gilt-framed oil paintings. Sir Rodney and his chums, Peter thought, for whom a party was simply business in another guise. And in between, circulating aimlessly around the hallway and the laden buffet tables of the dining room the other side of the stairs, those like himself who didn't quite know where they belonged.

He tossed a mental coin and it came down tails. East first, then, to see what he could make of the made-to-measure dinner suits flattering Sir Rodney. He sidled through the panelled door and checked the settings on the Nikon. There would be no mucking about with special high-speed film tonight. He was here to play the common or garden photographer, to be seen, categorised and then instantly forgotten like a waiter or a car-parking valet. That cloak of professional anonymity was his best chance of picking up any indiscretions if alcohol should loosen tongues, as well as his insurance if he was caught poking his nose in where it didn't belong. That was the theory, anyway. It was time to put it to the test. At the first flash, a pair of steely eyes jerked round and fastened on him with instinctive hostility, which his second shot caught perfectly. Peter shuddered. That was another one for his private collection, he thought as Sir Rodney relaxed and nodded slightly at him. Expressions like that belonged in the jungle, not at a house party in Oxfordshire and weren't the stuff to generate client goodwill. He was here to find images that flattered, that would portray the generous host and man of distinction. It was a shame that Sir Rodney would never appreciate that photographing a lie was a much more skilful business than capturing the truth.

Then his wandering lens caught a familiar profile and his heart missed a beat. The man from the Jaguar had appeared in the doorway, wearing the same plain black business suit that Peter remembered so well from his previous encounter. He was looking confidently around and clearly feeling not the slightest embarrassment about the absence of a dinner jacket. Peter kept the Nikon pressed to his face, knowing that it almost completely obscured his features and hoping that would be a sufficient disguise. His finger hovered over the shutter release. He desperately wanted to press it and capture that face on film, but all his instincts told him that this was another predator, whose eyes would automatically look for a potential threat if a flashgun fired. It would be lethal to attract that sort of attention, only a complete fool would assume otherwise. Peter eased himself backward into the crowd, bending his knees to make himself less prominent and twisted the zoom ring to widen his angle of view. The lens captured a moment of eye contact between the man and Sir Rodney, who acknowledged it with a fractional jerk of the head towards a door at the back of the room.

Several people had already disappeared discreetly through that door, Peter realised, although he'd attached no importance to it amid the comings and goings of the party. But when he saw Sir Rodney make his excuses to the group he'd been chatting with and follow the black-clad figure, it acquired a new significance. His stomach churned. Something was going on under cover of the party and the chances were it was connected to his own quest. But did he dare try and find out what? There was at least one person behind that door who would recognise him immediately and going through it could be a fatal mistake. On the other hand, it could be a unique opportunity. And the decision had to be made now.

He eased the door shut behind him and leaned back against it. An empty corridor stretched away in front of him and he let out his pent-up breath with a heartfelt sigh. It had taken all his self-control to walk confidently across the crowded room and enter this private part of the house as if he had every right to do so. But nobody had noticed, or if they had, they had not chosen to interfere. Perhaps they just assumed that a photographer, obviously working at Sir Rodney's behest, had the freedom to go where he wished.

Whatever the reason, he was unscathed. The sound of the party barely penetrated here and the silence was unnerving. The panelling lining the corridor smelt faintly of polish and the only illumination came from the lights over the paintings hanging on the walls each side. Peter peered at the nearest one and grimaced. A Hieronymus Bosch by the looks of it, worth a fortune if it was genuine. But the misery it depicted spoke volumes about the mind of both the painter and anyone who would purchase and display such things in the name of art.

At the far end of the corridor there was a glow and a murmur of conversation. Peter tip-toed his way towards them, praying that the floorboards wouldn't give him away by groaning in protest and that nobody would choose this moment to come the other way. In either event, there would be no hiding place. The passageway opened into another reception room, with yet more rooms connecting off to both sides. The house was like a maze and he began to feel disorientated, realising that he must have taken some sort of servant's short cut into the heart of the East Wing living quarters. This room, too, was empty and dark, but flames flickered in the carved stone fireplace, casting scurrying shadows that made his nerves twitch. The glint of crystal glasses abandoned on the low table in front of the fireplace spoke of recent occupancy, which might be resumed at any time. To his left, bright shaft of light and the sound of voices came from a door standing ajar. Through the gap, he glimpsed bookshelves extending from floor to ceiling filled with leather-bound volumes and he edged along the wall in the direction of what must be the library. His eyes kept flicking towards the other side of the room, where immense sash windows overlooked the grounds. The sense of danger was palpable. There would surely not be anyone outside watching on a winter's night like this, when the festivities were concentrated at the other end of the house, though anything was possible. His knees weakened at the thought. He had no idea of what sort of security surrounded the building and might be alerted by the sight of someone creeping about. But the risk had to be taken, now that he'd got this far. There would at least be time to take evasive action if an alarm was raised out there. The more pressing danger was here, on the inside, where the retribution would be instant if he was discovered. He concentrated his mind on moving silently and breathing as shallowly as possible.

Through the gap of the doorjamb he saw Sir Rodney and a group of six men sitting round a table. Their conversation was animated and the words carried clearly to his ears as one of their number leaned forward in his chair, stabbing his cigar towards the others to emphasise the point he was making.

"It's too soon, old boy." The overtones of Eton and Oxford were unmistakable and it was a voice accustomed to command. "It takes time to set up a market position like that. If we try and move too fast, we risk raising suspicions."

"You'll just have to give your people a kick up the arse," Sir Rodney responded crudely and Peter saw a majority of the other heads nod in agreement. "We've all got a lot at stake here. We're over-exposed and the market is beginning to move against us. If you haven't got the balls for it, we'll have to go ahead without you."

"I agree," another of the group chimed in. "I can't hold the line with my board much longer. Some of the Bank's institutional shareholders are already questioning our judgement in going short on Oil and Gas stocks. If we don't burst the bubble as planned, I can't answer for the consequences."

"Aye, well, we can't have a load of bloody sheep questioning your wisdom, can we?" Sir Rodney chuckled fatly. "You'd look a right fool." His tone suddenly hardened and he shot a penetrating glance at a bespectacled man on his right who had a vaguely academic air about him. "Is the media operation all set to go?"

"It just needs the code word."

"And the rest of the arrangements?"

"The subjects have all been fully prepared and we are confident that responses will be within the defined parameters."

"Right, let's put it to the vote. All in favour of launching 'Project Icarus' on Monday, as planned?"

Peter scratched his head in puzzlement as the majority of hands round the table were firmly raised. The owner of the plummy voice who'd objected earlier kept his firmly in his lap, Peter noticed, but made no further protest beyond a sour look at his colleagues. The professor type didn't appear to have a vote, but a faint nod seemed to signify his approval. None of it made much sense, but it sounded disappointingly like some sort of routine business transaction. An impromptu board meeting, perhaps. Then his attention focused again on the table. Sir Rodney was pushing his chair back and Peter looked round for somewhere to hide in case he was heading for the door. But instead, he turned towards the wall of books at the back of the room.

"No more buggering about, then," he said, reaching for one of the volumes and pulling it towards him. "I'll give the go-ahead right now."

To Peter's amazement, a section of the library wall swung back, shelves, books and all, to reveal a hidden room. If he hadn't seen it, there would have been no way to tell it existed. At the far end, a sophisticated-looking computer terminal sat on a desk, flanked by rows of display cases and filing cabinets. Sir Rodney deposited himself in the chair and tapped commands into the keyboard with one finger while data scrolled down the screen in front of him. After a couple of minutes, he grunted in satisfaction, switched the machine off and turned back towards his colleagues.

"That should get the bloody establishment choking on its morning cup of Earl Grey," he chortled. "Time we rejoined the party, gentlemen, unless there's any other business. And for Christ's sake try to look surprised on Monday when you read the headlines, won't you?"

Chairs scraped as they were pushed back and people started to head for the door. Peter was already on the move towards a large folding screen in the corner of the room. It was about six feet high, covered in embroidered silk on an ornate mahogany frame and would no doubt fetch a fortune in auction at Sotheby's. But at the moment it was literally priceless as a hiding place. He scuttled behind it and crouched low, hoping that nobody would take it into their heads to linger. Whatever was in that secret room, it was bound to be important. And he was determined to take a good hard look. He held his breath as footsteps marched past and faded. The thumping of his heart sounded like thunder in his ears, shouting his presence if there was anybody left to hear it in the sudden silence. Peter strained his senses, but could detect nothing. He risked a quick glance round the edge of the screen. Light still streamed from the library door, but otherwise there was no sign of life. He took his courage in both hands and stepped out into the room.

Chapter 9

"Jesus, you took a hell of a chance, didn't you?"

Anna Stein pushed her hair back out of her eyes and stared hard at Peter, who was perched on the arm of a rickety chair looking as though a puff of wind would blow him over. His peremptory demand to come and talk had been a right pain in the neck. The back office of the bookshop was airless and oppressive this Sunday afternoon and there were piles of books everywhere, evidence of her interrupted stocktaking. It was bad enough having to come in at the weekend and checking the inventory was a nightmare at the best of times. Now she'd have to finish it tomorrow, which was bloody. There was nothing worse than winding herself up to do one of her least favourite tasks, only to face the prospect of starting over. But he'd insisted and she'd given in. She rather regretted now that she'd been so grumpy about it, though. Looking on the bright side, it was a fascinating story he was telling.

Anna shook her head unconsciously. Peter Conway didn't look like the stuff of which intrepid investigators were made, but it never ceased to fascinate her what people were capable of, given the right motivation. It wasn't a surprise that he'd reacted to what he'd learned about his father. His letter, tucked away in the office safe, had been clue enough to that. But she hadn't expected him to move so quickly, or take such risks. There was unsuspected grit underneath the surface, judging by what she'd heard so far. Either that, or he had a streak of foolish stubbornness a mile wide. Perhaps both, she smiled fondly, inherited from his father who'd had those qualities in spades.

"What's so funny?" Peter said, misinterpreting the smile.

"Nothing. I was just thinking how easy it is to misjudge people. I'd never have figured you for an escapade like that."

Peter smiled wryly. "That makes two of us. But the opportunity was there, so I just sort of took it without thinking, really."

"So what happened next, then?"

"Well, I couldn't get any joy out of the computer. It was password protected and I didn't think it would be too smart to hang around trying to crack the security."

"You mean after all that it was a waste of time? I thought from your phone call there was something urgent. I mean, it's an interesting story, but..."

"No," Peter interrupted. "I found something else. Something important, I think. That's what I wanted to see you about."

"Well spit it out, for goodness' sake."

"You remember I said there were display cases? They were full of Nazi stuff from the last war, daggers with swastikas, badges, armbands, that sort of thing. It seems Sir Rodney is a collector."

"For crying out loud, that's not so uncommon. What are you getting at?"

"It got me thinking about the Kaiserhof story. So I started to check out the filing cabinets and I found these." Peter pulled a sheaf of eight by four photos from his bag and tossed them on the desk. "I took them with the digital camera, so I could print them off myself on the computer."

Anna picked one up and wrinkled her nose. "It's all in German. If these are original Nazi papers, they look as though they're in remarkably good condition. Fetch a high price at auction, I shouldn't wonder. There's a strong market for this sort of stuff, you know, not just the military hardware."

"Yes," Peter said impatiently, "but these are different. If I'm right, you couldn't buy them at any price. Look at the heading at the top of the page."

Anna fumbled for her reading glasses and Peter fidgeted while she scanned the typescript. She drew in her breath sharply.

"It says 'Kaiserhof'. But... But that means..."

"They must be part of the Kaiserhof Archive," Peter finished the sentence for her. "I hit the jackpot. He must have got hold of them after Maxwell died. There were thousands of files, I reckon, masses of it. I could only photograph a few pages here and there, though, they'd have smelled a rat if I'd been out of circulation too long."

"But that implies..."

"Yes," the words burst out of Peter like a dam breaking, "It's proof that Dad was right all along about Maxwell and the deal with Oberberg. If I can show they're genuine, that is. That's where you come in."

"Me?"

"I need an expert opinion, independent confirmation these are authentic. That'll make it watertight, don't you see? You know all about old manuscripts and so on and you can do that for me."

Anna glanced up in alarm. "Whoa, there. Just hold your horses. I can't do anything of the sort."

"What do you mean?" Peter snapped. "You promised me you'd help. It's not much to ask, dammit."

"It's not that. I said I can't, not I won't."

"You're splitting hairs. I know what you said."

"No, listen. I buy and sell old manuscripts, but that doesn't make me the kind of expert you're looking for. Authentication is a very specialist business."

"Nonsense. You have to do it every day otherwise you couldn't trade. Everyone says you've got a nose for what's genuine."

"Maybe I have. You learn fast in my business and getting palmed off with a fake can wipe you out. But that's a long way from saying my opinions would stand up in court. In any case, you'd need the originals. Photographs are no good for that sort of thing."

"There must be something we can do," Peter snarled. "You've got to know someone who can help, even if it's just to translate the bloody things, for God's sake."

Anna pursed her lips and thought hard. You could in fact tell quite a lot from photographs if you knew enough about the way things were done back when a document or book was supposed to have been produced. It was little things, details, which usually gave away forgeries. Layout, typefaces, printers' marks, things like that. You could tell a lot from the ink and paper, too, though that was out with photos. Even so, there might be enough to work with if you knew what you were looking for. Her range of contacts was pretty broad, she mused. You met all sorts of strange people in the antique book trade. But who would know enough about the history of the Third Reich?

"Well, I suppose there's old Jacob Cohen," she said pensively. "He's a regular of mine. I don't normally deal in this sort of stuff, but he's heavily into material from the thirties and forties. He might know someone, if he can't give an opinion himself."

"Well give him a call and get him round. I suppose he lives locally if he's a frequent customer?"

"What, just like that? It's Sunday afternoon, Peter. Be reasonable."

"I don't care about that," Peter said impatiently. "Look, I've got to be back at Media Associates tomorrow and it's damned important to be sure of what I'm dealing with. Please try at least."

Anna rubbed her chin doubtfully. "I'll have to look him up and there's no guarantee I've got his number in the book. Even if I have, there's no telling how he'll react."

"Tell him you've come across something unique that's just up his street, the opportunity of a lifetime or whatever. Hell, use your imagination. Tell him anything, just get him here."

When Anna put the phone down, Peter was almost dancing with excitement.

"See, I told you it'd be OK if you tried," he said smugly. "Did he say when he'd be here?"

"About twenty minutes," she said reluctantly. "But it was bloody odd, the way he reacted. I hope you know what you're doing."

"Odd? What do you mean, odd? I could hear you had to twist his arm a bit, but like you said, it's Sunday.

It's understandable he'd need a bit of persuasion to drop everything."

"No, it's more than that. He's got his grandchildren there for the weekend and there was no way he was going to come. He wouldn't budge until I mentioned the Kaiserhof."

"So? That's good, isn't it? He must have heard of it, which means he can help us for sure."

"Maybe. But I've got a bad feeling. The way he reacted was... I don't know... unnerving, somehow."

"You're being over-sensitive."

Anna shook her head. "I don't know how to put it into words, exactly. It was as though he was scared to death and captivated at the same time. It gave me the creeps." She shuddered and came over to perch herself on the desk beside Peter. "Anyway, enough of that. Tell me the rest of what happened last night, after you found those manuscripts."

***

When the doorbell rang about half an hour later, they were both giggling helplessly. The previous evening's events had taken on the characteristics of a farce under the lash of Peter's self-deprecating wit. It was easier to play the comedian and poke fun at himself than to dwell on the realities of dry-mouthed terror. Every time the flash fired, his hands shook so badly that half his pictures were blurred and useless. Later, the realisation that it would be impossible to return the way he'd come, emerging in the full view of Sir Rodney and his entourage, paralysed him with indecision. Stumbling around darkened rooms looking for an alternative escape route was the stuff of nightmares, playing hide and seek in the maze of kitchens and storerooms below stairs. But he kept all that to himself. He told Anna instead about things where, in retrospect, it was possible to see the funny side. Playing the drunken fool in search of a toilet, for instance, when he was finally cornered near the back door by a frock-coated butler. And later, when he found the birthday girl was spaced out on drink or drugs or both and hardly an ideal candidate for photographs in the family album. That was actually a blessed relief, something he was professionally equipped to handle. There was, in fact, something genuinely comical about finding a selection of strong young men to prop her up in decorous poses while he fussed about attracting attention to his endeavours. The icing on the cake was roping Sir Rodney himself into the final shots, despite his obvious reluctance. His recollections, if any, would be of an overly officious photographer busy about his work, rather than of a stranger who'd been mysteriously absent at critical moments.

"I was laying it on a bit thick," Peter chuckled. "But under the circumstances I'd rather he thought I was a harmless idiot. Anyway, he'll like the results. I got some good pictures, despite everything."

"I wish I could have seen his face," Anna said, laughing, as she went to answer the door. "You're a scream when you're doing your bossy act like that."

Jacob Cohen was a short, grey-faced and painfully thin man, in his eighties Peter guessed, though it was hard to tell. Illness had a way of aging people and there seemed little doubt that this was someone seriously, if not terminally sick. Cancer, perhaps, Peter thought, hearing the hacking cough, smothered in a white linen handkerchief clutched to his mouth. He was waving Anna's concern away with the impatient but resigned air of someone who knew there was nothing left to do but suffer.

Peter held out his hand and introduced himself.

"I'm Peter Conway. Thanks for coming round."

A pair of dark brown eyes fastened on him, peering with lively interest through old-fashioned spectacles with heavy, tortoiseshell frames. There was nothing wrong with the mind inside that decrepit body, Peter realised, feeling the intensity of the scrutiny. It would be a mistake to underestimate the man's intellect, despite outward appearances. The charcoal Sunday-best suit had seen better days, giving Jacob Cohen an air of faded gentility. But the agitation of his fingers as they fretted with his hat contrasted strangely with the tension that gripped the rest of his body. It wasn't uncertainty or nervousness. It was more like the focus of a bird of prey about to pounce and flexing its claws in anticipation. The image was powerful and Peter found himself reaching for his camera to capture it on film. His hand grasped futilely at his empty shoulder and he felt a flush of embarrassment as he realised that he hadn't brought the Nikon with him today and that anyway this was hardly an appropriate moment for such activity.

"So you think you have seen some documents from the Kaiserhof Forschungsanstalt, young man?" the visitor suddenly said without preamble. His voice was soft and well educated, but incisive and carrying a hint of a European accent. "Nobody has claimed that in more than fifty years."

"I'm sorry, the Kaiserhof what?"

"Ah, you don't speak German? Research Institute. Or to give it its full title, 'The Kaiserhof Research Institute for Cultural Awareness'. They had a clever way with words, those Nazis, don't you think?"

"How do you mean?"

"You cannot begin to imagine the truth behind that pretty title. For your own sake, I hope you never do." There was a depth of passion and pain in Jacob Cohen's words that made Peter shudder and wonder what the hell he'd got himself into. "But enough, already," Jacob continued tiredly. "Show me what you brought me here to see."

"On the desk," Peter gestured, feeling out of his depth with this unpredictable old man, who simply nodded politely and shuffled across the room. He slumped into the swivel chair and picked up the first of the photographs in silence, pushing his glasses up onto his forehead and holding it a few inches from his face. The silence lengthened as he went through each one with a fierce concentration. It was maddening and Peter was just about to speak out when a glint of a reflection from the desk lamp caught his eye. A tear was rolling down the old man's face, leaving a glistening trail in its wake. The sight shook him rigid and he knew he had no need of a camera to capture that image of grief. It would stay with him more surely than any mere photograph. It also told him beyond any possibility of doubt that he'd found more than he'd bargained for and he felt worms of apprehension begin to wriggle in his stomach.

"Where did you get these?" Jacob wheezed, struggling to catch his breath.

"Er... I don't think I want to go into that," Peter replied. "I just want to know if they're genuine and what they're all about."

"And why do you want to know?"

"It's a long story. Personal. I just need to know, that's all."

"Personal. I see." Jacob looked at him with an unfathomable expression. "For me, too, it is personal. I will say this much. These documents are indeed from the Kaiserhof. Part of an evil I've prayed for half a century had been wiped from the face of the Earth. Tell me, is there more where these came from?"

"Yes. So far as I could tell, a whole roomful."

"Ah." The sigh burst from Jacob's lips as though he'd been punched in the gut. "It is the Archive, then. The rumours were true after all."

"What rumours?" Peter was starting to lose patience. "Look, are you going to tell me what this is about, or not?"

The old man pushed back his chair and struggled unsteadily to his feet. Despite his frailty, his presence suddenly seemed to fill the room.

"I will tell you nothing more, except that you should leave this thing alone. Walk away while you still can, if it is not already too late. It is too... dangerous."

"I can't do that." Peter's vehemence stopped Jacob in his tracks and he cocked his head to one side, staring intently at Peter's face.

"Can't? Your commitment is so strong, to come from your heart like that?"

Peter squirmed under Jacob's gaze, which seemed to be penetrating his innermost thoughts.

"I owe it to my father," he said reluctantly.

"So." There was a long pause before Jacob Cohen continued. "I too owe things to my family. Come," he beckoned Peter towards the desk, "tell me your story. Then we will see."

The only interruptions as Peter talked were occasional bouts of coughing which racked the old man and a muttered interjection in what sounded like Hebrew at the mention of the name of Klaus Oberberg. Darkness was falling outside by the time Peter finished, matched by the deepening despair emanating from the hunched figure behind the desk.

"Their work continues, then," Jacob whispered as if speaking to himself. "I have feared this. I had hoped it was not possible, that there had been an end." He looked up at Peter with a haunted expression, his pallor deeper than ever. "That was foolish of me, was it not? And now you want revenge, am I right?

"Justice," Peter said. "I want justice and to clear my father's name."

"A fine word. But I prefer the older, deeper instincts. An eye for an eye, that is justice. A name will not bring your father back to you. Nor my family to me."

"Your family?"

"My parents, my brother and his family, my sister... they stayed behind in Germany when I escaped, before the war. We were Jews, you understand and there was only enough money to pay for one of us to be smuggled out. I was the youngest, so they sent me. They stayed and they died in the Kaiserhof."

"Died?" The word hit Peter like a hammer. "Are you saying it was a concentration camp?"

"No, worse... far worse. Your journalist friend, Simon, he was nowhere near the truth of it, although your father might have realised what he was dealing with at the end. Oberberg and his fanatics were seeking the keys to the mind. For that, they needed human subjects to experiment on. Thousands, maybe tens of thousands, were sacrificed to their obsession."

"My God, you can't be serious?"

"Oh yes. Not much is known about it now. Or at least, it seemed so until today. But in the concentration camps they broke only the bodies. In the Kaiserhof they broke the minds. What do you know of the history of the National Socialists in Germany before the war?"

Peter was taken aback by the change of subject. "Er... not much. Only that they rose to power surprisingly fast."

"It was no surprise to the few who understood what they were doing. My father was a professor of psychology, you see and he saw it clearly. You think it was all about posters and censorship, storm troopers beating people up and smashing windows. What they did was much more sophisticated than that. They learnt how to control people's thoughts."

"That's not possible," Peter said bluntly.

"You think so, young man, with all the certainty of your youth and inexperience? You should start by studying history and look at the facts."

"What facts?"

"The fact that it took Hitler less than three years between 1929 and 1932 to persuade millions of ordinary people to vote for a fascist dictatorship in democratic elections, for one. And don't tell me he was lying to them about his policies; he spelled out exactly what he intended to do. Or that a few thousand bullies in brown shirts could achieve that sort of result out of nowhere. 'The Will and the Way' Josef Goebbels called it. Most thought it was merely a slogan, something for the mindless masses to daub on walls. But it was more, much more, than that. It was the mainspring of the National Socialist propaganda machine, their weapon for seizing power.

Jacob Cohen paused as a cough racked him.

"Make no mistake," he said, "the nation marched willingly into that darkness. Unwittingly, perhaps, but willingly. History has many examples of mass aberrations, though none so sudden and so complete. But then, those responsible were scientists who had unravelled the workings of the mind. They understood not only what could be done, but also how to make it happen at their command and that was something the world had never seen before."

Peter leaned forward to interrupt, but Jacob held up a hand to silence him.

"You ask yourself how is it possible," he continued in a cold, flat voice. "Listen, then and I will tell you. In its simplest form, it is the age-old technique of bullies and gangsters. First, you create an elite and adorn it with the trappings and symbols of power. It is attractive, is it not, to be part of such a group, to feel superior? So then you bind others to your clique with threats and rewards, while branding outsiders as inferior. After that it is easy to stir up fear of those inferiors and provoke hatred. What could be more natural than to protect your privileges from those who seem to threaten them? Next you exploit that hatred to legitimise persecution, dressed up as self-defence. Little things, initially, you understand, which are sanctioned by authority figures so they leave no inconvenient feelings of guilt. Then finally, you extend that persecution into a beating here, a killing there, until it ceases to be repugnant, becomes extreme - it is truly remarkable how quickly that can be made to happen - and then, my friend, you are at the doorway to the Holocaust. Those five easy steps to tyranny are buried in human nature, you see. All you need is the key to unlock them."

Jacob paused again and took a deep breath.

"These principles are well-known to experts today," he said, "but then they were revolutionary. It was the Kaiserhof team, with Josef Goebbels as the mouthpiece and Klaus Oberberg as the mastermind, that first understood them fully and put them into practice. And that was sufficient to bring Hitler to power."

"But if the principles are known," Peter objected, "what's the great mystery about the Kaiserhof Archive?"

"What I have described was only the beginning. When the Nazis achieved power, the project went underground and changed its focus radically. Until then, the work had been empirical; all that mattered was how to manipulate the masses into behaving as they wanted. Once they'd done that, they moved on."

"Moved on? How?"

"They put the cream of their biochemists, neurosurgeons and psychologists into the Kaiserhof project for the duration. Just as they did in other places with their nuclear physicists for the atomic bomb project and their engineers for the rockets at Peenemunde. Their real goal, you see, was unlocking the deeper secrets of why those techniques were effective, the very essence of the mechanisms of the human brain..."

Peter's horror mounted as Jacob Cohen's quiet voice described the indescribable. There was no shortage of experimental subjects and no constraints on what could be done with them, as the pogroms against the 'untermenschen' gathered pace. Insanity was the kindest outcome, as minds were driven to breaking point and beyond by scientists unfettered by ethics or morality. Finally, the ultimate secret was torn from the tortured flesh. The underlying mechanism of the human mind. And with that knowledge came the understanding of how to control and manipulate the thought process. Not crudely, by trial and error, but with the precision of scientific logic.

"You can't be serious," Peter said. "That's... I mean, the implications are..."

Cohen's gaze was full of sadness, but did not waver.

"Appalling, yes. But I assure you, it's true. The Kaiserhof Archive is the mental equivalent of the human genome. A map of how everyone's brain ticks and how to program it as you will."

The silence that fell was deathly and seemed to go on forever.

"Come on," Peter said uneasily, "this is crazy. Are you trying to tell me that somebody can tell us what to think and we've got no choice in the matter?"

"Why not, young man? Everybody thought genetic engineering was impossible till the scientists started doing it, but now we accept they can manipulate our bodies with their 'magic bullets' however they wish. What makes you think the mind is any different?"

"But if the Nazis could do that," Peter protested, "surely they would have won the war? It would be impossible to fight against."

"Oh yes, there's no doubt of that," Jacob said calmly. "It was the fourth of their 'V' weapons, more deadly than the flying bombs, the rockets or maybe even the atomic project and a much better kept secret. It would have been devastating. There is no defence against mental warfare."

"So why did they never use it? What happened?"

"The same thing as with the other wonder weapons. They merely ran out of time. When they finally made the breakthrough, there was no infrastructure left to deploy it effectively. They needed radio, newspapers, any form of mass communication. But by 1945 all that was gone."

Peter's instincts rebelled against what the old man was saying.

"I'm sorry," he said. "It can't be feasible to control the way people think. Humanity is just too diverse for that."

Jacob smiled wearily. "I must assume, then, that

you've never experienced a football match, a mass demonstration or a thousand other situations where crowds behave irrationally in unison. Perhaps you even believe as an individual that you're immune to advertising and political propaganda and that every decision you make is entirely free of external influence?"

"Well, okay," Peter admitted grudgingly, "I suppose you're right as far as it goes. But they're the exceptions. You can't claim emotional reactions like that amount to mind control."

"I don't suggest they do. What I'm saying is that those reactions are evidence of deep instincts, which we are helpless to resist. They arise from the way our brains work at the cellular level. Find the keys to trigger them at will and then you have got control, at least of the behaviour of the masses. Those keys are what they discovered at the Kaiserhof."

"But how can they possibly, er, what's the word - program people to do what they want?"

The old man shrugged and waved his hand dismissively.

"You ask too much of me, I do not know their methods. But the evidence that behaviour and ideas can be and are being manipulated is all around you every day of your life and these papers you have photographed prove that it is underpinned by hard science. The Nazis had their own word for it. We, in our ignorance, merely call it 'Spin'."

When Jacob Cohen departed he left a grim silence behind him. Peter looked at Anna helplessly. Knowing the truth was one thing. What to do about it was something else. His battle wasn't over, he realised. In fact, he hadn't even been fighting in the right war. The real struggle had barely even begun.

Chapter 10

"You look as though you're enjoying all this," Anna Stein said accusingly through a mouthful of Doner kebab.

"Mm." Peter agreed, reaching for his wineglass and waving it airily to take in her flat. "Nice place you've got here. And you were right about these kebabs being the best in town."

Anna reached over and smacked him on the shoulder. "Stop playing the fool. You know what I mean. And you didn't drive me all the way home to Catford just to make a pig of yourself. This thing you've got involved in sounds horrendous."

The smile faded from Peter's face. She was right and it was stupid to sit here feeling smug about putting one over on Hardcastle. There was no denying the glow of satisfaction from getting away with the risks he'd taken, but the dangers were real enough. If anything, they'd just got greater.

"Yes, I know," he said. "I came because I need someone I trust to talk to about all this. Someone with common sense who can convince me I'm not going mad. You believe what old Jacob had to say, then?"

"Didn't you?"

"Unfortunately, yes, I did." He shook his head. "It's just hard to swallow, that's all. I mean, the whole idea is... well... devastating, somehow."

"I know what you mean. It's like being raped. You think you're in control, but suddenly you realise that it's just an illusion. Somebody else is pulling the strings and there's nothing you can do about it."

"It's worse than that. It's like... Hell, I don't know. It's as though the last million years of evolution counts for nothing. If he's right, the whole idea of 'Homo Sapiens' is just a sick joke. We're just prisoners of our instincts, being jerked around by our biological programming like rats in a bloody laboratory maze."

"Come off it. It's not that bad."

"Isn't it?" Peter growled. "It means that free will, judging right and wrong, all the things that supposedly make us civilised, they're only figments of our imagination."

"Not entirely. They're still there. They're real. It's just that they're not as strong as we like to believe, compared to the biological programs evolution has given us."

"That doesn't help much, does it? Especially if those basic instincts are being manipulated, programmed even and we can't help but react. If somebody can plant ideas in your head that you have no choice but to obey it makes a mockery of the idea that we're rational beings, capable of independent choices."

"I'm not so sure. Perhaps that's only true if we don't know what's happening."

"What do you mean?"

Anna's brow furrowed in thought. "Well, people do things all the time that must be against their instincts, don't they? Take risks when they don't have to and so on?"

"I suppose there are exceptions to any rule."

"But what if they're not exceptions?"

"What are you driving at?"

"I'm not sure... Maybe it's something to do with being able to control your instincts if you're aware of what's going on." Anna shook her head impatiently. "Oh, I don't know. I can't put it into words. It just seems to me that there's a reason for the secrecy around this stuff and not just the obvious one. As though it only works properly if people don't know how they're being manipulated."

"Well thanks for that masterful analysis," Peter said. "Am I supposed to feel better now?"

"Get stuffed, you supercilious bugger. I'm telling you, if some prick in a white coat tries to persuade me that black is white, I'll send him packing to think again, Kaiserhof or no Kaiserhof."

"Maybe you would at that." Peter grinned. "So would I, I reckon. I just needed to hear someone else say it."

"Well, then," Anna huffed, still not completely mollified. "Does that mean you're going to carry on with this crusade of yours?"

"What do you take me for? Of course I'm going to see it through after what they've done to Dad and me. The bastards haven't got inside my head yet."

Anna's eyebrows twitched and she gave him an odd look.

"Are you sure you'd know if they had?" she said.

"That's a bloody silly question. Do I look as though I'm ready for the funny farm?" he retorted, then grinned. "On second thoughts, you'd better not answer that. But I can guarantee you if they've tried to change my mind, it hasn't worked."

"I'm pleased to hear it," she said. "If you've finished

feeding your face, then, you'd better go and get on with saving the world. I need my beauty sleep." Her face softened and she took his hand. "I'm sure you're doing the right thing. Promise me you'll be careful, though, Peter. I don't want to lose you."

He took the hint and got to his feet. As he left, he glanced back. She was sitting upright in her armchair with an unfathomable expression on her face, her eyes fixed on him. The sight made him shiver. She was nobody's fool and she was worried, which was the scariest sign yet.

***

Later, weaving the Porsche through the traffic on the A21 towards Tonbridge, Peter kept coming back to Anna's idea that secrecy was the key. Could it be that simple? All that was needed was to expose the Kaiserhof secrets and they would lose their effectiveness? It seemed unlikely. But there was precious little else to hope for and even that was a tall order. Understanding the theory of spin was one thing, but figuring out how it worked in practice would be much tougher. After that, hardest of all would be finding a way to expose those secrets in a way that couldn't be glossed over or ignored. The old Jew had been dead right when he warned of the difficulty of fighting against this kind of mental warfare. And, more surprisingly, Anna had been dead right, too, when she had accused him of enjoying himself, despite the danger. The last few days, he'd felt more alive, more alert than he could remember. He'd never been truly scared before, knowing his life was on the line.

Until it happened, it was impossible to know how it would feel. Now he knew. The adrenalin surge of fear created a high where all his senses seemed magnified. Colours were brighter, vision sharper and even small details seemed to reach out and shout for attention. Smells, textures and tastes were accentuated, as though long-dormant parts of his brain had opened new channels of communication. Nerves pulsed with information that once might have been vital for survival but which the dead hand of civilisation had rendered obsolete. It was how he imagined cocaine or heroin might make you feel, with a rush of pleasure and a belief that you were capable of anything. But this was from within, free of the sordid baggage of drug addiction. Perhaps it was what drove people to take part in extreme sports where life was lived on the very edge of what was possible. He'd always reckoned them to be fearless, either madly brave or moronically stupid. But that missed the point completely. The fear itself was what provided the thrill. Peter's knuckles whitened on the steering wheel at the premonition that someday he would pay a high price for his newfound awareness. But the future would have to take care of itself. For now, it was enough that his old placid, one-dimensional existence was a thing of the past.

The tyres of the Porsche squealed in protest as he took the slip road to Tonbridge South faster than usual and he smiled at the sensation of the back end stepping out as he rounded the left-hander onto the downhill stretch to home. The faster he moved the harder it would be for the opposition to catch up with him. After today's revelations he had a much better idea of what he was looking for and he was ideally positioned with David Tyler's team, who were about to start their latest project. Tomorrow, the real work would begin. It would be difficult, he had no doubt. Dangerous, too. He smiled again, this time in anticipation.

***

At nine o'clock the following morning there was an expectant buzz in the third floor meeting room at 46, Bevis Marks as the team waited for David Tyler to arrive to begin the project briefing. Peter sat quietly towards the back of the room, his camera at the ready, watching. The curiosity engendered by last week's introductions was gone and now he was accepted, part of the furniture, just as he'd hoped. It was hard to envisage any of them as the front-line troops of an evil empire. They were nice people, or so it seemed on first impressions. Bright, confident and friendly, without even the arrogance that you so often found in high-flyers. That probably had something to do with the nature of the business they were in, he thought cynically. It would be self-defeating for a PR consultant to come across as a nasty piece of work. Presumably they were trained to exude bonhomie and to hide their real feelings and intentions. Or perhaps they just knew how to manipulate his thinking to make him see whatever they wanted him to see. Peter shifted uneasily in his chair and tried to pull himself together. It was a nightmare trying to get to grips with the concept of mind control. They were just ordinary people, he told himself, with ordinary loves, hates, ambitions and worries. He had to believe that, or he'd go mad.

A large coffee trolley arrived, china cups rattling as it was pushed to its parking spot against the far wall and he was grateful for the distraction. He hung back politely from the scrum that immediately developed, not quite sure of the protocol.

"Dive in, Peter," somebody said, "it's every man for himself. Don't worry, they'll be bringing refills around later. Help yourself to a biscuit, too, before the gannets snaffle them all."

"Thanks. I didn't know they treated you to five star service round here. I thought that sort of thing died out with Noah's Ark."

"I guess the accountants have overlooked it. Make the most of it, though, you only get the red carpet treatment in the meeting rooms. Anywhere else, you'll have to slum it round the coffee machines with the chattering classes."

"Even so it must take a bit of organising, catering for the right numbers and getting it all delivered," Peter observed, making conversation while he filled his cup.

"I've never really thought about it. But there's a booking system and every meeting room's got its own trolley, so I guess that makes things easier. See the number there, 3-21? That's us."

"It probably knows its own way here, then."

"Yeah, perhaps there's a built-in autopilot or something. You never know these days. Good coffee, though."

Peter added milk and sugar, sipped and nodded polite agreement. Then he wandered off to a quiet corner with his cup, preoccupied with his thoughts. This was a small group by the standards of Media Associates, so David had insisted, though to Peter's mind five people was a lot of firepower to bring to bear on creating a public image for a single individual. It must be a damned important project, he mused and money was clearly no object. But frustratingly, David had refused to elaborate on the background, insisting that Peter would have to wait for the briefing like everybody else. 'Wait and see,' he'd said with a grin. 'But I guarantee it'll give you exactly the kind of action you're looking for. Much better than one of the boring corporate identity or product launch assignments, take my word for it.' The question was, would it provide the answers he was really seeking? Peter glanced up as David Tyler strode in and the chatter died away. One way or another, he'd soon know.

"Morning, all," David said cheerfully, grabbing some coffee in passing and taking his position at the front of the room next to the overhead projector. "Let me start by saying this is a code-word project, which as you know means that nobody outside this room is to be briefed on it without my specific authorisation."

A buzz of excitement ran round the room and David held up his hand to quell the noise. "And that applies particularly to the identity of our client," he continued, "who will be referred to as 'Zeus' in all correspondence and working papers."

Peter felt a nudge in his back and turned to see the bespectacled face of Mark Jones, one of the two research analysts, thrust close to his ear.

"You must have some heavyweight connections," Mark whispered. "It's unheard of to have an outsider in on one of these jobs. We don't do much political stuff nowadays, not since the party gurus got their own spin-doctors on board. You're in for some real excitement."

Peter's frowned in puzzlement. "What..?"

Mark shook his head and put a finger up to his lips. "Just wait. You're a lucky bastard. This'll be one for the men in black. You'll see."

"I don't understand," Peter whispered back, but Mark had already leaned back into his seat and simply gestured towards the projection screen where David Tyler's first slide had just sprung into focus.

"This is Zeus," David announced, pointing at the screen. "Most of you will recognise him as William Cookson, the millionaire industrialist. Our job is to build his public image to position him for a prospective Ministerial appointment in the Labour government, so you'll understand the need for extreme confidentiality."

"Er, David?" A hand went up in front of Peter, belonging to Joanne Barker, the senior consultant of the group.

"Yes, Joanne?"

"I don't quite understand. The Labour team at Millbank are fanatics about this sort of thing. They always and I mean always, spin their own candidates these days and control the message script. Aren't we heading for a conflict here?"

"Good question. Millbank have okayed our involvement on this one, though. They've had too much political flak recently and they want to appear to have clean hands, at least in the early stages. Naturally there'll be close liaison behind the scenes on the big picture issues and key messages. The plan is they'll take over once we've laid the groundwork and killed off any potential controversy."

"Sounds messy to me," Joanne said. "You're saying those bastards will be controlling the agenda. That means we're just a front to carry the can if anything hits the fan while their man's being groomed for his big move. I thought we'd moved on from that sort of crap years ago."

"Cool it, Joanne," David responded tetchily. "There isn't going to be a problem. So far as the media are concerned there's nothing political about the project or our involvement. While it stays that way, Millbank will stay out of our hair. Trust me."

Peter's jaw dropped in amazement as the briefing continued. William Cookson, it seemed, was a man with an unsavoury past. Massive donations to party funds apart, he was on the face of it a most unlikely candidate for a politically prominent role in a socialist government. But the matter-of-fact way that inconvenient realities were to be swept aside was breathtaking. Joanne Barker's role was to 'sanitise' his image, which appeared to mean rewriting history into a more palatable form and burying beyond recall anything that could not be twisted to fit the new, squeaky-clean character the script called for. After that, she would be 'creating the news agenda' and 'spinning the rat pack', which Peter understood to mean planting appropriate stories in the media and persuading journalists to present Cookson as God's gift to the Nation. Forgetting his determination to stay in the background, Peter felt compelled to interject.

"You can't possibly expect reputable reporters to print stuff you make up, surely?"

A titter ran round the room and David looked up.

"I'm sorry, Peter. I'd forgotten we had a novice in the room," he said. "You seem to have decoded the jargon, but we, er, don't exactly make stories up."

There were a few smothered guffaws.

"Anyone seen a reputable journalist lately? I seem to have forgotten what they look like," a voice piped up from the back of the room. David's face reddened with annoyance amid intensifying mirth.

"All right, that's enough," he snapped. "Joanne, will you spell it out for him, please?"

She cocked her head to one side and fastened her brown eyes on Peter. She was fresh complexioned, demurely but fashionably dressed and looked young and innocent enough to be barely out of school, but those eyes riveted him. They contained the world-weary cynicism of someone much older, whose illusions had long since been consigned to life's graveyard of unfulfilled hopes. He fixed the picture in his mind and resolved that the next time it appeared he'd be ready to capture the poignancy of the contrast on film.

"You're a professional photographer, right?" she said. "It should be easy for you to understand, then. Your career depends on getting great pictures, not just now and then, but every time, yes?"

"I guess so."

"And great pictures aren't just a straightforward 'this is a building' or 'that's an avalanche', are they?

There's more to it. The picture has to tell a story and give an insight into some aspect of the truth that you've chosen to highlight. That's your way of delivering a message and influencing how people think about what you've photographed. It's actually what you're trying to do here with us, right now."

"I've never thought of it that way, but I suppose you've got a point."

"You bet I have. Well then, reporters are just the same, whether it's newspapers, TV or whatever. They have to produce great stories day in, day out. Their careers depend on it and if they're not up there on top of things, they're finished, fast. It's a cut-throat business, more than most and the pressures are remorseless."

"Yes, but..."

"There aren't any 'buts' about it. Like your pictures, a great story isn't necessarily about facts. It's about angles and interpretations, some perspective that grabs the readers' interest and makes them see things in a different way. That's what we mean by creating the news agenda. We're not making things up. We just find those perspectives on reality that get our message across and will make people think the way we want them to, in this case about our friend Zeus."

Peter scratched his head. "I thought journalists were supposed to be independent. What if they don't buy your slant on the truth? How do you get round that?"

Joanne snorted in amusement. "This is media land we're talking about, not the real world. Truth barely comes into it. It's all about seizing the agenda and dominating the news cycle with opinions and presentations that fit each outlet's editorial policy."

"Policy? What do you mean? I thought the media's job was reporting the news."

"Jesus." Joanne ran her fingers through her hair in despair. "Look, reporters and editors don't give a toss about news as such. All they care about is getting hold of material that will keep their readers, viewers, advertisers or whatever happy. That's what keeps the profits rolling in.　So that's what we give them, on a plate. If we scratch their back, why shouldn't they scratch ours?"

"That's pretty cynical."

"No, just human nature. Besides, reporters need information like a car needs petrol. As I said, their careers and salaries depend on it and they know we can cut off access if we choose. It's in their own interest to keep us sweet."

"So from now on, think a bit harder before you believe what you read in the papers," David said to Peter with a grin. "But enough of the kindergarten stuff. We need to get back to work, here."

He turned to his notes and addressed himself to the team, putting another slide on the projector.

"Now, our man's been a bit of a walking PR disaster in the past, so we've got some salvage work to do as a first priority. Here are the big picture messages we're going to push. We're going to have to fuzz it on some of the nastier issues and as you can see from this next slide, the preliminary grid of events I've put together spells out how we'll create the media opportunities to start the process..."

Peter's attention wandered as David got deeper into the technicalities. His mind was buzzing with the awareness that nobody in the room doubted that they could create whatever public perception they wanted of William Cookson and with the casual way in which truth was brushed aside as an irrelevance. Even more frightening was the fact that their confidence must be born of experience. Many apparently unimpeachable public figures must be the products of similar treatment by the spin-doctors. But even so, nothing he'd heard yet could be linked to the Kaiserhof techniques. There might well be a cartel operating amongst media insiders to look after each other's interests and be economical with the truth, but that sort of conspiracy wouldn't justify murder. Nor was it the sort of arrangement that could generate the certainty of success that was radiating from the faces around him. It was more than just hype. These guys had no doubts. None. That had to be down to the Kaiserhof techniques, but Peter still had no idea how they were being used. There was nothing in David Tyler's project plans so far that gave the game away.

He thrust the puzzle to one side temporarily. There was no way he was going to get those answers from David's briefing and it was time he started cementing his own credentials. His cover wouldn't last long if he kept on asking stupid questions instead of taking photographs. He picked up the Nikon and discreetly checked the settings. Then he edged out of his seat and made his way to the vantage point he'd chosen, by the coffee trolley towards the front of the room. From there he had clear sight of everybody's face without being in their direct line of vision and the zoom lens would do the rest. The first few clicks of the shutter drew the customary aggressive looks, which he met with a shrug, a friendly grin and assurances that any embarrassing moments caught on film would never see the light of day. After that, his subjects relaxed and he captured some passable shots. None, though, had the impact of that moment earlier with Joanne. Patience, he thought. Film was cheap and it was still early days.

Thirty-six exposures later, Peter rewound the film and tucked it into his jacket pocket. Stupidly, he'd left his camera bag under his chair and disrupting the presentation by scrambling back there to retrieve a fresh film wouldn't earn him any brownie points. He hovered indecisively and glanced at his watch. To his amazement it was nearly lunchtime and he decided not to bother. The meeting would be breaking up soon anyway. He'd got all the useful pictures he was likely to get in this particular setting and there was no point in drawing unnecessary attention to himself.

His thoughts turned to ways to dig deeper into the specialist world of Media Associates and he eyed Mark Jones thoughtfully. There was something about a camera lens that exposed a person's character to an experienced eye and Mark's weak chin and air of schoolboy bravado suggested he might be tempted into indiscretions. When the meeting adjourned a few minutes later, Peter took him to one side and put his theory to the test.

"You were certainly right about it being a fascinating project," he said. "I couldn't follow a lot of what David was saying, but you all certainly seem to know your stuff. I guess it must take a long time to learn the ropes, though, to get to your level of expertise?"

Mark preened at the implied compliment. "It's not really that hard," he said with false modesty. "Of course, we're the best agency around, so we get the pick of the recruits and we train them better than anybody. I do quite a lot of teaching and it doesn't take that long to knock them into shape."

"Ah, that explains it."

"Explains what?"

"Sorry," Peter said, trying to look abashed. "I couldn't help noticing you've got a special air of... well... confidence about how this all works. Teaching a subject does that for people. I imagine you're in great demand for the training courses."

"Well, I do my share..."

"Oh, come on. Don't be modest, I bet you've got a real knack for it." Peter paused as though an idea had just struck him. "Say, maybe you could help me out, if you're willing?"

"In what way?"

"Like I said, I've been struggling to understand exactly what's going on. If I buy you lunch, do you think you could run over some of the basics for me? You know, as if I'd just joined the firm? It would have to be pretty elementary, of course, words of one syllable and all that. I'm not as smart as you lot."

Mark shook his head doubtfully. "I'm not sure..."

"Please," Peter interrupted. "I'd be really grateful. I mean, I felt like a real prat asking that question earlier on and everybody laughing at me."

Mark sniggered. "Yes, well, it was funny you know. We didn't intend any harm by it, but I see what you mean." He rubbed his chin thoughtfully. "Come on then. Let's get a bite to eat and I'll have a go at bringing you up to speed."

***

The cafeteria in the basement was an interior designer's dream with its pastel colours and functional but elegant wooden furniture. Peter eyed the equally fashionable food in the self-service counters and wrote off any prospect of a hamburger. Wholemeal pasta, low-fat cottage cheese with smoked salmon and Perrier water seemed to be the main themes of the day. But his smugness at discovering the makings of a couple of cheese rolls, albeit in granary rather than white bread, evaporated on reaching the checkout.

"I'll pay for both," he said, offering a twenty-pound note and waving at Mark's tray alongside his own.

"No cash, sorry. Only cards."

"Er... what? Sorry," he reddened in confusion, conscious of curious eyes in the queue behind. He reached for his wallet again. "Is Visa OK?"

"Sorry," the reply was uncompromising. "Company cards only."

"Here, let me," Mark interrupted, handing over a white plastic card embossed with the corporate logo. "I forgot about this. They changed the system a few months back to this stupid 'pay as you go' card. You have to keep topping up your credit, like those mobile phones. They obviously haven't got round to giving you one yet."

"I'm sorry," Peter said helplessly. "It was supposed to be my treat."

"Forget it. The stuff's all subsidised anyway. It won't

break the bank."

It wasn't a great start, Peter thought, as they made their way towards a table, but Mark didn't seem at all put out. In fact, it seemed to have the opposite effect, as though the blunder had triggered a vein of sympathy. Whatever the reason, when they sat down Mark plunged straight in.

"I suppose the place to start is with the firm's basic methodology," he said. "I take it nobody's bothered to walk you through that?"

"No."

"Right, then. The thing to remember is A.L.E.R.T., the so-called five steps to paradise. It's how any PR project works in this place, though the individual stages vary according to the type of project, of course."

"Alert?" Peter repeated doubtfully.

"Yes. It stands for 'Associate', 'Legitimise', 'Exclude', 'Repress' and 'Terminate'. Applies to anything, products, corporate positioning, or individuals like our friend Zeus. That's the framework David was setting out this morning."

"You could have fooled me."

"Yeah, well, it's easy when you know how. Take this morning, for example. We're trying to position this bloke for a top job, right?"

"Seems to me you've got your work cut out. From what I've heard he's a classic fat cat. You don't make millions by being Mr. Nice Guy."

"Exactly. So the first thing is, we've got to change that image. We associate him in the public mind with things that people accept as morally or socially superior. Charity, health, education, patriotism, you name it. There are plenty to focus on in this case. If there aren't, you create new ones."

"Create them?"

"You really are a babe in the woods, aren't you?" Mark laughed. "Yes, sure, you can create pretty much whatever associations you want if you go about it right. Take so-called organic food for instance, that's a classic. If you're Global Vegetables plc and your profits are suffering, what do you do? You hire us to make people believe that your particular veggies are healthier than your competitors' products. Nobody wants to risk feeding all those nasty pesticides to their kids, do they, even if there are no facts to back up the claims that it's bad for the little dears? Bingo. Suddenly your cabbages or whatever are associated with motherhood and apple pie, you sell them at a premium and you laugh all the way to the bank."

"So you make people think organic food is all about better health and caring for your kids, is that it?"

"Yes, that's the idea. Who could disagree with that?"

"Presumably quite a few people, if it's not actually true," Peter said tartly.

"Now you're getting there. That's where 'alert' comes in again. The next step is to legitimise. People have a natural respect for authority figures, so you find professors, doctors, politicians and so on who'll underwrite your messages, give them substance. The majority of people will accept that as gospel. If enough of them believe something, for most practical purposes it becomes the truth."

"But reputable experts won't do that, surely?"

"There you go again with that 'reputable' stuff," Mark grinned. "This is the real world we're talking about. It's amazing how a well-paid lecture tour or a juicy research contract seems to clarify the mind. There are always ways."

"But..."

"I know, I know. You're going to tell me some folk can't be bought or pressured. You'd be astonished how few they are. Perceived wisdom has a hell of a lot of momentum and it takes a rare kind of courage to stand up against it. Besides, we take care of that. Exclude and repress, remember? It's like the first two stages, but in reverse."

"You mean you discredit any opposition?"

"Sure. If they're against the good guys, they must be bad guys. And if you're a bad guy, who's going to listen to you or complain if you get hurt?"

"I don't understand."

"OK, take organic food again. We've created the opinion it's a good thing, right? Now you come along and say it's all a con. So we can immediately exclude you from the group who believe in food safety and looking after children's health. That makes you an outsider and a pretty heartless one at that. Worse than that, you're defending the interests of the big chemical companies who produce all these toxic pesticides, which means you're also a profiteer and a wrecker of the environment. That more or less excludes you from the human race. Pretty soon, we've got public opinion saying people like you should be locked up and nobody is listening to anything you have to say. That's repression. See how it goes?"

"Sounds all very well in theory, Mark, but I bet you can't give me any real life examples that were that simple."

"Are you saying I'm bullshitting?" Mark said indignantly. "I'll tell you what, it'd make your hair curl if I told you some of the things we've done."

"Oh yeah?" Peter said, injecting a sneer into his voice. "I think you're just having me on." He paused and mentally crossed his fingers. "Although I did hear a rumour that Media Associates pulled off some kind of coup on a company in the Biotechnology sector a while back. But I suppose you're going to say you can't talk about real examples."

Mark's face reddened. "Well that's where you're wrong. Have you heard of Holt Biotechnologies?"

"You mean the company that was all over the papers for doing those dodgy experiments with human embryos? They went spectacularly bust, didn't they?"

"That's the one. That was one of my projects."

"Well that's hardly an advertisement for your methodology, is it? I thought you were saying you could do miracles for your clients."

Mark bared his teeth in a grin. "We do. Our client wasn't Holt. We were hired by someone who didn't like what they were up to and we made sure the problem went away. And you remember the hostile takeover of Armitage Holdings, where their chairman got the elbow? That was one of ours, too. Don't forget what the 'T' in 'alert' stands for."

"Bloody hell." Peter struggled to keep the elation off his face. There were two new lines of enquiry to follow up and if one of them was the same biotechnology company that Simon Milward had mentioned he might even be following his father's footsteps. "I'm impressed. I'd no idea."

"Not many people do," Mark said, looking smug. "We don't broadcast it for obvious reasons. But getting results in our business is as much about tearing things down as building them up. That's the beauty of spin. It works just as effectively either way."

"But how the devil do you control the media to get that kind of result?"

Mark tapped the side of his nose knowingly. "The men in black. I told you this morning."

"Sorry, I'm not following you."

"Haven't you seen the Stephen Spielberg movie? You know, the one where aliens have colonised the Earth and the men in black go round wiping out the memories of anybody who accidentally finds out? They're like thought police, shine this sort of ray gun in your eyes and zap, you can only think what they tell you to think."

"Yes, I saw it, but what's that got to do with anything?"

"Sorry, it's an in joke. The guys who handle the behind the scenes stuff for us, they always wear these black suits, you see, like some kind of uniform. I'm surprised you haven't seen them. There's usually a few knocking about around Rodney Hardcastle."

"I thought they were just security guards."

"Yeah, that's what us plebs are supposed to believe. Some of them are just muscle, true enough. They've got cameras and stuff everywhere and their control room up on the twentieth floor is like a bloody fortress."

"But you reckon there's more to it than that?"

"You bet there is," Mark said with a snort of derision. "It's the brainy looking ones you've got to watch out for. You don't see them in any of our project plans or activity networks, but they're always around. Nobody quite knows how they do it, but whatever ideas you want to put in people's heads, they seem to be able to deliver. Just like the characters in the film."

Chapter 11

The project room was buzzing when they got back to the third floor and so was Peter's head. He'd found his quarry, but the revelation that he was like a fox trying to hide in the midst of the hounds had him twitching. He was a hell of a lot more exposed than he'd bargained for and his plan suddenly didn't look quite so clever. Then Mark was whisked away into a huddle around a computer screen and Peter overheard a few pointed remarks about some people having to make do without a fancy lunch. He chose to ignore them, but he'd have to be more careful there, too. Mark was a potential goldmine, but there'd be no more pay dirt if the rest of the team got on his back. Peter picked up his camera bag, slung it on his shoulder and looked around hesitantly. He needed to get busy, not just stand here like a spare part. But it was impossible to concentrate. His head was full of the implications of what he'd learned. Things were beginning to come together and what he really needed was some time alone to think it through and figure out the connections. Well then, why not? He wasn't on the payroll here. Peter spun on his heel and strode towards the door. He'd give David Tyler some excuse about needing to get back to the studio and then make himself scarce for the afternoon.

His next thought was that he'd run headlong into a brick wall and Peter staggered back slightly winded. The man he'd just collided with as he rushed into the corridor seemed quite unmoved by the experience and the deep voice was all of a piece with the impression of solid muscularity.

"Steady on, there. Are you OK?"

"Er... yes," Peter gasped, doubled over and trying to catch his breath. "Sorry..." His voice tailed away as he registered the polished black shoes and dark trousers in front of his eyes and his stomach lurched. There was only one group amongst this cosmopolitan crowd that dressed like that. God Almighty. Peter's mind froze and his legs went leaden, refusing to respond to the instinctive urge to run for it. From the corner of his eye he noticed a second black-suited figure a few yards further down the corridor, swinging round to see what the commotion was about. The distinctive profile was unmistakeable. It was the driver of the black Jaguar, who'd been so confidently at ease in that curious meeting at Sir Rodney's country home. The man who'd already come within a whisker of having him killed and who would recognise him in an instant if he got a clear sight of his face.

Peter averted his gaze and with the desperation of a trapped animal cast around for an avenue of escape. His paralysis yielded to a surge of adrenalin. Keeping his head down, he mumbled another apology and started walking away from the two men, willing his feet to keep moving. There were no safe, dark corners to hide in, just the brightly-lit expanse of carpet leading to the sanctuary of another corridor and the promise of anonymity if he could just get round that corner and out of sight. But it seemed like a million miles and he could feel their stares like the spotlight on a cabaret performer. He fought back the urge to run. Panicky flight would be the confirmation they needed and every yard was precious while they hesitated, unsure of what they'd seen.

"Hey, you. Hold it right there."

The command cracked like a glacier calving and Peter's nerve broke. As he sprinted round the corner, he risked a glance back over his shoulder, half expecting to see a hand reaching out to collar him. Things were bad enough, but not quite that bad. It was small consolation, but his subterfuge had bought him a lead of perhaps thirty metres over the two grim-faced figures now pounding down the corridor after him. That was just a few seconds for a decent athlete, his brain unhelpfully prompted him and from what he'd seen both of his pursuers fell into that category. He had to find a hiding place, fast. But there was nothing... nowhere... no time.

His thoughts, astonishingly, remained calm. Make time, then, dummy, they said, more constructively this time. Create a diversion. He spotted a fire exit onto a stairwell, slammed an arm against the bar and raced on past as it flew open with a distinctive clatter. Closed office doors stretched ahead of him, each a potential trap whose occupant would give no sanctuary to a wild-eyed stranger bursting in. One, he counted, sprinting past the walnut veneered slab with its uninformative nameplate. Two... Three... The sounds of pursuit were very close, now. The instant they turned the corner, he'd be done for. Last chance, then. Peter grabbed the handle of the fourth door and shot inside, swinging it shut behind him as quietly as possible. Empty. Thank Christ for that. He leaned back against the cool timber, his shoulders heaving as he tried to catch his breath. There was a crash from outside as the fire exit was flung open a second time and the noise of running footsteps receded onto the staircase. One going up and the other going down by the sound of it, with no sign of any hesitation. They were nobody's fools, then and his ploy wouldn't keep them at bay for long. Nor would skulking in an empty office, he thought grimly. He had to move again and fast. But where? The corridor was out of the question. There wasn't a prayer that he'd be able to get out of sight down there before they came back.

His gaze flickered around the room, looking for options. He was trapped in a standard middle-management cubicle and there was nothing to inspire hope. The only thing even notionally big enough to hide in was the four-drawer filing cabinet and he'd have to be a fully paid-up member of the magic circle to get in there. The windows were sealed units and a quick glance confirmed a lethal drop down three floors to the road outside even if he could smash his way through the glass in time. Then Peter's heart missed a beat at the sound of returning footsteps from the stairwell, followed by a peremptory knock on an office door and the mutter of a conversation. Two more doors to go, he thought in renewed terror and then it would be his turn. Whatever he was going to do, it had to be now.

He climbed. Standing on the desk, he lifted one of the square polystyrene ceiling tiles out of its frame, sliding it aside to reveal an eighteen-inch service space that ran under the slab of the load-bearing floor above. There was just room to crawl in amongst the ducts and wires, but would the flimsy-looking framework of the false ceiling support him? The sound of urgent voices from the next-door office made any such doubts academic and he heaved himself upwards, hooking his feet and hands over the pipework above to reduce the load as best he could. It was like climbing into a coffin and at that moment the comparison seemed apt. Sweating, flat on his back and fighting the urge to sneeze as dust clogged his nose and lungs, he scrabbled with one hand to retrieve the loose tile. Twisting his head awkwardly so he could see what he was doing, he worked it into what he hoped was the right position, knowing that if he dropped or misaligned it the game would be over. As the square of polystyrene fell into place and darkness overtook him, the last thing he saw through the gap was his camera bag, lying behind the desk where he'd forgotten it in his haste.

He could feel a trickle of blood running down his cheek from a graze where he'd scraped his forehead on the rough concrete a few inches in front of his face. His pulse was hammering and he felt sick. That bloody bag was a dead giveaway. Idiot. How could he have been so stupid? Peter pushed the thought from his mind and concentrated on trying to maintain his precarious balance. With luck they might overlook the bag or assume it belonged to the authorised occupant of the office, but if he dropped through the ceiling on top of them it would be the end, even if he didn't break his neck in the fall.

It was only yesterday he'd reckoned he was enjoying the thrill of the chase and the danger. He shivered and clutched the pipework more tightly. What a hollow bloody joke that was. Why on earth hadn't he just turned round and walked back into the safety of the project room? There were people there... it would have been safe. Surely they wouldn't have wanted to make a scene there, in front of everybody? It was crazy to have marooned himself up here, scared witless and at their mercy. Then there was a knock on the door below and he twitched, almost losing his grip. The door opened and he heard footsteps. The sounds carried clearly through the thin tiles and Peter went rigid, holding his breath.

"Shit." The frustration in the voice just beneath him was unmistakeable. It was so close the expletive might have been spoken to his face. "Nothing. Look, Mike, are you sure it was him? I mean, we can't afford to draw too much attention to ourselves round here."

"I'd know the skinny little bastard anywhere. It was Conway alright."

"It doesn't make sense, man. Think about it. What the hell would he be doing here, of all places?"

"Christ, Sam, how should I know? I don't believe in coincidence, though. If he's got this far, he already knows way too much. He's got to be stopped and bloody quick. No more pissing about with fancy 'accidents', we need to nail him any way we can."

There was a chilling silence. Peter clenched his teeth and tried to ignore the pain of metal cutting into his back and buttocks where they rested on the ceiling supports. He'd never imagined people talking about murder as though they were swatting flies and the callousness of it made his head swim. It took every ounce of his determination to cling on to his precarious perch and stay motionless.

"Where the fuck is he, then?" Sam Garvey said. "He can't have got much further than this, he didn't have time."

"He must have got out onto one of the other floors from the stairs."

"You'd better be right about this." The implied threat crackled in the air.

"I'm telling you. It was him."

"Right then." Decision time, Peter thought, quaking. The sudden authority in the voice was unmistakeable. "That leaves us with no choice. You get down to the front desk, Mike, right now. I want all exits blocked immediately and a full-scale search mounted. Then you get up to the control room and use the CCTV to spot if he breaks cover. But he's to be taken as quietly as possible, you hear me? The last thing we need is to turn it into a fucking three-ring circus. I'll go and give Hardcastle the bad news and get him started on covering our backsides with the Research Council."

"Rather you than me. But what do I tell the security team it's all about?"

The sounds started to recede as they moved back out into the corridor.

"Use your sodding initiative. You can tell them there's a homicidal maniac in the building for all I care. Just get on with it. If you'd been quicker off the mark in the first place..."

There was a clatter of feet on the staircase, then silence.

Peter felt icy cold. It wasn't given to many to hear their own death sentence being passed like that. He stirred, trying to pull himself together. The urgency of the threat was greater, but the bottom line hadn't changed. They'd been trying to kill him anyway. But the obituary was premature and he wasn't about to wait around for it to be fulfilled. He listened again, as though his life depended on it - which it did, he recognised with grim certainty. Nothing. They'd gone, unless it was a bluff. The thought was insidious and he hesitated. Then he thrust it aside. One way or another, he had to move. He had to gamble they weren't that smart.

Casting caution aside, he lifted a tile from beneath him, slid out of his hiding place and dropped to the floor in a crouch, ready to lash out if necessary. The sight of the empty room was a blessed relief and he straightened, feeling his body creak in protest. His limbs were cramped and painful, but the effort of brushing the filth off his clothes took care of the worst aches and pains as the blood started to flow again. Peter took a last look round. A black hole gaped in the ceiling. Damn. He climbed shakily onto the desk and slid the tile back into place. It was probably futile, but keeping his refuge hidden might buy more time to get out of the building. If he could figure out how to go about it, that was. All the exit doors would be guarded any second now and his chances were slim at best.

He jumped down and stumbled over his camera bag, still lying where he'd dropped it earlier. He stifled a curse and picked it up. Lugging bloody equipment around was the bane of a photographer's life, but there was no way he was going to abandon a couple of thousand quid's worth of Nikon. Pity Jack Howson wasn't around to take care of it for him this time, he thought as he swung the bag over his shoulder. Then he paused. Wait a minute. His brain raced. He was missing something. Something important... something to do with Jack... with equipment. Trouble with getting past security. Then he had it. There was a back way out, which might not yet be sealed off and which they certainly wouldn't expect him to know about. The service lift to the executive car park, which the commissionaire had been moved to let them use that first time when he'd wanted to get Jack Howson and the van off the front doorstep. Peter put his hand into his pocket, then smiled. The little square of plastic with his photograph and that all-important magnetic strip was still there. He pulled it out and stared at it, wondering. The question was, would his pass operate the electronic locks on the lift and the car park doors? He eyed the plastic card quizzically, but it offered no enlightenment. There was only one way to find out and he was fresh out of alternatives.

Shutting his eyes and thanking his lucky stars that they'd given him a tour of the place on that first day, he conjured up a mental picture of the building. It was a knack he'd always had, even as a child, knowing where he was and memorising layouts, though he'd never imagined it might one day help save his life. He held his breath and concentrated as the image swam into focus in his head. Then he sighed with relief. The service lift was nearby. He fixed the route in his mind, then eased open the office door and peered cautiously round it. There was nobody about. He took a deep breath and scuttled out. The two minutes it took to reach the lift seemed like forever, but he encountered nobody. He swiped his card through the slot on the wall and pressed the call button. Nothing seemed to happen and his heart sank. Then, distantly, electric motors hummed to life as the machinery responded to his summons. He tried not to dwell on the possibility that others might be responding, too, if the system was smart enough to register whose identity was encoded on that thin black stripe. He had more than enough worries, without inventing more.

A few moments later he emerged into the gloom of the underground car park. He stood stock still with his back pressed against the wall, eyes and ears straining to detect any other presence. The air smelt damp, stinking of oil and petrol fumes, but it was still and lifeless. So far, so good, then. Reaching back, he pushed the button to return the lift to the top floor. The noise of the doors clanging shut echoed like thunder, but nothing stirred. Empty, it whirred upwards, the sound fading quickly and he let his gaze wander. The ceiling here was claustrophobically low, dotted sporadically with unshielded neon tubes and the walls still bore the striations left by the shuttering into which the concrete had been poured. Squat columns shouldered the weight of the building above, marked here and there with paint-smeared gouges that testified to the fallibility of even the most senior executives and between them gleaming limousines were packed into every available space. To his right, at the far end, a dim light shone through the glass panel of a door marked 'Maintenance'. Directly in front of him, a heavy metal roller blind sealed off the exit, flanked on one side by a smaller door for pedestrian access. Freedom beckoned.

Peter started forward, then shrank back into the shadows, heart pounding, as the door to his right clattered wide. A man emerged, anonymous in greasy cap and overalls and headed towards the exit, whistling tunelessly. Reaching it, he turned, making a gesture half way between a wave and a salute before swiping a card through the sensor on the wall. There was a pause, then the small door obediently swung open. He stepped through and disappeared. The boom of the door slamming shut behind him reverberated like the death knell of Peter's hopes. The greeting had been aimed at a closed circuit TV camera nestling almost invisibly just under the ceiling. It was focused inescapably on the only way out. And it was clear that somewhere, someone was monitoring it.

Would it matter if he was spotted, though, so long as he was out? The temptation to go for it, to make a getaway even if the hounds of hell were baying at his heels, was overwhelming and he took a couple of steps before his brain forced him to a reluctant halt. What he'd seen was more complicated, more significant than that. The wave had come before the pass card had been inserted to open the door. Farewells normally came after that, as you stepped outside, not before. Peter cursed under his breath, feeling paranoid, but his mind wouldn't let go. It was such a small thing, of no importance. Unless... what? He rubbed his forehead in frustration and tried to dig out the source of his unease.

Then it came to him. Unless the hidden watcher also controlled the lock. What if there was a remote override of some sort? Bugger. It made sense. Why else would this place be left unattended, when the whole building must be alerted by now? The certainty swept over him that if he walked up and used his pass, nothing would happen. He'd be trapped like a fly in the spider's web and that would be the end.

The light was still on in the maintenance workshop and Peter tiptoed across, keeping well out of the camera's line of sight. He reached for the door and gently pushed it open with his fingertips, praying the hinges wouldn't creak. Inside, a short corridor lined with lockers and coat hooks led to a second half-open door, through which he could see the outlines of tools and workbenches. He shuffled towards it, scarcely daring to breathe and peered through the gap. His heart sank. Daylight was seeping in from two long, horizontal windows set high up near the ceiling, but they were far too narrow to offer any chance of escape and the concrete walls were otherwise unbroken. The only good news was that the place was deserted and even that wasn't particularly reassuring. There had to be staff on duty at this time of day. They must be out on a call, which meant that they could return at any time. He glanced nervously over his shoulder at the lift. As if on cue, it groaned into life and the floor indicator light started to flicker as it descended.

Beads of sweat burst out on Peter's forehead and he searched for inspiration. A grubby boiler suit and an old baseball cap hanging on one of the hooks caught his eye. The watchers were looking for someone in jacket and tie, not a mechanic and contractors must be going in and out all the time. There was no time to think about it. He grabbed the garment and fought his way into it. Thank God it was a zip-up job. Buttons would have been a nightmare, his hands seemed to be all thumbs. It hung on him like a sack and he wrestled with the folds of cotton festooned around his ankles. The damn thing must belong to a giant and he'd get nowhere if he fell flat on his face. He was hopping about on one leg, trying to pull the trapped cloth over his other shoe when there was a clunk and the sound of lift doors opening. His heart leapt into his mouth and the involuntary jerk as he turned to look sent him staggering, arms windmilling to keep his balance.

The indicator light shone through the gloom. It said '3' and the relief was like a reprieve on the brink of the gallows. But even as the thought flashed through his mind, he heard the doors slide shut again above him. The light blinked and the figure '2' shone out. Whoever was coming would be here in moments and it was now or never to make his move. He crammed the cap on his head and pulled the peak down over his face. The walk to the exit seemed to last a lifetime and Peter kept his eyes on his feet as he waved clumsily in the direction of the camera. The pass card slid easily through the sensor and he held his breath, waiting for the click that would signal the release of the lock. Behind him, the sound of the lift stopped. This time, there was no mistaking the fact that it had reached the end of the line.

Chapter 12

Jack Howson unlocked the door of Spectrum Studios, then froze at the sight that met his eyes, whistling hollowly through his teeth. The place had been comprehensively trashed and debris was scattered like the aftermath of a hurricane. Shards of glass from the broken window glinted in the early-morning sunshine and he swore viciously, searching his memory for reassurance that he'd set the alarm system properly last night. He was sure he had. Almost sure. It was a routine he'd gone through a thousand times, but the trouble with routine was that in the end you stopped thinking, you just did it on auto-pilot. Last night was no different, but he was bound to be quizzed about it and he couldn't specifically remember. His breakfast congealed into an uncomfortable lump under his breastbone and he stirred uneasily as he took in the scale of the destruction. The furniture was matchwood, seat covers and even the leather desktop slashed to ribbons with a sharp knife. The filing cabinet drawers were ripped out and Peter's carefully organised paperwork scattered to the four winds. The metal carcase lay abandoned in one corner, with a dent in one side where a boot had crashed into it from frustration or malice. Even the wallpaper was ripped, in places hanging in ribbons as though someone had probed for a safe or hidey-hole that might contain valuables. There'd be hell to pay for this and plenty of people waiting to point the finger of blame. Then his eye caught the tangle of wires ripped from the alarm system control box and he felt a surge of relief, which quickly turned to anger.

"Bastards," Jack muttered. There was no call for such mindless savagery, though he knew it was a common enough by-product of burglary. Then he stiffened as he recognised the broken remains of a Hasselblad lying against the wall underneath a deep gouge in the plaster. That was odd, to say the least. You were talking thousands for equipment like that and no self-respecting thief would overlook such a prize. But it looked as though it had been hurled against the wall in rage, which was a bloody stupid thing to do. What kind of idiot would go to all this trouble and then smash the most valuable item in the place?

Unless they were after something else. The thought popped unbidden into Jack's head and he frowned. That was daft. What else was there in a photographic studio worth pinching? Apart from the camera equipment there was nothing except... well... photographs. Who'd want those? He scratched his head. Best to leave that kind of thinking to the fuzz. Not that they'd be anything but a pain in the arse if his past brushes with the law were anything to go by. Bloody useless, the lot of them. Like as not they'd try to pin it on him, with his track record. The thought troubled him and his hand, which had been reaching for his mobile phone, dropped indecisively back to his side. Sod it. He had to do something, but there was no way he wanted to get caught up in that sort of hassle. Phone Peter, he decided. Yes, that would be for the best. Peter would know what to do.

Jack glanced at his watch and saw that it was still barely quarter to eight. It was the last sodding time he was going to use his initiative to make an early start, he grumbled, but there was a fair chance Peter hadn't left home yet to catch the train to the city. He punched in the number and listened to the ringing tone, wondering how the job with that PR firm was going and whether anything had turned up about that story with Peter's old man. Toffee-nosed lot of bastards, he thought derisively, feeling glad that he wasn't involved. Anything was possible with wankers like that...

His thoughts were interrupted by the click of the receiver being lifted.

"Hello?"

"Uh..." Jack grunted with surprise. It was a strange voice. Damn. Must be a wrong number. "Sorry. I was trying to get Peter Conway."

"This is Peter Conway's phone. I'm afraid he's not here at the moment. Who's calling?"

"What the hell...? Who am I speaking to?"

"This is Detective Constable Wilkins of the West Kent Constabulary..."

Jack hit the disconnect button, cutting the conversation off in mid sentence. Jesus wept. He stared at the instrument as though it was a poisonous snake that had just bitten him. Police at Peter's house? Something must have gone seriously pear-shaped there, too. And where the hell was Peter? He shuffled his feet, trying to work out what to do next. Then the phone in his hand rang, making him jump. He pressed the button to accept the call and lifted it cautiously to his ear.

"Jack? Listen, I need you to drop everything and..."

"Peter," Jack interrupted with a huge sigh of relief. "Man, am I glad to hear your voice, I'm in deep shit here. I just got in to the studio and somebody's broken in and wrecked the place. I tried to call you, but there's police at your place in Tonbridge, I don't know what the hell's happened there. It's a total shambles..."

At the other end of the line, Peter suppressed a shudder. He'd been half expecting something like this. Even so, the speed and efficiency of the retaliation was frightening. One false move and these people would need no second chance.

"Never mind all that," he interrupted, oblivious to Jack's agitation. "Look, I've got bigger troubles and I need your help right away. Can you bring your car and meet me at the Grand Hotel in Hastings?"

"Hastings? What the hell are you doing there? Are the police after you?"

Peter laughed shakily. "No, not the police. It's a long story, I'll tell you when you get here. But make it fast, can you?"

"Yeah, OK, how about if I bring the van? That's parked just down the road and it'll be quicker. My own wheels are back at the flat."

"Forget the van," Peter said. "Someone will be watching that. You'd just lead them to me."

"Lead who, for Christ's sake? Have you dropped yourself in it with those funny buggers at that agency?"

"You could say that, but there's no time to explain now. They'll have the studio staked out, which puts you in the firing line too."

"What do you want me to do about this place, though? Like I said, it's a shambles."

"I don't give a toss about that. Just leave it."

"But I can't just walk away..."

"Look Jack," Peter interrupted. "You're in danger, take my word for it. Get out of there right now and try to make sure you're not followed. I'll see you in a couple of hours and I'll fill you in then."

There was a click as the line went dead. Jack put the phone down and kicked idly at a file lying on the floor, scattering its contents. A few more bits of paper wouldn't make any sodding difference, he thought disgustedly. The place was a right mess, though and it didn't seem right to simply walk away. But Peter was the boss and it sounded as though he was in some real bother. Best follow orders, then. His eyebrows knitted in concentration as he tried to figure out how to avoid being tailed. Then his eye caught the broken glass and his brow cleared. The answer was staring him in the face. Getting in and out unseen was the first rule of burglary, so all he had to do was take the tip from the experts. Ignoring the crunch of glass under his boots, he strolled over to the window, ducked through the empty frame and vanished.

***

A little over two hours later, Jack parked his RS2000 Turbo on the Hastings sea front. The Escort might be old, he thought smugly, but he tuned it himself and it would still see off most things on the road. And he'd given it enough welly on the way down the A21 to be sure that nobody was sitting on his tail. He'd not had that much fun for ages. Then his grin faded. Burning a bit of rubber was all very well, but he wished he knew what the hell was going on.

The view through the windscreen was bleak. A Northeasterly was driving scudding clouds and the swell was pounding on the shingle to his left, behind the railings. The promenade, not surprisingly, was practically deserted. A few brave souls, shoulders hunched against the wind and spray, strolled under the festoons of Christmas lights, but none spared more than a casual glance at Jack. Those that did, he reckoned, were acting more out of incredulity that someone else might be daft enough to join them than from any more sinister motive. His gaze moved to the hotel a hundred yards or so down to his right. The steps leading up to the entrance were deserted and above them the ranks of balconies overlooking the beach stood empty behind their ornate ironwork. Here and there the white paint of the facade was peeling, giving the building an air of neglect that belied the five stars on the sign by the door. Jack shivered, despite the warmth of the heater and reached for his anorak. It wouldn't be smart, he figured, to pull the car right up to the entrance, but all the same it wasn't a day for walking further than you had to. Nor was it a place you'd choose to visit at this time of year without a compelling reason. Peter must have got himself into something very nasty indeed, unless he was just playing silly buggers.

Jack marched across the road, bounded up the steps two at a time and pushed his way through the revolving door, bringing a gust of winter into the foyer with him. The felt seals made gentle slapping noises as the door spun to a stop behind him, but nothing else disturbed the silence. Even the receptionist seemed to have despaired of any custom and deserted her post. He looked around and caught sight of a solitary figure waiting in the lounge. One look at Peter Conway's haggard face dispelled any thoughts of silliness.

"Jack, over here," Peter beckoned. "Jesus, am I glad to see you."

"You look like shit," Jack said bluntly, dropping into an armchair next to him. "What the hell's this all about?"

"I asked one question too many at Media Associates."

"So you were right about that lot. Can't say I'm surprised." Jack sniffed disdainfully. The way the doorman had treated him still rankled. "I never liked the look of them. I suppose they kicked you out, then. What's the big deal? It was always on the cards if they caught on."

"You don't know the half of it. Did I tell you what I found at that party I went to?"

"What, at Hardcastle's place last weekend? No, I haven't seen you since, have I. I figured you were nursing a hangover."

"Damn, I'm losing track of things a bit. I..."

Peter paused, interrupted by the approach of a white-coated waiter offering morning coffee. Jack shook his head. Peter followed suit, waving a dismissive hand to emphasise the point when the young man continued to hover nearby. The waiter took the hint and disappeared behind the wooden screen that shielded the service door. Jack opened his mouth to speak, but Peter held up his hand to silence him, waiting for the sound of the door to signal that they were alone again. It duly came and Peter relaxed.

"Sorry," he said. "This isn't something I want anyone else to be listening in on. Let me bring you up to date, then..."

Jack stiffened and sat forward in his chair as the story unfolded.

"Stone the crows," he said disbelievingly when Peter paused for breath. "You reckon that old Jewish bloke was right, then? There really is somebody out there screwing around with our minds?"

"Oh yes, they're using the Kaiserhof material, that's for sure. When that guy Mark at the agency described the way they work, it was like he was reading from the same script as Cohen. Except I don't think he knew anything about what was behind it. It's the other lot, what he called the men in black, who do all the clever stuff. That's where I came unstuck..."

Peter felt sweat trickling down his back as he related yesterday's nightmare. He was finding it hard to cope and sleep had eluded him for most of the night. At times panic would overwhelm him, leaving him trembling and seeing traps everywhere. Then his mood would swing and it felt like a fantasy he'd wake up from to find the world had gone back to normal. That was how it had been when he heard the lock click open on that basement door yesterday and made his escape. He'd walked away - it hadn't crossed his mind to run - down the street and then caught the train for home, without thinking, as though his problems were over. The stupidity of turning up at Woodside Road only dawned as he was about to get off the train at Tonbridge. Thirty seconds with Rodney Hardcastle would have been all it took to confirm who he was and how far he'd penetrated their organisation. A few minutes more and they'd have found out his address. He'd have walked straight into their arms.

"I guess you were right about that," Jack said. "That must be why the plod were there when I phoned. I bet the same guys did the studio, too. Jesus, though, I never thought things would get that heavy. You're bloody lucky you didn't end up in the river tied to a block of concrete, by the sound of it."

"You're not kidding." Peter held up his hand, thumb and forefinger a centimetre apart. "It was that close. Just the width of a bloody ceiling tile."

"So how did you end up here?" Jack asked.

"It just happened to be the end of the line," Peter said. "Hastings, I mean. It was where the train I was on ended up. I came to the Grand because it was the only hotel I knew. I photographed a wedding here a few years back. There's no way they'll trace me from that, though."

"Sounds to me like you ought to keep moving anyway," Jack said, tugging thoughtfully at his lower lip. "They'll pull out all the stops to find you and no mistake. I mean, they've got to reckon you've got the goods on them by now. They must be shitting bricks that you'll take it to the cops."

"Take what?" Peter snorted. "I've got no proof of anything. There's not a hope in hell that the police would take a story like this seriously."

"Why not?" Jack said indignantly. "I do. It's bleeding

obvious you're not here for the good of your health."

"Maybe so. But you're hardly an unbiased judge. The fact is, everything's hearsay and conjecture."

Jack shook his head and scowled. "You can't sit here on your backside hoping it'll all go away. I wasn't joking when I said you might end up in the river."

"Mm," Peter said. "I know, they've tried already. Didn't I say? I heard them talking about that stonework that nearly took my head off at the studio. It was no accident."

"Effing hell." Jack's eyes went wide and he struggled for words. "But I thought... I mean you're not serious..."

"I'm deadly serious. They're trying to kill me, no holds barred."

"Christ almighty, Peter. What are you going to do?"

"That rather depends on you."

"Me?" Jacks eyebrows shot up in astonishment.

"Yes. How far you're willing to get involved."

Jack gave Peter a hard look. "All the way, pal. You should know that."

"Not so fast, Jack. Just think about it for a minute. We're talking about dangerous people here and they're not fooling about. It's not your fight. You'd be smarter to stay out of it."

"Are you saying you don't want me with you?" Jack's face was thunderous and Peter could see his neck reddening as the blood rose. It was a sure sign, he knew from bitter experience, that Jack was about to lose his temper. He held up his hand to ward off the explosion.

"No, I'm not saying that. I'm asking you to think about it while you've still got the chance. I reckon they wouldn't hesitate to take you out to get to me. I'm dangerous company and I wouldn't blame you if you'd rather steer clear, that's all."

"Stop talking crap," Jack said. "You should know me better than that. Just tell me what you want me to do."

Peter leaned over and put his hand on Jack's arm. "Thanks," he said simply, but with all the sincerity he could muster. There weren't really any words to express how he felt.

Jack wriggled uncomfortably and glanced away.

"Cut it out, there's no need for that. You've got something figured, I can tell. Are you going to let me in on it, or what?"

"It's a question of logic. There's only two ways to stop something like this... public opinion or the law."

"How do you mean?"

"I mean you either splash it all over the media so enough people get mad and force them to pack it in, or you find out what laws they're breaking and screw them in the courts instead. I figure we'd be wasting our time going after public opinion, so it'll have to be the law, at least for starters."

"Why's that? There's a lot of people out there who'd get hot under the collar if they knew someone was frigging about with their minds."

"You're missing the point. We can't go that route because they control the media. No coverage, no impact. It's as simple as that."

"Ah," Jack said, open-mouthed. "I hadn't thought of that." He looked up, the effort of concentration plain to see on his face. "We're buggered then. They're not breaking the sodding law, even if they are a bunch of liars. Unless," he added hopefully, "you think we can pin those murders on them?"

"I don't see how we can, unless we can prove a motive and we can't do that without making people believe what they're up to. It's a circular argument."

"I thought you said you had something worked out," Jack said grumpily. "Sounds to me like they've got it all sewn up tight."

"Maybe not. The law's a funny thing. Telling lies for political purposes is called freedom of speech, something to be defended to the death. But doing it for financial gain is different. That's fraud. You can go to jail for that."

"It is political, though, all this spin. Like that project you wormed your way into. Whitewashing another of Tony's cronies to make out like he's Mother Theresa. Makes you sick, it does."

"That's what I thought at first. But that guy David I was working with, he said they don't often do jobs like that these days. I think they've moved on from politics. And when I tweaked his nose a bit, all the examples he came up with were commercial."

"That doesn't help." Jack shrugged. "It's not a crime for companies to use PR firms."

"No, but what if it's more than PR? What if they're using these mind control techniques to manipulate the financial markets, for example? That could change everything."

"Don't be daft. I can't see how that would work."

"I'm not sure either. But I reckon it's where we've got

to start looking. Remember how they bankrupted my Dad? Some funny business with shares? And how did Robert Maxwell make his fortune? Or Rodney Hardcastle, come to that?"

"Well... maybe. So what do we do, then?"

"Find out more about Holt Biotechnologies, for starters. That's one of the cases they threw at me. There's a reference library round the corner from here and I wasn't just kicking my heels while you were driving down. According to the business directories, they're based just down the coast near Brighton. Are you up for paying them a visit?"

"I'll drive, you navigate," Jack said. He stood up, the car keys chinking as he tossed them from hand to hand. "Are you all settled up here?"

"Yes, I checked out before you came."

"Well let's stop pissing about then and get on the road."

Peter smiled and followed Jack towards the door. After all the running, it felt good to start fighting back.

***

Behind Peter Conway, unnoticed, the coffee waiter peered cautiously round the wooden screen, then strolled across to the window and watched the two men climb into their car. It was an old trick, kicking the service door and letting it swing shut again to make the customers think you'd gone, then settling down out of sight behind the screen, listening to the gossip. Usually, it didn't mean much, beyond having a laugh with the other staff about the odd little secrets that people sometimes let slip. He grinned to himself.

This was different, though. He didn't understand it all, but with a bit of embellishment it would make a great story. Good enough, perhaps, to impress that chambermaid he fancied up on the third floor, the new one with the blonde hair and big tits. His grin broadened at the prospect and his imagination began to run riot. Later, when two men in black suits turned up and stuffed a pocketful of cash into his hand to relate the story, his grin was broader still.

***

The chances of finding out anything worthwhile were slim, Peter acknowledged to himself as the Escort screeched to a halt outside an uncompromising security barrier. Beyond, a futuristic aluminium and glass edifice was tucked back from the road in its own grounds, with what looked like a lake glinting through a copse of trees along one side. The air of twenty-first century high-tech prosperity was a far cry from the run-down bankruptcy he'd been expecting.

"Hang on here a second," Peter said, unclenching his fist from the hanging strap he'd been clinging to in self-preservation. Jack's driving technique could charitably be described as assertive, although terrifying was nearer the mark. "I'll go and have a word with the gateman."

The man in question was emerging from the gatehouse and Peter stepped out of the car to greet around six foot three of immaculately uniformed muscle. Close-up, he was older than first impressions suggested, perhaps mid-forties, with an authoritative manner that would have been intimidating but for the twinkle of good humour in his eyes and the faint west-country burr softening his voice as he enquired how he might help.

"I'm here to see Mr. Jonathan Holt, the managing director," Peter said confidently. He fished in his wallet for a business card and held it out. "I'm from Spectrum Studios. It's about some photographic work I'm doing."

An official eyebrow twitched and the twinkle beneath it vanished.

"I'm sorry, sir, you must have been misinformed. Mr. Holt no longer works here."

Disapproval, Peter thought. Well-disguised, but definitely there in the voice. But was it of the man or of the fact that he'd gone?

"Damn, that's a shame. We got on really well, he was a nice guy. What happened? I understood he owned the business."

"Takeover, sir." A gloved hand gestured towards the sign just inside the barrier. 'A Division of Zetec Holdings plc' it said, underneath the Holt Biotechnologies banner. "You know how it is. These things happen."

Regret on top of the disapproval. Peter looked at the impassive face in front of him and hoped he wasn't misreading the situation.

"Must have been a bit of a shock all round, something like that."

The stern figure unbent a little and leaned forward confidentially.

"You could say that. I've been here ten years and Mr. Jonathan was always good to us, like family, you know? All changed now, of course. But that's life. You've got to make the best of things. Just the same, it wasn't right, what happened to him. Being forced out, like."

"How did it happen, then?"

The air suddenly seemed to cool a couple of degrees and Peter felt a wave of suspicion washing over him.

"I couldn't rightly say, sir. If you're one of those reporters, I'll have to ask you to move on."

"No," he protested quickly, "I told you, I'm a photographer, got a business proposition for Mr. Holt. Nothing to do with the press, I assure you. If he's not here, where can I contact him?"

"Sorry, sir, I'm not allowed to give out information about company staff."

"But if he's gone, that doesn't apply, surely? Look, it's something I'm sure will do him a bit of good. Sounds as though he could do with some good news for a change."

The level brown eyes narrowed and Peter felt like a specimen under a microscope. Then the twinkle returned as the guard smiled.

"Perhaps you're right at that," he said. "Have you got a map in the car? I'll show you where he lives."

***

Two hours later, Jack turned the car into a cul-de-sac lined with middle-income town houses packed cheek by jowl into miniscule plots. Peter wrinkled his nose in instinctive compassion. It was a stark contrast to the elegant Victorian farmhouse in its own few acres, whose location the gateman had divulged as the Holt family residence. All they'd found there was a faint echo of its former owner, tucked away as a forwarding address in an almost forgotten drawer. The decline in Jonathan Holt's fortunes could hardly have been more dramatic and Peter felt his pulse begin to accelerate in anticipation as Jack brought the Escort shuddering to a halt in front of No. 23, Windsor Close. He felt a sudden illogical certainty that behind the curtains, drawn tight against the winter evening, he would find some of the answers he was looking for.

There was no car on the short concrete driveway leading to the garage, but the light shining through the glass panel in the front door suggested reassuringly that someone was at home. Peter pressed the bell and his confidence suddenly evaporated. He'd make a lousy encyclopaedia salesman, he thought ruefully. Jack was the one with the gift of the gab when it came to chatting up total strangers. He shuffled his feet nervously, and then turned to give Jack a call, but before he could get the words out the door clicked open behind him and a soft, well-educated voice spoke. "Can I help you?"

Caught off balance, he stumbled as he turned back and felt like an idiot. The hint of amusement in the level grey eyes taking in his antics was salt in the wound.

"Um… er… Mrs. Holt?" he managed.

"Yes." The wary monosyllable implied visitors were frequent and usually troublesome.

"My name's Peter Conway. I was wondering if I might speak with your husband? I'm trying to find out … um… that is, I want to…"

Her eyes blazed in sudden anger.

"For God's sake, haven't you reporters had enough?" she snapped. "We're sick of your lies. Go away and leave us alone."

She looked like a lioness defending her pride and Peter took an involuntary step backward at the intensity of her reaction. Jesus, he was making a right mess of this.

"Wait a minute," he yelped. "I'm not from the press. Give me a chance, I'm on your side…"

The crash of the door slamming in his face echoed round the Close like a gunshot and he found himself talking to a glass panel inches in front of his nose.

"Dammit," he yelled, "the bastards who screwed you are after me, too. I need your help, here."

Silence. So much for that, then. A day wasted. He was about to turn away in frustration when the lock clicked and the door opened just a crack.

"What do you mean, they're after you too?" she said suspiciously.

"Look, these people, they ruined my father, destroyed my family. I'm trying to find other victims, more information, anything that might help me expose what they're doing. Please. I know how painful it is, but I need your help."

"Did you say your name was Conway?"

"Yes, Peter Conway."

"We had an old guy here a while back giving us much the same story, he said his name was Conway. Come to think, he looked a bit like you. Was that your father?"

Peter's heart leapt. Finally, he had a firm connection to Frank's investigations.

"Yes, it would have been. He mentioned your name."

"Well then, we told him everything we know. You should go away and talk to him. We gave him our files. We even answered his questions on video. There isn't anything else we can tell you."

The door started to close again in Peter's face.

"Wait," he said despairingly, "Please. I can't do that. He died recently, you see and all his records went missing. I think the same people were responsible, and I'm trying to put his investigation back together."

"You can't fight the press," she said. "You're wasting your time."

"It's not the press I'm after. There's more to it than that."

"He's got that much right, at least." Jonathan Holt's deep voice carried from inside the house. "Let him in, Jessica."

"But…"

"Oh, for goodness' sake, what harm can it do? Let's face it, we've got nothing left to lose."

Jessica Holt stood aside reluctantly and let the door swing open.

"You'd better come through, then, Mister Conway" she said. "We're in the lounge, just here."

The room was cramped and sparsely furnished. Jonathan Holt looked like a broken man, shoulders hunched with the weight of his misfortunes and defeat clinging to him like a shroud. Peter was reminded of his father just before he'd turned to the bottle. The memories of confidence and success could still be seen, but like an old photograph in strong sunlight the image was becoming faint and would soon be gone altogether. His wife, prowling protectively in the background with her claws temporarily sheathed, was handling it better, he thought. But that too would probably change as the rage turned to bitterness and, finally, despair.

Despite appearances, the ashes of Jonathan Holt still contained some smouldering embers. A few direct questions fanned them to life. His back straightened and a hint of the arrogance of a successful scientist and entrepreneur crept back into his voice as he described the rise and rise of his business. The breakthrough originated from his research as a postgraduate student at Oxford, where he had seen and become entranced by the potential of genetic engineering. While his contemporaries had devoted their energies to the apparently more promising, but infinitely controversial, experimentation with embryo stem cells, the young Jonathan had cajoled and charmed his way into the wallets of potential investors with a different vision.

The venture capitalists' faith was repaid a thousand-fold with the flotation of the company on a tide of optimism and confidence. It wasn't riches that drove him, he insisted, though riches had come. It was the prospect of turning back the tide of human misery that genetic disorders and degenerative diseases carried in their wake. Adult stem cells, he discovered, had the same multipotential flexibility to transform themselves into heart, brain, nerve or sinew and could be extracted without ethical or other complications from bone marrow. The techniques he'd developed and patented for in vitro genetic manipulation, leading to the creation of 'magic bullets' for the delivery of therapeutic genes, were world-beating, he claimed.

Peter's eyes began to glaze over at the technicalities of

dysfunctional cell replacement, tissue engineering and organ regeneration and Jonathan instantly spotted it. He was getting a bit carried away, he apologised with a rueful grin. In layman's terms, he explained without appearing in the least patronising, it meant things like fixing up your heart after a heart attack, repairing the spinal cord so you can walk again if you're paralysed, things like that. Maybe even growing new kidneys and other organs for transplant as well as curing genetically inherited diseases like Alzheimer's or multiple sclerosis. Peter nodded, impressed. Experts rarely possessed that kind of sensitivity to the difficulties of ordinary mortals in understanding their jargon and even fewer had the ability to express themselves clearly in plain language. It explained much about how the proverbially hard-nosed moneymen had been persuaded to back the budding Holt empire. But it told him nothing about why everything had fallen apart.

"Sounds too good to be true," he said sceptically. "What went wrong?"

Jonathan Holt's face crumpled and for one dreadful moment it seemed as though he might burst into tears.

"Hardcastle," he said. "Sir Rodney bloody Hardcastle. That's what went wrong."

Chapter 13

Bingo, Peter thought, then felt immediately ashamed of his elation at finding the link he was looking for.

"Tell me about Hardcastle," he said gently, trying to ignore tweaks from his conscience at Jonathan's obvious distress.

"I... er, we... thought he was a friend. Good advice and so on, do you see? The business was undercapitalised. It was Rodney who suggested... arranged..." Jonathan swallowed hard, his throat working as he struggled to find the words. "I'm sorry... I can't..." He stuttered to a halt and flapped his hand as if to brush the memories aside.

"Please," Peter encouraged him, "it's important. Do go on."

Jonathan stared into the middle distance, seemingly lost in a quagmire of 'what if' and 'might-have-been' and unable to face harsh reality. Jessica, though, was made of sterner stuff and Peter turned to her in mute appeal. Her toughness might be the salvation of them both in time, he thought, but it would be an uphill struggle.

"Jonathan's work was revolutionary," she said reluctantly. Her face was a rigid mask and the words emerged painfully, like shrapnel being extracted from deep wounds. "The patents were... are... potentially worth millions. And of course, biotechnology was the coming thing... everybody in the city wanted to get on the bandwagon. But that kind of research is terribly expensive… we needed fresh capital… we were so relieved when Rodney Hardcastle took us under his wing, said he'd help us through the financial jungle… he seemed such a nice man, different from the others. His advice made all kinds of sense to us at the time."

"What exactly did he suggest?"

"It seemed so simple. Float the company on the stock market. We'd retain a controlling interest, of course, so there was no risk. He had contacts with this merchant bank in Liechtenstein… he made all the arrangements, wouldn't even take a fee… he said it was between friends, only too glad to help."

"But the flotation went wrong?"

"No, quite the opposite, it was a huge success. We used the money to expand, build the sophisticated lab facilities Jonathan needed… no more scrimping and making do with out-of-date equipment… it was a dream come true for both of us, you see."

"Yes," Peter said and indeed he did see. The memories had lit a glow in Jessica's eyes that spoke of ambitions fulfilled and the heady pleasures of a lifestyle revolving around more than just well equipped research laboratories. For her, it had meant the reflected glory of a successful husband and the social standing of being the mistress of a fine country house with all the trappings of wealth. If anything, her loss might be the harder to bear, he thought in sudden empathy. "But it didn't last?"

The glow faded and disappeared as though a curtain had been drawn.

"No," she said heavily. "It didn't last. Oh, everything was fine for a while… but it all took so long, got so complex. Jonathan's work, I mean. Every time he thought he'd cracked it, there was another hoop to jump through. It wasn't his fault," she added fiercely, as if challenging Peter to disagree.

"No, of course not," he said, treading warily. Plainly, the dreadful temptation to blame her husband was there, deep down, gnawing at her very soul and threatening destruction. There was no way Peter wanted to have on his conscience that he'd encouraged that particular genie out of the bottle. "I'm no scientist, but even I know how unpredictable leading-edge research can be."

"Yes, well. We needed to raise more money. The mortgage on the house helped, but wasn't nearly enough. We didn't want to sell any shares; that would have meant losing our overall control and the pot of gold at the end of the rainbow was so close. We talked it over with Rodney, he'd been so helpful before, you see and we trusted him completely. The shares were doing well… on paper we were worth millions by that time… he said there'd be no difficulty, we could use our shareholding to secure a short-term loan, he'd arrange things, the same as before… businesses like ours do that sort of thing all the time, apparently."

"Sounds reasonable."

"Oh, it was all very… reasonable," she said, spitting the word out as though it was a slug in a mouthful of salad. The tendons in her neck stood out as she fought against tears, head still held resolutely high. "It was only afterwards we found out the bastard had set us up."

"Afterwards?"

"The bottom fell out of the stock market," Jonathan intervened dully. "Or at least our sector of it. You probably remember all those lurid headlines about using dead babies, creating Frankenstein monsters and so on. All garbage, of course. But investors dumped biotechnology shares and ran for cover like scared rabbits. Just like they're doing now," he gestured at the business section of the Telegraph lying open beside him on the settee, "with the Oil and Gas sector stocks because of all the sudden scaremongering about global warming melting the icecaps and all that garbage."

"Er... I don't quite see..."

"Don't you read the papers, man?" The flash of irritation was short-lived and he slid back into the morass of self-pity. "The same thing's happening again. Started yesterday with rumours and innuendo. Share traders are like lemmings. Somebody's told them what to think, so they've wiped billions off the market valuations..."

Jessica interrupted, protectively stroking his arm with her fingers. "I don't think that's quite what he meant, dear." She glanced at Peter, who nodded encouragement. "Ordinarily we could have ridden out a slump in the share price," she continued. "But we'd used our shares as security for the bank loan, you see."

Suddenly, Peter understood. "So when the share price fell the loan wasn't covered any more?" he said slowly. She nodded. He saw her knuckles whiten as she gripped her husband's shoulder. "There was something in the small print... foreclosure, I think they called it, something like that... of course, when they demanded the money we couldn't pay them back, not at such short notice… we tried, but no other banks would touch us. And… and that's when we found out the bank we'd been dealing with, the one in Liechtenstein, was owned all along by Rodney Hardcastle. But when we asked… begged…" She dried up, her throat working but no words coming out at the vivid memory of humiliation.

"Go on," Peter said, feeling embarrassed. "Please."

"I'm sure you can guess the rest. He took the company from us, our shares, everything. Even the patents on Jonathan's discoveries… he'd advised us to transfer them to the company to boost the share value for the flotation, you see. 'Just business,' he kept saying, 'nothing personal', though it was. Personal, I mean. He enjoyed every minute of it, I could tell. It was as though he'd seen it all coming, though that's impossible, of course."

Perhaps not so impossible, Peter thought, his mind seething with the implications. Sharing his suspicions about Media Associates' role in the affair would only be an added cruelty, though. There had to be some comfort for them, however thin and cold, in blaming their disaster on fate rather than trickery. But if he was right, there would be a final twist.

"What happened after that? I mean, I went to the laboratories and things look pretty prosperous now."

Jessica laughed bitterly. "That's the worst part of it. The bad publicity all died down after a few weeks and the share price bounced right back up. Too late for us, you see, but he was laughing all the way to his Liechtenstein bank. We heard he'd bought most of the rest of the stock, too, while the price was on the floor and then he touted the business around the big pharmaceutical companies we'd been fighting off for years. Zetec Holdings bought him out lock, stock and barrel. God knows how many millions they paid, money that rightfully was ours…"

In the gloom that followed, Peter assured them what they'd told him had helped. He couldn't promise that retribution would be visited on Sir Rodney Hardcastle, but he'd give it his best shot. Maybe one day soon, he said, knowing that for them it was already too late. It wasn't much, but it was all he could offer. When he left, they were clinging to each other, staring desolately into their broken dreams.

***

Sam Garvey was a worried man, though he'd be damned if he'd admit it to Mike Arnold who was sitting in the passenger seat beside him, any more than he'd allowed it show to Sir Rodney Hardcastle and his partners the previous evening. Being head of security at Media Associates wasn't entirely a bowl of cherries. The people he reported to tolerated no excuses and never handed out second chances. Sam's face twisted into a mirthless grin. Deflecting their irate accusations over the farce with Conway had taken some nifty footwork, but ironically it was the fact that Hardcastle himself had approved Conway's photographic project that was the clincher. The old man hadn't been able to wriggle out of that. Sam's expression hardened. Pointing the finger was a dangerous game. Hardcastle's glance at him across the table had been pure poison and the man's vindictiveness was legendary. Whatever credit he may have had in that quarter, he'd used it all up and then some. He shrugged and pushed the thought aside. He wasn't in this for the pension rights and watching his back was second nature anyway. One more rich bastard with a score to settle wasn't going to make much difference in the short term. Except that it meant he couldn't afford any more foul-ups. Which was why he was out here dealing with the mess personally instead of enjoying the bright lights. He grunted irritably.

"You sure we've got the right place, Mike?"

"Escort RS Turbo, just like the man said." Mike held out the powerful night vision binoculars. "See for yourself. Right outside the house. The plates check out, too, registered to Conway's assistant."

Sam pushed the glasses away edgily.

"Yeah, all right, I don't need chapter and verse. He's been in there too sodding long, that's all."

His boss was rattled, Mike thought. He shifted uneasily in his seat. Nobody told him a damn thing, but it was obvious some sort of serious shit had hit the fan. Sam had been like a bear with a sore head ever since they'd found those photographs at Conway's place in Tonbridge. They hadn't looked much, just old documents, some sort of foreign crap. But Sam had reacted like he'd had a red-hot poker shoved up his ass. Anger was okay, though. He could handle Sam's explosive fly-off-the-handle fury; he'd seen it all before. But this was different.

Mike shivered and put the binoculars back to his eyes. He wouldn't want to be in this guy Conway's shoes. The skinny little bastard was smart, he admitted. They still hadn't worked out how he'd escaped the tight security net round the building yesterday. But not smart enough to know that credit cards could be traced. Perhaps he didn't know what he was up against, or simply didn't realise that in these days of electronic banking using plastic was like sticking up a big sign saying 'here I am'. If you had access to the right databases, that is. He thought of the banks of computer screens in the Media Associates' control room and shivered again. Access was no problem, not when half the movers and shakers in London were on the payroll. You couldn't take a leak these days without it showing up on a computer somewhere and they'd picked up the hotel charge within minutes of Conway checking out. The spotty young waiter at the Grand who was now fifty quid richer had done the rest, that and a quick phone call to check out these Holt people.

Mike stiffened suddenly. "He's coming out," he said. "Do you want to take him now? Could get a bit messy, mind," he added, doubt creeping into his voice. "He's got his mate sitting there in the car."

"Not here," Sam snapped. "We're going to have to take care of the Holts as well, now. Any trouble and some nosy bastard might put two and two together."

"Where then?"

"They'll have to hole up for the night soon, won't they? Somewhere quiet and out of the way, with a bit of luck." He chuckled maliciously. "Somewhere safe, where they think we'll never find them in a million years."

A few minutes later the chuckle was a distant memory as Sam wrestled, cursing, to keep control of the speeding Jaguar on the twisting country road. The wash of the Escort's headlights on the hedgerows was drawing away again. The bastard was driving like a maniac. At this rate they'd lose him and that was one thing he couldn't afford to let happen. He gritted his teeth and eased his right foot further towards the floor. With any luck they'd fucking kill themselves and save him the trouble. The heavy car twitched as the rear tyres lost adhesion for a second and he felt his heart pound. That's if he didn't kill himself first, he thought. His knuckles whitened on the wheel and he narrowed his concentration onto the thin ribbon of tarmac and the cats-eyes flashing hypnotically as they whipped towards him out of the darkness.

***

Peter Conway was once again hanging for dear life onto the strap above the passenger door and regretting his decision to entrust himself to Jack Howson's tender mercies. His pleas to take it easy had fallen on deaf ears. The smile on his companion's face told its own story. Incredibly, Jack was actually enjoying himself, caressing the steering wheel one-handed while he worked the gears like a rally driver. Relax, he'd said, this is fun! Don't fight it. Let the bucket seat take the strain, that's what it's designed for. Peter reached across with his right hand and cinched his seatbelt even tighter. Anything had to be better than the constant wrenching of his arm muscles and the incipient cramp in his bloodless fingers. He tentatively let go of the strap and felt the seat grip him round hips and neck as he pushed himself deeper into it with his feet.

The change was instantaneous and reassuring. Now that he was no longer fighting the motion of the car, the sensation of breakneck speed and imminent disaster diminished. At least so long as he kept his eyes averted from the perils ahead. They strayed to the wing mirror instead and Peter contemplated the road unwinding behind. They weren't the only lunatics out tonight, he saw with surprise. Another pair of powerful headlights was scything through the blackness about half a mile back. He watched with mild curiosity as they lurched across the landscape, now bright, now vanishing for a moment as hedges and hollows intervened, but neither gaining nor dropping back. Must be in a hell of a hurry, he thought, to be keeping pace like that.

"You seen those lights behind us, Jack?" he said thoughtfully.

"Yeah, been there quite a while. Don't worry, though," he said smugly, "there's no way anyone's going to catch up with us in this baby."

"Slow down a minute, will you?"

"Aw, come on. I thought you'd given up on that. I told you, just relax. Speed is what life's all about."

"No, I mean it. I want to check something out."

"You're a real pain," Jack grumbled. He reluctantly lifted his foot slightly and the roar of the turbocharger dropped a few decibels. "Check what out?"

Peter kept his eyes on the mirror and ignored Jack's question. The pursuing headlights surged towards them. Then his heart skipped a beat as they checked and dropped back.

"Bugger."

Jack glanced sharply across at him. "What's up?"

"I think maybe we're being followed."

"No way. That's impossible."

"See for yourself. Those lights back there. They were going like a bat out of hell till we slowed down. Now they've slowed down too."

"You're being paranoid. They've probably had a bit of a skid or something, scared themselves. It's a tricky road, this."

"OK, clever Dick. Crank it up again and let's see. Gradually, though. If they're following us, I don't want them to know we've spotted it."

Five minutes later, Jack grunted in annoyance.

"You've made your point. The buggers are still there. What the hell do we do now?"

"Christ knows. You can bet they're not following us for fun, though." Peter felt his guts twist into an uncomfortable knot. "If they've worked out I've been talking with the Holts, they'll throw everything they've got at us."

Jack absorbed the judgement without noticeable concern.

"I hate to tell you this," he said quietly, "but we're going to have to stop for petrol soon."

"Good. Pull in at the next service station."

"What do you mean, good?" He shot Peter a sharp glance of disapproval. "We stop and it gives them the chance they're looking for."

"I don't reckon so." Peter grinned briefly at the puzzled expression on Jack's face and then relented.

"Not among the bright lights," he added, "They seem to specialise in accidents. It's hard to do that with witnesses around. Besides, I need time to think."

Jack's brow cleared.

"Right. I'll pull in up there, then." He pointed through the windscreen at a glowing green BP sign that had just come into view at the end of a long straight.

There were a couple of other cars and a minibus on the well-lit forecourt, Peter saw with relief as they pulled to a halt alongside a self-service pump. A queue of old-age pensioners, presumably from the minibus, was lined up waiting to use the solitary toilet and a few others were milling about aimlessly inside the shop. It wasn't likely that his pursuers would try anything in front of that sort of audience. He leaned on the roof of the car, watching the road from the corner of his eye while Jack unscrewed the fuel cap. The approaching headlights were dazzling, but he saw a momentary flash of red reflecting off the road behind. An instinctive dab on the brakes, just as you'd expect when they realised he'd stopped. Then the slight surge of acceleration as the decision was made to go past. Peter nodded to himself. It was what he'd have done in their shoes. All they had to do now was park up out of sight, then fall in again behind as their supposedly unsuspecting quarry caught up.

The whir of the pump stopped as Jack crammed the nozzle back into its holster.

"I'll get this," Peter said without turning round. "You wait in the car."

"OK. Do you think that was them, just now, going past?"

"Yes."

"Well, then, why don't we just take off in the other direction? I can lose them for sure if I really put my foot down."

Peter shuddered at the prospect. "I doubt if they're dumb enough to fall for that, they'll be watching for it. Anyway, the most important issue is how the hell they found us in the first place. Until we figure that out, we've got to assume they can do it again even if we give them the slip now."

"Well I'm damn sure I wasn't followed to Hastings this morning," Jack said defensively. "Maybe it was that bloke you were talking to at Media Associates? He'd have had a right grilling after you disappeared, so they'd know you'd talked about the Holt place. Maybe they just put two and two together."

"Hm." Peter frowned doubtfully. "Bloody long shot, that. We talked about a lot of things. I could have gone anywhere and they couldn't cover every possibility on the off-chance."

Jack shrugged. "Beats me, then."

"Me too." Peter reached for his wallet. "I'll go and settle up for the petrol. Want anything from the shop?"

"I could murder a can of coke and a sandwich. Ham if they've got it."

Peter piled his purchases on the counter and wondered how Jack could possibly feel hungry at a time like this. His stomach churned at the mere thought and he struggled to suppress his queasiness as he offered his Visa card to the bored-looking attendant. "Pump number five," he said and tapped his fingers idly on the counter as the laser bar code scanner beeped up the item descriptions and prices.

"That's thirty-five pounds twenty pence altogether."

An expert flick of the wrist sent the card through the EPOS scanner and after a short pause the printer started rattling and a tongue of paper emerged detailing the transaction. An indifferent finger pointed to the dotted line. Eye contact, it seemed, was not part of the job description.

"Sign here."

So bloody simple, Peter mused. A few million quid's worth of electronic wizardry, a bit of plastic and magnetic tape and Jack's ham sandwich was immortalised in bits and bytes on some computer. As a result, stocks would be replenished, money moved about and God knew what else, all without any further intervention. It was scary when you thought about it. He grabbed his purchases and screwed up the obligatory receipt, looking for the nearest waste bin. The scraps of paper always irritated him, but he never quite had the bottle to walk away without taking them. Surely, though, nobody ever had any use for all that printed detail, the evidence that big brother was patiently recording your every move.

Hm. Something nagged at him. He opened his hand and stared at the crumpled receipt. Suddenly, he laughed out loud, earning puzzled looks as he hurried past the remaining few pensioners who were straggling out towards their bus. Peter ignored them and yanked open the car door, waving his credit card in Jack's face. "I reckon this is how they found me," he said excitedly. "I paid the bill at the Grand with it."

"So what? I don't see what that's got to do with

anything."

"No, listen. I've just realised. When you use a credit card the details go straight to a computer, right? Look," he held out the crumpled debit slip, "it's all there - date, place, time, card number. Suppose they could access the Visa database? They'd know exactly where I was within seconds of the card being swiped. It wouldn't be hard then to make the connection with Holt Biotechnology like you said."

"Christ Almighty. Can they do that?"

"I don't see why not. It'd take money, expertise and the right contacts, but this lot have got all those in spades. But let's get moving. I think I've figured out how to give them the slip..."

The tyres squealed as Jack took the first sharp bend a fraction too fast and the lights of the service station vanished behind them, cut off by the dense trees that suddenly crowded in on either side. Peter was still talking intently, but struggling to make himself heard above the rising whine of the turbocharger. The road here was eerily deserted, the bare winter branches reaching out for them like claws in the light of the headlamps before vanishing again into the blackness. Not total blackness, Peter registered from the corner of his eye. A light was flashing feebly from the undergrowth just ahead, like a hand-held torch. Strange. The wash of the headlights dimly picked out a figure leaning on the roof of a large black saloon car, pointing something at them. Another flash. Christ. Not a torch...

"The bastards are shooting..."

Peter's shout was drowned by the explosive noise of a

tyre bursting. A kaleidoscope of sensations engulfed him, each sharp and distinct, yet merging like the frames of a slow-motion film. The wet, slapping sound of shredded rubber flogging the road. A lurching, sliding, high-speed skid. Jack's hands frantically seesawing the steering wheel. A despairing grunt of failure and an earthquake transition from tarmac to trees. Branches reaching, slashing and the gritty texture of shattered safety glass. Then blackness. Silence.

It seemed like forever before he realised that it wasn't death. Not even unconsciousness. Just darkness.

"Jack?" he whispered.

"Yeah." The reply was slow in coming and sounded like a distant sigh.

"You all right?"

"Jesus." Peter heard a brief rustle of movement. "Yes." The voice was firmer this time. "I think so. Everything still seems to be attached in roughly the right place, anyway. You?"

Peter stretched his arms and legs and flexed his neck. Plenty of bruises, he judged, but basically functional.

"Yes. Bloody miracle we didn't hit a tree."

Silence descended again. He should be moving, Peter knew, but his brain felt like it was stuffed with cotton wool. A sharp tang of petrol assaulted his nose. If the freshly filled tank had gone, one spark meant incineration. Somehow, it didn't seem important, as though he was a mere spectator. Move, his brain insisted. They shot out the goddamned tyre and they'll be coming to finish the job. Get out, now. Run.

His right hand moved jerkily to release the seat belt

buckle and he turned his head to bully Jack into doing the same. Night suddenly turned to day. He craned his head further round and saw the powerful beams of twin headlights shining through the intact rear window. Through slitted eyes he made out a shadowy black figure scurrying purposefully down the track the Escort had torn through the undergrowth. Peter let his head drop in despair. If there'd been any chance to escape, it had just evaporated.

Chapter 14

"Shit."

The fury in Sam Garvey's voice hung quivering in the air as he lowered the binoculars from his eyes and ground his teeth in frustration. The arrival of a minibus on the scene at the critical moment was sheer bad luck, though even so he'd had every reason to suppose that the ferocity of the crash would have done the job. But the black and green picture in the image intensifier told a different story. There was no mistaking the two stumbling figures being helped out of the trees into the back of the crowded bus and there wasn't a damn thing he could do about it, short of massacring a bunch of what looked like elderly tourists. He fingered his automatic pistol and fought back the temptation. A fatal accident was one thing. A nationwide hue and cry after a mass murderer, with all the attendant publicity, was something else entirely.

"What's wrong?" Mike said, reacting nervously to the venom in his companion's voice and the dangerous twitching of the gun in Sam's hand.

"Looks like the bastards have come out of it without a scratch."

"You're kidding." Mike said incredulously. "After a smash like that? It's fucking impossible."

"See for yourself if you don't believe me." Sam tossed the binoculars across the bonnet.

"What now, then?"

"What do you sodding well think? We try again, that's

what. Their luck can't last forever. Get in the car."

Twenty minutes later they watched in silence as the minibus swung between ornate stone pillars and chugged up a gravelled drive. Farnsham Court hotel looked every inch a class establishment, not one of the great country houses but nevertheless an architectural gem of honeyed stone and scrambling creepers. A uniformed porter marshalled the baggage while the occupants of the minibus straggled up the marble steps into the foyer. The place was lit like a film set and at this distance Sam didn't need the binoculars to spot his quarry. Peter Conway's silhouette was unmistakeable as he limped through the doorway, camera bag slung carelessly over one shoulder. The question was, what would he do next? Sam glanced at his watch. It was getting late. Shaken up from the crash, unaware he'd been followed and without transport, it was a near certainty that he'd call it quits and stay. Sam grinned wolfishly. At least Conway's last night would be a comfortable one. His luck had earned him that much.

"Out you get, Mike," he said. "I figure he'll be checking in. Give it fifteen minutes, then go in and have a drink. Take your chance to find out quietly which rooms they've put him and his mate in."

"Where will you be?"

"I'll park just down the road and keep an eye on things in case they decide to make a run for it. I don't think it's likely, but don't hang about in there, alright?"

"Suppose he calls the cops to report the crash?"

"You see the police, get the hell out, fast. But I don't see why he should. So far as he knows it was just a blown tyre, nobody else involved. If he wants anybody, it'll be the local garage for a recovery truck is my guess."

A lay-by a few yards further on provided a decent vantage point and Sam Garvey killed the lights, settling down to wait. Traffic on this minor road was light and nothing else was moving. After a while, he saw Mike Arnold make his way up the drive and disappear inside. Sam's pulse quickened momentarily when a small white van bearing the hotel logo appeared from the back of the building, but the binoculars showed nothing alarming. Just an employee, alone, off on some errand. Sam stretched and yawned. He'd forgotten how boring this kind of work in the field could be and to take his mind off it he began to run through his options.

He picked up the binoculars again and started a careful survey of the property. The car park was nearly empty. That figured, given the time of year. Few guests and minimum staffing meant easy entry and low risk of detection. Not from the front, though. That was too exposed even if the lights were doused later on and the creepers covering it made for uncertain grip when climbing. His gaze moved on, following the line of first floor windows to the twin gable end. It was heavily shadowed and a solid-looking drainpipe ran from the central gulley, conveniently close to a balcony outside a large sash window. So far, so good, he thought. That would be his way in, but what then? Old folk were often light sleepers. The presence of those pensioners ruled out breaking into the room and dealing with Conway directly, much as he'd like to get his hands personally round the little bastard's throat.

The risk of some sort of noisy struggle was too great, especially with two of them to deal with. It had to be something indirect, then. He let his imagination wander. It would be difficult to engineer a convincing accident. Falling out the window, breaking their necks down the stairs, that sort of thing. Again, too noisy. And too suspicious. How often did two people have the same accident at the same time? Unless it was part of something else, like a car crash or an explosion. A gas explosion, perhaps? He shook his head. Out here in the sticks it was unlikely the place was on mains gas and you never saw gas appliances in hotel bedrooms anyway. A fire, then? That was more like it. Hotel fires were common enough. And if a blaze in the room didn't do the job, the ensuing chaos would provide ample cover for a discreet accident or two if necessary. Sam Garvey smiled. A spot of arson was always exciting and it was a while since he'd had the chance. It would be a gratifying end to a lousy day.

A tap on the car window made him jump. Mike had crept up on him unnoticed and he cursed as he released the door lock.

"You asleep in here, or what?" Mike said accusingly as he slid into the passenger seat.

"Watch your lip," Sam growled. "There's bugger all been going on my end. How about you? You smell like a goddam brewery."

"Just local colour. I couldn't go in for a drink and not have one, could I?"

"You were supposed to be finding out what's happening, not guzzling beer."

"Get stuffed," Mike retorted. "You're just jealous.

Anyway, you were right. They've checked in for the night. Went straight upstairs. And get this, they're sharing a room. Number fifteen, on the first floor. The bar staff were having a right giggle, reckoned they were a couple of poofters."

Sam scratched his head. "I didn't reckon them for that."

"Me neither. Makes it easier for us, though. Have you figured out how to take them yet?"

"I've got a few ideas, yeah. Have to wait till everyone's tucked in and fast asleep, though. Meantime, you can tell me about the layout in there..."

***

A faint scuffling disturbed the deep silence of the small hours as a black-clad figure swung itself onto the small first floor balcony. There was a click as the blade of his knife flipped back the catch of the sash window and Sam Garvey eased it open, sliding athletically through. A dimly lit corridor stretched out in front of him and he moved down it silently, like a cat. He froze at a sudden creak of protest from a warped floorboard. Nothing stirred and he lifted his foot carefully to step around the danger area. Outside room fifteen, he knelt down, cautiously and put his ear to the door.

The silence was reassuring and he reached into the poacher's pocket of his jacket. The thin plastic soft-drink bottle, salvaged from the litterbin in the lay-by, was slightly damp where petrol was leaking from the crude duct-tape joint fixing a short length of rubber tubing in place of the cap. No matter. It would last long enough to get the job done. He gently slid the tube under the bottom of the door, inverted the bottle and squeezed once, twice, three times to expel a litre of petrol into the room. The acrid fumes made his eyes water. If anybody was awake in there it would be having the same effect, he knew and his movements became hurried. The empty bottle and tube were tucked away and a match flared. Petrol vapour ignited with a whoosh. Blue and yellow flames danced briefly, casting reflections off the walls. He stood for a moment, watching, as they reached through the gap at the foot of the door, greedy for the sustenance that lay beyond. Satisfied, he melted silently back down the corridor, skirting the loose floorboard and eased himself back out onto the balcony.

Crouching there, invisible against the darkness, he watched gentle wisps of smoke drift down the corridor like a spider's web and heard the sudden urgent clanging of the fire alarm as smoke detectors triggered. Doors opened and sleepy heads peered out, followed by shouts and the sight of a panicky, pyjama-clad exodus. But number fifteen stayed firmly shut. He waited patiently until he saw the paint on the outside of the door begin to blister and smoke. Inside, it would be an inferno and nobody was coming out of there now. The sound of a distant siren racing towards the scene carried through the deepening roar of the fire digging its way deeper into the fabric of the building. Time to go. His teeth gleamed whitely in the contented smile of a job well done as he slid soundlessly over the balcony rail, reached for the conveniently placed drainpipe and disappeared into the night.

Peter Conway woke. The light in his eyes was blinding and he was racked with pain. He groaned, shifting his head muzzily out of the shaft of sunlight streaming through the East-facing window. He felt as though he'd been beaten all over with a pickaxe handle and despite the dead weight of tiredness, further sleep was impossible. Throwing back the sheets, he squinted morosely at the blue, black and yellow blotches of the ripening bruises covering his body, each of which was shouting its individual message of protest at him. It could have been a lot worse, he thought philosophically, hobbling gingerly towards the bathroom in his underpants. He could be dead.

A steaming bath eased the worst of his aches and pains, but the sight of the two-day stubble sprouting on his chin reminded him of some urgent practicalities. Apart from the immediate lack of a razor, there was the unsavoury prospect of cramming his clean body back into unwashed clothes. Trailing into the kitchen with a towel round his waist and gagging for a hot drink, he discovered some further essential additions to the shopping list. The fridge was switched off and empty and the cupboards were bare of coffee or any other makings of a potential breakfast.

He fought to suppress his irritation, which smacked of ingratitude. Last night, he'd been at his wits' end for somewhere to go, short of cash after bribing the porter to smuggle them to the nearest railway station in the back of the hotel van and fearful of using his all-too-traceable credit card. God knows what had made him think of the converted warehouse at St. Katherine's Dock and the furnished flats he'd been commissioned to photograph for the developer, Viscount Stanfield. But he'd known Billy Stanfield for a long time and Peter knew that the much-feared bark of the successful entrepreneur disguised a generous nature. And so it had proved. There had been no 'ifs' or 'buts' when he phoned his stammering request. 'Be my guest, old chap,' Billy had said immediately, as though desperate calls from beleaguered friends were commonplace. 'There's several flats still empty. I'll call the security people, they'll give you the keys to one when you get there.' He cut off Peter's thanks and attempted explanations. 'Don't worry about that now. Sounds as if you've got enough on your plate for the moment. I'll drop by in the morning in case there's anything else you need. You can tell me all about it then.'

As if on cue, there was a sharp knock on the door. The rotund figure of Billy Stanfield stood there, eyes twinkling behind his heavy-rimmed spectacles and his Savile Row suit straining as usual to contain his exuberant waistline.

"Coffee and croissants," he said triumphantly, holding up two brown paper carrier bags. "I thought you might be in need." The smile faded from his face as he took in Peter's battered appearance. "Christ, old boy, you've been in the wars, haven't you?"

"It's a long story. Great to see you, though and I'd kill for some of that coffee. Come in."

Jack was stirring in the other room and Peter took him a cup of coffee before settling down on the living room sofa and diving into the croissants. The last food he'd had sight of had been that ill-fated ham sandwich the previous night and he was starving. The first barely touched the sides and he was well into the second when a discreet cough made him look up.

"Sorry, Billy, I'm being an absolute pig," he apologised, proffering the bag across the table. "I've not eaten since I can't remember when. You want one?"

"No thanks, you carry on. I've already eaten. But look, Peter, have you seen the breakfast TV news this morning? You'd better tell me exactly what I've got myself into here."

There was iron in the voice all of a sudden and Peter stopped in mid-bite. Friend in need or not, it was a salutary reminder that Billy was nobody's fool and hadn't made his millions by accident, despite the advantages of inheriting a title.

"TV? No, why?"

"Are you telling me you don't know the police are looking for you?"

"Police?" Peter said in amazement. "Christ, no, what would they want with me? Is it about the car going off the road? That's not the sort of thing TV reporters would get involved with, surely." Unless, Peter realised with a start, someone had spotted bullet holes.

"I don't know about a car crash," Billy said suspiciously, his instincts aroused by the shifty look that had flashed across Peter's face. "All I know is that some exclusive country hotel was burned to the ground last night. Arson, they reckon. That and the fact that the police are looking for a certain Peter Conway and his companion," he jerked a thumb in the direction of the bathroom where Jack was splashing noisily in the tub, "presumably your pal in there, to help them with their enquiries into the said incident. Luckily, it seems nobody was killed, otherwise I might be aiding and abetting a couple of murderers. I don't much appreciate being put in that position."

The blood drained from Peter's face and Billy Stanfield's confidence in his own judgement wavered uncharacteristically. He'd been certain that Peter wasn't the sort to do anything criminal, otherwise he'd already have called the police and had done with it. He wanted no truck with arsonists and wasn't about to put his good name on the line by getting involved some sordid little conspiracy. On the other hand, he wasn't one to abandon friends easily and his instincts about people were rarely wrong. You didn't survive long in business otherwise. He weighed Peter Conway's reactions carefully. Shock and surprise, those were plain. Knowledge, too. Guilt, though…? Perhaps not.

Peter squirmed under the accusing stare of icy blue eyes, from which all traces of camaraderie had vanished. This was a side of his friend he'd not seen before, the tough, calculating man of the world and it wasn't a pleasant feeling to be in the spotlight of such critical appraisal.

"Jesus, you don't think that I'd have anything to do with something like that, do you?"

"I wouldn't take up Poker if I were you," Billy said coldly. "You haven't got the talent to carry off a bluff."

"Er… I…," Peter stuttered unhappily. Sod it, he thought. What was he hesitating for? He was already well out of his depth and could sure as hell use some heavyweight help, no pun intended. But there was no telling how far the rot had spread, how many of the great and the good in the city were involved. Billy moved in the same circles as Hardcastle, might be part of it. On the other hand, Billy knew how the city and the markets worked. If he could be persuaded to lend a hand, his knowledge and contacts would be invaluable. Peter's head started to ache. He just didn't know who to trust any more.

Billy Stanfield read the inner conflict on Peter's face and was intrigued. He unfolded his arms from his chest and leaned forward with a glimmer of a smile.

"Come on, Peter, I'm not asking the earth. Just give me one good reason why I shouldn't turn you over to the police. I've already gone out on a limb for you, I think I'm entitled to that much."

Peter returned the smile tentatively. "I suppose so," he said. "I was at Farnsham Court last night. You've already guessed that. But it was fine when I left."

"Can you prove that?"

"Yes, I think so. It depends when the fire started. Did they say on the TV report?"

"Early hours of the morning, I think they said."

"Well, then. We'd already left when I phoned you about the flat. That must have been what, nine o'clock? The hotel porter took us to the station in his van, he can testify to that. Oh and we got here about eleven. The security people downstairs can tell you when we picked up the keys."

"So why are the police after you?"

Peter laughed bitterly. "My guess is because the fire

started in the room we were supposed to be occupying."

"Steady on old boy." Billy leaned back in his chair with a frown and clasped his arms behind his head. "How do you know that if you weren't there?"

"Easy. It's not the first time someone's tried to kill me in the last week or so."

"Kill you?" For the first time Billy was genuinely shaken. "What the hell are you talking about?"

"It's a long story. Are you sure you want to know? You might end up in the same boat as me."

"You bet I want to know."

Peter shrugged. There was armour plate just underneath Billy's pink-cheeked, disarmingly frivolous exterior and he could use a friend right now.

"On your own head and all that, then," he said. "Perhaps you can make more sense of it all than I can. I got tangled up in it when my father died, but the real story seems to have started long before that…"

***

While Peter talked, net curtains were twitching fifty-odd miles away near Brighton. A minor drama was unfolding in Windsor Close and Jessica Holt wondered what on earth was going on. Two grey vans marked 'Transco' were parked up, one at each end of the small cul-de-sac. The noise that had attracted her attention seemed to emanate from an overalled figure at the entrance to the close, who had just finished banging in metal posts either side of the road and was now stringing red plastic tape between them to block it off. Several other men were pulling equipment of some sort from the back of the vans. Their air of urgency piqued her curiosity. Workmen rarely displayed such energy and purposefulness these days. Nor were they usually so smartly turned out in clean grey overalls and peaked, baseball-style caps. They fanned out along the street, each with a bulky box slung over their shoulder on a strap and waving some sort of long metal wand. It looked as though they were spraying something, but that couldn't be right, surely. One of them started to head in her direction and she let the curtain fall, moving back from the window. She felt a bit silly, but she didn't want to be caught staring, it didn't seem quite proper.

Jonathan looked up from the morning paper and wondered aloud what was going on. She was about to explain when the front doorbell rang, making her jump. A burly man was standing there, anonymous in his cloak of officialdom. A hint of a practiced smile was barely visible under the peak of the cap shading his face.

"Morning, Ma'am," he said. There was a brief flash of an identity card, which she barely had time to register before he slipped it back into his pocket. "Sorry to trouble you. I'm from Transco. We've had a report of a gas leak in the vicinity."

Jessica's hand flew to her mouth. "Oh, Lord," she said nervously. "Is it dangerous? We've not smelt anything here."

"Nothing to worry about, Ma'am," he said reassuringly. "It's probably nothing, but we've got a legal duty to check it out."

"Yes, of course. Er... what do you need to do?"

"Just give your place a quick once over with this here sniffer," he waggled the metal rod in his hand for emphasis, "and check your appliances. It won't take a jiffy, we're doing all the houses down here as a precaution."

Jessica craned her neck over his shoulder and saw the same conversation being replayed at front doors all down Windsor Close.

"You'd better come in, then," she said, reassured.

"Thanks. If you can just show me where your meter and the main appliances are?"

"The meter's in the garage. This way." She led the way down the narrow, carpeted hall to the spotless kitchen and pointed to the connecting door to the garage. "Just through there, on the right."

He vanished, emerging a few minutes later shaking his head and clipping the sensor rod back to his belt.

"All clear in there. Where's the central heating boiler?"

"Upstairs in the airing cupboard. First on the left at the top of the stairs."

"I'll have a look at that, then. What about gas fires?"

"Just the one in the living room."

"Right, I'll start upstairs. I'll just have to take off the casing and check the burner, to make sure, like. Don't want to risk missing anything, do we?"

"I'd best leave you to it. Would you like a cup of tea?"

"That's very kind. Milk, no sugar, please."

It took Sam Garvey less than a minute to remove the boiler covers, exposing the flue pipe and burners. By the time the tea arrived he'd made the necessary adjustments and was retightening the last of the screws. "Ta very much," he said appreciatively, taking the mug from Jessica's hand. "Just the job. No problems here. I'll come down and have a quick look at your fire, then I'll be out of your way."

Ten minutes later, Sam Garvey cast a searching glance around Windsor Close before climbing into the waiting van. Good. Everything was as they'd found it.

"No problems your end?" he asked Mike Arnold as he settled into his seat.

"No. Like falling off a log. You?"

"All done. I reckon a couple of hours with the heating going should finish the job nicely and the timer's set to come on at six. Let's get out of here."

"You sure this time?"

Sam scowled. The fiasco last night rankled and he still hadn't worked out how Conway had given them the slip. It was the second time the slippery little bastard had vanished into thin air. To cap it all, he seemed to have stopped using his plastic. If he'd figured that one out, it would be the devil's own job to track him down. But at least the Holts were taken care of and there'd be no comebacks. Carbon Monoxide poisoning from faulty gas burners and blocked flues was commonplace enough and there'd be no evidence of anything other than poor maintenance.

"Shut your face and drive," he snarled. "We've still got work to do."

Chapter 15

Viscount Stanfield was pacing up and down the expensive Axminster carpet with a vigour that bade fair to leave permanent scars. Peter had expected scepticism. Instead, he was being subjected to a fierce interrogation. It was like sitting beside a dynamo sparking as it ran close to overload and he could almost taste the tension in the air.

"You must have some idea how they do it," Billy snapped. "You're saying their operation goes well beyond normal PR and media management techniques."

"They can target a campaign like a bloody cruise missile, judging by what the Holts told me. But as to exactly how," Peter shrugged and shook his head, "your guess is as good as mine. I'm a photographer, not a shrink."

"Don't give me that bullshit. You've read this Kaiserhof stuff, seen how these people put it together. Tell me what you think."

"I can only guess, really. But OK, I reckon it this way. Suppose the brain is like a computer. Everybody gets more or less the same model, all wired up and ready to go. The trouble is, though, there's no instruction manual, so we all learn to bash away by trial and error. It works, after a fashion, but normally we all come up with different results because we're pushing different buttons and putting in a lot of random data."

"I don't follow. Everybody's got the same five senses,

we all gather the same information about the world around us. That's not random."

"I don't think it works like that. We all interpret things differently."

"Precisely. That's why your argument doesn't stand up. It's perfectly obvious that our minds don't all work the same way."

"I agree we don't use them the same way. But that's not the point."

"Go on."

"Take photography, for instance. You're into that, like me. Why is it that we can look at something and see a perfect photograph, but most people can't?"

"I've never thought about it."

"Well, there's nothing special about our eyes, is there? So we must be using the information differently."

"I suppose," Billy said impatiently. "But so what?"

"What if everybody's got this program we call photography in their brain, but only a few of us have discovered, by chance, how to use it?"

"Well then you'd better keep your mouth shut about it, or everybody would be David Bailey and you'd be out of a job. Life isn't like that, though, is it?"

"You're still missing the point," Peter said quietly. "I think we do all have the same mental programs and these guys have figured out how they work. All you've got to do then is arrange the input in the right way and you can get whatever result you want. Feed the same instructions into the same program on a million different computers and you'll get the same answer from them all."

"Jesus." Billy's jaw dropped and there was a

momentary silence. "Is that what you think they're doing?"

"I think that's what 'spin' is all about, yes," Peter nodded. "It's about organising information and presenting it in a way that pushes the right buttons. The key is knowing for sure which buttons produce the results you want."

Billy heard unspoken reservations in Peter's voice and pounced. "But you don't think that's all there is to it, do you?"

"I'm scared it might not be," Peter admitted reluctantly.

"Go on, spit it out."

"What really terrifies me is taking the analogy one step further. The thing about computers is, if you know how they work at the technical level you can change the programming."

"How do you mean?"

"I mean you can write new programs, or modify the existing ones. It's easy when you know how. You can make a computer do almost anything if you load up the right software."

Billy Stanfield whistled under his breath. "If you could do that to people's minds..."

"Exactly. Then you'd really have a secret that was worth killing to protect."

"But..." His voice tailed away as he considered the implications. "Dear Lord, the power..." He glanced sideways at Peter and forced himself back down to earth. "You're right, of course. If there's even the remotest possibility that what you suspect is true, it must be stopped. How can I help?"

"There are two things I need to get a handle on," Peter

said, thinking rapidly. "First, am I right in thinking the financial markets are vulnerable to spin, like politics? Second, if they are, I need to know whether it's illegal to manipulate share prices in that way."

"Dear me," Billy said, shaking his head in mock reproof, "you're not suggesting these people are stealing our money as well as our free will, surely?"

"How else can you explain what happened to Holt Biotechnology? It can't have been coincidence."

"It could have been, dear boy, it could have been. Strange things happen in the city and your man wouldn't be the first to lose his shirt there."

"Well I don't think so," Peter said doggedly. "You must know someone, a stockbroker or whatever, I could talk to. Someone who could fill me in on how a scam like that might work."

Viscount Stanfield smiled a trifle condescendingly. "I can do better than that, I think. Roger Collins runs my own investment management company. He's one of the best brains in the business, even if I do say it myself."

"That's great. When can I talk to him?"

"My chauffeur's downstairs, probably bored to tears. I dare say we could prevail on him to take us now, if you like. I'm overdue to pay Roger a visit in any case."

Peter accepted the offer with alacrity and after a hurried explanation to Jack he followed Billy Stanfield down in the lift. The drive to Cannon Street took only a few minutes, barely enough time to appreciate the pleasures of travel in a Rolls-Royce and nowhere near long enough for Peter to organise his thoughts, but he'd asked for help and could hardly complain about the speed of its delivery. Feeling breathless, he followed as Billy bounded up the steps and through the doors, conscious of the stir that their arrival was causing. The scenario at reception reminded Peter briefly of Sir Rodney's visit to Media Associates, except that this time he was at the centre of the whirlwind instead of a mere observer. There was the same deferential nervousness, the same bustle of underlings smoothing the path. It was an intensely flattering experience that he could easily get used to, Peter thought, as they were whisked to the boardroom. Coffee appeared as if by magic. Spode china cups and saucers, he noted approvingly, with matching milk jug and sugar bowl on a silver tray. No common or garden disposable plastic or chipped mugs to mar the elegance of the vast mahogany table and padded leather chairs.

***

The door would have crashed against the wall if the spring-loaded brass door closer fitted to the frame had not smoothly arrested it, but even so the suddenness with which it flew open nearly made Peter spill his coffee. He looked up to see a stocky man in shirtsleeves marching in wearing an angry expression, the red of his face clashing uncomfortably with the lurid maroon of his braces. The newcomer stopped, hands on hips, in front of them and looked accusingly across the table.

"This is most inconvenient, Billy," he said without preamble, radiating ill humour. "I told you on the phone, I've got a bit of a crisis."

"Hello Roger," Viscount Stanfield said imperturbably. "I'm sure your team can manage without you for a few minutes. Peter, this is Roger Collins. Roger, meet Peter Conway. He's got a few questions about how the markets work and I'd like you to take care of him for me."

"What sort of questions?"

"Oh, I don't know," Billy waved his hand airily. "Anything he wants. I've told him you're the best in the business." He stood up and headed for the door. "I'll leave the two of you to sort it out while I run through the latest financials with the accountants. Peter, you can find your own way home when you've finished, I expect?"

"Yes of course. Thanks for your help."

There was an uncomfortable silence as the door closed behind him and the two men took stock of each other. Roger Collins looked to Peter as though he was bristling with reservations and not just about being dragged away from whatever crisis was brewing back in his office. He was also broadcasting signs of prolonged stress, red-rimmed eyes moving restlessly in his sallow face, hands fidgeting at the wide braces. On the surface he seemed to be in his middle thirties, but few lasted that long in the front line in the city and at least ten years of that was most likely down to sheer pressure. Peter knew how he felt and ventured a wry grin at the thought that after the last few days his own appearance was probably pretty similar.

"I'm sorry I've been dumped on you like this," he said apologetically. "I'm sure you're extremely busy."

"Yeah, well, can't be helped." A reluctant smile

appeared. "When His Nibs says jump, we jump, you know." The smile broadened revealing an unsuspected boyish charm and Peter revised his estimate of Roger's age further downwards. "Truth is, it's a kind of game we play. I don't want him thinking he can jerk me around too easily."

"Mm," Peter said. "He can be a bit overpowering once you've scratched the surface. Must be those aristocratic genes, I suppose."

"So how come he's doing you favours?"

"We're friends, that's all. We're both interested in photography, that's how we got together in the first place."

Roger narrowed his eyes and looked quizzically at Peter.

"I thought you were a writer. He told me on the phone you wanted some help researching a plot for a novel."

"Er... yes," Peter said uncomfortably, wondering how aspiring young writers were supposed to operate. It had seemed like a good cover story in the car on the way over. Now he wasn't so sure.

"I don't recall reading any of your stuff. What sort of thing do you write?"

"So far mainly articles and short stories," Peter lied fluently. It was a skill in which he was becoming disturbingly adept and he wriggled uncomfortably at the thought. "This will be my first full length novel."

"Rather you than me, old son," Roger laughed. "I've heard that getting a book published is like trying to sell snow to the Eskimos. You'd have a better chance of fame and fortune putting a quid on the national lottery."

"So would you, I reckon, the way the stock market fluctuates," Peter said pointedly

"That's different." Roger tapped the side of his nose and gave a knowing wink. " Anyway, what's it about, then, this book of yours?"

"It's about spin-doctors and what might happen if we lose the ability to distinguish between spin and reality."

"Mm," Roger said doubtfully. "Sounds a bit far-fetched. How do you think I can help?"

"Well, it seems to me that the financial markets are highly dependent on perception. Confidence, I suppose you'd call it. My theory is that if you could create or undermine that confidence at will, I mean with certainty, then you'd be able to manipulate the market as you choose. If you can do that, you've got the power to do almost anything."

"What, get mega-rich, you mean?"

"Yeah, if you want. Or put people out of business, wreck them financially, you name it."

Roger leaned back in his chair, stuck his thumbs under his braces and twanged them against his chest. "You don't have any idea how these things work, do you?" he said with a hint of scorn. "That's crap."

"I don't see why. A couple of journalists got fired recently for using their financial column to push shares they'd bought in advance. And I've heard about people doing it on the internet, starting rumours then cashing in when shares rise."

"Pumping and dumping, you mean? Sure, it happens, but it's strictly small beer, amateur hour stuff. Professionals don't fall for that kind of thing."

"What makes you so sure?"

Roger heaved himself out of his chair. "Come with me," he said. "Ever been in a dealing room?"

"No."

"Look and learn, then, look and learn. Outsiders always imagine it's either some kind of black magic or equivalent to chucking money at whatever you fancy in the two thirty race at Epsom. That couldn't be further from the truth."

He led the way through a swing door into a vast open-plan room packed with computer terminals, several to each desk. The stale, flat smell of tension and static electricity filled Peter's lungs. Shoulder-high grey partitions, festooned with a bewildering variety of objects ranging from printed listings to Playboy centrefolds, divided the room into small bays. All were occupied by intent young men, sleeves rolled up and flamboyant ties casually at half-mast below unbuttoned collars, each with a phone clamped between shoulder and ear as though they had grown there. Their eyes were flickering from screen to screen as they talked, fingers scuttling simultaneously across the keyboards and phone pads in front of them. Nobody looked up, except a middle-aged man in a glass-walled office at the far end, who gave Peter a hard stare then turned away to talk urgently into his telephone. Their bodies were here, Peter thought, but their minds were eerily far away in cyberspace, surfing through the densely packed data scrolling down the monitors. No individual noise was loud enough to disturb their concentration, but the cumulative buzz of clicking keys and muffled voices was loud enough to force Roger to raise his voice slightly.

"I wasn't kidding when I told Billy things were a bit hectic at the moment. The bottom's dropped out of Oil and Gas stocks since Monday and they're starting to drag other share prices down with them. We're having to rebalance our portfolios so our clients don't get creamed."

There was something about what Roger had just said that nagged at him and Peter's brow furrowed as he tried to put it together. It slithered out of his grasp as Roger continued.

"Over there," Roger gestured towards the far right hand corner, "that small group are the actual traders. They do all the dealing, you know, the buying and selling. Down the centre here, those are analysts. They do the grunt work, monitor trends, assess company financials, evaluate sector economics, that sort of thing and feed their recommendations to the dealers. That's done through our senior analyst, Fred Watkins. That's him back there in the office, he's sort of the lynchpin, making sure we balance our trades and adjust our portfolio for any sudden shifts in the market. Then at the back there, you've got the gophers, who supply the raw data off the networks."

"What networks?"

"You name it, we've got it. Computer databases, press agency feeds, company reports, economic surveys, the lot. We deal in hard facts here, fundamentals, you know, like profitability and asset values. That's where your novel won't cut it. There's no way a team like this will get suckered by spin, they've been round the block too many times."

"Why the press agency links, then?" Peter said mildly, pointing at a bank of screens on the far wall. "And the TV newsreels running over there? You can't say that stuff's all fact."

Roger's eyebrows beetled and he shot Peter a hard glance. "You're an expert all of a sudden, are you?" His voice had an edge to it, as though he'd been accused of something distasteful. "Real things happen out there. If an earthquake in Japan wipes out half the world's production capacity for microchips, you'd better believe that's an important fact affecting share prices. And I didn't just make that up, either. It actually happened a few years back and CNN were the first to report it."

"Yes, OK, I'll buy that. But what about more subjective stuff? Rumours, popular bandwagons, that sort of thing. They must have some impact, surely?"

"Yeah, I suppose," Roger admitted reluctantly, running his hand through his thinning hair. "You've got to watch out for major swings in investor sentiment. That's just common sense. But it's only a small part of the equation, short-term stuff. You don't bet the farm on rumours, even if the great unwashed get in a panic and run for cover. It's a sure-fire way to get screwed."

Just like Jonathan and Jessica Holt got screwed, Peter thought. Jonathan's bitter comment about investors dumping shares popped unbidden into his mind and he felt his subconscious give him another powerful nudge. Something about Oil and Gas stocks. Damn, what was it?

"So what caused the internet bubble?" he probed,

fishing for the elusive memory. "That's a classic story of hype, surely, the way prices rocketed recently. The way I understand it, none of the dotcom companies have any profits or assets to speak of, do they? Where were your fundamentals then?"

"New technologies are a special case. You've got to look at the wider economic issues."

"Oh yeah?" Peter said sceptically. "And how come those have changed all of a sudden?"

"Smart for a novelist, aren't you?" Roger stared at him through narrowed eyes and cocked his head to one side as though listening to an inner debate. Then he nodded decisively. "Billy Stanfield seems to think the sun shines out of your arse, so I'll tell you a few trade secrets. No attribution, mind. Strictly hypothetical, for your book. Let's go back to the boardroom, get some privacy."

The empty coffee cups had been spirited away and there were no distractions except the reflections off the gleaming table and a faint lingering smell of expensive cigars that pervaded the room. The silence was oppressive after the hubbub of the dealing floor.

"Trade secrets, you said," Peter prompted. Roger was looking a trifle shifty, as though he was already regretting his indiscretion and it was vital not to give him the chance to back off. The opportunity wasn't likely to come again, or even to materialise at all if he was given too much time to think about it. "What did you mean? Hypothetically, of course," he added with a reassuring grin.

The braces twanged again as Roger's hands picked at them pensively, looking like a schoolboy wondering whether to share a playground secret. "How do I know I can trust you?" he said abruptly.

"You don't, I suppose. I give you my word I won't drop you in it, though." Peter stretched across the table. "Here's my hand on it, if that means anything in the city these days."

The handshake was firm. "It does to me," Roger said decisively. "All right, then. You can forget all that crap about spin. That's strictly for politicians and lobby journalists. Money's much more serious than votes and tabloid headlines."

Peter stifled his objections. Money and power were two sides of the same coin, but this wasn't the time to split hairs.

"Go on," he said.

"You've got to understand how the market works. It's no bullshit what I said about analysis and facts. But that's not the whole story. There's instinct, too. Call it gambling if you like, but there's always been a few people, like Billy Stanfield, who can spot when the market's about to turn."

"Why's that so important?"

Roger looked at him in disbelief. "What planet have you been living on? Buy low and sell high is what making money's all about. The trick is in the timing. Making your move at the turning points, see?"

"Yes, I think so."

"The thing is, Billy's been losing his touch recently. Things like this collapse in Oil and Gas stocks, he just didn't see it coming. Neither did most of the rest of us, for that matter, but for him to get caught, that's really odd."

"Why odd? Surely nobody can get it right every time, however good their instincts are."

"Well somebody sure is at the moment. And that's not all. The markets may be cruel, but they're logical. There's always a solid reason for major shifts, even if you can only see it afterwards. But that doesn't seem to apply any more."

"What are you suggesting?" Peter said, puzzled. "Has this happened before?"

"You bet. The last time was just a few months back when the biotechnology companies all went down the pan. No reason, but... Hey, are you OK?"

Peter's grunt as two and two made an explosive four had been involuntary, but sounded as though he was in pain. Roger's face was full of concern.

"Yes...yes, I'm fine," he said distantly, his brain racing as pieces of the puzzle dropped into place. Project Icarus, he thought. Standing behind a half-open library door listening a plummy voice complaining about market positioning and being overruled. Feeding instructions into the computer. Jesus. He knew who'd been responsible for wiping out the Holts. The conclusion that the same people were behind the current market crisis was inescapable.

"You sure?" Roger said doubtfully.

"Yes, really. Go on, please."

"The bottom line is I'm beginning to think somebody's changed the rules, like in your book. Not in the way you were talking about, though. The media couldn't swing this kind of action."

"How, then?"

"It would have to be the market makers, probably

more than one, downgrading stock ratings to start a run. The thing is, though, it shouldn't happen like that. Not unless all the other key indicators lined up, pressed the right buttons with all the other senior analysts. They're an independent-minded bunch; that's one of the main checks and balances in the market."

"But if you fed them the right data, surely they'd all come to a similar conclusion?"

"It could be something like that," Roger admitted. "But it would have to be a hell of a sophisticated operation. I mean, you'd have to crawl inside their heads, figure out how their minds worked and hit each of them where they live. It might work in a novel, but not in real life."

Peter suppressed the gleeful urge to enlighten him. "What do you reckon's happening, then?"

"I don't know," Roger said edgily, looking as though he wished he'd never started the conversation. "Perhaps nothing. It doesn't feel right, that's all."

"Come off it. You had something specific on your mind."

"I can't prove anything, see," he said with a strange blend of apology and belligerence. "But there seems to be some sort of cartel going with a few of the big investment banks. They always seem to be in the lead and they always seem to have their positions covered. Collectively, they've got enough muscle to move the market, then everyone else has to jump on the bandwagon."

"Isn't that sort of thing illegal?"

"Rigging the market? Bet your ass it is. But you try and prove anything. They'd just say it was sour grapes because they were smarter at spotting the trends than anyone else."

"That's what regulators are for. I mean, if these people are making a fortune, it must look fishy."

"Oh, sure, they'd be down on you like the wrath of God if you tried it on as a private investor, or like those journalists you mentioned. But it's different if you're talking about the great and the good. The big boys," he spat out distastefully, "they're untouchable, oozing professional ethics and all that crap. They're too smart to get caught with their fingers in the till. In any case it's almost impossible to pick the bones out of a run on the market, especially after everyone else has piled in to protect their own positions."

"Who do you figure is behind it, then?"

"What's it to you?" He looked up abruptly, suspicion suddenly oozing from every pore. "We're only talking about a plot for a book, aren't we?"

Peter decided to chance his arm. "It wouldn't be Sir Rodney Hardcastle by any chance, would it?"

Roger's face went blank. "I never said anything like that."

"No, you didn't," Peter agreed calmly. "Am I wrong?"

The face across the table remained inscrutable. "I think that's enough," Roger said bleakly and stood up. "I've got work to do. And take my advice, if you even breathe that sort of accusation outside this room the very least you can expect is you'll get sued to within an inch of your life. He's not someone you want to tangle with, believe me."

Peter nodded his thanks and made for the door. He'd only gone a few steps down the corridor when he felt a hand on his arm and found Roger had followed him.

"Off the record," he said quietly, "what would you do if you found proof that Hardcastle was behind it all?"

Peter looked at the level eyes set in a face that was worldly-wise beyond its tender years.

"Off the record," he said, "I'd do my damnedest to destroy the bastard."

The ghost of a wintry smile flickered over Roger's face and was gone as though it had never been.

"Send me a copy of your book when it's done, then," he said. "I think I might enjoy reading it after all."

Chapter 16

Peter was still pondering the implications of that enigmatic smile as he pushed his way out of the building. The heavy wooden door swung shut behind him with a thud and he stood on the marble steps wondering what to do next. Mere accusations wouldn't inconvenience Rodney Hardcastle in the slightest. Roger Collins was right about that and about the likely reaction if he approached the regulators or anybody else without hard proof. And despite Roger's tacit admission that he knew at least some of the answers, it was clear enough that there was no hope of any more help from that quarter. He looked around, feeling depressed. Cannon Street was emptier than usual at middle day, but strips of tinsel in the office windows opposite gave the clue to that. It was nearly Christmas, he realised without enthusiasm. The normal crowds of sandwich seekers were probably already ensconced in festive lunches, escaping from their problems with false bonhomie and cheap wine. Lucky them, he thought tiredly. There was no sign of any such rock, however illusory, to cling to in his own particular patch of quicksand and time was running out.

Sam Garvey watched his quarry hover indecisively on the steps of Stanfield House then drift towards Cannon Street tube station. He muttered a curse. They'd likely lose Conway again if he went in there, which would be a disaster after the sterling efforts of the informant in Stanfield's dealing room. Whoever it was must be a sharp cookie to spot the face and make the connection. The encrypted e-mail with a copy of the photograph from Conway's security pass only went out on the private network yesterday. Keep going, he urged silently, his knuckles whitening on the steering wheel as the distant figure approached the station entrance. Obligingly, Peter Conway ignored the inviting steps and turned instead down the narrow link road to Upper Thames Street. Must be heading for the river walk, Sam thought with satisfaction. There was bugger all else down there. More importantly, there would be hardly any people. He smiled and put the Jaguar into gear.

***

Chloe Pearson drew herself up to her full five feet four inches and declined the barman's leering offer of another drink. The cocktail bar of the Riverside restaurant was all but empty now and a few of the groups in the crowded dining room were already becoming raucous. She made a small moue of distaste. Next thing, they'd be getting out the Christmas hats and throwing streamers and then no doubt the drunken gropers would start flexing their lustful fingers. Time to move.

She glanced for the hundredth time at the clock on the wall, which mutely confirmed her conclusion. Her contact wasn't going to show. She tossed her long blonde hair back from her face and arched her shoulders in frustration, indifferent to the barman's rising blood pressure as the pose emphasised her shapely figure. Bloody men, she thought, noting the direction of his gaze. Instead of the scoop she'd been hoping for, she'd now have to go back and face the patronising smile of her editor and the knowing grins of her fellow journalists. As if they never had a source chicken out on them. Chloe studied her reflection in the wall mirror and abstractedly smoothed out the wrinkles in her tight skirt. The image staring back at her was peaches and cream. The steady pale-blue eyes were fractionally too far apart, she thought critically and the nose a shade too prominent above the determined set of the chin. But it wasn't her looks that were holding her back, far from it. It was her failure to come up with front-page material, the kind of indiscretions she'd been expecting to tease out of a dusty civil servant over today's aborted lunch.

She leaned forward towards the mirror and smoothed the incipient crow's feet at the corners of her eyes with her fingertips, the rings glinting on her delicate fingers. Time was getting short, she thought a trifle desperately. Her twenty-fifth birthday was looming and another generation of aspiring investigative reporters would soon be snapping at her heels. She needed a big break and soon. Looks and talent were fading assets and they weren't enough to get her to the top and keep her there without the right sort of scandal to work with. Then she shrugged and headed for the door. Wherever that was to be found, it wasn't here, at least not today. Out on the walkway, she turned left past the picture windows overlooking the river and sensed heads turning as the revellers were distracted from their Christmas fare. She smiled and let her hips swing a fraction more provocatively. At least some things were still predictable, she thought smugly and tomorrow was another day.

The canyon of Upper Thames Street was gloomy and oppressive, hemmed in by high-rise buildings and the ugly lump of Cannon Street station. There were few people and little traffic and Chloe searched in vain for the yellow beacon of a vacant cab. She crossed the road towards the more promising pastures of Cannon Street, scuttling the last few yards with a muffled curse as a large black car shot out of the murk threatening to collect her along the way. From the safety of the pavement she turned to flash two indignant fingers at the driver. Her heart lurched when the brake lights flashed ruddily in response and tyres squealed in protest as the car swerved violently to a halt, mounting the pavement just ahead of a solitary pedestrian a few yards further on. The doors flew open and two large men leapt purposefully out. Shit, she thought nervously, reaching for the highly illegal can of Chemical Mace she kept in her handbag as a precaution against muggers. The guy on the pavement looked pretty weedy and wasn't likely to be much help even if he had the guts to try. How could she have been so bloody stupid as to provoke this?

Time slowed and her pulse raced. The stranger had some chivalry after all. He was wrestling with the two men, preventing them from getting to her. He shouted something frantically, before a meaty hand clamped over his mouth and silenced him. Telling her to make a run for it? Chloe turned to comply, then stopped in confusion. It had sounded awfully like 'help' rather than 'run'. She swung back. The slightly built young man was still struggling furiously, but was being dragged inexorably towards the car. Nobody was paying the slightest attention to her. Damnation. She'd got the whole bloody thing back to front. He was the intended victim, not her. A gangland beating, a turf war perhaps? She forced herself to think. No, more like a kidnapping. Either way, potential front-page news and here she was shaking in her boots like a blushing virgin fresh from the cloister while it happened in front of her eyes. They'd have a real belly laugh about that back at the paper. Well sod that, she thought, her face burning at the imagined derision. The mist of uncertainty burned away in a sudden flare of adrenalin. She was a reporter, damn it and sometimes you had to make your own breaks.

Chloe flipped the top off the Mace and sprinted towards the melee. The two bruisers had their backs to her, preoccupied with pushing their victim into the back of the car. A few more seconds and they'd be clean away. She screamed at the top of her voice to let him go. Their heads turned, staring blankly, taken by surprise. Standing close together, they made a compact target. She angled the nozzle of the canister upward and let them have it. Perfect. A double whammy, up the nose and in the eyes, just like the instruction leaflet said. The results were spectacular, also as advertised. They staggered away, retching and pawing at their faces. She reached past them and grabbed their victim's arm, tugging urgently.

"Follow me," she hissed, "and run like hell."

***

The back of the taxi was silent except for their ragged breathing and the rattle of the diesel engine as they turned onto London Bridge and Cannon Street disappeared behind them. Peter Conway was shell-shocked and it was Chloe who took the initiative.

"Just what the hell was that all about? You seem to keep some very strange company. I'm Chloe Pearson, by the way," she added.

"Peter," he said, shaking the outstretched hand and gathering his wits. "Peter Conway. I... er... I don't quite know what to say. 'Thank you' seems a bit pathetic under the circumstances. You took a terrible risk."

His voice was smooth, well educated. The accent was mainly London, she thought, but with a hint of something else. Not foreign, a soft regional burr. Gloucestershire, perhaps, or Herefordshire. Not the sort of pedigree you'd expect of a gangster. He was still an unknown quantity, though, she reminded herself sternly. There had been a murderous intensity about the assault and assumptions were dangerous. Chloe shivered. Especially any assumptions that she was safe in his company.

"I know how to look after myself," she said, with a confidence she didn't feel. "A squirt of Mace cuts anybody down to size," she added defensively.

Peter spotted the twitch of her hand towards the canister in her handbag and got the message. The slight quaver in her voice told him she wasn't as tough as she'd like him to think, but that was okay. He eyed her speculatively. She was a real looker and so far as he was concerned she could come to his rescue as often as she liked. He put his hands up submissively.

"I'm sure," he said. "And damned lucky for me, too. Those guys weren't fooling around."

"Who were they?"

"It's a long story. Let's just say they're trying to stop me blowing the whistle on a nasty scam they're up to. Believe me, you don't want to get involved any deeper than you already have." Peter paused, searching for the right words. "I mean, you saved my life back there and I don't want to seem ungrateful. It'd be poor thanks, though, to drag you into my troubles. In fact, it's probably best if we pull over and I get out right here."

"Oh no you don't," Chloe snapped as he turned towards the glass partition to speak to the cabbie and he looked back in astonishment.

"What do you mean? I told you, this is dangerous. I don't want you getting hurt on my account."

"I'll make my own decisions about that, thank you very much. Besides," she gestured at his shirt where a red stain was spreading soggily on the right hand side of his chest, "you look like you've got a nasty cut under there somewhere. We need to get you to a doctor."

Peter looked down in surprise. He remembered the wicked-looking knife, the deadly menace of the command to stop struggling and the unmistakeable intention to inflict whatever damage was necessary. After that, events were a blur and he'd not felt a thing. Now she'd pointed it out, though, it started hurting with a perverse insistence. He unbuttoned his shirt and stared at a gaping gash across his ribs. A glint of white bone showed fleetingly underneath the slowly pulsing blood.

"Here." Chloe held out a clean handkerchief she'd extracted from her handbag. "Press down on it with this, it'll slow the bleeding."

She didn't much like the sight of blood, but she'd been wrong to call him weedy, she saw with a stir of interest. His chest and stomach were smoothly muscled, suggesting he was much stronger than she'd given him credit for. Quite dishy, really.

"Not like that," she said, distracted by his awkward attempts to compress the wound. "Give it here. You need to make a pad." Her fingers moved busily. "There." She pressed it against his chest. "Hold it like this."

The mat of fine black hair brushed silkily against her hand. She felt her body tingle in response and suddenly found it hard to concentrate.

"What are you, a nurse or something?" he said with a wince.

"Never mind that now." Chloe glanced up at the grey concrete bulk of Guy's Hospital towering over London Bridge Station on their left and leaned forward to speak through the partition behind the driver's head. "Is there an A and E department at Guy's these days?"

"Yes, I think so," the cabbie said without turning his head. "You got a problem back there?"

"We'll survive. Just take us there, please, as quick as you can."

She saw a pair of worldly-wise eyes staring back at her in the driving mirror.

"Yeah, anything you say," the driver said phlegmatically. "But if that's blood I can see, keep it off the goddam upholstery, will you? It's a twenty-five quid surcharge for you and a pain in the arse for me if I've got to get the cab cleaned up."

As good as his word, he dropped them a few minutes later outside the hospital entrance. Medically speaking, South London was apparently having a quiet afternoon and the ranks of plastic chairs in the down-at-heel reception area were empty. Peter was whisked into a curtained cubicle, where a taciturn doctor shook his head briefly over the knife wound and the yellowing bruises. He had clearly seen it all before too many times to display any curiosity about the cause. After some rather perfunctory sewing and bandaging Peter found himself back outside, clutching a small bottle of painkillers. The local anaesthetic would wear off in a couple of hours, he'd been assured and then it would hurt. The pills would help and could be replenished if necessary by his GP, who should be consulted anyway in a few days. And good riddance, don't bother us again, was the unspoken impression. The mood was catching and he frowned to see Chloe was still there, waiting.

"I thought you'd be long gone," he said tactlessly.

"Charming," she said indignantly. "What did they do in there, give you a charisma by-pass?"

"Sorry, I didn't mean it like that. I assumed you'd have to get back to work or something."

Chloe thought quickly. There was a story here and she wasn't going to let go until she'd extracted it.

"Actually, I'm on my Christmas holidays," she lied smoothly. "I thought I'd better hang around at least until you called the police, they'll want a statement from me I suppose."

"Police?" Peter was taken aback. Hours of suspicious questions and unsatisfactory answers about arson and burglary beckoned. "Er... I don't see much point in getting them involved. I mean, those thugs will be long gone by now."

Chloe hid her satisfaction. He obviously had reasons for not getting the authorities on the case, which gave her the leverage she needed. She proceeded to turn the screw.

"You must be joking," she said. "You as good as told me you know who those men were and that they were trying to kill you. And what if they report me for assault? I could find myself in real trouble."

"I'm pretty sure they won't."

"What sort of answer is that?" she said indignantly. "I think I'd better call the cops if you're not going to."

"Er... hang on a minute," Peter said wretchedly. "Look, believe me, getting the police involved will only make things worse. You don't know... that is, you could get hurt... I told you, I don't want that on my conscience."

"Don't you dare patronise me. I'm the one saved your bacon back there and I don't need any chauvinist crap about protecting my delicate female sensibilities." Chloe waved her mobile phone in his face. "Now, do I make that call, or are you going to tell me what the hell this is all about?"

The colour was high in her cheeks, her body tensed with the challenge and Peter thought she looked stunning. It wasn't difficult to make his decision.

"You win," he said. "Don't blame me if you live to regret it, though."

"Let me worry about that. First things first, let's find another taxi. Come on."

Peter followed her lead towards Borough High Street, but he'd only gone a few steps before a sudden wave of giddiness, a combination of the injections and delayed shock, made him stumble. He instinctively grabbed hold of her and they both staggered as she took his weight. His face ended up just inches from hers and he could feel the warmth of her skin under his hand through the silk blouse. Her blue eyes were laughing at him, but he sensed something deeper move behind them for a second before she pushed him gently away and twisted out of his grasp. Before he could protest, she was at the edge of the pavement waving her arm at a taxi that had just turned the corner and it screeched to a halt beside them.

"Where to?" the cabbie said through the lowered window, his voice full of boredom and Peter damned him silently to hell for turning up at just the wrong moment.

Chloe smiled sweetly and glanced up at Peter. "You need to rest and put your feet up for a bit," she said. "Why don't we go to my place? We can sort things out once we get there."

"I suppose it's as good as anywhere," he said ungraciously and followed her into the back of the cab. The flat was all Scandinavia and Tate Modern, in sharp contrast to the drab exterior of the row of nineteen-thirties semis squatting in their suburban ranks. They were somewhere in the unfashionable East End, Peter reckoned, though the barrage of questions he'd been subjected to had distracted him from following their precise route. It was a strange area for a single woman to choose to live, the streets litter-strewn and exuding that indefinable aura that made the hairs on the back of your neck prickle and discouraged walking alone after dark. He wadded his bloodstained, torn shirt and tossed it in the waste bin under the sink, staring critically at his reflection in the bathroom mirror. The white slash of the bandage across his battered chest looked dramatic and the face above it peered back at him looking pale and drawn. The strain was telling, he thought grimly, fingering the gauze. It was the closest call yet and he'd have a permanent scar to remember it by. Assuming he had a future in which to enjoy the luxury of remembering. For all his efforts so far, he was no nearer figuring out how to stop them and they wouldn't give up now. His father's fate was grim testimony to their persistence.

He grabbed the soapy flannel and started washing himself down vigorously, wishing that he could have used the shower without ruining the bandage. Life was full of frustrations at the moment. And Chloe Pearson was another enigma he needed to sort out before things got out of hand. The good news was, she was attractive and definitely single; the bathroom cabinet was full of exclusively feminine perfumes and potions and there were no signs of lingering male influences about the flat. The not so good bits of news were her seemingly insatiable curiosity, the skill with which she evaded his attempts to discover what she actually did for a living and the thoroughness with which she'd swept him under her wing. He had his share of vanity, but it couldn't all be down to his masculine charms.

He dried himself and fingered the new clothes still in their Marks and Spencer bags. She'd insisted on stopping off to buy them, but why would a relative stranger do that? Fair enough, he'd explained his inability to use his own credit card and his need for a change of attire was obvious, but even so. He wasn't sure he'd have done the same for someone he hardly knew, let alone take them back to his home. He frowned. The temptation was to ride his luck, but the last few weeks had made him incorrigibly suspicious, with good cause. Or was it paranoia? He shook the shirt out of its wrapping and pulled it on, wincing as the stitches in his chest stabbed a protest and the dull ache sharpened into a throbbing pain. Peter finished dressing and swallowed a couple of painkillers, wishing his other problems were so easy to treat.

"Feeling better?" Chloe eyed Peter calculatingly as he emerged from the bathroom. He looked better, she thought. Cream linen trousers and matching open-necked shirt set off his dark good looks and that air of wrinkled, slightly grubby dishevelment had vanished. The strain lines on his face were still there, though, together with that wary shadow in the eyes that told her he was still keeping things back. We'll soon see about that, she thought smugly.

"Mm," Peter nodded, strolling over to the settee and flopping down next to her. "Have I told you recently how grateful I am?"

She laughed and ran her fingers through his curly hair. "Only half a dozen times. It's my pleasure, believe me."

"Really?" he said, leaning closer. "Do you make a

habit of rescuing strangers in distress?"

She pushed him away teasingly. "Don't be silly. I could hardly ignore what was going on in front of my eyes, though, could I? And you looked as though you might be worth saving."

"I hope you still think so."

"Of course I do. I haven't had so much fun in ages." Which was true, Chloe reflected, but beside the point. She needed the rest of his story and more facts before she could get a piece put together for her editor. She tucked her feet casually under her thighs and wriggled comfortably into the cushions. "But why don't you tell me more about yourself," she said persuasively. "You never know, perhaps I can help in other ways."

As afternoon turned to early evening, Peter's reservations melted. She was an attentive and sympathetic listener as well as charming company. The combination was irresistible and he found himself holding nothing back.

"Look," she said eventually, "this is all very well, but you've got no hard evidence to back you up. Without that, it seems to me you're snookered."

Peter arched an eyebrow at her. "Don't you believe me, then?"

"Of course I do. That's not what I meant. But officially, what have you got? A suicide, a car accident, a couple of burglaries and a mugging that you haven't even reported and a few ups and downs on the stock market. You can't prove any of them are even suspicious, let alone connected."

"You're forgetting at least three attempts to kill me," Peter said dryly. "Coincidence has its limits."

"I hadn't forgotten. But those could all be put down to accidents or bad luck, too, couldn't they? You know that, otherwise you'd already have gone to the police yourself. Except the hotel fire, perhaps," she corrected herself, "but you seem to be in the frame for that, not anybody else."

"Perhaps I should just shoot myself, then and save everybody the trouble."

"Don't be silly," she said firmly. "I think you're right, the way to get the evidence you need is through the way they're playing the markets. Once you've got something concrete there, you've got a credible motive for the rest of it."

"That's not much help. I tried that with Roger Collins this morning and got nowhere."

"Perhaps you were asking the wrong questions. I mean, what you need is records of who made a killing every time the markets went crazy. Share dealings are all recorded, they have to be. If there's a consistent pattern there, you'll have some serious ammunition."

"Those records must be highly confidential, though, protected by all sorts of professional ethics and suchlike. Nobody's going to break ranks and show them to an outsider like me."

Chloe smiled. Any serious newspaper had its own ways to twist arms to get hold of confidential information and the resources to dig as deep as necessary in the pursuit of a headline.

"I've got an idea about that," she said. "As it happens, there's an old friend of mine who's quite high up in the stock exchange. If I talk to him nicely, he might be willing to help."

Peter saw the smile and felt an irrational stab of jealousy. An ex lover, he guessed, or maybe not so ex.

"No," he said stubbornly. "I don't like it. This was just between the two of us. Any sort of leak about what we're looking for and we've had it, they'll just destroy the evidence and run for cover."

"You can't have it both ways. You've just said you can't get the information yourself. If you want to go any further, you're going to have to find somebody on the inside."

The logic was incontrovertible, Peter was forced to admit. "I suppose so," he said grumpily. "But how do I know I can trust this friend of yours? For all we know, he might be part of it."

Chloe's conscience pricked. The kind of leak she had in mind would blow the whole thing wide open, whether he liked it or not. But a story was a story, she told herself sternly. She had a duty to report it, even if Peter got hurt and a few villains escaped the net in the process. He was a nice guy, but there were plenty more fish in the sea and a scoop like this would make her career if it panned out.

"No way," she said. "He's definitely one of the good guys."

"You'd better be right. They've been trying to kill me just on the off chance that I know too much. They'll be down on me like the hounds of hell if there's even a sniff that I've got hard evidence. You too. What's happened so far will look like a Sunday School picnic if anything goes wrong on this and you'll be right there in the firing line."

"You worry too much," Chloe said uneasily. She

shrugged off her sudden doubts and glanced at her watch. "Look, there's no time like the present. I've just got time to catch Derek if I leave right now. You make yourself at home here. I shouldn't be gone more than a couple of hours."

She was like an elemental force, Peter thought with foreboding, as he watched her march down the street in the gathering dusk, dust and litter blowing around her ankles. She was right that there was no alternative and he had no reason to mistrust her. But all the same, he had a bad feeling about it.

Chapter 17

Derek English hid his consternation behind an editorial tantrum of the kind for which he was notorious. It was a technique he had assiduously cultivated and had proved its worth on more than one occasion when he'd needed to deflect attention from inconvenient facts. A psychiatrist might have told him that his vindictiveness was rooted in over-compensation for a short stature, but he'd never had truck with such people. He simply enjoyed making his victims suffer and derived a bitter satisfaction from knowing his staff referred to him as 'the malignant dwarf' behind his back. The more they mocked, the sweeter his revenge. He glowered at Chloe Pearson and let his face redden, then banged his clenched fist again on the desk, sending papers flying.

"Well?" he spat contemptuously. "You heard the question. Do you believe in fairy stories? Perhaps you still believe in Father Christmas, too, the way you found this Conway fellow all nicely gift-wrapped? That would be a nice seasonal touch."

Chloe stared back at him across the massive black desk. Ordinarily there would have been something faintly ridiculous about the wizened figure perched behind such a monstrosity, but she felt no inclination to snigger. The force of his personality more than filled the space and the combined effect was intimidating. As it was meant to be, she supposed. The atmosphere in the glass-walled office was fairly crackling with sarcasm and she was conscious of the audience in the newsroom beyond, following every move while taking good care not to be obvious about it. They knew the signs and would be relishing her discomfiture.

Not for the first time, she wondered why the hell she put up with it. The daily diet of sneers, innuendo and intolerance might sell newspapers when translated into print, that was what editors were paid for. There was no disputing that the Globe was his creature in that respect. But there was no call for the same nastiness to spread its tentacles like a cancer through every aspect of her working life. Her private life, too, if the way she'd treated Peter's confidences was anything to go by, she thought with a wince.

"What do you mean, fairy story?" she said as aggressively as she dared. "Give me the support I need to research the background and it'll be a sensational scoop."

"Scoop?" His eyes bulged and the tendons in his neck quivered with the force of his derision. "God save me from ambitious fools. You wouldn't recognise a scoop if it put you over its knee and spanked you. You're being conned, you bloody idiot."

"That's outrageous."

"Is it?" He held up a scrawny hand and checked off the fingers. "Point one, anyone with half a brain knows you'd kill to get your name on the front page..."

"It's not like that..."

"Shut up and listen," he snapped. "You might just learn something about being a journalist. Point two, you just happen to be passing when an attractive young Sir Galahad needs rescuing by the Lady of the Lake. I presume he is young and attractive?"

Chloe reddened and looked away.

"Yes, I thought so. Point three, this knight in shining armour gets your hormones in an uproar, then spins you a tale about fighting off the forces of evil, which gets you on the hook without a shred of evidence to back it up."

"That's not fair. I told you, I want to check it out, find the evidence."

"Bah! Evidence? It's the oldest trick in the book, girl. He's got you wanting this drivel to be true so bad you can taste it and your objectivity's gone straight down the toilet. The mood you're in, you'd find evidence that the Pope's an atheist and ignore any pointers to the contrary."

"No, I..."

"Point four," Derek continued grimly, ignoring her protest. "The only thing in this sorry shambles that does add up is that the media do influence the financial markets. What do you think would happen if we splashed headlines about share price manipulation and fraud all over the front page tomorrow morning?"

"Er... I hadn't thought about that," Chloe mumbled, taken aback by the sudden shift of direction.

"I hadn't thought about that," he parodied in a vicious falsetto. "Seems to me you haven't bloody well thought about anything. The first thing that would happen is the market would take a dive. Anybody who knew that was coming would make a fortune. The second thing would be a howling pack of lawyers beating a path to my desk wanting to sue the shit out of us."

He pushed over the last finger on his outstretched hand and clenched the fist till his knuckles whitened.

"Point five. Whoever's behind this informant of yours has been playing you for a sucker, trying to get their own agenda printed for their own purposes. You've been naïve and unprofessional enough to fall for it. Q.E.D. Now get the hell out of my sight."

The door clicked shut behind her and he watched her trudge across the newsroom, head bowed, avoiding the smirks and curious glances from her colleagues. He allowed himself to relish her discomfiture for a few moments before his bushy eyebrows came together in a thoughtful frown. Derek English hesitated for a moment and then reached for his telephone.

***

Peter Conway heard the front door slam and footsteps clattering urgently down the thinly carpeted hallway. He stretched and put the novel he'd been reading down on the coffee table. It was a pity that in real life the heroes and the villains were so much harder to detect and the clues about what to do for the best so much more obscure. He glanced at his watch. She'd been quicker than he'd thought and he wondered if that was good news or bad.

Bad, he decided, as the sitting room door flew open and he got a look at Chloe's pinched, angry face.

"What's up?" he said in alarm.

"I want you out of here right now."

His pulse started hammering. "Christ, are those thugs back again? They haven't had a go at you, have they?"

He craned his neck, half expecting to see black suits charging down the hall behind her.

"Don't give me that bullshit," she spat furiously. "I was stupid enough to take your pack of lies to my editor and he saw through your little game right away. You've made me a laughing stock, you bastard."

"Editor?" His heart sank. "Oh, shit, don't tell me you're a reporter."

"You can stop pretending you didn't know. That's what this is all about, isn't it?"

"I don't know what the sodding hell you're talking about," he exploded. "All that sweet talk and concern, you've been after a bloody headline all the time, haven't you, you cynical bitch. You've just been using me."

"Me, using you? That's a laugh. I'm the one you've been trying to con. You and your precious pals, you make me want to puke. Go on, get out. The game's over"

Peter grabbed her by the arms and shook her angrily. "This isn't a fucking game," he yelled. "Some bastards out there are trying to kill me. What have you done?"

Tears started leaking from the corners of her eyes and Chloe blinked furiously. She wouldn't give him the satisfaction of seeing her cry, if it was the last thing she did.

"Don't waste your breath. It may have cost me my job, but you won't get what you're after from me." She grabbed his wrists and broke his grip. "And keep your hands to yourself, you son of a bitch, or I'll have you for assault."

She backed away, scrabbling in her bag for the can of

Mace and struggling to remember how much she'd already used. Surely there'd be enough left for another burst? Christ, what a mess. How bloody stupid, inviting him into her home like this. He was stronger than she was despite his knife wound, she realised, remembering the smooth ridges of muscle on his slim torso. Maybe she could tear open those stitches, though. She flexed her nails. That would slow him down fast enough if it came to a struggle.

"Wait a second." Peter got a grip on his fury and backed away, hands held out in a calming gesture. There was something terribly wrong here, something he needed to get his head around. He was the one who'd been betrayed, but she was acting as though it was the other way around. More than that, she was obviously scared half to death of him. It didn't add up. "Wait just a second," he repeated. "Let's calm down. I don't understand what's going on here."

"You attacked me, that's what's going on." Chloe whipped the Mace out of her bag and waved it in his direction. "Come near me again and I'll give you a dose of this."

"Look, I lost my temper. I'm sorry, all right? You never told me you were a journalist, I thought you really wanted to help. I suppose it gave you a good laugh playing me for a fool to get your story, but you can't expect me to like it. If it's all over the papers tomorrow morning you've blown away any chance I might have had to get the goods on these people."

"You've got a bloody nerve. You knew all along what I was."

"Of course I didn't. I'd have kept my mouth shut if I

had."

"Oh, stop lying. I know you were using me to plant that story. That's what this charade is all about. Well you can forget it. The editor threw it out and me along with it."

"You mean it's not being published?" Peter said incredulously.

"No and it won't be. I'm sorry to disappoint you, but you might as well just bugger off and tell your friends they can forget their scam. I hope you're all going to lose a fortune."

"What the hell are you talking about? I never wanted anything to get out in the first place. I told you, I must have hard evidence before I can make any sort of move, even with the police."

"Yes, but that was just to egg me on..."

"Now you're being ridiculous," Peter interrupted in exasperation.

"No I'm not. Derek explained it all to me."

"Explained what, for Christ's sake? And who's this Derek character? You lied to me, he's not really some friend of yours in the stock exchange, is he?"

"My editor at the Globe. Derek English. He saw through you straight away and figured out your plan."

"Give me strength," Peter sighed and ran his fingers through his hair, resisting the urge to start tearing it out. "Start at the beginning, will you? Perhaps it'll make some sense then."

Chloe looked at him, uncertainty beginning to gnaw at her. This wasn't the reaction she'd expected. But unless he was a superb actor, his air of puzzlement was genuine and there were no signs of guilt at being found out. You'd expect something to show. Logically, the only thing he could do was cut his losses and run. He couldn't be foolish enough to believe he still had a chance of getting away with it, could he? Well, she could knock that on the head easily enough. Derek's analysis was burned into her memory and she let it flood out in a cathartic torrent. The scars were deep, but there was a bitter satisfaction in pouring the invective on its proper target. When she'd finished, there was silence. That had shown him, she thought. Perhaps now he'd get lost and she could begin to pick up the pieces.

She saw his shoulders begin to shake and his cheeks redden. Then Peter Conway tilted his head back and roared with laughter.

"That's... that's brilliant," he spluttered, gulping for breath and clutching his ribs in pain as the stitches in his wound threatened to rip. "This Derek must be quite something."

"What are you laughing at? It's not a joke."

"Oh yes it is. It's hilarious. He's really done a job on you and I thought reporters were supposed to be smart."

"Don't you dare poke fun at me, you pig. I should have left those men to carve you up."

"So you don't believe they were pals of mine putting on an act for you, then?"

"Yes. I mean no. Damn you," she stamped her foot in fury, "This isn't funny. You've wrecked my career with your bloody nonsense. Nobody will take me seriously at the paper after this."

"I'm sorry, but you can't blame me for that. It's all

your own doing. You're the one who tricked the story out of me and tried to take advantage. I told you it wouldn't stand up without evidence, that's the whole point."

"No..."

"You still can't see it, can you? You've got to admit it's ironic for a reporter to be a victim of spin."

"So you admit it, then?"

"No, I mean this bullshit your editor's come up with. He tears you apart for believing the truth because you've got no proof, then makes you believe a version of events he's invented with no facts at all to back it up. That's classic spin-doctor technique."

"He wouldn't lie to me."

"No? Well one of us must be." Peter unbuttoned his shirt and pointed at the bandage across his bruised ribs. "This is a fact. You must be mad if you think I'd let somebody take a knife to me on the off chance of making a few quid. What facts has he produced?"

"But he's the editor. He's a professional, with years of experience. He must have seen this sort of thing hundreds of times."

Peter shrugged and re-buttoned his shirt. "You're a professional too. I thought journalists were supposed to be objective, print the truth without fear or favour and so forth. You saw what happened to me today. It's up to you whether you trust his judgement or your own eyes."

"You're confusing me. How am I supposed to know what the truth is?" She looked appealingly at him and instinctively Peter stepped forward and hugged her. Hesitantly, she slid her arms round his neck and then clutched him fiercely, pressing her face into his shoulder.

"Christ, what a mess," she said in a muffled voice. "I don't know what to do."

Peter caressed her hair and smiled. "What any top class journalist would," he said gently into her ear. "Keep an open mind and dig out the facts."

She arched her head back and looked him in the eyes. Her face was expressionless and he feared he'd said the wrong thing. Then her lips curved into a smile and she moved her hips slowly against him. "You're right," she said dreamily and took his hand. "But it won't do any harm to leave that till later, will it?"

"No harm at all," Peter agreed happily and followed her into the bedroom.

***

Some hours later, Peter was dragged from a dreamless sleep by an insistent shaking of his shoulder and a voice whispering urgently in his ear.

"Wake up, for God's sake," the voice was saying.

He prised open a bleary eye and was rewarded by the sight of Chloe's face a few inches from his, dimly lit in the reflected glow of streetlamps through the gap in the curtains. He smiled lazily, then realised with a start that she wasn't lying beside him, but standing by the side of the bed.

"What's the matter?"

"I couldn't sleep and I was looking out of the window. A big car's just pulled up out there, like the one those men were in yesterday."

"I'm sure it's nothing. Come back to bed."

"No, something's not right. There are two people in it, just sitting there and I'm sure they're watching us. Come and look for yourself."

Peter heaved himself reluctantly out of bed and padded across to the window. He kept his body concealed behind the curtain and peered carefully out through the gap.

"I can't see anything. Where are they?"

"Up the road a bit, on the right. They probably think we can't see them from here."

Peter shifted his stance and delicately moved the curtain aside with his finger. Sure enough, a big saloon car was sitting beside the curb, in the shadow between two street lamps. It was hard to see who was inside, but a wisp of exhaust smoke drifting up from the rear meant the engine was running. It might not mean anything, just somebody coming home late from a party, but he suddenly felt wide-awake and nervous. He turned away from the window and grabbed his trousers.

"Get dressed," he whispered, "and for goodness' sake don't turn on the light. I don't know what's going on, but we can't afford to take any chances."

He heard the rustle of clothes behind him as she complied and put his eye back to the gap in the curtain while he buttoned his shirt. A dark coloured van was coasting down the road towards them, showing only its sidelights. The waiting car pulled out silently as the van passed and followed. Both vehicles eased to a halt outside the front door and Peter caught a glimpse of men piling out from both vehicles as he frantically pulled on his shoes.

"Shit, there's a bunch of them coming up the drive now," he said urgently. "Is there a back way out of here? We need to get out, fast."

Chloe, to her credit, didn't hesitate.

"Follow me," she said and ran out through the sitting room, grabbing her handbag on the way. Seconds later they were through the back door, down the overgrown garden and clambering over a rickety wooden fence. As Peter let himself drop into a narrow, unlit footpath running behind the row of houses, he heard the splintering crunch of the front door being forced and caught a glimpse of a shadowy figure coming round the side of the house to cut off any escape at the rear.

"Where now?" he hissed. "They'll be on us any second."

"This way," Chloe tugged his sleeve urgently. "There's another alley just down here, then we'll be out of sight."

A few seconds later, Mike Arnold peered over the fence and stared at the weed-strewn path beyond. Nothing moved in the gloom and he stood for a moment, head cocked to one side, listening intently. The shrubbery rustled and he tensed, ready to pounce, then cursed quietly and relaxed as a cat slunk across the path and disappeared. He turned away and went back towards the house. The back door swung open at his touch and he paused for a second, raking the garden with another stare. Then with a slight shake of the head he disappeared inside.

The alley was narrow and dank, hemmed in by larchlap fencing either side and smelling of mildew laced with pungent whiffs of urine where the local toms had marked their territory. At least, Peter hoped it was only the cats. Not that it mattered, he thought, stumbling over the uneven surface. In the blackness the alley felt like an open coffin, with only the narrow strip of marginally lighter sky overhead giving reassurance that the lid hadn't yet been nailed down. He glanced over his shoulder again, but there was still no sign of any pursuit. But that meant nothing. The hounds of hell could be ten yards behind ready to tear them to pieces and he wouldn't be able to see them through the murk. His shoulder blades itched at the thought and he hissed at Chloe to go faster ahead of him. Speed was more important than silence now, they needed to get as much distance as possible behind them before the net widened.

Peter's foot caught a pothole and he staggered, suppressing a shout of pain as his flailing hand collected splinters from the rough timber of the fence and the stitches in his chest threatened to tear open. Better than a twisted ankle or a broken leg, though. That could be lethal. Keep going, that was all that mattered. There was a glow ahead now. Streetlights, where the alley decanted into another suburban backwater much like the one they'd left behind. He grasped Chloe's arm and tugged her back. They stood panting, the shadows suddenly welcoming rather than oppressive. Peter glanced cautiously round the corner of the fence and scanned the road. Rows of parked cars glistened frostily under the lampposts and the darkly curtained windows of the houses stared like blind eyes at emptiness. He checked the alley behind and nothing stirred in the blackness. They were safe, then, for the moment. But not for long.

"Have you got any idea where the hell we are?" Peter whispered.

"Can't be far from Commercial Road," she said. "We should be able to find a taxi there even at this time of night, if we had somewhere to go."

Her voice sounded strained and Peter looked up in alarm. She was trembling from head to foot, her arms clasped tightly round her chest.

"Are you all right?"

"Terrific," she said acidly. "Nothing I like better than being chased by a bunch of murderous maniacs in the middle of the night and freezing to death out on the streets. Any other smart-alec questions?"

"Sorry," he said and put his arms round her. Her skin felt icy through the thin material of her blouse and the white plumes of their breath hung heavily in the still air. It wasn't a night to be outside without a coat, but there'd been no time and there'd been more urgent priorities. There still were.

"Commercial Road?" he prompted. "Which way's that?"

***

The waves of warm air blasting from the heater in the back of the cab were a blessed relief. Perversely, now that he was warmer his body was shivering, not with cold but with fright. He peered nervously over his shoulder at the street unwinding behind them. It was reassuringly empty, but somehow that didn't help. Media Associates seemed to have an uncanny ability to track him down and each time they were getting closer. His luck couldn't last much longer.

"Why Tower Bridge?"

"What?" Chloe's question dragged Peter back to the present with a jolt.

"You told the driver to take us to Tower Bridge. What happens when we get there?"

"There's a flat I've been using, just down the river at St Katherine's Dock. Jack Howson, a colleague of mine, should be there."

"Is it safe?" The alarm in her voice was crystal clear, even above the roar of the heater fan. "Surely these people know where you live."

"It's not my place. I've sort of borrowed it from a friend."

"Can you trust him, this friend?"

Peter stared blankly at his hands. They were still shaking, he noticed abstractedly.

"I don't know who the hell I can trust any more. But there's not much choice. I can't think of anywhere else to go."

"What about a hotel? Wouldn't that be safer?"

"Maybe, but I don't think so. I've no idea how they're doing it, but wherever I go they seem to be able to catch up with me. I mean, nobody could have known I was at your place and look what happened."

"I've been thinking about that," Chloe said seriously. "You didn't phone anybody, did you, tell them where you were?"

"Christ, no, I'm not that stupid. What are you getting at?"

"Well, after we got away from Cannon Street I can't

see how we could have been followed. And there was nothing to link you to me, I mean it was just an accident I happened to be there, wasn't it?"

"Yes of course it was," Peter said hotly. "You don't still believe any of that crap about me setting you up, do you?"

"Hardly." She laughed shakily. "Those people back there didn't look to me like friends of yours. But don't you see that that means?"

"No I don't. I'm not in the mood for riddles, either."

"Keep your hair on. We're looking for facts, right? Well here's one. The only person I told was Derek English. Nobody else could have connected you to me and given them my address."

"But that means..."

"The editor of at least one of the national dailies is part of your conspiracy, yes." She smiled at him sweetly. "You were pretty rude to me a while back about the responsibilities of a journalist and I was wrong to go behind your back. I trusted the wrong person, that's all. The story just got a whole lot bigger, though and I won't make that mistake again. It's strictly facts from now on and you'll find I'm pretty good at digging. Am I forgiven?"

Peter grinned. "Do I have a choice?"

"Do you want one?"

He laughed. "Not really. But whatever happens, we work together from now on. No more solo efforts. Deal?"

The rest of the journey seemed all too short. He reluctantly untangled himself from her embrace as the cab driver tapped sharply on the partition and repeated his question.

"This is Tower Bridge, mate. Where do you want me to drop you?"

"Uh, sorry." He looked out and saw the huge stone arch of the Northern end of the bridge looming. "Just along here will be fine, thanks."

The hairs on the back of his neck started to prickle as they made their way down the slippery steps to the riverside walkway. The air was cold and clammy in the shadow of the bridge, the chop of the incoming tide echoing eerily off the glistening stonework. Nothing moved on the deserted riverbank, but Peter couldn't rid himself of the feeling of being watched. They skirted the warm splash of light from the reception area of the Tower Hotel, instinctively keeping to the shadows. The scrunching of shoes on brick paving seemed to shout their presence and the urge to walk on tiptoe became almost irresistible. Peter fought his increasing unease as they made their way furtively across the swing bridge and past the dark outlines of the boats in the marina. Logically there was nothing to worry about, he knew, but logic didn't help. He was afraid and it was only the greater fear of seeming cowardly in Chloe's eyes that prevented him from turning tail and running.

The lights by the entrance to the flats were just a few paces away when Peter sensed a sudden swirl of movement. His cry of alarm was stifled as a hairy hand clamped itself over his mouth. From the corner of his eye he glimpsed Chloe kicking and struggling in the grip of a stranger. He twisted violently and brought his arms up to break the headlock, then something hard and cold jabbed him sharply in the ribs.

"Enough of that," a deep voice growled menacingly in his ear. "I'd rather not have to shoot you here, unless you insist."

Chapter 18

Peter's skin went clammy with shock and he felt sick. Chloe, too, had stopped struggling though her terrified eyes were staring at him vainly for help. He felt his arms being pulled roughly behind his back and twitched involuntarily at the bite of cold steel on his wrists as handcuffs clicked over them. His reward was another painful jab in the ribs with the gun barrel and a harsh reminder not to try anything. Somewhere deep in the paralysed mush of his brain there was a thin trickle of amusement at the futility of the command. His muscles were frozen in terror, all except his legs. They had turned to jelly. The idea of resistance was absurd, though the danger of collapsing on the spot was real enough.

The sound of a number being punched into a mobile phone slid across his awareness, followed by the mutter of a brief conversation. There was a third man, then, still out there in the shadows, reporting their capture. It didn't require much imagination to guess what instructions he was receiving. His bowels loosened at the thought of what was about to happen. Not just to him, but Chloe too. She didn't deserve to die. He should have stepped out of that cab in Cannon Street and walked away, kept her out of it. Was it only yesterday? Less than twenty-four hours. It seemed like an eternity. But it was his fault she was caught up in this. He felt a surge of regret. She was special, deserved better. Suddenly the blood was running hot in his veins and the fog cleared from his brain. Half a chance, he prayed, just show me half a chance to break her free. It doesn't matter what happens to me.

"The boss says to take them upstairs," a voice said from the shadows. "He wants to talk to them."

"Move." The jab in the ribs left no room for debate and Peter stumbled forward, his legs still behaving as though they belonged to someone else. Upstairs? His brain raced. It would be the cruellest coincidence if they were based here, of all places. But Jack Howson was up there too, in Billy's flat and perhaps they didn't know about that. There might be a glimmer of hope after all.

A firm push in the back propelled him past the deserted security desk and into the waiting lift. Peter's spirits faded again as a muscular arm reached out without hesitation to push the third floor button. It was beyond coincidence that they were being taken to the same floor where he and Jack had taken refuge. It could only mean they'd taken Jack too and had been lying in wait for his own return. And he'd been fool enough to walk into their arms like a lamb to the slaughter. Stupid, he cursed himself. A curt command brought him to a halt facing the familiar door and his last faint hope died. But how in God's name had they traced him? Perhaps the answer lay inside, but it wasn't going to help. Not any more. His head dropped to his chest and he heard the rattle of the deadlock being released. The door swung open and he stepped falteringly through like a condemned man onto the scaffold.

"Peter!"

The voice sounded familiar and there was surprise where he'd expected triumph. He lifted his head and felt the breath go out of him as though he'd been punched in the stomach.

"Billy," he gasped. "What the hell...?" He stuttered to a stop, his brain refusing to take in the implications.

Viscount Stanfield stood there in his dressing gown, eyes narrowed menacingly, his plump face red and angry.

"What the hell is this?" he exploded. "Get those handcuffs off them immediately."

Peter was still struggling to get to grips with the words when he realised they were not addressed to him.

"But sir..." his captor protested.

"Don't be a bloody fool, man." Billy shook his head in disgust. "This is Peter Conway. You're supposed to be protecting him, not frogmarching him up here at gunpoint in the middle of the night. Let them both go at once, I tell you."

With a click his hands were free and the pressure of the gun barrel vanished. Livid red marks circled his wrists where the cuffs had cut into his skin and he felt his hands begin to throb with returning circulation. He massaged them gently, strangely grateful for the pain. It was the only thing that proved he wasn't dreaming.

"My God, Peter," Billy said, advancing with a deeply worried expression on his face, "I'm dreadfully sorry about this. You must have been terrified." His gaze hardened as he looked over Peter's shoulder. "And as for you, what the hell do you think you were playing at? You're supposed to be a professional."

Peter turned his head and found himself looking into a

pair of ice-cold eyes containing not the slightest trace of embarrassment or apology. They were set in what looked like six feet of roughly hewn granite under a military style crew cut.

"Just following your instructions, sir. These two were behaving suspiciously, so we apprehended them. No harm done."

He sounded crisp and efficient, without a trace of the chilling menace with which he'd threatened to shoot without hesitation. Peter shivered. Even so, he still had no doubt this man would have killed him with no more compunction than swatting a fly. No harm done? That was a laugh.

"Hm," Billy said dubiously. "Perhaps you're right. Anyway, Peter, this is Max Johnson, head of a firm of private investigators I use from time to time."

"Pleased to meet you." Max inclined his head towards Peter, but didn't offer to shake hands. "Sorry about the mix-up."

Like hell he is, Peter thought, seeing the glint of sardonic amusement in Max's eyes. He knows he scared the shit out of me and he's letting me know he enjoyed it.

"So am I," he replied with an equally cursory nod, struggling to keep a quaver out of his voice. "I'll try and give you a better run for your money next time."

"And who's this charming young lady, Peter?" Billy demanded.

"Chloe Pearson. Chloe, meet Viscount Stanfield, an old friend of mine."

"Less of the 'old', if you don't mind and it's Billy to my friends." He looked her up and down appreciatively and Peter felt a tiny prickle of jealousy as Billy took her by the hand. "I'm sure we are going to be friends, aren't we? How did you get involved in all this?"

"It's a long story," Peter interrupted. Chloe was still pale and shaken and she could do without the third degree. "But what the hell are you doing here and with a private army? They nearly gave us both heart failure out there."

"Yes, yes of course. I'm sorry. You must both be shattered. What am I thinking of, keeping you standing here in the hall? Come in. Make yourselves comfortable and I'll explain."

In the sitting room, Jack had already gone straight to the essentials. Two life-savingly large brandies materialised in crystal goblets, accompanied by a broad grin and a clap on the back that eloquently conveyed his relief at Peter's reappearance. He waved the decanter invitingly, but Peter and Chloe were the only takers. Not at three in the morning, the others said, but coffee would be welcome and Jack obligingly shuffled off towards the kitchen. Billy ignored him, leaning forward earnestly towards Peter to begin explaining the situation.

By the time he'd finished, the dregs of the coffee were cold and nothing remained of the brandy but fumes and a warm glow. It was hard to believe that Billy had hired private investigators solely to help out a friend in need, although he'd done his best to make it sound plausible. But his manner was a little too unctuous, with a hint of the doorstep salesman and Peter wasn't buying. He wondered what was really going on in that calculating brain. Billy's baby-pink face gave nothing away, but these guys must be costing serious money and he wasn't noted for his charity.

"If I get you right," Peter said slowly, "you want me to run through everything I've found out with Max and his team and then work with them to nail the people who are after me."

"In a nutshell, yes. They're experts at this sort of thing, take my word for it. I've used their services before in some of my trickier business ventures. Of course, they'll give you protection, too. It's obvious you're mixed up with a very nasty situation, to put it mildly and I figured you could use some support."

"I'm certainly grateful for any help I can get, but this is a bit overwhelming. I mean, er... I don't doubt their expertise..." Peter floundered for a moment, "look... don't take this the wrong way, for God's sake... it's just that... well, why?"

"Why what?"

"Why are you doing this? I know we're friends and all that, but I hadn't expected... I mean I can't quite see... damn, I know it sounds bloody ungrateful, but there must be more to it than you just feeling sorry for me, surely?"

Billy had the grace to look slightly shamefaced. "You're right, of course, he said, "I shouldn't keep anything back. The truth is, I've been worried for a while that odd things were happening in the financial markets." He laughed mirthlessly. "Thought I was losing my touch, don't you know? I've missed a few tricks on the investment management side lately and some of my clients have been drifting away, losing faith. In my business, your reputation's only as good as the last deal. Anyway, when you told me your story yesterday morning, a few pieces of the puzzle started to drop into place."

"So you knew what was going on all the time?"

"Suspected, maybe, no more than that. But what could I do? The markets are so complex these days it's impossible to know where to start looking for problems unless somebody points the finger. You did that for me."

"The bottom line is, you're aiming to protect your business, then?"

"In a way, yes," Billy said with a frown, "though you've chosen a pretty uncharitable way to put it. I'm doing you a good turn as well, damn it. As I understand it, these bastards have been trying to shut you up permanently. This way, we both get what we want. There's nothing to apologise for in that."

There was a ring of truth in the words this time, although behind the bluster Peter suspected he still wasn't getting the whole story. What the hell, he thought, Billy's motives didn't really matter. He'd be a fool to turn down the offer of help, even if it wasn't entirely altruistic. For now, it was enough to feel safe and get a good night's sleep. The rest, despite Billy's impatient protestations, would have to wait.

***

Peter woke with a stiff back and the gritty-eyed, brain-dead symptoms of a restless night. He and Jack had ended up with lumpy cushions on an unforgiving floor after Billy grandly commandeered one bedroom and

Chloe laid claim to the second. There had been bad dreams, too, though thankfully he couldn't remember the details. All things considered, it was a lousy start to the day and things quickly began to get worse.

"Police?" he said crossly, still nursing his third cup of coffee, which was making no headway against his general malaise. "Don't be bloody stupid. I'm deep enough in the shit without letting them get their hooks into me."

"I'm deadly serious, Peter. Jack, you too. You've both left a trail behind you and the question marks won't go away. The longer you leave it the worse it'll get. Much better to go in voluntarily and make statements, clear things up." Billy's tone was uncompromising and Max nodded his agreement.

"You're heading for more trouble otherwise," he said. "Besides, a police investigation will start to put some pressure on the opposition, get them looking the other way while we sneak up on them from behind."

"I don't like it," Peter said stubbornly. "You're forgetting how my dad was framed to shut him up when he first got hold of the story years ago. I did tell you about that, didn't I Billy?"

"Yes, but that was different."

"Was it? He couldn't prove anything, so nobody believed him. We should wait until we've got some hard evidence, otherwise I'll be in the same boat. What do you think, Chloe?"

She opened her mouth to speak and was interrupted by Max's mobile phone.

"Sorry," he muttered. "I'll take it in the kitchen."

Her eyes followed him as he left the room, then

swivelled back to Peter.

"I don't know exactly what happened to your father," she said, "But he wasn't prepared for it, I guess. You're luckier; at least you're aware they might be trying to set you up, if they can't take you out of the game permanently, that is."

"Lucky?" Peter snorted. "That's a bloody odd way to look at it."

"Is it? You've got a chance to get your retaliation in first, give the police your side of things. That way, at least they'd have another angle, some sort of motive to think about if the finger gets pointed at you."

"You're already in the frame," Billy interrupted. " The police want to talk to you about the hotel fire, don't forget. And they'll surely have found Jack's car by now, they'll be suspicious about why you haven't reported that, too. The longer you leave it, the more you look as though you've got something to hide. You can hardly blame them if they draw the obvious conclusions."

"They'd never believe my story in a month of Sundays. Besides, how am I going to explain ferreting around in Hardcastle's house and all that stuff in the Media Associates offices?"

"Nobody's suggesting you tell them everything," Chloe said in exasperation. "Use your head. All they need to know is that you've inadvertently got mixed up in a stock market fraud. You don't have to go into the rest of it."

"Are you suggesting I lie to them? That'll just make things worse."

"What planet have you been living on? There are

shades of grey, you know, real life's not just black and white. All I'm saying is, stick to the parts of the truth you want them to know."

"I'm still not sure..."

"You've got witnesses for most of it, damn it," she said. "Jack, here for one and me come to that. And you'd hardly burgle your own studio and flat. I don't see your problem."

Peter's reply was cut short by Max's sombre voice as he came back into the room.

"You've got no choice now," he said with finality. "You need to get your side of things over to the police right away."

"Why?" Peter said, looking up in alarm. "What's happened?"

"That was one of my operatives," Max said, gesturing at his phone. "I sent him down to Brighton first thing to check with those people Billy told me you'd been talking to, the Holts. I wanted more details of exactly how Hardcastle took them to the cleaners so we could track back the share dealings and so on."

"So?"

"So he tells me they're dead."

Peter felt his guts freeze. "No," he protested, as if denying it would change the blunt inevitability of the words.

"Carbon Monoxide poisoning, apparently, from faulty gas burners. He says they were found in front of the TV in their sitting room, dead as doornails. They wouldn't have known a thing about it."

"It was an accident, then?" Peter said, relief mingling with the shock.

"My man couldn't ask too many questions, for obvious reasons. But no, not an accident. The cops were all over the place and he managed to get chatting to one of them. They're treating it as a suspicious death, something about evidence of tampering with the gas appliances."

"Jesus."

"Quite. It looks like Hardcastle's people are tidying up their loose ends."

"But that means it's my fault," Peter said wretchedly. "I must have led them there, stirred things up."

"You can't blame yourself. In their shoes, I'd have shut those two up anyway, regardless." Max swept Peter's self-recrimination aside callously and the icy expression on his face left no room for doubt that he meant what he said. "But it gives you a real problem. The police will be looking for someone to pin it on and they won't take long to find out you were there recently. If they come after you on a murder rap, you'll have nowhere to hide."

"But that makes it worse. If I go and talk to them they'll lock me up and throw away the key."

"Not if we play it right," Max said calmly. "I've got some contacts. Let me make a couple of calls, see if we can keep it unofficial. No lawyers or anything, mind. You prepared to handle it like that?"

Peter hesitated.

"Trust me, he knows what he's doing," Billy urged.

"Jack?" Peter raised a questioning eyebrow. "You're as deep in this as I am. What do you reckon?"

"I'd say we've got no choice," he said seriously. "We've got to trust someone and this bloke sounds as though he knows his way around."

With a heavy heart, Peter turned to Max and nodded.

***

Detective Inspector James Urquhart was as thin as a chapel hat peg and the beaked nose that dominated his face seemed to be quivering as it swung suspiciously round the room.

"This had better be good, Max," he said, the trace of a Scottish accent softening the words. "You've used up all your favours getting me here like this. Which one's Conway?"

"There," Max pointed. "This is Jack Howson, Chloe Pearson. And Viscount Stanfield."

Urquhart's head bobbed briefly on his scrawny neck in acknowledgement of the title.

"Aye, we've not met, but I've heard of you, of course," he said briefly to Billy. His nose swivelled towards Peter like a battleship's guns being brought to bear. "Not half as much as I've heard of Peter Conway since Max called me, though. You've got a hell of a lot of explaining to do, young man. And God help you if you give me any bullshit."

The snap of command forced Peter to revise his opinion of Inspector Urquhart. The measure of the man wasn't his wrinkled, ill-fitting suit or the vacuous expression generated by his drooping eyelids and weak chin. Those were camouflage, to trap the unwary. He suddenly felt guilty and nervous and it didn't help in the slightest to realise that it was exactly the reaction that Urquhart intended.

"Er... I'm not quite sure where to start," Peter

mumbled. "I mean, I don't know how much you've been told."

"The beginning would be a good place. Assume I know nothing. I'll tell you soon enough if you're boring me."

"It's a long story."

"You'll find I'm a patient man and I've got plenty of time." He suddenly smiled warmly. It transformed his face and Peter felt himself instinctively responding with a smile of his own. "Just tell me your story, the way it happened. That's what you got me here for, isn't it?"

"Yes," Peter said unenthusiastically, "I suppose it is."

James Urquhart cocked his head to one side and looked quizzically at Peter.

"No," he said with unexpected insight. "That's not it at all, is it? The first thing you want to know is whether you can trust me." He leaned back in his chair and spread his arms. "I can't help you with that. You've got to make up your own mind. I will say this much, though. My job is to catch and prosecute people who break the law, whoever they are and I take my work seriously. To me, that doesn't mean fitting up the most convenient suspect, it means finding out the truth, all of it. If you're innocent, you've got nothing to worry about. All I ask is that you don't hold anything back."

Peter glanced at Chloe and thought about her advice, conscious of the calm eyes of the policeman staring at him as though reading his mind. He'd know, Peter was suddenly certain, if anything was left out or covered up. The message in those eyes was unmistakeable, the product of years of listening to evasions and half-truth.

But beneath the cynicism Peter thought he could detect a core of icy determination, of integrity. Perhaps it was wishful thinking and he was only seeing what he wanted to see. There was only one way to find out for sure, though and the silence was already beginning to stretch uncomfortably. His mind drifted back to the day he'd heard the news of his Dad's death. By the time Peter realised his subconscious had taken this strangely compelling little man at his word, he'd already been talking for several minutes.

Chapter 19

"What an odd fellow," Chloe said as Max came back into the room after showing Inspector Urquhart out. "Not at all like a policeman, really. Where on earth did you dig him up from?"

Max grinned and tapped the side of his nose. "Not much of your average Mr. Plod about our Jimmy, is there? Did you expect size fourteen boots and a hearty 'Let's be 'aving you, then' while he felt your collar? I told you to trust me."

"Do you think he believed me?" Peter said. "He didn't say much."

"You're not under arrest, are you? He believed you all right. Didn't you see him twitch when you mentioned the Kaiserhof? I'll bet my pension he knew exactly what you were talking about."

"Can't be much of a pension, then. How would an ordinary Inspector know anything about that? More to the point, I can't see how he's got any clout to deal with the other stuff either. I reckon it was just a waste of time."

"Do you, now?" Max said knowingly. "Well let me tell you, you're dead wrong. Don't let the rank fool you. He's no ordinary copper, he's in charge of one of the Met's spookier Special Operations units. When he says jump, the uniform jobs just ask how high."

"How come you know so much about him, then?"

"Let's just say our paths have crossed a few times. The point is, if he's satisfied you're clean, that's the end of it."

Peter shrugged. "I'll have to take your word for it, I suppose. So what do we do now? Relax and hope for the best while he does whatever it is he's got in mind?"

Max grinned. "Not on your life. Spook or not, he's still got to work more or less within the law. We haven't got that disadvantage."

"What the hell's that supposed to mean?"

"It means we get down to business. I'll work the outside, do some serious arm-twisting to find out who's orchestrating the markets. There'll be a pattern behind the trading and that will give us the names we want if we dig deep enough. Meantime, you and Jack will be figuring out how to hack into Media Associates' communications network from the inside, with the help of one of my technical gurus."

"Where do I fit in?" Chloe interrupted. "I've got a stake in this, too."

Max looked across at Billy, who smoothly picked up the ball.

"That rather depends on you, my dear," he said. "Your boss, Derek English, is already on our target list, you see. That gives you a serious conflict of interests."

"But I..." Instinct prompted Chloe to bite off her protest. She didn't like his glinting, piggy little eyes, or his patronising arrogance. Powerful men were all the same in her experience, selfish and dangerous beneath their expensive suits and superficial charm. Peter was a fool to trust him or this creature of his, whose loyalty would be entirely to his paymaster. She glanced at Peter and suppressed a fond smile. His naivety was appealing, but he needed protection and she couldn't do that unless she was part of the team. Nor, she reminded herself, would she get her story, the breakthrough into the big-time she wanted so badly. Whatever Derek English had said, she'd learned a thing or two fighting her way through the journalistic ranks. She could smell a deal when it was being dangled in front of her and Billy Stanfield was fishing for something. More fool him, she thought gleefully, if he reckoned she was easy meat.

"I don't understand," she said. "How can you say it depends on me? You must realise I'm finished at the Globe after this. I can't go back... they'd never take the risk..." She let her eyes fill with tears. "My career's over, everything I've worked for... surely you can see that?

"I wasn't certain you'd grasp your position quite so clearly," Billy said. "It's not so uncommon for journalists to have a falling out with the editor, you know and carry on afterwards."

"I'm not a fool and despite what you may think I've got principles. Anyway, the man's a pig. I couldn't possibly go on working for him." Chloe paused and gnawed at her lower lip as if considering the implications for the first time. "I suppose that means I'm out of a job."

"Not necessarily. How would you like to come and work for me instead?"

"For you?" Her eyes widened in surprise that wasn't altogether feigned. "I'm intrigued. But I'm a journalist, not a charity case. The last I heard, you don't run a newspaper."

Billy hesitated for a split second and Chloe's instincts gave her a hefty nudge. He was hiding something.

"Well, no," he said. "I was thinking of taking you on as a freelance. A consultant if you prefer. Max can find out who's behind the dealings in the market, but we need the same sort of job doing on the press and media. You can bet Derek English isn't the only one who's up to his neck in this and you must know how to go about finding any other rotten apples in that particular barrel. After that, well, who knows? Maybe something else will turn up."

Like what, she wondered, knowing it would be a waste of time to push him. Whatever his hidden agenda was, she wouldn't winkle it out of him easily. Step one, though, was to sign up as part of his team.

"Go freelance? That's a big step. I mean, I can do the investigation you want, but there'd have to be more in it for me than just that and a vague promise."

"From where I'm sitting, you've not got too many options," Billy said acidly. "What more did you have in mind?"

Chloe took a deep breath. It was a gamble, but she reckoned playing the selfish bitch was the way to hook him and if he bought it, he'd not look for any other motives.

"I'd want exclusive reporting rights on whatever we find," she said bluntly. "I mean the whole thing - Peter's story, whatever Max comes up with, the works. That's not unreasonable. I wouldn't stand a chance going it alone without something big to build my reputation on."

"I've got no problem with that," Billy said with a

quick sideways glance at Peter and Max. "Provided, that is, nothing gets published without my prior agreement."

"And I get to keep any fees, including syndication rights."

"You must be joking." Billy's expression hardened. "I'm the one putting up the money for all this. I'll take fifty percent. Think of it as an agency commission."

"Twenty," Chloe shot back, calculating quickly. "But in that case I want a retainer up front. I've got to live off something while I'm doing your dirty work. Call it a consultancy fee, that way I'm sure your accountants can find a way to write it off against your tax bill."

For a moment, she thought she'd gone too far. His lips clamped into a thin line and a muscle in his jaw twitched. Then he put his head back and laughed, before naming a sum sufficiently generous to take her breath away. And that, to Chloe's amazement, was that, apart from some haggling over whether getting his agreement to publish meant censorship. No editorial veto, they settled, but he'd have the final say on when the story could be released. She'd seen at first hand the consequences of letting the cat out of the bag too soon, so she had no problem about being careful there. In any case, she thought smugly, there was no real downside for her. Resigning from the Globe wasn't such a big deal. If the worst came to the worst, the malignant dwarf wouldn't hesitate to have her back if she came bearing information that might save his bacon. Finally, she thought with mounting excitement, I've got it made. Whatever happens.

***

Two frantic days later, Peter put the phone down with a sigh and massaged the back of his neck, which had developed a crick. He shuddered, wishing he'd never started his foolish crusade. He wasn't cut out for this sort of thing, but somehow he kept getting sucked in deeper. Like the latest plan Max's people had fastened on. It was crazy, dangerous. The bugger of it was, he'd dreamed up the basic idea himself, but hadn't had the sense to keep his mouth shut. Now, unless one of the others had devised something better, there was a real risk they might decide to go for it. And if that happened, there was only one logical way for things to develop...

A shout from the next room interrupted his thoughts. They were all in there, waiting to start a council of war and the demand to know whether he had finished his bloody phone calls yet had a distinct overtone of exasperation. They wanted to get on with it and he was fresh out of excuses.

Max had already started his briefing when Peter walked leadenly into the room. He frowned and carried on, waving at Peter to take a seat.

"In a nutshell, then, we've tracked share transactions on four unusual market upheavals in the last six months," he said, "and found a consistent pattern. That includes our reference case involving Biotechnology stock and the events surrounding what happened to the Holts, so it's pretty clear that they're all linked. By my reckoning, Hardcastle and his cronies have made tens of millions just from those four and we don't know yet how much further back it goes."

"So it's conclusive, then, that the markets are being rigged?" Billy interrupted.

"I'd say so, yes, if you accept the basic premise that it's being done deliberately by insiders. And Chloe's come up with a similar pattern of media activity that suggests close coordination to deliver the required messages to analysts and investors."

"You're saying we've got the proof we need, then?"

Max shook his head slowly. "Unfortunately it's still mostly circumstantial," he said. "A good lawyer would tear our case to pieces and you can bet they'd hire the best if they needed to."

"We're not talking about the Old Bailey, for God's sake," Billy said impatiently. "Surely there's enough to convince the regulators? That's all we need."

"I'm afraid not," Max shrugged an apology. "You know how the market works. It's all about timing. When a bandwagon starts to roll, everybody tries to jump on board and the dealing rooms go crazy. It's too complex to track with certainty. All they'd have to do is claim they were fractionally quicker off the mark than everybody else, a bit smarter or more professional and who could prove for sure they were lying? You've done that sort of thing often enough yourself."

"That's different," Billy said hotly. "I work on instinct, experience and careful research. Insider deals aren't like that."

"Maybe not, but it's a thin line to walk. Anyway, this isn't classic insider trading. That sticks out like a sore thumb because it's based on specific information known only to one or two people. Here we're looking at widespread shifts of market sentiment, backed up by extensive media coverage."

"But if we can show the media are being orchestrated...?"

"I've got the same problem as Max," Chloe interjected. "All the signs are there, but proving a conspiracy is something else entirely."

"For Christ's sake. Haven't we got anything we can work with?"

"We've got a pretty clear idea of who's in on it," Max said. "That's a start."

"Well who, then?"

Max passed over a typewritten list. It barely filled a single page and Billy's face flushed with anger as he glanced down the sheet.

"Is this all?" he shook the paper disgustedly in Max's face. "You must be joking. There can't be more than twenty names here. What the hell are you playing at? There must be more to it than this load of... of..." He spluttered to a furious halt.

"No, boss, think about it," Max said calmly. "There may be a few we've missed, but it doesn't take many key players to exert one hell of a lot of leverage in the financial markets. All the rest go along for the ride if the message is believable and according to Peter these people know exactly how to make sure of that. Same for the media, all that's needed is three or four of the popular dailies and a couple of the leading TV stations spinning the same line and away you go. That doesn't add up to an army. You can keep a group like that real tight."

"I can see that, I suppose. But it doesn't explain what my company's doing on the list. It's outrageous to suggest I've got anything to do with this."

"Sorry, we can only work on the evidence. Your people definitely seem to be involved. We're not suggesting you are, personally, of course. But that's our other problem."

"What do you mean?" Billy snapped. "It sounds to me like you're saying I'm part of it. Unless you're suggesting I don't know what's going on in my own business, which is just as bloody offensive."

"I mean we can't be sure which individuals are involved. You trust your staff to run day-to-day operations; you've got no choice, just like anyone else in your position. There's probably three or four of your people with enough clout to start a run, buying or selling. Any one of them could have done a deal with Hardcastle's mob behind your back."

"Impossible. Most of them have been with me for years. You're barking up the wrong tree, I tell you."

"No need to try and shout me down. You may not like it, but the facts say you need to think again about that. We're talking big money here, don't forget, wads of cash in the back pocket wouldn't be a problem. The same with the press, the proprietors or editors could easily twist an ambitious reporter's arm to slant a story, but equally one of the top journalists could get away with it on his own initiative."

"We're buggered, then. That's what you're saying."

"Not exactly. The real problem is, we don't know how they operate their network. If we could crack that, we'd know precisely who was in the loop. It'd give us the kind of hard evidence we need, too."

"Brilliant. Any more glimpses of the obvious?"

"Save your sarcasm. Thanks to Peter, here, we may have found a way into the Media Associates computer system. It's risky, but I think I can pull it off."

All eyes turned on Peter and he wished the ground would open up and swallow him.

"You told me the security software was too tough to crack," Billy said accusingly.

"It is," Peter said. "I mean, we could get lucky eventually, I suppose, but we've tried just about everything to hack it and we've not managed to get through yet."

"Well what the hell is Max talking about, then?"

"Tony had to replace a disk drive the other day and it just occurred to me there might be a simpler way..."

The idea had come to him out of the blue at the end of a long, frustrating morning with Tony Darwin, Max's technical whiz kid. The sophisticated password protection and software firewalls in the Media Associates' system were still stubbornly resisting all attempts to persuade them to cooperate. Tony was a hacker 'par excellence', but even he was running out of ideas. Logging on to the system through the external modem was a piece of cake, Tony reckoned, although how he did it baffled Peter. But once on line, there just wasn't enough time to figure out how to by-pass the next layer of electronic guardians before they triggered an unauthorised access alarm.

The latest attempt ended in another tense and sweaty failure and as Tony cut the telephone link his computer suddenly went dead with an expensive-sounding crunch. The burst of obscene invective he let rip was astonishing for such a mild-mannered man and Peter watched in fascination as he reached for a screwdriver and started attacking the computer case, muttering furiously. People forgot that effing computers had mechanical moving parts, he said and hard disk drives were delicate bastards. The heads picked up data by moving across a spinning magnetic disk and the tolerances were very fine. Like a jumbo jet flying full speed six inches off the ground. On that scale, a speck of dust was equivalent to hitting a brick wall. That was more than enough to make it crash, with spectacular and terminal consequences. Tony ripped the ribbon cable off the back of the defunct drive, pulled it out of the case like a rotten tooth and tossed it disgustedly into the bin.

"Peter," Billy's voice cut impatiently across his recollections, "what's a broken disk drive got to do with anything? Get to the point, will you?"

"Sorry." Peter came back to the present with a jolt. "That is the point, really. It only takes a minute or two to replace the disk drive. Just a few screws and a plug-in cable connector. Most people think computers are incredibly complicated, but they're not, not at that level, anyway."

"I'm still not following you."

"It's simple enough. The data we want is electronic, so our thinking's been focused on trying to get hold of it electronically. But it's stored on a disk drive. That's just a metal box, something we could get our hands on physically. Why not steal that instead?"

"A bit of old-fashioned burglary, you mean?" Billy chuckled. "I like it. Everybody's spending millions on security software to lock the front door and you want to go in the back door with a swag bag and a screwdriver." He looked quizzically at Max. "It can't be that simple, though can it?"

"It could be done. People get over-reliant on technology. It's easy to let the basics of physical security slip."

"And if Tony had this disk thing, he'd have all the time he wants then to crack the passwords and whatever?"

"It's better than that," Peter said. "We might be unlucky, but Tony tells me that most of the protection usually goes into stopping hackers accessing the hard drive in the first place. That's where we were blocked. Apparently there are ways to by-pass that entirely if you plug it into another machine. All you need to worry about then is whether individual files are password protected. Tony reckons most people are too lazy to do that, though."

"It still won't work," Chloe chipped in. "You've forgotten something fundamental. They'll know right away if a chunk of one of their computers is missing and have plenty of time to cover everything up. You might as well send them a postcard."

"I've thought about that," Peter said, "and I'm pretty sure we can cover our tracks if we play it smart."

They listened intently as he explained.

"That's bloody clever," Billy said finally. "I don't suppose we could slip a bug into Hardcastle's machine while we're at it? I mean, if we could listen in on him as well, we'd be miles ahead of the game."

"Out of the question," Max said firmly. "We're not dealing with amateurs. They'll scan the offices for bugs before any important meetings, as a matter of routine. They'd find it for sure."

"There may be another way to do that," Peter said diffidently. "I presume the devices are pretty small and you can stick them more or less anywhere?"

"About the size of my fingernail. What have you got in mind?"

"I'm not sure... How does this scanning business work? I mean, you wouldn't do it at random, or while people were actually there, would you?"

"Well, no, you wouldn't want technicians barging around in the middle of a confidential discussion, now, would you? My people do Billy's security and we scan first thing in the morning, before meetings get going. That takes care of any uninvited overnight visitors. I imagine it's the same at Media Associates."

"So if there was a way to get a bug in at the beginning of a meeting and out again at the end, you wouldn't pick it up?"

"No, I guess not," Max said, puzzled. "But how the hell would you do that? The only traffic in and out is the people and there's no way we can plant a microphone on Hardcastle himself."

"There's one other thing that might work. Something so commonplace I doubt anyone over there even notices any more."

"Go on."

"How about on a coffee trolley? Don't forget I've been in those offices. They wheel in coffee just before meetings start and each room has its own trolley, they're numbered to make the administration easier. If we could find out which meeting room Hardcastle normally uses and bug the one assigned to that room..."

His voice tailed off as Max leaned back in his chair, forehead creased in thought. The silence was uncomfortable and Peter began to think he'd made a fool of himself.

"Er, it may not be practical, of course," he said apologetically to nobody in particular. "The trolley would be parked in a corner. I don't know how sensitive these microphones are, whether they'd pick up anything at that range. I expect one of you can come up with a better idea."

No one could, it seemed.

"Max? What do you think?" Peter said.

"I'm thinking what a difference detailed inside knowledge makes. It'll work, if we can plant the bug. In fact it's bloody clever. I'd just forgotten you know your way around in there, that's all."

"Mm," Peter said. "I thought you might have."

Max looked at him sharply and Peter swallowed hard before continuing.

"I'm hoping you can come up with a better way to do this," he said. "You're the expert. Can't you bounce lasers off the windows or something?"

"'Fraid not. They've got a top class security team who'll have built defences against the latest surveillance technology. The old ways are still the best, if you can find the sort of loophole you've put your finger on."

"If their security's that good, it'll be pretty bloody dangerous getting in there."

"Yes. Taking risks is part of my job, though. I've got

to go in anyway to get at Hardcastle's computer."

"Do you know how to swap out a computer hard drive?" Peter forced himself to ask. "I mean, have you ever done that sort of thing?"

"No."

Peter stared at the impassive face and Max stared calmly back. The silence lengthened.

"I've built a couple of my own computers up from components," Peter said eventually.

"Have you, indeed?"

"Yes."

"That's good, then. You can show me what I've got to do."

"How are you planning to find your way to Hardcastle's office?"

"You can help me there, too. You've had the guided tour. And I can use your security pass to get in. We can doctor the photograph."

Peter thought of the confusing maze of corridors and offices and of the chances of a security guard finding a dodgy photograph on a stranger's pass.

"We'd be more likely to succeed if I did it, wouldn't we?" he said, feeling sick to his stomach.

"I think you already know the answer to that," Max said bluntly. His face seemed craggier than ever and his eyes bored mercilessly into Peter's. "But you know how dangerous it is. I won't ask you to take that kind of risk. It's up to you to decide how badly you want revenge for your father."

"You're a real bastard."

He smiled coldly. "So my mother always told me," he

agreed. "But she also told me I was a good judge of character. I figured you'd find the guts to volunteer, in the end."

Chapter 20

Sir Rodney Hardcastle felt not the slightest premonition of disaster when he strode into the foyer of number forty-six Bevis Marks. On the contrary, despite the unaccustomed earliness of the hour he felt good. It was a crisp, dry morning, winter darkness still lingering and for once it was gratifying not to be met by a crowd of sycophants trying to curry favour. They were drones, frequently irritating with their petty concerns and demands. The pleasures of tormenting such pathetic victims had grown thin over the years, though it amused him briefly to think of them all still snoring in their beds while he manipulated the wider canvas of their lives. The smile broadened on his lips as he ignored a salute from the uniformed security guard and headed to the lifts, savouring the deeper excitement of impending battle. Today would see the closure of another major deal. It wasn't the money that made his heart pump faster. Not any more. It was the satisfaction of bringing down another of his rivals, of watching the man crawl humiliatingly to him for help. He'd give it eventually, of course. The proposition was attractive and however rich you were, you didn't walk away from millions out of spite. But Charles Guthrie was one of the old guard, a supercilious snob who made his distaste for the lower social classes plain enough. Today, though, he'd have to grovel. That was the price for a succession of insults and slights over the years, none of which were forgotten or forgiven. A bog standard comprehensive education might not teach you much about the finer points of social etiquette, Sir Rodney thought smugly, but it sure as hell gave you a good grounding in how to exact revenge. The lift sighed smoothly to a halt at the fifth floor and he walked briskly down the corridor, still preoccupied with his thoughts. A hunched figure shuffling the other way, pushing a cleaning trolley, did not even register on his consciousness as he strode past and flung open the door to his office.

Underneath his grubby overalls, Peter Conway's pulse was still hammering with shock. The fact that he'd left the office door ajar was all that had saved him. If it weren't for that, he'd not have heard the bell announcing the arrival of the lift and been caught cold. What the hell was Hardcastle doing here at this time in the morning? A glance at his wristwatch confirmed he was well within the planned time parameters and he ran his hand shakily over the stubble on his chin. There should have been a huge safety margin according to Max's calculations and Peter wondered grimly what else they'd got wrong. Not that it mattered. It would all be over anyway if Hardcastle noticed the screw he'd dropped in that panicky rush to get out into the corridor and got curious. Sod it, he cursed, he'd been so close to finishing the job. It was such a small thing, the last of four screws to refasten the outer panels on the computer case, but he'd fumbled it and then there'd been no more time. Nothing to be done about it now, though.

Peter trudged on down the corridor, his thin face showing nothing as he concentrated on maintaining the dull-witted expression that was a vital part of his camouflage. A slow trickle of sweat ran stickily down his spine while his brain worked furiously. Instinct screamed at him that discovery was inevitable, but reason insisted the job was only half done and nothing terminal had happened yet. The odds were still good that nothing would. He fought back the urge to abandon the trolley and run for the exit. Stay cool and get to the lift, he thought desperately. If you make it that far, you're in the clear. If Hardcastle is going to spot anything, he'll have raised the roof by then. He almost believed it. But it was still the longest walk of his life.

As the doors of the service lift slid shut behind him, Peter slumped against the wall and flexed his aching back. His eyes were fixed on the basement button, the one that spelled exit and freedom. But it was the one above that he'd pushed and was glowing brightly to signal his destination. I must be bloody mad, he thought, feeling a reckless exhilaration bubbling to the surface. But revenge was sweet and suddenly he felt invincible.

A dull ping from the lift announced his arrival at the ground floor. His tour of the offices hadn't included the service areas, but the staff canteen where he'd had lunch was on this level. It was a fair bet that the coffee and biscuits originated round here too. Pulling himself together, he ignored the renewed ache between his shoulder blades and peered cautiously round the open doors. No home comforts here, he saw. The vinyl floor tiles and bare concrete walls of the corridor contrasted starkly with the designer decor of the Executive floors.

Another and potentially disastrous difference caught his eye and his heart missed a beat. Closed circuit TV cameras were mounted high on the walls, red lights blinking to prove they were active. Peter swore violently under his breath. It was blindingly obvious in retrospect that if the basement was covered, the same would apply to the other back-room areas, but they'd missed it. He'd got no plan for this contingency and he was caught like a rat in a trap.

As he watched, the nearest camera swivelled towards him. He was already on display, then. It would be suspicious to back away, nor could he stand here looking stupid. He gave the camera what he hoped would pass for a casual wave and stared down at the floor, thinking furiously. His eye caught faint ridges in the vinyl tiles, highlighted in the cold glare of the fluorescent lights. Wheel marks, perhaps, from the daily passage of coffee carts? They led away towards scarred swing doors at the left hand end of the corridor. There were no other clues and it was imperative to move, to give the appearance of knowing what he was doing and having every right to do it. To the left, then, he decided. He swung his trolley out of the lift and abandoned it against the wall, grabbing a bucket and a mop. Head down and swinging the mop industriously from side to side, he backed his way slowly along the corridor and away from the prying lens. The acrid smell of industrial disinfectant stung the back of his throat and made his eyes water, but he didn't dare lift his head. He risked a sideways glance. The camera had stopped following him, though the fish-eye lens would have a wide enough field of view to keep him in sight.

He swabbed faster. Time to get the bug planted was running out. The cleaning staff would be knocking off soon. He couldn't afford to be far behind them when they left and there was still a lot to get done.

Four floors above Peter Conway's growing worries, Rodney Hardcastle struggled unsuccessfully to keep his temper. When he had switched on his computer, none of his files had come up - a big, fat zero. Just a load of incomprehensible technical start-up data followed by one of those infuriating error messages on a black screen, saying 'Invalid System Disk', which was sitting there blinking infuriatingly at him. And of course the technical support teams were not yet in the office. Nor, apparently, was anyone else at their desk to vent his growing fury upon. He slammed the phone down on the third polite but useless electronic invitation to leave voicemail after the tone and swore to fire whatever damned idiot had installed that particular system. He didn't want to leave a goddam message like some junior clerk requesting permission to blow his nose. He wanted action, someone who'd get off their arse and do something, right now. Sir Rodney snatched up the phone again. There was at least one son of a bitch who'd better be at his desk, or he'd be out of a job so fast he wouldn't even feel the pain.

Fred Garrett felt uneasy. The job of night shift duty officer in the control room was a well-paid sinecure. His relief would be arriving soon and he was more than ready to call it a night. The bunions on his sixty-four year old feet were playing him up again, despite having been comfortably propped on the desk for the majority of the past seven hours and the last thing he wanted was trouble. But there was something definitely odd about that cleaner down in the first floor service corridor. He leaned forward with a grunt to take a closer look at the TV screen in front of him, ignoring the creak of protest from the waistband of his trousers as it bit deeper into his paunch. Fred's suspicion began to harden. He couldn't quite put his finger on what was wrong, but impending retirement hadn't completely dulled the instincts from forty-odd years of security work and they were nagging at him insistently now. Better safe than sorry, he decided and reached for the two-way radio. One of his team shouldn't be far away and it would only take a few minutes to get the situation checked out.

As his hand closed around the radio, the phone at his elbow rang loudly, making him jump. Bugger, he thought with mild annoyance. If this was another idiot who'd forgotten to recharge the battery on his walkie-talkie, he'd give him a piece of his mind. They were getting careless and it was high time he made an example of someone.

"Control room," he said irritably.

"Who am I speaking to?"

Fred's spine stiffened and his feet fell off the desk with a thump as he sat upright. Sir Rodney Hardcastle's voice was as unmistakeable as it was unexpected.

"Uh... Garrett, sir," he spluttered, searching his conscience and wondering what the hell might have gone wrong. "Duty officer."

"There's a fault with my computer. Send a technician

up to my office right away, will you?"

"Er... shall I transfer you to the technical support help line, sir?"

"Don't be a bloody fool. They're not answering. Why do you think I'm calling you?" Fred blanched as the angry voice rattled his eardrums and eased the phone away from his ear. "Get upstairs and find someone immediately."

"Yes, sir. But... er..."

"What is it, man?" Sir Rodney bellowed testily. "Can't you understand a simple instruction?"

"I'm not supposed to leave the control room unattended, sir," Fred muttered nervously, "and I'm not sure anyone will be in this early."

"I don't give a bugger about any of that, Garrett. Drag somebody out of bed if you have to. Get off your backside and sort it out, or you'll be looking for another job."

The receiver at the other end slammed down and Fred stared at the dead instrument in his hand. The bastard would fire him, too, he thought, forty years' service or not. He'd done it before. Fred broke out in a cold sweat at the vision of his pension disappearing and mopped his brow with a grubby handkerchief. He hastily pulled on his uniform jacket and buttoned his collar. By the time he reached the door, he'd broken into a lumbering trot.

Behind him in the empty control room, the bank of television monitors flickered. The diminutive figure of Peter Conway backed through a set of swing doors and disappeared from one screen only to reappear on another. Fred Garrett's empty chair was the only audience as he slowly mopped the floor alongside a row of trolleys, then bent down next to one of them with a cleaning rag in his hand, as if to tackle a particularly stubborn stain.

***

Liam Donovan drew the short straw that morning and was soon wishing he'd stayed in bed instead of conscientiously coming in early to tackle the backlog in his in-tray. It was bad enough being ordered about by a flabby old fart in a wrinkled uniform, who was in a muck-sweat about a computer problem without being able to give the faintest idea of what was wrong. As it turned out, though, he'd been nothing more than the warm-up act. Sir Rodney Hardcastle made the other guy look like motherhood and apple pie. This one was a dyed-in-the-wool bastard, he thought, behaving as though he was going to nail somebody to the wall for making his computer break down. And those snide remarks about not answering the phone were uncalled for - it wasn't his job to man the bloody help line, he wasn't even supposed to be in the office for another hour or so.

"It looks like a head crash," he repeated patiently. "It happens sometimes. I know it's a pain, but it's nobody's fault - just one of those things."

"Well just get on and fix it then," Rodney snapped. "I've got some urgent work to do and I need the machine right now. You've wasted enough of my time already."

The technician frowned as his eye caught something odd in the start-up diagnostics display. It looked like this machine was fitted with a type of disk drive the firm did not normally use. How would …

"How long will it take?" Rodney interrupted the technician's thoughts peremptorily. "I haven't got all day."

"I'll have to take it downstairs and swap out the drive. It'll only take a few minutes to fix the hardware, but …."

"Good God, man, I won't put up with this sort of incompetence, d'you hear? You've been fiddling about for twenty bloody minutes already. I'll be back in another ten and if you know what's good for you you'll have it back on my desk and working before then."

"No, wait, listen" Liam said desperately as Sir Rodney turned to leave the office. "It's the software." He struggled briefly to find the words that would convey the bad news to a layman. "I'm really sorry, sir, but you won't be able to use the machine for at least four or five hours. The drive is easy to replace, but then I'll have to set the machine up and reload all your software and data from the back-ups. That's what takes the time."

Liam bent over the back of the machine and concentrated on unplugging the peripherals while a stream of invective blasted over his head. If the old sod wanted to fire him, that was fine by him, there were plenty of other people out there who'd be glad to take him on. He bit back the temptation to tell Sir High-and-Mighty Hardcastle to stuff his job and walk out. He didn't have to put up with this sort of crap and he'd be damned if he was going to grovel when none of it was his fault. But wisdom, fuelled by the thought of the loan repayments on his new sports car, prevailed. Liam kept his mouth firmly shut, though it was by far the hardest thing he'd done so far this morning. The last connector came free and he scuttled gratefully out of the office with the computer tower in hand, pursued down the corridor by the sounds of Sir Rodney's displeasure.

When the door of the IT support workshop finally swung closed behind him, Liam Donovan was still fuming and rehearsing all the things he'd like to have said - should have said, he corrected himself angrily - to that arrogant shit upstairs. He'd had his belly full of this place, he decided and its toffee-nosed management could get stuffed. He'd start looking for another job this evening, on the internet and let his actions do the talking. They were a pretty useless lot anyway, he reckoned and his opinion was immediately confirmed as he set about dismantling the computer case. One of the screws was missing and that just about summed up the whole place. Not that it made any difference to the functioning of the machine; it just seemed to him to symbolise the fact that the people at the top didn't give a toss about looking after the equipment. Or their staff, come to that. The side panel popped off easily and he laid it tidily on the bench before reaching into the guts of the machine to disconnect the hard disk, nursing his resentment and forcing himself to concentrate. The ribbon cable connector was sometimes a sod to shift from the slot on the back of the drive and you had to be careful not to break off the pins. He worked it gently from side to side, then smiled in satisfaction when it slid free as though it had only been put together yesterday. It took a few seconds more to remove the power cable and the retaining screws, then he slid the unit from its rack and looked at it thoughtfully. It was awesome how they could pack all that sophistication into something no bigger than a paperback book, but there was something niggling away in the back of his mind about this one. Then, outside, he heard the rattling of a coffee trolley heading down the corridor for the first meeting of the day. The sound made him realise that he was ready for a cup himself and amazing technology or not, the drive was just so much junk now. He tossed it in the bin and headed for the drink machine with the beginnings of a smile on his face. He reckoned he'd earned a break and it would do Sir Rodney bloody Hardcastle no harm to be kept waiting.

***

Peter Conway kept his eyes fixed on the pavement as he scurried along close to the wall. Out here amongst all the city suits his overalls and cap seemed about as anonymous as a flashing neon sign, but he somehow felt less visible if he avoided eye contact. A shoulder knocked him off his stride and he looked up in annoyance. The offending young man who had pushed past seemed oblivious as he made his way on through the crowds, eyes fixed on the screen of the mobile phone in his hand and thumbs twiddling to respond to a text. Earplugs in, too, listening to God knows what on social media or some other app. Peter almost laughed as he saw most others on the street were similarly absorbed. His worries about avoiding eye contact were pretty far off the mark; he could have been naked and he doubted anyone would have noticed. Technozombies the lot of them, their machines and software interfaced with their minds far away in cyberspace like the input peripherals of a computer. The image nagged at his subconscious as though he'd seen something important, but he pushed it aside. It was still dangerous out here and delivering the package in his pocket safely was the priority.

He swung down a litter-strewn alley and through a nondescript doorway. A board on the wall displayed tarnished company nameplates, the gaps between them pockmarked with empty screw holes as testament to the impermanence of the businesses that utilised the rented offices. Peter supposed their aim was to lay claim to an apparently prestigious city address on their letterhead. It certainly wasn't to impress any clients that might drop by; the narrow stairs creaked alarmingly under the threadbare carpet and there was an unpleasant, pervasive smell of mildew. Neither the address nor the decor was important to the present project, though. What mattered was the clear line of sight between the second-floor room and the rear of Number 46 Bcvis Marks, plus the fact that they were within the half-mile transmission range of the bug he'd planted.

Chloe was waiting for him outside the open door of their temporary bolthole and grabbed him in a bear hug as he stepped forward onto the landing.

"You're late," she said accusingly, though the fervour of her embrace transmitted a warmer greeting. "What happened? We thought something must have gone wrong."

Peter kissed the top of her head gently. "I'm glad to see you, too," he said. "Are the others in there?"

"Yes, we've all been worried sick."

"Let's get inside, then and I'll bring everybody up to date."

Inside the room, there was an expectant silence as Peter stepped out of the overalls, wadded them and flung them into a corner like the remnants of a bad dream. The background hum of cooling fans and the intermittent rattle of disk drive heads from the bank of computers against one wall seemed deafening and he could smell overheated plastic overlaid with coffee and burnt toast. Tony sat watching, like a hungry spider surrounded by his electronic web.

"Did you get it, then?" he said. The reflections from the monitor screens on his glasses made him look eerily like part of the machinery.

"Yeah." Peter produced the disk drive he had removed from Hardcastle's computer. "I hope it was worth the effort."

"Give it here." Tony snatched the package, indifferent to the mechanics of the theft or Peter's state of mind. It was the twenty Gigabytes of confidential data, equivalent to the contents of a fair size public library, which interested him. "What about that drive of mine that crashed?" he added as an afterthought. "I presume you got it slotted in OK?"

"Sure. I'd like to see his face when he tries to boot his machine and it all goes tits up. It was a close-run thing, though. The bastard came in early and nearly caught me at it."

"Hardcastle was there?" Max Johnson stiffened in his chair near the window and there was alarm in his voice. "Did he see you?"

"Of course he sodding well saw me. I could tell you what after-shave he used this morning, he was that close. Your people got their homework wrong."

"He's never come in that early before," Max said defensively. "Not while we were watching, anyway. But how come... I mean, er, you got out OK, so you must have fooled him somehow."

"Sheer bloody luck. I'd nearly finished when I heard him coming. I managed to slip out into the corridor and make like I was part of the wallpaper."

"He didn't suspect anything, then?"

"I don't think so, or he'd have collared me there and then. He must be used to seeing cleaners about the offices first thing."

"Good job you kept your nerve." There was grudging approval in Max's expression and Peter wondered what it would take to drag a real compliment out of him. "What about the rest of it, though?" He gestured at the reel-to-reel tape recorder sitting on the battered desk under the window. "Did you plant the bug?"

"Yes, but your people screwed up there, too. There were CCTV cameras all over the service areas, you never warned me about that."

"Shit."

"That's what I thought."

"But how..."

"I couldn't just turn tail and run for it, could I? Not with the cameras on me. So I showed them what they expected to see."

"What do you mean?"

"I scrubbed the goddamned floor, didn't I. That's what cleaners do. Gave them their money's worth, too. It was a fucking long corridor."

Max looked at him blankly for a moment, then started to chuckle.

"It's not bloody funny," Peter said indignantly.

"No of course it's not," Max spluttered, his shoulders shaking with mirth. "It's brilliant." He reached out and clapped Peter on the back. "Bloody brilliant," he repeated. "I misjudged you. If you ever want a full-time job, just say the word. You're a natural."

"You must be joking. I just hope it's paid off, that's all," Peter said, glancing across the room at Tony, who'd already deftly fitted the stolen drive into the cage on the test rig and powered it up. Standardisation was a two-edged sword, he reflected. Anything that fit one computer would work just as well in another these days. 'Plug and Play' was the marketing jargon and it was amazing that nobody seemed to have realised the full implications. Technology blinded even the cleverest people to the obvious at times. He wandered across to have a closer look.

"What exactly are you doing?" he said, looking at the festoon of wires sprouting from back of the equipment.

"I've set up my disk drive as the Master and running theirs as a slave. With luck, that'll get round all their security and we're home free."

"I don't follow."

"It's simple. Look, see here, the wiring and connectors are already in place to run two hard drives, if you want, that's standard on most machines these days. You just have to set up the operating system to recognise one as the master, which boots the system and runs the application software and the other as the slave, which you can use for data."

"But the applications are all on their disk, surely?"

"Exactly. That's where they've got all their passwords and security routines to prevent you using those programs to access the data. But this way, I don't need to go down that route. I run them from my drive, not theirs."

"Hang on a minute. How did you get hold of copies of their programs?"

"Easy." Tony gave Peter a scornful look. "They use standard packages, Microsoft Office and so on, like most businesses these days. You can buy them in any halfway decent computer store. I've loaded the same stuff, except I've set it up with my own passwords. That way, I can access the data on the slave drive without ever starting up their version of the application program. All their front-end protection's irrelevant then."

"We still need to crack their security if we're going to hack into their network from outside, though, don't we?"

"Yeah, sure," Tony waved Peter's objection away, "there's plenty of time for that later. It won't be hard to unravel now I've got my hands on the disk. Meantime, though, we should be able look at whatever Hardcastle's downloaded from the network servers, plus his own personal stuff. That's not bad for starters. Look, I'll show you." Tony tapped a few keys and file names started scrolling down the monitor. "There," he said triumphantly, jabbing the screen with his finger. "How does a directory called 'Media Associates' grab you?"

Chapter 21

Later that day, back at the flat in St Katherine's Dock, Billy Stanfield was lost in thought as he listened to the recording of Sir Rodney Hardcastle and Charles Guthrie. Their voices were so clear he might have been sitting in the meeting room next to them.

"This is a rare privilege, Charles," Sir Rodney was saying, his voice oozing saccharine. "You don't often go visiting without your gaggle of bright young men around you. Have they decided you can be trusted off the leash today?"

"I think you know why I'm here, Rodney. What I have to say is best kept between the two of us."

"It's this takeover bid from Athena, I imagine. They've really caught you with your pants down, by the sound of things. I tried to warn you, but you gave me the brush off. That hurt, you know. You should pay more attention to your friends."

"Look, I know we've not exactly been close..."

"Not a bit of it, lad, I know how the old boy network operates and it's not your fault if I'm a peasant in a flat cap, now, is it? But even the best of us makes a muck of things sometimes. That's when you find out who your friends really are."

"I've not got too many of those at the moment," Charles said tiredly. "You know that my institutional investors are threatening to sell me out?"

"That's a damn shame." Sir Rodney suppressed a smirk at the thought of all the strings he'd pulled to ensure exactly that outcome. "They're a fickle lot. Perhaps if you'd been a bit more, er, attentive towards them? I've never gone in for arse-licking much myself, it leaves a nasty taste in the mouth, don't you know. But I'd always figured your charm was one of your strong points."

"I can do without the cheap jibes, thanks all the same."

"Don't get tetchy with me because your aristocratic chums have dropped you in the shit." Sir Rodney growled. "I may not have their breeding, but at least I'm still prepared to talk. I take it you need help. What did you have in mind?"

"I need to protect my share price. It's under pressure at the moment..."

"Dropping like a stone, old fellow, the last time I checked. Athena will pick you off for a song unless you can put some muscle behind the stock."

"Yes, quite," Charles said sourly. "I need to find some buyers in the market to push the price back up."

"You need a bloody sight more than that, I reckon."

"What do you mean?"

"With all due respect, your group's not exactly in sparkling shape, is it? Your profits are off and your assets are under-utilised. Too much time poncing about on the grouse-moors and not enough getting your hands dirty behind your desk, I suspect, eh? Easy trap to fall into, that, if your tastes run in that direction."

"And yours don't, naturally."

"You know me, Charles. Muck and brass, lad, that's the way I was brought up."

"I can turn the business round. All I need is some

breathing space."

"Aye and a bloody miracle. What you need is for Athena's shares to crash while yours rise. They're only offering paper and that would stop the bid in its tracks."

"That's not likely to happen, though, is it, without some heavyweight backing."

"No." The monosyllable was delivered bluntly, like a door slamming.

"You could do it, though. It wouldn't be the first time you've played the white knight."

"Yes, I could." Sir Rodney's voice was creamy with satisfaction. "If I wanted to. But why the hell should I, eh? At my time of life, one of the few remaining pleasures is watching bastards like you go to the wall."

" You're my last chance. I'm asking... for God's sake, man, I'm begging if that's what you want... will you do it?"

The silence was broken only by the background hiss of the tape as the reels slowly turned.

"That depends," Sir Rodney said eventually.

"On what?"

"On how far you're prepared to go, old boy. What sort of risks you're prepared to take."

"Suppose the group pension fund happened to be reviewing its investment strategy," Charles said. "The trustees might consider, for example, placing up to twenty million pounds in a discretionary fund with your Liechtenstein bank to be invested as you see fit. A sum like that could make a significant impact on the market, don't you think? And I'm sure they would be flexible on the question of your fees for the service."

"You're suggesting using your own pension fund to buy back shares in your company and push up the price?"

"Don't pretend to be shocked, Hardcastle," Charles Guthrie snapped. "You've done worse than that in your time and got away with it."

"Aye, maybe I have and you've turned up your priggish little noses at me for it, you and your establishment cronies. The boot's on the other foot, now though, isn't it?"

"I'm sorry, I didn't mean..."

"I know exactly what you meant. All right, this is how it goes. I'll need fifty million, not twenty, to invest and the management fee will be ten percent, up front, plus I get to keep any profits on the trades if we succeed. Oh, yes and I'll need your signature on a waiver that I'll carry no liability for losses under any circumstances. After all," he sneered, "shares in the Guthrie Group aren't exactly what you'd call a blue-chip bet at the moment."

"Fifty million? I... I'm not sure..."

"Do you want to save your miserable little company or not? There's one other thing, too. It'll only work if there's a credible reason for buying Guthrie shares, otherwise it'll be obvious what's happening. I don't give a toss if you end up in jail, but I'll be damned if I'm going to join you there."

"What sort of reason?"

"Well it's not going to be the strength of the management or your profitability, is it? We'll have to attack Athena. If we can push their share price down, that undermines the basis for their bid. Once that's in doubt, it will seem reasonable that other investors might gamble on you turning things round on your own. You've got the asset base, you're just not leveraging it properly."

"Can you do that? Undermine Athena, I mean?"

"You'll sign up the Guthrie Group for a PR campaign through Media Associates. That'll be the vehicle I use."

"Public relations? You must be joking, that's all bullshit."

"Those are my conditions. By the way, there'll be a flat fee of a million for the PR contract, on top of the other arrangements. You can put that through your group accounts in the normal way, though, along with the fees for your other professional advisors. I don't imagine anyone will question that your image needs polishing up, under the circumstances"

"I'm not prepared to piss money down the drain. And I can't swing fifty million from the pension fund. I might be able to go to twenty-five."

"No. That's not enough to move the market."

"Too bad." There was the sound of a chair being pushed back. "Give me a call if you decide to get serious."

"If you go out that door you're on your own and you know damn well what that means," Sir Rodney said viciously. "I'll settle for forty million plus the PR stuff. I'll undertake to buy in shares up to another ten million from my own resources if needs be, but the price for that will be a seat on your board after the dust has settled. Last chance, take it or leave it."

"You're a hard-nosed bastard, I'll give you that."

There was a pause before Charles Guthrie continued. "Deal. I'll get my people to set up the arrangements."

"No need. I've got the contracts here. You're chairman of the pension trustees as well as chief executive, aren't you? You can fill in the numbers and sign them now."

"You were bloody sure of yourself, weren't you?"

"It wasn't hard. You high and mighty types are no better than the rest of us. I knew you'd try to save your skin any way you could when it came to the crunch. We're two of a kind, Charles. The only rules that matter are winning and making sure you don't get caught."

"Show me your damned papers, then and let's get on with it."

Peter reached forward and clicked the tape machine off.

"That meeting finished just two hours ago," he said matter-of-factly. "And the written agreements you have there," he pointed at the table, "are the final drafts from Hardcastle's computer as of this morning. Guthrie signed them both and like the man said, all you have to do is fill in the numbers."

There was silence in the room, apart from the faint hooting of a boat on the river. Peter ran his finger nervously round his shirt collar. Then Billy's eyes swivelled to fasten on him. There was a strange blankness about them and he shivered involuntarily.

"You're certain that they don't suspect we've got hold of any of this?"

"Positive," Peter said firmly. "It stands to reason. There's no way they'd have struck a deal like that if they had the slightest hint of a leak. I mean, it's illegal to try and rig your share price during a takeover battle, isn't it?"

"Oh, yes, it's certainly that." Billy's face twitched and began to redden, then his body started shaking. Peter's alarm turned to astonishment. Billy Stanfield was laughing, fit to bust, gasping for breath as he tried to hold it in. "Illegal," he spluttered and dissolved again into helplessness. "That's not the half of it... I'm sorry..."

Peter waited patiently until Billy finally got a grip. "Are you going to let me in on the joke?" he demanded. "I risked my ass to get this stuff and I don't see what's so funny."

Billy pulled out a large monogrammed handkerchief with a flourish and wiped his streaming eyes.

"I'm truly sorry," he said, breathlessly, " It's just that those two have been at each other's throats for years and Charles Guthrie is such a self-righteous bugger. It was... it was..." Another explosive titter shook his fleshy frame. "It was priceless to hear him crawling around with his begging bowl and swallowing humble pie. Nobody dishes it out better than Hardcastle when he's got the upper hand and you could tell he was enjoying every millisecond. I'm ashamed to say it, but so did I."

"It just seemed plain nasty to me."

"You don't know Charles. Believe me, it's poetic justice. But the best bit is Hardcastle. It's beautifully ironic, don't you think, that in humiliating Charles Guthrie, he's also destroyed himself? Not that he knows it yet, of course."

"How do you mean, destroyed himself? We obtained this stuff illegally, so we can't use it in a court of law. Anything else we find will just be circumstantial, the same as before."

"Not this time. The rules in takeover situations are draconian, you know, much more so than for normal trading and we know exactly what's going to happen. We'll be able to track and document it every step of the way."

"I'm not so sure. And what about the thugs that killed my father? There's nothing we can pin on them yet."

Billy clapped him on the back. "Don't be such a pessimist, Peter. Take my word for it, Hardcastle will be going down for fraud. Take him out and the rest of them will be finished. Cheer up, for Christ's sake. You've won."

It wasn't enough, Peter thought, not by a long chalk. But this wasn't the time or the place to take issue.

"What's the next step, then?" he said.

"I think I'll go out and buy myself a newspaper."

"What the hell for?" Peter said, frowning. "You can catch the news on the telly, if you want."

Billy laughed delightedly. "No, I didn't mean that. The Globe is part of the Athena group. I've always fancied owning a national daily and something tells me the shares will be going cheap in a few days."

"You're kidding... you can't mean it. That's insider trading, isn't it? The regulators will have you for breakfast."

"Oh, I don't think so," Billy said airily. "What inside information are you talking about? You and Max may be privately investigating Hardcastle, but I couldn't possibly know anything about that, could I now?"

"But that's..."

"That's just business," Billy interrupted. "Besides, I've got to find a new job for Chloe Pearson. She'll have a juicy scandal to write about before long and the Globe would be a perfect outlet for her talents. It'll make her name and you wouldn't want to deny her the chance, would you?"

"It would make you a tidy fortune in increased circulation, too, you crafty sod. You're as bad as the rest of them."

"You're not being fair," Billy said, looking at Peter reproachfully. Then his eyes started to twinkle. "But it would be a shame to miss the opportunity to give a bastard like Hardcastle a good kicking while he's down. You of all people can't argue with that."

***

The next few days saw Peter becoming increasingly irritable. Chloe, after a brief period of euphoria over the prospect of writing leaders for the Globe, buried herself in research and was moody and preoccupied. If that wasn't bad enough, Max's goons were a constant reminder of the threat they were still living under, spoiling what few moments they had together. Max, meanwhile, was immersed in a mountain of printouts from Hardcastle's files, when he wasn't rushing off on mysterious errands to follow up the most recent revelation from the bug. Peter's demands for information met with short shrift, though Max seemed to have plenty of time for secretive briefing sessions with Chloe and Billy. Even James Urquhart, who put in a brief appearance in the shabby office, was poker-faced and unhelpful. Enquiries were proceeding satisfactorily, he said and Peter was not to worry, he was no longer considered a suspect, though witness statements might be required in due course. Peter took it to mean that progress, if any, was minimal, which added to his frustration and puzzlement. What was Urquhart doing here anyway, he wondered, in the midst of what was clearly a surveillance operation of highly dubious legality? Max clearly had no qualms about any potential consequences. Quite the reverse, he and Urquhart seemed thick as thieves, which raised all sorts of unanswered questions about their relationship. Scouring the financial pages of the newspapers was equally unrewarding. After a few largely speculative reports of a takeover battle between Athena and the Guthrie Group, the matter had seemingly vanished into a black hole.

The only things to brighten his mood were the arrival of his new Hasselblad camera, courtesy of the insurance adjusters and the fact that Tony, the computer technician, was the sort who enjoyed an audience for his arcane skills. Peter quickly gave up on his attempts at social chitchat, which earned him nothing more than blank looks and awkward silences. But bits and bytes, it seemed, were different. Press those conversational buttons and Tony was happy to talk for hours, oblivious to Peter's lack of comprehension of much of his monologue. It beat staring at the peeling paint on the ceiling, though and passed the hours between the takeaway meals. Gradually Peter found his grasp of the technicalities improving and when Tony finally cracked the codes and hacked his way into the Media Associates network he felt a genuine sense of elation. Maybe now, he thought, they could get to the underlying issues, instead of just skimming the surface. There was still something fundamental missing. They might know what was going on. They might even have found a way to stop it. But they still had little idea of how these people were exercising their control. At the back of his mind something stirred as though he knew the answer, but when he reached for it, it vanished.

Chloe came into his bedroom on the third night while he was deeply asleep and woke him, putting a hand over his mouth so he made no sound.

"The others are all asleep," she whispered. "We need to talk."

Her face was a blur in the darkness and he reached out to gather her into his arms.

"I thought you'd forgotten about me," he said softly.

"No," she giggled, wriggling away from his embrace. "Stop it. I'm serious. I need to talk to you. There's something really strange going on around here."

"You mean apart from you creeping into my bedroom in the middle of the night?"

"Quit playing the fool, will you? We may not have much time before someone notices I've gone."

"So what? There's nothing to be embarrassed about."

She shook her head abruptly. "They don't want me talking to you. Haven't you noticed? And I don't think Max's men are protecting us, I think they're keeping us prisoners."

Peter thought of the constant presence at his shoulder

and alert eyes watching his every move.

"They take their work seriously," he admitted. "What makes you think there's more to it?"

"I'm hitting a brick wall every time I try and follow up on this mind control theory of yours. All they want to talk about is old-fashioned fraud and putting Hardcastle in the frame, like it's personal, somehow."

Peter frowned and sat up. "The issues go much deeper than that," he said. "Are you saying they don't believe me?"

"No, I'm saying I think maybe they're trying to bury it. I've been around long enough to spot a cover-up when it's staring me in the face. You must have noticed too, surely?"

The frustrations of the past few days paraded through his mind. He'd met his share of brick walls, too. Media Associates' computer systems were the key to the whole affair, an electronic trail to the Kaiserhof techniques and the secrets of how they were being used. Chloe's accusation would certainly explain why was it so difficult to get Max to exploit their success in accessing the network, or even consider it. But what if those systems weren't so important after all? The sudden thought startled him. Where the hell had that come from? An image of a city street full of people staring at their mobile phones popped into his head and he straightened with a sharp intake of breath.

"Ouch," Chloe said. "Watch what you're doing with your bloody elbows."

"Sorry. I've just realised I think we're on the wrong track. I've never been able to figure out exactly how these bastards are getting inside people's heads. I've always assumed it was their computer systems. But what if it's not their systems, but ours?"

Chloe raised herself and stared down at him wide-eyed. "What are you talking about?"

"It occurred to me the other day, watching all these City types walking along the street staring into their mobiles as though their brains were on another planet, but it's only just come back to me. Half the reason all this mind control stuff is so hard to believe is that it depends on a practical way to push particular buttons in individual people's heads, right? Well what better way to do that than to have them all plugged directly in, like a keyboard into a computer?"

"You're kidding."

"No. Think about it; Google, Facebook and the like collect personal information and tailor their services actively back to individuals. That's not so different from a programmer interfacing with his computer and giving instructions. Or take these new gaming apps that are so addictive - what's the difference between putting that into people's heads and downloading a new program into a computer? Back in the day the Nazis had to work through mass media and we've been stuck in that mindset. But technology has moved on and the Kaiserhof people surely will have too. Suppose they have figured out how to control the behaviour of individuals, not just mass reactions? We voluntarily plug ourselves in and all they have to do is download their programs, press our buttons and away we go."

Chloe snorted.

"That's rubbish. These big tech companies would spot

it a mile off if outsiders were fiddling with their software like that."

Peter shook his head.

"No, why would they? First they're not looking for that sort of thing and any clever hacker can find ways to hide code in other people's programs. Second, it's virtually impossible for them to monitor in detail the content sent over their platforms anyway. And third, it's not a million miles away from what the tech companies are trying to do themselves with their algorithms and targeted advertising."

"Well in that case we're screwed, aren't we." Chloe slumped down on the bed with a sigh. "Whether I'm right about a cover up or not makes no difference. Nobody's ever going to root the bloody stuff out if it's buried deep inside Google or Facebook."

"There's still one way left to stop them."

Chloe raised an eyebrow.

"Oh, yeah? What's that then?

Peter was about to reply when he heard a faint scuffling noise. Her absence apparently hadn't gone unnoticed and if she was right about Max's real role in all this the consequences of being caught whispering in the dark didn't bear thinking about. His brain raced. There was only one other innocent explanation for her presence. Well, not innocent, exactly, but understandable and not inherently suspicious. He threw back the covers and hauled her unceremoniously into the bed beside him, his hand over her mouth to still the squeal of surprised indignation. He clamped his lips to her ear.

"There's someone listening at the door," he muttered

urgently.

He felt her body relax and he took his hand away as she nodded her understanding. He felt a leg slide silkily between his and the touch of her teeth nibbling his earlobe.

"We'd better not disappoint them, then," she whispered wickedly, before covering his mouth with hers.

***

The following morning, back in the dingy rented office, little seemed to have changed. Chloe's distant, slightly aloof manner remained intact, though there was perhaps a hint of a sparkle in her eyes where there had been none before. Tony was silently preoccupied with his incomprehensible computer game. Peter, as usual, felt like a spare part, but more conscious than ever of watchful eyes following him as he prowled up and down trying to figure out what to do.

"Sit down and relax, Peter, for God's sake," Max finally snapped at him. "You're driving me mad wearing out the carpet like that."

"I can't help it. I'm bored and none of this," he waved his arm disparagingly around the room, "seems to be getting anywhere."

"Patience, man, patience," Max said reassuringly. "We've got to wait for Hardcastle to make his move. It'll only be another day or two."

"There's nothing stopping us trying to nail those killers in the meantime. That pal of yours, Urquhart, seems a waste of space to me."

"That's police business now. We can't interfere in his

investigation, there'd be hell to pay. Don't worry. He's a good detective. He'll get there in the end, you'll see."

"He's come up with bugger all so far. We don't even know who these guys are."

Max frowned irritably. "As a matter of fact we do," he said. "Sam Garvey is the head of security for Media Associates and Mike Arnold is his number two. But knowing their names and proving they've been going round killing people are very different. Now drop it, will you? Leave it to the experts."

Like hell I will, Peter thought as he gave his grudging assent. Chloe was right that you couldn't destroy the delivery mechanism, so the only way left was to get rid of the people giving the instructions in the first place. There must be some way to smoke the bastards out, evidence or not and he wasn't about to let Max or anyone else brush things under the carpet. His eyes strayed to Tony and his computer. Things needed stirring up and there was the means to do it, if only he could figure out what and how. He went back to his seat and bowed his head in thought.

When Max's phone rang a while later, it was quickly apparent from the sudden tenseness of his muscles that something significant was happening. He barked a few staccato questions, then hung up.

"Problems?" Peter asked.

"That was Roger Collins. It looks as though Hardcastle's making his move. I told you it wouldn't be long."

"What's happening?"

"There's been heavy selling of Athena when the

market opened and apparently now there are rumours circulating about undisclosed liabilities in one of their subsidiaries. Billy wants Chloe and me over there in the dealing room so we can follow developments on the spot. You can hold the fort here."

Peter's face betrayed no emotion, but his heart leapt at the prospect. With Max out of the way he'd have a free run at Tony and he could put that to good use. He nodded obediently and followed them to the door.

"Make sure you don't let the bastard off the hook," he called after them as they clattered down the rickety stairs. His only reply was the slam of the front door and he turned back into the office.

"Looks like you and me have drawn the short straw," he said to Tony with a shrug. "What do you say we try and have some fun, liven things up a bit?"

"Like what?" Tony said indifferently.

"Like seeing what you can do with that machine," Peter waved towards the computer keyboard. "You claim to be able to get into Media Associates' systems, but I've seen precious little to back it up."

Tony bridled. "Are you saying I'm a liar?" he demanded.

"Well, I don't know, do I? Why don't you show me? There must be plenty of useful stuff in there we could get at, if you're as good as you say."

"I dunno," Tony shuffled his feet and looked awkward. "Max said I wasn't to pinch any of their stuff, in case they cottoned on."

"I thought you were supposed to be better than that," Peter said scornfully. "It's all been a bit of a waste of time if you can't get in without leaving dirty great footprints all over the place, hasn't it?"

"They'd never catch me. I can get in and out clean as a whistle, but Max said..."

"Yeah, I know, they might notice if some of their files got nicked. Gives you a ready-made cop-out, doesn't it?" Peter crossed his fingers and hoped for the best. "He didn't say you couldn't put something in, though, did he?"

"What would be the point of that?"

"It'd be good for a laugh, at least. And it would prove you're not just full of bullshit."

"I'm telling you, it would be a piece of piss. But..."

"Come off it, there's no way anyone would notice something like that," Peter interrupted. "I don't reckon you're as smart as you think."

"Oh yeah? You want to put your money where your mouth is? How about a tenner on it?"

"Make it twenty. It'll be like taking candy from a baby."

"You're on. This is just between you and me, though, right? Just for a laugh. What have you got in mind?"

Peter put his chin on his hand and pretended to think. After a couple of minutes, he looked up at Tony and grinned. What he had to say wiped the answering smile off Tony's face and replaced it with a frown.

"That's not fair," Tony complained. "You're talking about system files there, not user files. And targeting one specific machine on their network, that's really pushing it."

Peter held out his hand and rubbed his thumb and forefinger together. "That's twenty you owe me, then."

"Not so fast, you sly bastard," Tony shook his head. "I didn't say it was impossible, it just means setting up a simulated network on my machine to create the transaction data before I start on their side of the fence. Actually, technically it's quite an interesting challenge." His eyes lost focus as his mind addressed itself to the problem. "Leave it with me. You're not getting my money that easily."

By five o'clock when Peter locked up the office and headed down the stairs on his way back to the flat, he was twenty pounds worse off and heartily sick of Tony's crowing. But with a modicum of luck, it would turn out to be the best twenty pounds he'd ever spent.

Chapter 22

It took two more days for events to reach a climax. They were strange days for Peter, who floated in a kind of limbo, largely ignored in the eye of a hurricane of activity. The dossier Max was compiling grew thicker by the hour, fed by ever more complex analyses of share dealings and Chloe's reports on partisan media coverage. Their satisfaction was oddly mirrored by that of Sir Rodney Hardcastle and Charles Guthrie, whose recorded meetings from the still undetected bug betrayed their growing confidence that their deal was working. Strident headlines in the financial press punctuated the battle like growls of thunder as the takeover struggle intensified, share prices soaring and plunging as investors' sentiments swayed first one way, then another. The underlying trends moved inexorably against Athena, though, as small investors ran for cover under the pressure of an orchestrated campaign of media invective while the market makers made seemingly more measured decisions to move from 'hold' to 'sell'. It was around noon on the second day when the voices on the tape agreed that the time had come for large-scale intervention to buy Guthrie shares and sound the death-knell for Athena's bid. Billy Stanfield was like a hungry shark as he listened to the two men laying their plans for the following morning. The markets would go wild, he chuckled gleefully and Athena would be wide open to his raid. Twenty-four hours and he'd have the Globe in his pocket. After that, he'd have Hardcastle for breakfast. Peter smiled broadly too, though nobody particularly remarked on it amid the general air of elation. His own move would have to be a little earlier, he thought and he was glad the waiting was nearly over.

That night Peter was wide awake when the door to his room opened quietly and Chloe slid into bed next to him. After a moment, she leaned back on one elbow and stared down at his unresponsive figure.

"What's the matter?" she demanded with a pout. "You got a headache or something?"

"Just listening to make sure there's nobody following you, that's all."

"Charming, I'm sure. You really know how to make a girl feel wanted, don't you?"

"Sorry."

"So what's on your mind? It's obviously not me."

"I want you to do something for me."

"It'll be a pleasure."

"No," Peter giggled despite himself as he pushed her hand away, "not that. Not yet, anyway. It's about the men in black. You said that Max and Billy weren't really interested in them, but I sure as hell am. It doesn't look like Urquhart's getting anywhere, so I've... er... set something up myself. But I need your help to make it work."

"Christ Almighty, Peter, they're dangerous," she said with alarm. "I hope you haven't done anything stupid."

"Keep your voice down," Peter hissed urgently. "Look, I haven't just been wasting my time the last couple of days, I've been watching Max and Billy carefully. You said the other night they're working to their own agenda and you're right. They're out to get Hardcastle, no question, but they're steering clear of everything else. I can't go along with that."

"You may not have a choice. Garvey and Arnold have covered their tracks bloody thoroughly, whatever it is they and their people have actually done. There's no way you're going to be able to pin anything on them."

"There is one way."

"What's that?"

"Get one of them to turn informer."

Chloe snorted in disgust. "Fat chance. They're thick as thieves, literally. In any case, if you're even half right about what they've been up to, they'd be banged up for life whether they turned queen's evidence or not."

"Not necessarily. Those two must know a lot about the Kaiserhof archive and how it's been used, right? In their position they'd have to."

"I guess so. But so what?"

"Can you imagine what would happen if all that came out in public? Damn it, with all the spin that goes on, half the bloody political and financial establishment must be tangled up with Media Associates one way or another. The powers that be would be falling over themselves to avoid a scandal like that. It wouldn't take a genius to negotiate a deal in exchange for keeping quiet about that side of it."

"I thought you wanted to expose all that, not see it hushed up?"

"I want to get even for what they did to Dad and me and stop it happening again. But I'm not crazy enough to think you can rewrite history. Get rid of the spin doctors and I figure most of their creations will self-destruct anyway. Puppets are pretty useless if there's nobody pulling the strings."

"Even if you're right," Chloe said doubtfully, "It doesn't help. There's no way you're going to persuade one of them to talk, deal or no deal."

"I won't have to. Hardcastle will do the persuading for me once we convince him Mike Arnold has sold him down the river."

"You're mad. Mike Arnold's done nothing of the sort, you know that perfectly well."

"That's beside the point. If I've learned one thing in the past few months, it's that for all practical purposes the truth is whatever you can manipulate people into believing."

"That's crap. Anyway, you can't spin your way round these people, they're experts at it. They'd spot anything like that right away."

Peter sighed under his breath, grateful for the darkness that hid his grimace of exasperation. Perhaps it wasn't fair to blame her, they were reasonable objections, but did she think he was stupid, or what? He'd had plenty of time over the last couple of days to think it through. The plan was crystal clear in his mind and he wished she'd just listen so they could get on with it. It was simple, really. As soon as the markets opened in the morning, Hardcastle would be committed, there'd be no way back once he'd taken the plunge on buying those shares in Guthrie's business. All they had to do then was feed him the bad news that his scheme was blown and point the finger at Mike Arnold. When

Hardcastle found the smoking gun Tony Darwin had planted in the computer system, his reaction would be fast and violent. Arnold would be squarely in the firing line and desperate to find a way to save his skin. Offer him protection and he'd talk. QED. But none of it would happen unless he got Chloe on side. Peter thrust aside his irritation, marshalled his thoughts and started whispering persuasively.

***

In the cold light of day, things didn't seem quite so simple and Peter shivered as he followed Chloe towards the ugly concrete and glass monstrosity housing the editorial offices of the Globe. Giving their bodyguards the slip had been relatively easy, but now he found himself missing their reassuring presence. The dangers crowding in on them both were anything but imaginary and while Chloe confronted the receptionist with a confident demand to see the editor, he struggled to keep his composure. The phone call seemed to take an age before two visitors' passes were pushed across the desk with a smile and a request to sign in.

"You can go right up, Ms. Pearson," the receptionist said sweetly. "Mr. English says you know the way. He's very busy this morning, though and says he can only give you ten minutes."

"That'll be all I need, thanks," Chloe said matter-of-factly and headed towards the lift as if she hadn't a care in the world. Peter followed, trying to ignore the itchy feeling between his shoulder blades. The starkly modern reception area was bustling with people even this early and it felt as though their eyes were crawling all over him. The garish primary colours of the walls didn't help, either, he decided. They created a restless, aggressive atmosphere, perhaps intentionally reflecting the callousness of an enterprise wholly dedicated to exploiting the worst sides of human nature. The visual impact was stunning and he wished for a moment he had his camera. It would drive him mad to work here, but there was no doubting the value statement that was being made loudly and clearly. You could almost hear knives being sharpened and taste the poison flowing onto tomorrow's pages. He glanced uncertainly at Chloe. She'd worked here, learned her trade here, he reminded himself. It wasn't a comforting thought.

The sight of Derek English behind his enormous desk was even less reassuring. Peter's fingers itched for his camera again, to capture the gloating expression on the man's face. Whoever had named him the malignant dwarf had got it dead right.

"Well, well, back so soon?" Derek said to Chloe. "Tougher than you thought out there, is it? If you've come crawling for a second chance, I'm not in the charity business."

Chloe allowed the sarcasm to bounce off her.

"I wouldn't come back and work for you if you were the last man on Earth."

"What are you wasting my time for, then? And who the hell is this sorry looking specimen you've got in tow?" he said, waving disdainfully in Peter's direction.

"I've got an exclusive for you, if you've got the balls to outbid the competition for it. Peter here has been researching it with me."

"It's not that sorry pile of garbage you tried to peddle last time, I hope," Derek said with a glimmer of interest.

"Oh no, this one's right up your street. Scandal in high places, fraud, corruption, you name it. And a couple of big names for you to flush down the sewer, I know how you love to do that. It's watertight. Facts, figures, documents, whatever you need."

"Who?" The word came out like a lover's sigh and there was something obscene about the way Derek's tongue emerged and slowly licked his thin lips in anticipation. Peter shuddered at the spectacle, but Chloe seemed unmoved.

"Sir Rodney Hardcastle and Charles Guthrie," she said. "They're in it together."

There was a choking noise and a muffled curse from behind the desk.

"Christ Almighty," Derek said finally, dabbing a thin trickle of blood from his mouth with a handkerchief where he'd bitten his tongue. "You must be bloody joking. Those two hate each others' guts."

"No joke. Like I said, we've got chapter and verse. Hardcastle's been sabotaging the Athena takeover bid, using money Guthrie's illegally diverted from his Group pension fund." Chloe glanced calmly at her watch. "The ten minutes are nearly up. Do you want the story, or not?"

"Sod the ten minutes. Athena you say? What's your source?"

"You know better than to ask that. I guarantee you it's impeccable, though. I've got more than enough to put them both in jail for a long stretch. Lots of dirty dealing and moral outrage for the Globe to get on its high horse about."

"Come on, Chloe," Derek said with a sly look on his face, "you know I've got to validate your source. I can't just take your word, not on something this big."

"Too bad." Chloe pushed back her chair and stood up. "I'll take it to someone who will, then."

"No," he yelped. "Sit down, damn it, I didn't mean..."

"You want to make me an offer, then? What have you got in mind?"

"If it checks out, I'll pay our top freelance rates and..."

"Forget it." Chloe turned to Peter, who was watching her performance with amazement. "Come on, let's go. This guy's a cheapskate. We'll do much better down the road."

"Double the usual rate, then," Derek growled furiously, "and guaranteed full front-page spread under your by-line for the initial exclusive, plus follow-ups if it runs. You won't do any better than that."

"It'll run and run, you can bet your wizened little arse on that. I want shared by-lines, too, on any related articles by your staff reporters."

"They won't stand for that."

"They'll stand for anything you tell them to," Chloe said bluntly. "I worked here, remember? You've fucked them all so often they don't even feel it any more, so don't give me that bullshit."

Derek chuckled.

"Dear me, what language. And here I was, thinking you hadn't learned a damn thing from my inspired leadership." His voice hardened. "All right, I'll give you your by-lines. But there's a condition. I get to see your evidence, right now and you give me the name of your source. Otherwise, no deal."

"No," Peter interrupted. "We promised..."

"Who's in charge here?" Derek snapped, looking hard at Chloe. "You or your poodle? You know how it works. I won't publish unless I'm satisfied the allegations can be substantiated. Or at least," he added with a twisted grin, "that the lawyers have got a fighting chance to keep us out of the shit if they can't."

Chloe glared at Peter. "You keep out of this," she snapped and turned her head back to Derek. "OK, then. But the usual conditions apply. This is for your eyes and ears only, strictly between these four walls."

"My word on it." He stuck out his hand. "Deal?"

Chloe had to lean forward awkwardly to clasp Derek's hand across the expanse of the desktop.

"Deal. Peter, show him the contract documents and the trading summaries."

Derek English scanned the papers quickly. His eyebrows shot up in surprise and he whistled.

"Are you certain these are genuine? Hardcastle's not the type to let anything like this out of his sight."

"They're genuine all right. Look at the share dealing analysis. The trades over the last few days follow the agreement with Guthrie exactly. He's making his final moves right now."

"How did you get hold of this?"

"Our source took it right off Hardcastle's personal computer via their internal network, then e-mailed it out to us through the Internet gateway. He's high enough up in their organisation to have access to the right passwords and most computer systems are amazingly vulnerable to internal compromise. Security's usually focused on preventing external access."

"That sounds suicidal. As soon as this hits the street, the finger will point right at him."

"What do you care? Anyway, you're wrong. Encrypted e-mail through an anonymous remailer is virtually impossible to track or decode and he's not stupid enough to keep copies his end. I'm told the only possible trail is in the automatic system and network transaction logs and nobody's going to think of checking those, they're strictly for the technical anoraks."

"So who is it?"

"A guy called Mike Arnold. He's the number two in their security division. You can check that easily enough."

"Why the hell would he spill this kind of stuff to you?"

Chloe wagged her finger at him warningly. "That's none of your goddam business. He's got his reasons, but that's strictly between him and me. You've got all you're going to get, apart from my first article by this evening's deadline. And if there's nothing else, I'll be on my way to get it finished."

Peter followed her out in silence, which persisted until they pushed their way through the revolving door into the street. Then Chloe's composure finally cracked and she turned and clung to Peter for support.

"Christ," she said, "I'm shaking like a leaf. I was scared stiff that bastard would turn round and tear me apart."

"You were brilliant," Peter said, hugging her close. "You even had me going and he fell for it hook, line and sinker."

"You reckon?" She looked at him dubiously.

"No doubt about it. I thought he was going to choke when you dropped Hardcastle's name on him. I'll bet he's on the phone right now pushing the panic buttons, though, so we'd better get a move on. Are you okay?"

She stepped back with a strained smile and patted her hair into place. "I'll survive. What the hell, give me time and I might even get to enjoy kicking bastards like that in the teeth. He's had it coming for a long while."

"Yes, well, don't go getting too macho on me. I like you soft and cuddly, just as you are."

"Get stuffed," Chloe said, laughing shakily. "Anyway, it's your turn now. I hope you're right that James Urquhart is an honest cop, that's all."

Half an hour later, in a cramped office in New Scotland Yard, Peter stared into the eyes of Inspector Urquhart and devoutly hoped he wasn't making a serious misjudgement. The signs weren't promising. Urquhart's arms were crossed tightly over his chest and his face was as unwelcoming as the meanly furnished, utilitarian surroundings. If he was a man of influence, Peter reflected, he certainly didn't flaunt the petty vanities of power. In a funny sort of way, the lack of ostentation was reassuring, though. Whatever motivated this man, it wasn't his ego. Nor, judging by his wrinkled, off-the-peg suit and cheap wristwatch, was it money. There was no telltale whiff of corruption, only a sense of unbending purpose. It was enough, Peter decided, trusting to his instincts. He began, quietly and persuasively, to explain the trap he had laid for Mike Arnold and how it could be sprung. As he talked, James Urquhart unfolded his arms and leaned forward in concentration. When the stern face finally cracked into a wintry smile, Peter grinned back, knowing his gamble had paid off.

***

Sam Garvey was in a cold sweat as he hurried towards Sir Rodney Hardcastle's office. One of the few certainties of working for Sir Rodney was that bad news triggered incandescent fury, vented as often as not on the nearest target without regard for guilt or innocence. And the news he was unwillingly bearing was not merely bad. It was catastrophic. Saving his own skin would take every ounce of persuasiveness he possessed, but Mike Arnold was a dead man, he thought grimly. Damn the man. Damn him to all the furies of hell. It was unbelievable. He'd counted Mike as a friend, in a business where friendship was a dangerous luxury and would have trusted him with his life. They'd been a formidable team, but that meant nothing now. There was no denying Mike's guilt, or his own disastrous error of judgement in allowing himself to be deceived.

He ground his teeth in rage as he strode down the corridor, the muscles in his jaw working spasmodically. The call from Derek English had been a bombshell and he'd been close, so terrifyingly close, to dismissing the possibility of Mike's treachery out of hand. It was only the calamitous nature of the leak and the fact that the information was accessible to so few, that persuaded him otherwise. He'd been reluctant, embarrassed even, to call in the system specialist to discreetly check out Mike's computer. Sodding computers, he thought. Who would have guessed that somewhere deep in their guts they recorded every action you took? He hated feeling foolish and the scornful expression on the spotty youth's face in response the question still rankled deeply. Perhaps he should have known about network transaction logs and system files, but there was no call for the patronising lecture and the thinly veiled implication that not knowing was tantamount to doddering senility. He'd not been treated that way for more years than he remembered and under normal circumstances he'd have rammed the little sod's teeth down his throat without a second thought. The temptation was still powerful and his fist clenched until the knuckles were white with the effort of restraining himself. There'd be time for a reckoning later. What mattered now was what those expert hands had revealed. Each click of mouse and keyboard was another nail being hammered into Mike's coffin. Dates, times and details of data transmitted springing to life on the screen, like footprints on a stretch of wet sand. Without Mike's personal key they couldn't break the encryption, but the file sizes matched the stolen data and that was conclusive enough. Computers couldn't lie and the evidence was cast iron. The only thing missing was why.

The question nagged at him, as it had ever since the call from Derek English. Why in God's name had

Mike betrayed them? Not from conscience, surely? There'd never been the slightest hint of any problem there. Money, then? It seemed unlikely. Loose ends bothered him and he wished he had more time to think it through. Then he shrugged. There was no more time. His only chance was to take what credit he could from exposing the treachery and it had to be done right away. There could be no hint of delay, of seeming to protect Mike, perhaps giving him a chance to escape. Understanding Mike Arnold's motives came a very distant second to protecting his own position. Stony faced, Sam rapped his knuckles on Sir Rodney's door and marched in without waiting for an invitation.

Moments later, the storm broke. Sam Garvey stood his ground, trying not to show his repugnance at the drops of spittle spraying from Sir Rodney's lips. He knew better than to retreat, or even flinch. The purple face and bulging eyes thrust within inches of his own were part of a measured performance, intended to intimidate and confuse. He'd seen it many times and he'd learnt to ride it out. What did scare him was the calculating brain behind those eyes, watching intently for the slightest sign of weakness or guilt and waiting coldly to pounce. He reached into his pocket for a handkerchief and wiped the moisture from his cheeks with as much calm as he could muster.

"Raving about it won't help," Sam said firmly. "You should count yourself damn lucky my security routines picked it up at all. If you want to kick the shit out of somebody, try your computer people. It's their bloody systems that have been leaking like a sieve."

"Aye, I'll have those incompetent bastards in my own

good time, when I've finished with you. But I'll have your fucking balls first. Arnold is your man." The accusation spat out like a bullet and Sir Rodney's rage threatened to engulf Sam Garvey like an avalanche.

"Yes, approved by you and the rest of the board. We've all got our share of responsibility for that." Sam kept his voice steady and matter-of-fact, resisting a powerful urge to raise his arms defensively against the naked threat. "But use your head, for God's sake. Save the inquisition till later. There may still be time to repair the damage."

Sir Rodney's eyes went blank and the rage seemed to evaporate like a door slamming shut. "How?" he said icily, taking a step back.

The hairs on the back of Sam Garvey's neck prickled and he suppressed a shudder. The temperature in the room seemed to have suddenly dropped a few degrees and the feeling of danger was heightened rather than diminished. There was something truly evil stalking the room, something that would not be satisfied until it had found a victim and taken its vengeance. For the first time he had cause to doubt the very sanity of his employer and he chose his next words with care.

"We get Arnold to talk. We must be sure how much of our operation he's blown."

"Break the bastard, eh?" Sir Rodney nodded his head dreamily and flexed his fingers in anticipation. "Yes... yes..." He glanced sharply at Sam. "He doesn't know we're onto him?"

"No," Sam said confidently, hoping it was true.

"And what then?"

"Then we kill the treacherous son of a bitch," he said

bluntly, "and clean house. Bury everything so deep you'd need a sodding archaeologist to dig it up. Let the lawyers try and pick the bones out of that without their precious witness."

"Aye." A sly look of eagerness flitted over Sir Rodney's face and his tongue slid across his fleshy lips. "But he's to die slowly, mind, slowly. That son of a bitch is going to suffer for crossing me and I want to see to it personally, you understand me? You'd better make damn sure of that."

"There must be no delay," Sam said urgently. "That would be a foolish risk."

"Foolish?"

Sam saw the colour rise threateningly again in Sir Rodney's face and cursed himself for making such an elementary mistake.

"I meant unnecessary," he interjected quickly.

"So be it, then," Sir Rodney said silkily. "No delay. We will start now. I take it you have a room where we can deal with Arnold without any, ah, protests being overheard?"

"Well, yes, but I didn't mean..."

"I don't give a shit what you meant. I will not be contradicted in my own office. Do as I say."

"But you can't... I mean, killing him here would..." Sam groped desperately for words. "We don't have the facilities to dispose of a body."

"Oh, very well, no killing then. Just questioning for the time being. I will allow you that much. Now go, damn you."

Sam went.

Chapter 23

Over the next few weeks, chunks of information came Peter's way like the flotsam from a distant shipwreck.

James Urquhart was the first to call, purring his satisfaction at the torrent of revelations flowing from Mike Arnold's hospital bed. The police had discovered him, trussed like a Christmas turkey, in the boot of Sam Garvey's Jaguar as he drove out of the underground car park at 46, Bevis Marks. Physically, Arnold would recover in time, Urquhart assured Peter with a distinct lack of sympathy, although he might not regain full use of his hands, where the fingers had been smashed to a pulp. The rest of his injuries were equally horrific, as though a wild beast had savaged him, but not critical. The officers at the scene had never seen anything like it, Urquhart said contentedly, but fortunately there was nothing wrong with Arnold's memory or his ability to talk. It was safe enough for Peter to go home and resume his normal life, he said. Hardcastle and Garvey were remanded in custody and would face further serious charges relating to the death of Frank Conway and others. A gratifyingly large number of their associates would be following the same route shortly and were much too busy trying to protect their own skins to pose any threat.

Taking him at his word, Peter moved out of the flat at St. Katherine's dock without regret and back home to Tonbridge. It felt strange at first, but the damage from the break-in wasn't as bad as he'd feared and the mundane business of fixing the place up with the insurance money brought a kind of normality back to his life. The studio, too, with Jack Howson's help, was soon up and running again. The news wasn't all good, though. Peter's enquiries about the Kaiserhof archive were universally met with stony silence and he wondered, cynically, what deals were being made behind the scenes.

Billy Stanfield, flush with his newfound status as proprietor of the Globe, seemed strangely preoccupied even while he stoked the headlines about fraud and corruption that were sending the paper's circulation to new and dizzy heights. It was understandable, Peter supposed, that he would want to steer clear of any suggestion that the press had been active participants in a conspiracy of spin. The truth would only harm his interests now. No doubt there were many others busying themselves with damage limitation, too, as old alliances unravelled and skeletons rattled threateningly in hidden cupboards.

Chloe, in contrast, fizzed and sparkled like a roman candle, revelling in her sudden notoriety as lead reporter on the Globe. The words flowed like a torrent from her pen, staying always one step ahead of the baying pack as the twists and turns of the downfall of a city giant unfolded. That apart, she too seemed content to ignore the deeper issues, brushing aside Peter's mounting frustration. Media Associates was finished without its key players, she said with a wry laugh, what more did he want? There was still no evidence of anything beyond a well-organised fraud, at least not enough to justify publication. She had a name and reputation to protect now. Why risk ridicule chasing after ghosts from the distant past? They were vanishing anyway of their own accord, she claimed airily and good riddance.

One of the oddest encounters came at an exhibition of his photographs organised at the studio in Buckingham Palace Road, designed to boost his business after the recent disruptions. Who should turn up but David Tyler and the sight of the familiar face gave Peter immediate palpitations as the circumstances of their last meeting at Bevis Marks flooded back. He'd never quite been able to figure out how much Tyler had known about what really went on at Media Associates. His immediate fear was that Tyler might be on some sort of revenge mission, especially as the collapse of the firm had probably cost him his job into the bargain. But as it turned out it was the photography that had drawn him to Spectrum Studios that day and Tyler had moved on from Media Associates. He'd never been comfortable with the way they did business, he said and had joined Blake and Moorfield, an international management consultancy firm whose ethical standards were more to his liking. Good luck with that Peter thought, as he wished David well. From what he'd seen of the big City partnerships they all treated ethics the way he used his lighting and camera angles to disguise unwelcome truths.

The malignant dwarf departed ignominiously, accompanied by recriminations and the whiff of sulphur. Loyal to the last, Derek English had reneged on his deal and attempted to bury the Hardcastle story before events and the change of ownership of the

Globe finally overwhelmed him. Chloe's farewell gesture, delivered with panache while the presses rolled beneath their feet, was a framed copy of her front page scoop, signed off for publication by his successor behind the editor's desk. Peter hoped that Derek would never learn exactly how it symbolised the trick that they'd played on him and Mike Arnold. Life was complicated enough without leaving hostages to fortune of that sort and Derek English was definitely the vindictive type, whose unpleasant talents would doubtless soon find another outlet in the murky world of tabloid journalism.

The same applied to Max Johnson, who'd faded back into the woodwork nursing deep suspicions about Peter's role in Mike Arnold's fall from grace. He didn't believe in coincidences, he muttered darkly with something more than just professional pique at being upstaged. But he was always on the look out for people who knew how to get results. The offer of a job on his team was still open, he said. Good pay, easy hours and more excitement than photographing weddings and suchlike. Coincidences did happen, Peter assured him blandly, while politely declining the offer. The way things had developed was just luck, long overdue. And photography wasn't as dull as he might think, thanks all the same.

At the time, Peter thought, it hadn't been a lie. The prospect of slipping back into familiar routines seemed comfortable and right, with VAT returns the only minor cloud on the horizon. He could pick up the traces with his clients, to whom his absence over the past few weeks were of no more significance than if he'd taken a brief holiday. The studio would continue to grow and prosper, which was all his ambition had ever been. Nothing to get the adrenalin pumping and the pulse racing, no risks to life and limb.

The reality turned out to be different as the weeks and months dragged by. The old ambitions were flat and stale, though for the life of him he couldn't figure out what was wrong. Under Billy Stanfield's benign influence, the commercial side of his business blossomed with impressive speed, to the point where Peter could pick and choose the most interesting and profitable work. Jack Howson effortlessly made the transition to studio manager, revelling in the unfamiliar challenges of knocking a new assistant into shape. Despite muttering occasionally about the growing need to take on a financial administrator, he was irritatingly happy in stark contrast to Peter's growing irascibility. Chloe's career at the Globe was burgeoning too, although the downside was that their relationship sparked and spluttered alarmingly under the increasing pressures. It was that which finally brought matters to a head on a fine spring day.

***

Frank Conway's gravestone was black marble, deeply incised with gold lettering. A carpet of wild April daffodils surrounded it, nodding gently in the sunshine and it seemed to Peter a kind of miracle that such delicate beauty could survive the ravages of winter to bloom unscathed. The thought moved him and acquired a deeper meaning. Perhaps he could blossom too, now, if the dark shadows over his life were finally gone. There would always be a lingering doubt, the possibility that fragments of the Kaiserhof legacy had survived and his aversion to mobile phones and their tempting apps was something he reckoned he would never shake off. But pursuing that road led only to obsession and despair. His father had found that out the hard way and it was time to leave those memories behind. Peter clutched Chloe's hand and turned his face to hers.

"Thanks for coming," he said softly. "I know it's stupid, but I had to tell Dad, let him know he could sleep easy now that Hardcastle and his cronies are behind bars. It was what he lived for, those last years."

"I don't think it's stupid," she said with a smile. "I think you both needed to make your peace. He'd have been proud of what you've done."

"I couldn't have done it without you. It's a shame you never had the chance to meet him, though, when he was in his prime. The two of you would have really hit it off."

"I read some of his stuff, you know, in the Globe archives," Chloe said wistfully. "He was a hell of a journalist. You gave me this story on a plate. Now it's over, I'll have my work cut out match him again."

"You're sure it's finished, then? All of it?"

"As sure as I can be. I told you, Urquhart dropped in on me last week. It was all off the record, of course, but he obviously wanted us to know that it didn't stop with the jail sentences. He said we could trust him to see it through to the end."

"The fire at Hardcastle's place wasn't an accident, then?"

Chloe laughed. "Not unless you still believe in Santa Claus, though I guess nobody could ever prove it. For what it's worth, my money's on the government spooks. I swear Urquhart's mob is tied in with them somehow and it would suit the establishment very well to destroy all traces of the Kaiserhof archive."

"What about the rest of Media Associates? I know the firm has folded, but there were twenty or more names on that list you and Max put together and there's no guarantee you'd spotted them all."

"I asked him about that, but he just smiled. Said I already knew the answer."

"And do you?"

"I suppose so, in a way. There's been a spate of resignations and retirements, mostly in the city, but a few politicians, too. Nothing particularly newsworthy; ill health, looking for a new challenge, wanting to spend more time with the family, that sort of thing."

"The same people as were on your list?"

"Most of them, yes. There have been a couple of accidental deaths, too, though that may just be coincidence. Either way, if you had a suspicious mind you could argue that there's some damn careful housekeeping going on behind the scenes. Nothing to make a printable story from, though."

"I wish Dad was still around to see the end of what he started," Peter gestured towards the headstone. Then he grinned. "But perhaps it's just as well he's not. He'd still be out there chasing down the last knockings of the story, not giving up on it like you have."

"It's best buried with him now," Chloe said. "The old bugger's caused enough trouble already."

"Great minds think alike. I reckon it's time we got to grips with our future."

"Our future? What do you mean?"

Peter turned away from Frank Conway's grave and gazed for a moment at the purple mist of heather softening the distant mountains. Then he slid his hands round Chloe's waist.

"Let's get back to the cottage," he said. "We need to have a serious talk about you and me."

"Is that right?" she said, with a mischievous twinkle in her eye. Then she twisted out of his arms, giggling and skipped away down the path. "You'll have to catch me first."

He took to his heels after her, the gravel crunching under his shoes. The gate was still sagging on its broken hinge, he noticed. Nothing had changed, but somehow everything was different. He was different. He'd tried going back, but it wasn't enough, not any more. Life was about moving on and the thought of growing old behind a dull, safe studio camera suddenly revolted him. And there was Chloe. He glanced up at her trim figure ahead of him and his heart skipped a beat, just as it had the first time he'd seen her. She'd never settle for a quiet life, he thought, any more than he would settle for being without her, if that was what she was trying to tell him. Whatever she had in mind, whatever it took, he felt the certainty settle within him that their destinies lay along the same path, together. He'd fight for that, just as he'd fought and won the battle to clear his father's name. A tingle of adrenalin flowed through his veins at the prospect. The feeling was familiar, welcoming, what he had been missing like an addict deprived of his needle. Memories of his father crowded in. He felt closer to understanding him than ever before, that at last he was truly Frank Conway's son. Peter stopped abruptly and laughed out loud.

"What's so funny?" Chloe turned and looked at him in bemusement.

"Nothing, really." Peter leapt forward and clasped her hands tightly, then swung her round until her long hair flew glinting in the sun. "I've just got this sudden urge to live dangerously, that's all."

Chapter 24

"It's finished, then?"

The question hung in the air of the small but richly appointed room like the smoke of a fat cigar and carried the same overtones of indulgent self-satisfaction. The Chief Scientist of the Kaiserhof Forschungsanstalt, the fourth in an unbroken line to bear that title since its foundation, stared at her interrogator dispassionately. Her jewelled hands fluttered and the lips thinned a fraction more as she suppressed her irritation. That much should be obvious from the experimental results she'd just finished presenting, even to a non-scientist.

"Yes Director," she forced herself to say with exaggerated politeness, reminding herself of the additional research funding she would need from now on. "The reactions of the subjects were within the predicted margins of deviation, given the number of variables we had to contend with. As you know, this was the first major field test of our new control techniques and the overall outcome was most satisfactory."

"Perhaps so." A stubby finger waved accusingly towards her. "But at one stage you lost control and as a result we have had to sacrifice more of our people than we intended. You assured me that would not happen."

"It would not have occurred if your security had been adequate," she said stiffly, bridling at the criticism. "I warned you of the need for tight surveillance of the primary subject. You know as well as I do that the techniques are not yet fully reliable when applied to individuals, despite my recent advances. The original Kaiserhof techniques dealt only with controlling the masses and we still have much to discover about directing individual thought and behaviour. That was one of the objectives of the experiment."

There was an eloquent silence, maintained just long enough for the Chief Scientist to grow uncertain of herself.

"And what of that subject now? What does your imperfect technique predict about him?"

"We are of course no longer manipulating his thinking. Now that he believes the Archive is destroyed and those behind it are neutralised, his mind will naturally turn to other things." She paused and cleared her throat apologetically. "The aggressiveness and propensity for risk-taking we implanted will remain, you understand. Once triggered, it is not yet possible to reverse such changes. But without the emotional leverage of his father as a focus, they will manifest themselves in more... er... conventional ways. His life will be changed, probably for the better. You might say we have done Peter Conway a favour."

There was a small grunt of laughter.

"You might say that, might you? Well, so be it. I can afford to be generous, under the circumstances." The voice hardened suddenly. "Where do things stand with the rest of the plan?"

"Er... proceeding smoothly, as you would expect," she said, hiding her satisfaction. There had been a low probability branch at this point in her equations where the Director might have decided to sacrifice the subject on security grounds, which would have been a pity. She had grown quite fond of Peter over the years, like his father before him. More importantly, though, it was another small success that her new methodology had predicted he would not do so. She dragged her thoughts back to the Director's question.

"The... ah... sacrifices you referred to have been successfully negotiated," she continued. "They naturally include all those who opposed your bid to replace Hardcastle as Director of the Institute last year."

"I understand a few of them proved difficult to persuade?"

"Yes, there is always a small percentage resistant to our methods. But James Urquhart's promotion as our new security chief has worked out well and he has taken care of that most ably. The deaths appeared entirely accidental and I expect no repercussions. The rest were, shall we say, encouraged by those examples to cooperate fully."

"Good. Go on."

"The somewhat larger than expected number of our people who have been exposed has in fact proved beneficial. In reality, of course, it will have little effect on our operational capability, but according to my latest calculations," her fingers scuttled through her papers and extracted the relevant sheet, "the probability that the civil authorities will believe they have completely eradicated our organisation has risen to over ninety eight percent as a direct result."

"The destruction of the original Kaiserhof documents

must have played its part in that."

The Chief Scientist bowed her head to hide the resentment in her eyes. That had been an act of historical vandalism she would not forgive, but this was not the time to exact her revenge for the insult to her eminent predecessors.

"Your decision to order that was inspired, certainly," she said silkily. Her hand strayed to the computer terminal at her side and her fingers possessively caressed the smooth plastic. "The papers were only of academic interest in this electronic age, the data was of course transferred to digital storage some years ago. But by applying the proper spin, we have been able to create the impression that the knowledge itself has been destroyed."

"You're certain of that? My plans depend on it and I won't tolerate any mistakes."

Fool, she thought. These arrogant men understood nothing of the science they used so casually. It was a fundamental axiom of the Kaiserhof technique that its nature and even its existence must remain unknown to those whose mental processes it was designed to manipulate. Even the lowliest recruit to her team of psychologists absorbed that simple fact with their basic training. Hardcastle's greed and impatience had compromised their precious secrecy. Her nose wrinkled in distaste. The widespread usage of the derogatory term 'spin doctor' was a monument to that folly and an affront to dedicated scientists practicing their skilled profession. The primary purpose of engineering Sir Rodney's downfall was to restore the anonymity that their science demanded, although only a few trusted colleagues knew that simple truth.

She looked expressionlessly at the fat, self-seeking face in front of her, with its smug grin. It was a necessary part of the plan that this man believed these things had been done for his personal benefit. Even so, it was hard, very hard, to swallow her pride and defer to such a creature. Perhaps this time, she consoled herself, the central experiment hidden at the heart of the overall project would succeed. They were the hardest subjects of all to control, these natural predators, though their ruthless talents were essential to the mission laid down all those years ago. Her fingers fondled the computer again. After integrating the latest enhancements to their methodology into her equations, the analysis showed a seventy-five percent probability of subjugating this one to the Research Directorate's will, higher than it had been for any of his predecessors. That figure could only improve as experience with the new techniques grew and their command of his mind became more precise. She moistened her lips and allowed herself a curt nod.

"Quite certain," she said respectfully. "My team is far too experienced to permit any mistakes now."

"And our international network?"

"That has not been compromised in any way. It was, of course, essential to our plan that there should be no suspicion of our ability to direct global affairs."

Viscount Stanfield leaned back in his chair and smiled into the flecked green eyes across the table. He enjoyed smiling. It cost him nothing and revealed even less. Anna Stein was a poisonous toad despite her benign disguise and had little grasp of the realities of power. Only her unquestioned scientific talent made her sycophantic manner tolerable; the Chief Scientist was, regrettably, too useful a tool to discard. But only a tool, nevertheless, to be used as he saw fit for his own ends. Billy Stanfield's smile broadened and he clenched his fingers into a tight fist of triumph. The power was in his hands now, where it properly belonged. And he knew exactly how to use it.

***

In an unkempt corner of a German churchyard, the wind whistled plaintively over an unmarked pauper's grave. The earth still carried remnants of winter's chill and the emerging buds of spring were not yet prominent enough to clothe the overhanging trees. Bare branches danced and rattled like harbingers of fate. If anyone had been listening, the noise might easily have been mistaken for the sound of Klaus Oberberg's distant laughter.

Printed in Great Britain
by Amazon